MARGARET FERGUSON

The Sign of the Ram

PHILADELPHIA

The Blakiston Company

MCMXLV

THE MONTH OF APRIL

"Born under this sign they are endowed with strong will power, determination, and obstinacy of purpose . . . they will stick at nothing to accomplish their purpose . . . and often meet a violent death . . . They have a magnificent store of health and energy, though their very excess of vitality is a danger. They desire to be looked up to and regarded as the 'head,' both in their homes and their careers."

You and Your Stars.

CHEIRO.

THE SIGN OF THE RAM

I

ON A WINDY DAY in late March on the coast of Cornwall the westerly gale came in from the Atlantic with the speed of a race horse coming down the home stretch, and with a prodigious leap and flourish, hurled itself over the towering barrier of Tremerrion cliffs.

Up on top it seemed to hesitate for an instant, gathering breath and impetus, and then the sight of the open country stretching ahead, heather-coloured under the petunia- and lemon-streaked evening sky, urged it on to even greater energy. The sea, dark navy blue frilled delicately with silver, and the jagged granite heights of the cliffs were behind it; in front was emptiness of moorland and gorse scrub with here and there a stone outcrop thrusting its squat and petrified shape out of the solid earth.

There was nothing between the wind and Tremerrion station, five miles inland, and it was away like a shot from a rifle, unchecked, until the square back wall of the bleak little station broke the rhythm of the wild stampede. The wind flung itself angrily against the small buildings with a noise like a cannonade; loose tiles rattled and threatened to cascade to the ground, and a sheet of corrugated iron lying near a shed flapped and clanged deafeningly, but nobody came to fasten it down, in a world of so much noise one more species didn't matter.

Sherida Binyon, getting out of the stuffy railway carriage that she had occupied alone for the last hour, seemed to step out into a world of wind and emptiness and strange fierce light that poured across the landscape from under a low bank of wine-coloured cloud, cut straight and sharply flat across the top like one of the queer Cornish hills she had seen from the window.

She stood on the tiny open platform looking about her, and still, as in the train, she seemed to be the only living creature in the vicinity. Someone had dumped her shabby trunk out of the guard's van, and it lay forlornly on the platform, the label fluttering wildly from the handle, but there was no one to move it for her, no one to meet her in spite of her telegram. Two milk churns and a hungry-looking sparrow scratching in a patch of dust were the only other wayfarers in the whole place, and for a moment she had, from tiredness and hunger, a nightmare sensation of having somehow stepped right out of the normal world into an unreal, alien one in some other dimension.

She put her suitcase down on top of the trunk and went to look over the low fence that leaned drunkenly in all directions, its apparent purpose being to separate the platform from the rest of the world. Beyond it there was a flat circle of rough grass and earth that might be taken for a station yard, and then the road, narrow and white, climbed steeply up the shoulder of a hill that cut off the view but did nothing to stem the rush of the wind. She could feel it tugging at her hat and wrapping her skirt round her legs so that she felt pinioned and cold.

"This is ridiculous," she thought angrily. "There must be someone alive somewhere about the place. This is Tremerrion station and I'm expected. I must do something sensible instead of standing here like an imbecile who's been dumped down in the wilds of Central Asia. There must be a stationmaster and a telephone."

She was just on the point of starting strong-mindedly in search of both behind the closed door of the station building when her eye caught something in the distance on the road, a car coming down the hill at what seemed a rather dangerous speed considering the steepness of the grade. It could only be coming to the station, since the road showed no sign of going any further, so she waited, taking off her hat because the gale threatened to waft it away at any moment and she didn't feel capable of chasing it down the empty track. The evening air was sharply cold, and it lifted her dark brown hair vigorously, like the hands of a masseuse, and pressed its fingers against her scalp. The

smooth dark fringe that lay across her wide forehead was twisted
up into little curls and horns.

The car shot down the hill and swung onto the flat ground
beyond the palings, and from it alighted a tall young man whose
ash-blond hair blew streakily into his eyes. He didn't bother to
come round by the supposedly official station entrance but
squeezed his long, thin shape through a narrow gap in the palings and came toward her anxiously.

"I say, are you Miss Binyon? I'm Logan St. Aubyn and I'm
frightfully sorry I'm so late in getting here, but I had a puncture
at the top of the hill. You must have thought we'd forgotten all
about you."

"I thought perhaps you hadn't got my telegram, but it's all
right. I thought I could telephone through." She smoothed down
her hair and pulled the little yellow hat on again and glanced
toward the trunk that lay on the platform with an air of abandoned forlornness. "I wonder—is there anyone who could move
that for me?"

"Yes, of course. Perowen must be somewhere about. He's an
odd bloke, he doesn't seem to like it when passengers get off at
his station. Perowen!"

He went down the platform toward the mysteriously closed
door, and Sherida waited. Logan St. Aubyn?—who was he?
Certainly not the husband; he didn't look more than twenty-
two or -three; but was there a son? She hadn't got anyone clear
in her mind yet; Leah St. Aubyn in writing to her hadn't gone
into any details about her family. And just at the moment her
brain felt too tired to struggle with conjectures and disentangle-
ments. It had been a long and complicated journey down from
Keswick, and travelling as cheaply as possible had meant odd
scraps of food, chiefly tepid tea and stale station buns snatched
at lengthy intervals. She felt cold and brittle, as though the wind
were blowing right through her body, and she wasn't conscious
of any great interest in the St. Aubyn family into whose midst
she was about to be plunged.

Somehow too the significance of human beings seemed to be
oddly diminished under this brooding sky that pressed its weight

of gigantic space and colour and cloud against the defiant earth.
The great humps of ragged granite seemed to be trying to
shoulder it back, to fling the dusk back into the sky, but they
weren't succeeding; at every second the light along the hillsides
grew dimmer and the purple canopy of cloud became more
closely part of the earth's darkness.

"Here's Perowen. You can put the trunk in the back of the
car and I'll take the suitcase. Come along, Miss Binyon."

Logan St. Aubyn had come back down the platform followed
by a dour and dark-visaged man wearing something that dimly
resembled a stationmaster's uniform.

"Oh, thank you!" Sherida murmured. "I hope it isn't very
heavy . . ."

He gave her an aloof and sullen stare, took the ticket she prof-
fered him, and then without a word swung the trunk up onto
his shoulder. Logan followed with the suitcase.

"You must be awfully tired," he said. "It sounds the dickens
of a journey from the North of England to here. Have you ever
been in Cornwall before?"

"No, never. How far is the house from here?"

"About six miles. It's right above Tremerrion Cove. Get in and
I'll put the rug over you, it's getting cold."

He tucked a shabby plaid rug round her knees in the front
seat, handed sixpence to the still entirely mute and glowering
Perowen, who didn't vouchsafe any reply to his cheerful "good
night," and then started up the car with a jerk.

"She's cold," he said apologetically. "She'll warm up in a
minute, but I hope she doesn't make a fuss about the hill tonight. You must be longing to get in and have some food and a
rest, and Leah would skin me if she knew I'd left you sitting on
the platform for hours before I turned up."

"It was only a few minutes," Sherida said, pulling the rug
closer. "Is Leah Mrs. St. Aubyn?"

"Yes, my mother—my stepmother I should say. We all call
her Leah except Andrew, who really is hers. Jane and Chris
and I aren't." He turned his fair head and smiled at her. "Did
you know that?"

"No, Mrs. St. Aubyn didn't go into many details when she wrote and engaged me as a companion-secretary. There was no reason why she should."

"But—you know about her, don't you?" he asked quickly.

"You mean that she's crippled? Yes, she told me that, of course."

"And I can guess what you're expecting to see," Logan said, almost angrily. "A soured, drab sort of virago all huddled up in a wheel chair, who makes life hell for everybody in the house with her tyrannies and tantrums. Well, you're going to get the surprise of your life when you meet Leah. She's—well, it's almost impossible to describe her without sounding like an extract from *What Katy Did* or one of those sickly-sweet Victorian novels for 'young people.' Leah's simply unique—at least we think she is, and I don't think we're the only ones."

"She writes charming letters," Sherida said slowly. "Are you and the others you mentioned all the family?"

"Yes. I'm the eldest, and then there's Jane who is nineteen and Christine who is sixteen and Andrew comes at the bottom, he's only nine. The accident to Leah happened only a year after he was born."

"Was it a car crash?"

"No. Jane and I, like a pair of fools, were bathing in the cove on a rather rough day, and we both got caught by the undertow. I managed to keep her up, but I was nearly done in when Leah came in after us, though she isn't much of a swimmer. She got Jane out, heaven knows how, and then came back to help me, and we both got swept onto the rocks—at least she did. She was smashed on her back right onto one of them—it was a miracle that she lived. There's the sea in the distance."

They had breasted the hill, climbing out of the dusk of the valley into a queerly brilliant afterglow. The air was twilit but shot through with iridescence as though gold dust were sprinkled on its surface. The sea was a dark triangle in a cleft in the cliffs, and in the wind now there was a salt tanginess.

"Is the house right on the cliff?" Sherida asked.

"Practically, but the grounds go down on one side into the

valley where the river is, and it's sheltered there. We can offer you quite a variety of scenery—but not much else in the way of amusements, I'm afraid. We're all hoping very much that you won't be bored and that you'll be able to stick it."

"That's kind of you." She smiled at his seriousness. "But it sounds rather sinister. What in particular is there to 'stick'? Family ghosts and things that go bump in the night?"

"Oh, lord no!" Logan swerved the car wildly to avoid a large rock that the gale seemed to have blown into the middle of the road. "We aren't that kind of family at all, though the house is pretty old and one could create a spooky atmosphere without very much effort. No, what I meant was that being Cornish we're rather a self-centred crowd—all except Leah, of course. We're isolated, and we don't mind it in the least, but other people do." He glanced at her again sideways, his light greenish-blue eyes unexpectedly scrutinizing. "But you don't look as though you're the type who'll wilt away into a decline because the nearest cinema and shops are five miles away."

"I certainly don't depend on cinemas and shops to keep me alive," Sherida answered coolly. "I was brought up on a farm in Cumberland, and you learn to be fairly self-sufficient there. I like walking and swimming and gardening."

"You've been sent straight from heaven," he murmured. "You should have seen the companion-secretaries poor Leah has been wrestling with lately. They ranged from a glamorous blonde who couldn't go within a mile of any cliff edge without turning green and fainting into the nearest pair of masculine arms, to a little, down-trodden creature called Miss Miffity—I swear I'm not making that up—who looked so terrified and persecuted that out of kindness of heart Leah couldn't bear to ask her to do anything at all in the way of work because she said it made her feel like a German S.S. man. By the way, you won't see Leah till tomorrow some time."

"I hope she isn't ill," Sherida said.

"No, she's gone over to see Granny St. Aubyn at Truro. The old lady's ill, and Father couldn't get away, so Leah felt she ought to go. Granny adores her."

"Isn't it rather a long journey for an—an invalid?" Sherida asked, and Logan jerked his fair head.

"My God, don't you ever breathe that word in earshot of Leah! It's the one thing that really does rouse what temper she's got, to be classed as a helpless invalid. But of course you're right, it is a long journey and tiring, even in the car Father's had specially built for her to travel in. We're nearly there now, but you don't see the house till you're almost on it."

The road had forsaken the gaunt uplands now and was curving along the side of a shallow valley at whose bottom ran a narrow, foamy stream between tangles of fern and tamarisk, blackthorn, and bramble. Here and there one of the small, quieter pools caught the last yellow glint of the sunset and looked like a fallen coin, and a rabbit, startled by the swinging head-lights, scuttered across the road and up the bank. The wind was gentler down here, and its saltiness was diluted with a scent of green undergrowth and opening leaves.

"You won't see much of it till tomorrow," Logan said. "The entrance is here."

He pulled the car to the left, and it swung through a stone gateway and began to go uphill again, but gradually, and there were trees on each side spreading dark branches against the first stars.

"The garden isn't bad really," Logan added casually. "Leah's very proud of the rockery and the azaleas. Here we are."

The house was a square, compact shape against the twilight, with gables at each end and a high chimney stack thrusting up in the centre, and light streamed out of the long windows and the open front door. Yet just for a second before she got out of the car Sherida hesitated, feeling a queer reluctance to face this decisive moment of walking into a strange house and the heart of a strange family. The St. Aubyns were simply names to her, and yet she had undertaken to live in their home, in close intimacy and contact with them. Leah, Jane, Christine, Andrew— they hadn't even got shapes or faces attached to them yet, only Logan had any reality. The lighted façade of the house was like a drop curtain that was slowly going to rise upon a play for which she hadn't got a programme.

"Come along in, you must be frozen," Logan said. "And starving. Beckett will see to your luggage."

She followed him under a deep stone porch thickly damasked with ivy, and through a small vestibule into a square hall, so brightly lit that after the outer darkness her eyes were dazzled and she stood blinking, her cheeks stinging with the touch of the warmth after the cold bite of the air upon them.

Mallory St. Aubyn, coming out of his study without hearing their arrival, saw her standing there in her loose camel's-hair coat and bronze tweed suit, against the hall's dark wood panelling. In the brilliant light her hair was dark and softly untidy, her eyes tawny brown, and her face flushed pink with the cold of the wind. She looked, he thought, like a bright autumn leaf that had blown unexpectedly into the hall.

"Here we are, Father," Logan said. "This is Sherida Binyon."

There was something faintly proprietorial in his manner, as though he personally were responsible for conjuring her out of the darkness. Sherida Binyon—Leah hadn't mentioned that her name was Sherida, but then why should she? Mallory held out his hand.

"Welcome to Bastions, Miss Binyon. I'm glad Logan got you here safely; he's rather a wild driver in the dark on these hills. I was wondering if anything had gone wrong, or was your train late? I thought you'd be here before this."

"That was my fault," Logan said easily. "The train wasn't late, but I had a puncture on top of the hill and I was horribly late. Sherida was waiting on the platform, at the tender mercies of Perowen, who was in one of his particularly Cornish moods. He almost pretended he couldn't speak English so that he shouldn't have to say good night, and it must have given Sherida a gloomy first impression of our manners and customs down here."

"Trust you to be late on any important occasion," Mallory said. "Come to the fire and get warm, you must be frozen if you had to hang about on our so-called station platform. I'm sorry my wife is away till tomorrow—I expect Logan told you—but Jane will look after you. Jane!"

"I'm coming," a girl's voice called from upstairs.

Sherida went over to the big carved stone fireplace and held out her hands to the red blaze of the apple logs. She had got over the difficulty of focusing from darkness to bright light. The drop curtain had, as it were, risen upon the first scene of the play, and she liked it. The hall looked as though it were used as a general living room. There were thick, amber-yellow stamped velvet curtains drawn across the windows, a number of rather worn leather armchairs drawn up round the fire, some good Persian rugs on the floor and dark oil paintings on the walls, and a number of family odds and ends lying about: books and magazines, an untidy sewing basket, some rolled-up knitting and a model aeroplane partially assembled. She had expected a different atmosphere, something rather chilly and sombre, perhaps faintly touched by the macabre, but that had only been because of her too vivid imagination. There was no reason why a house perched on the Cornish cliffs should be any less comfortable and cheerful than a home tucked cozily away in some London suburb.

"Here's something to warm you up," Mallory said and came over to her with a glass of sherry. "I should drink it down quickly, Miss Binyon—or are we allowed to call you Sherida? Logan seems to have decided that he can."

"Of course he can—I'd like you all to call me that," she murmured. "I hate Miss Binyon."

"It's better than Miss Miffity or Miss Sheepshanks at any rate," Logan put in as he came over to the fire to join them with his glass of sherry. "By the way, Dad, has Leah rung up from Truro all right?"

"Yes, she got there safely, but I think she was rather tired. I told her to go to bed very early; Mother won't want to talk for long, but she'll like knowing she's in the house. I'm afraid I'm inclined to worry when my wife goes off travelling," he added to Sherida. "We try and make it as comfortable as possible for her, but it's always a strain. However, she insisted on going, and my mother's pleasure is quite enough to make up to her for the effort. That's our difficulty, to keep her from doing too much, and that's where you'll be a great help, provided you don't exert your influence too obviously."

"I've warned Sherida about that," Logan said. "Hullo, here's Jane."

A narrow-hipped girl in a dark red dress came running lightly down the wide, curved staircase. She was as dark as Logan was fair, with a thin, sun-burnt face framed in restlessly flying raven-black hair, but her eyes were an unexpected, clear silver-grey set under very delicately curved black eyebrows.

Sherida wondered what the first Mrs. St. Aubyn had been like, since both her children were so totally unlike their father. Mallory St. Aubyn had a solid, nut-brown squareness and sturdiness that showed no sign of reproduction in his two eldest children, who were thin to the point of tautness and almost feverishly energetic in their movements.

"Sorry I've been so long, Father," the girl said, and her voice was very light and clear and restless too. "Andrew found some spots on his chest and insisted it was measles, and we had to have a great sitting with the doctor's book to make sure he was wrong."

"Andrew seems able to make himself come out in spots at a moment's notice when there's a question of doing something he doesn't particularly want to do. This is Sherida Binyon, Jane, and Logan left her sitting for half an hour on Tremerrion station, so she's cold and hungry and I should think exhausted. Will you look after her?"

"It wasn't as bad as that," Sherida protested. "I had to wait about five minutes before he arrived. It must have been a nuisance meeting me if Mrs. St. Aubyn is away."

"Oh, all our visitors arrive either after dark or at some unearthly hour in the morning," Jane said. "Logan's quite used to it. I'm very glad you've come, Sherida. I've been trying to do secretary to Leah, but I'm a complete fool at anything like that, and she must have been suffering agonies of impatience while I take down letters in longhand and type them with two fingers. And my idea of arranging flowers gives her fits. Here are all the others."

The hall suddenly seemed to be full of people; another girl, younger than Jane with vivid red hair swinging flatly and silkily against her cheeks and a wide, mobile mouth, and a stocky schoolboy with thick freckles spattered over his square forehead and short nose. He was the only one of them who was unmistakably Mallory's child. In the background a stout maid and a lanky manservant of sorts were taking Sherida's luggage upstairs, with three dogs, a spaniel, a golden setter, and an Aberdeen terrier, prancing and yapping round their heels.

"Shut up!" Mallory shouted at them, and they subsided in front of the fire, their round amber eyes fixed on Sherida in earnest and puzzled scrutiny. "These are Christine and Andrew, Sherida, and that's all of us, for the present at any rate, for which you must be thankful. Jane, I expect Sherida would like to see her room."

"Daddy, is Leah all right?" Christine put in quickly. "I heard the phone ring and I just wondered . . ."

"Of course she's all right. She rang up to say she's had quite a good journey, though it was rather cold, and she'll be back at teatime tomorrow. Granny may want her to stay longer, but I've told her she's to come home, because we want her here."

"You bet we do!" Andrew said in a deep, solemn voice. "I may have some more spots by tomorrow."

He gave Jane a dark, warning look, and she shook her head.

"You certainly won't if I have anything to do with it, Andy. What I'm going to give you at bedtime will put an end to any suspicion of spots for weeks to come, and well you know it. Come along upstairs, Sherida, and I'll show you your room."

"We'll have dinner as soon as you're ready," Mallory said. "But don't hurry down."

"I shan't be long," she called back as she followed Jane up the wide stairs. She was wondering if having all her meals with the family was to be a regular procedure, or whether this was just a special way of making her welcome to the house.

Upstairs there seemed to be innumerable passages leading in

different directions and a great many big windows let into the thickness of the walls. They were all curtained now, but she could imagine the unexpectedness of the views that would burst upon one through their massive frames. The house must be very old, she thought; the immense solidity and strength of its grey stone walls could be sensed even inside it, and she was conscious of a curious silence, though the wind must still be hurling itself against the house and the sea was very near.

"These are Father's and my rooms," Jane said as they passed two doors, side by side. "Christine and Logan and Andrew are in the other wing, and of course Leah's rooms are all on the ground floor. This is yours."

She opened a door and switched on lights, and again Sherida had that odd sensation of seeing a stage setting leap into view. It was a very pleasant room, square and big and oak-panelled, but without any effect of darkness or sombreness. There was a fire burning in the low open hearth, and the furniture suggested a bed-sitting room, with armchairs and a bureau and book-cases mingled with the bedroom furnishings. The curtains were a light golden brocade, patterned with sprays of red and bronze leaves, and the bedspread matched them.

"Oh, it's lovely!" Sherida said, and Jane gave her a swift, pleased smile as though she were relieved about something.

"Leah wants you to do exactly as you like up here, arrange things as you want them. And if you find it too noisy you're to tell us at once and we'll give you another room."

"Too noisy?"

"Well, it's right on the cliff side of the house, and when there's a gale there's rather a row going on outside, though the walls are thick. But Leah thought you might like to look out over the sea."

The curtains were drawn over the long windows, but Sherida moved over toward them.

"It sounds lovely. Do you mind if I have a look out now, Jane? It sounds exciting, to have the Atlantic so near."

"It is rather a marvellous view, especially when it's rough, but mind the wind. I'll hang onto the curtains."

Sherida pulled them back and unlatched the window, and the wind swooped triumphantly into the room, catching her breath and flinging the curtains high in the air. There was even fine, ice-cold spray driving against her face, and now in the darkness she could hear the boom and crash of breakers and catch a glimpse of ruffles and pools of silvery white foam almost under her feet. For a moment the nearness of the cliff edge and the sea startled her; it was like being in a lighthouse. Jane was saying something, lifting her voice above the noise.

"This side of the house is right on the cliff, but it isn't as near as it looks. The cove is just below down there"—she pointed into the darkness—"and there's a private path going down to it. We always bathe there before breakfast in summer. Don't you think you'd better shut the window? You'll get awfully cold."

They struggled with it for a moment while the wind resisted, wanting to stay in the room, and then at last it gave in and there was quietness again.

"Why is the house called Bastions?" Sherida asked as they went back to the fire. "It's an unusual name for a house."

"Yes, but it isn't the English word. In sixteen something or other the house was built by a mysterious Spanish gentleman whose name was Don Ramón Sebastiano, and I suppose the local people simply called it 'Sebastiano's' and that turned into 'Bastions' and that's what it's been ever since. There's a portrait of the Don on the stairs, and he does look rather a sinister individual. I expect he was a wrecker or something." She sat on the side of an armchair, swinging one slim leg and looking at Sherida with her curiously light and brilliant eyes that had something birdlike about them. "You know," she went on suddenly, "we're all terribly glad that you've come, and you can't imagine how pleased we are that you're—well—like you are. I mean, young and nice to look at. It's going to mean such a lot to Leah." She bent forward eagerly, her thin hands linked round her knees. "You see, Leah's a person who hates ugliness so much that it's almost like a physical pain to her to be with it, though she'd never admit it; she's much too kindhearted for that. Only of course we all know her so well that we know exactly what she's feeling about everything. And the last two women she's had here were so dreadfully ugly, the sort of drab creatures who wore grubby collars on their dresses and always had hairs sticking to their shoulders, and bad teeth. It was agony for her having them round her, and yet she was so sorry for them that she couldn't bring herself to giving them notice. It was Providence who made them decide after a few weeks that they didn't like the wilds of Cornwall—or us—very much after all."

"Providence—with a little outside assistance?" Sherida murmured, and Jane's eyes twinkled.

"Well, we didn't exactly hug them to the bosom of the family, and Leah had to be helped out of the mess her softheartedness got her into. So you can imagine how nervous we all were, waiting for you to arrive, even though Leah told us you were young."

"I hope I'll be able to do the work all right," Sherida said. "But of course I told Mrs. St. Aubyn that I quite realize I'm only on a month's trial. I haven't had a lot of experience as a secretary, and I hope she won't feel too softhearted to tell me if I'm no use."

"Oh, you'll be able to do it standing on your head," Jane said comfortingly. "And Leah is the easiest person in the world to work for. I'll put some more coal on the fire and leave you to unpack; but don't hurry, we shan't be having dinner till eight."

She added another lump of coal to the cheerfully glowing fire and departed downstairs. Sherida went back to the long window and stood for a moment holding back the curtain from the jet-black square of glass and listening to the roar of the sea. It made one a little dizzy to feel that sheer drop and tumult so close to the house, and it struck her that here the sound of the sea would always be in one's ears, like the background of music in a film drama. Odd and rather silly how her thoughts ran so persistently on drama in connection with her arrival here, simply because the house was old and the Cornish setting a little wild and noisy. It was the effect of her own tiredness and that square of wetly shining, pitch blackness framed between the curtains.

She pulled them sharply across again, and instantly the sense of melodrama was left outside and she was conscious of the warm friendliness of the fire-lit, low-ceilinged room. As she unpacked a suitcase and changed into a dark red crêpe frock and brushed out her wind-curled hair, her thoughts went back to the St. Aubyn family, and it seemed to her that her luck had changed a little in bringing her here into the midst of them. But of course she hadn't met the most important person yet—Leah St. Aubyn, who had sacrificed her health and youth in saving her stepchildren from drowning, who seemed to be such a gay, gallant person even from the eternal bondage of an invalid chair.

And yet in spite of that portrait that the family had etched so sharply and vividly for her, she couldn't feel sure of the permanency of this job until she had met Leah St. Aubyn in the flesh. She brushed her darkly tawny hair back from her square forehead vigorously, brushed some powder over her still wind-flushed face, and started out to find her way downstairs again, conscious of a feeling of adventure.

The length and crookedness of the low passages were a little confusing at first, and she took two wrong turns, but found herself back at last on the square landing at the top of the stairs. There was a portrait hanging there in a shallow alcove with a concealed light below it, and she stood for a moment to look at it. It was a painting of a swarthy, saturnine-looking man in a crimson satin coat and pointed lace collar and a curled black wig, and she guessed that it must be a portrait of the mysterious Don Sebastiano who had built the house three centuries ago. What had brought him from the sunshine and golden plains of Spain to this wild strip of Cornish coast, where he must have lived perpetually in a state of cold-shrivelled homesickness and loneliness? His heavy-lidded eyes seemed to follow her as she went on down the stairs, her hand sliding along the dark, rich slant of the banisters. She was tall, and the light caught in her hair, powdering it with gold, and there was something like a gleam of approval in the painted eyes as she passed out of sight.

For a second as she came down she thought the hall was empty, and then she saw that there was one person in it, standing vaguely in front of the fire and swishing over the pages of a *Sphere*. It was a large, billowy woman wearing a shapeless, greenish-yellow tweed coat and skirt and a faded mustard-yellow felt hat, and she stood in such a way that her shadow sprawled gigantically across the wall behind her. There was no sign of anyone else, and by the fretful impatience of her page-rustling she looked as though she were annoyed about it, so Sherida felt she ought to say something.

"Good evening. Are you looking for somebody?" she asked hesitatingly, and the woman gave a wild movement as though a ghost had addressed her.

"Good gracious!" she said in a startled voice, and her eyes were round and protuberant. "I—no, I was just waiting to see Major St. Aubyn, and he knows I'm here, but of course if he's too busy . . . But who—oh! I suppose you're poor Leah's new companion."

"Secretary," Sherida corrected her gently, and she wondered how any woman could manage to be so utterly colourless, so that unless one kept one's eyes fixed firmly on her she tended to melt out of sight altogether into the background. Everything about her matched the sickly gooseberry colour of her tweeds; her limp hair was greenish yellow, her marble round eyes yellowish green, her face suet-coloured, and her eyebrows and eyelashes of an almost invisible sandiness. The only touch of colour about her that wasn't yellowish was her full-lipped mouth, and that was a very pale, damp-looking prawn pink. "Yes, I'm Sherida Binyon," Sherida went on hastily, dragging herself with an effort out of a half-hypnotized fascination at the woman's quite unique ugliness. Funny how ugliness could be as fascinating as beauty sometimes.

"Oh well, I'm Mrs. Brastock from Cliff End House, and I just popped in to hear if poor Leah got to Truro safely. We're all so anxious about her when she goes away from home. Of course this journey was quite unnecessary, just to satisfy the whim of a selfish, spoiled old lady, but it's typical of Leah that she went. But of course you haven't seen her yet?"

Mrs. Brastock's voice was pitched very high, and one could imagine how, as a girl, she had been told she had a "fluting" voice and how strenuously she had cultivated that particular note of rising, ear-piercing melodiousness ever since.

"No, I only arrived late this evening after Mrs. St. Aubyn had left," Sherida said. "But I believe Major St. Aubyn had a telephone message to say she had arrived safely and expected to be back some time tomorrow afternoon."

"Oh, I am so glad!" Mrs. Brastock's voice rose higher on a note of lilting joy. "That's one part of it over for her, at any rate, poor darling. But it's a pity she was away when you arrived, Miss-um—Binyon, because it makes such a difference to the atmosphere of the house. It feels half dead when she's away from it; one senses it the moment one comes in at the front door. I should have thought to myself in a second when I came in, even if I hadn't known about her going to Truro, 'Leah is away.' There's a sort of chilly emptiness everywhere."

It was on the tip of Sherida's tongue to reply that to her when she arrived the house felt anything but chilly or empty or dead, but she guessed that Mrs. Brastock wouldn't even hear the interruption. Her globular, pale eyes were alight with a kind of fanatical devotion, and her plump hands were clasped together.

"You know Leah is quite the most wonderful person I—eh!" She broke off sharply as a door at the end of the hall opened and Mallory St. Aubyn came out of it, and before he could even say "good evening" she made an excited clutch at him. "Oh, Mallory! I was just passing on the way home, and I had to look in to hear if Leah was all right. Miss Binyon says you've heard that she is— is that true, and will she really be back tomorrow? She shouldn't go away when she knows how terribly you all miss her and how lost you all feel till she comes home." She gave a melodramatic little shiver as though the warm air of the hall had suddenly turned dungeon cold. "Has she really got to Truro safely?" she asked again, and Mallory frowned.

"Yes, of course she has; she rang me up about six to say she'd had a very comfortable journey and wasn't tired."

"Of course she'd say that even if she were nearly dead," Mrs. Brastock said almost resentfully. "She must have several days' real rest when she gets back. Is your mother very ill, Mallory? It must be very worrying for you not being able to go over yourself because of that stupid Conservative meeting, and it must have been an added anxiety for you having to let poor Leah go alone. But I suppose she insisted on going, whatever you said."

"Yes, she wanted to go. Will you have some sherry, Mabel? It's in the library."

"No, thanks, Mallory, I must be getting along; I'd no idea it was so late. Oh, here's Jane! How are you managing with the housekeeping while your mother's away, Jane? Can I do anything to help? You know you've only got to ask me."

"I don't think so, thank you, Mrs. Brastock." Jane looked at her with deliberately widened eyes. "It's only twenty-four hours, and I don't think much can go wrong between tonight and tomorrow afternoon. Sherida can help me if anything does."

"Sherida—? Oh, of course!" Mrs. Brastock's flat, full face looked a little blank and hurt. "You've got someone very efficient and highly trained now to look after things, haven't you? Mallory, would it be a dreadful bother for one of you to ring me up to-morrow when Leah arrives, just to say she's all right? One can't help being a tiny bit anxious; it's a long time since she made such a strenuous journey, isn't it? But of course if it would be a nuisance——"

"Of course it won't be. Jane will give you a ring. Logan, turn on the porch light; I put it out. Good night, Mabel, and thanks for looking in."

Logan, looking bored and indolent, escorted Mrs. Brastock outside, and Mallory said in a faintly apologetic tone of voice:

"Mrs. Brastock keeps an eye on us if Leah is away. She's known her for years, and she's a very kindhearted soul. Let's go in to dinner, shall we?"

The dining room was square and low-ceilinged, with cream walls above glossy dark wood panelling, and the oval polished table was lighted by red-shaded candles in tall crystal candelabra. At the head of the table there was one high-backed carved oak chair with a faded red velvet cushion on the seat and a red velvet footstool at its base, and without being told Sherida knew that it was Leah's chair and that no one else would ever dream of sitting in it. It had an expectant and faintly arrogant look.

There was a square cream pottery jar in the middle of the table, packed with wallflowers, tawny gold, flame, copper, and wine red, and Mallory St. Aubyn, glancing down the table at Sherida, thought suddenly that she was rather like a wallflower herself, with that dark tawny-bronze hair and those copper-brown eyes and lashes and that faint clear pink in her cheeks. One couldn't have called her in the least degree beautiful; her features were too irregular for that. The shape of her face was square at the cheekbones, with a firm jaw line, a pointed chin, a blunt-tipped nose, and a long, mobile mouth that smiled crookedly. An uneven face that was full of character that was, in a way, bafflingly contradictory. Her eyes were gentle but her chin obstinate, her mouth gay but her expression rather serious. He wondered how old she was—older than she looked, he thought—and what she and Leah would make of each other.

2

WHEN SHERIDA OPENED HER EYES in the morning she lay still for a moment, puzzled by something that she couldn't quite name at first.

Then, after those few seconds of blinking at the sunlight on the wall, she realized what it was that was so odd—the quietness. Not that it was completely quiet—that would never be likely in this cliff-perched house—but when she went sleepily to bed the night before, the whole room had been shaken and wrenched by the violence of the gale and the breakers might have been dashing themselves desperately against her windowpanes. But now there was only a low-pitched, rhythmical "swoosh-swoosh" down below, and the room was flooded with morning light as piercingly clear as spring water.

She dressed quickly and opened the window and took a deep, heady breath of salty air that was so strong that it made her feel dizzy. In the darkness the house had seemed much nearer to the cliff edge than it really was; now she saw that the low grey stone wall of the garden was set back fifty yards from the razor-sharp edge where the ground vanished and empty blue air took its place. But from the height of her room she could look well out over it to the sea that was a cloudy horizon blue, streaked suddenly with peacock and jade. There was a path running along the cliffs beyond the wall, and to the right the ground seemed to slant less precipitously. The real gardens and grounds were all on the sheltered valley side of the house and protected by a thick hedge of tamarisks; on this side there was only a strip of slightly wind-bitten lawn and a rockery.

Up the cliff path two people were swinging side by side with the dogs running in circles round them, and Jane and Logan both looked up and waved to her.

"We've been down to test the water in the cove for a swim," Jane shouted. "I think it's absolutely freezing, but Logan says he's going in before lunch. It's a matter of pride with him to bathe before the first of April, even if it kills him. Breakfast is ready if you're on the way down."

"I'm coming. I'll be down in two seconds—if I can find my way," Sherida called back. "It's the most glorious morning."

"It always smells rather lovely after a gale," Jane sniffed appreciatively. "Leah says it's worth ten bottles of old Dr. Sherman's horrible tonic. Hurry down before Logan and Andrew eat up all the kidneys."

The big dining room looked less formal in the morning sunlight and without the austerities of drawn curtains and lighted candles. There were letters and papers scattered all over the table amongst the toast racks and marmalade jars; Andrew between mouthfuls was earnestly studying the instructions for putting together a model aeroplane, and the telephone bell was ringing impatiently in the hall.

"Oh, curse it!" Jane went to answer it and came back with a worried look. "It was Mrs. Gale wanting to know if she can put us down to take in ten evacuated children from Shoreditch, if it comes to evacuation. I said I didn't know but I didn't think we possibly could, it would half kill Leah, and she said Leah had told her we could manage fifteen and she was letting us off lightly. You shouldn't have let her, Daddy."

Mallory, who was examining the *Times* with a not too cheerful expression, shook his head and sighed.

"I didn't know anything about it, and anyway I couldn't have stopped Leah from offering. If she wants to take in fifteen slum children, she will. Let's hope it never comes to that. Did you sleep well, Sherida?"

"Marvellously. I loved the noise of the sea." She looked across the table at Jane, who was sighing helplessly over a small pile of letters. "If Mrs. St. Aubyn isn't coming home till this afternoon, you must show me what to do and let me start on something."

Logan got up from the table and strolled over to the radio-gramophone, and the rushing rhythm of Smetana's "Vitava" filled the room like the river it pictured.

"Gosh," Andrew murmured, "if we must have music at break-fast it might be something decent like that new 'Stainless Stephen' record. Jane, you didn't come in to look at my spots, and they're still there, and I'm positive I've got measles and I can't go back next week."

"And I'm more than positive that you'll be on your way on Tuesday when your quarantine is up," Jane said. "You'll always be covered in spots if you eat marmalade and bramble. jelly on the same piece of toast. Take away one or other pot, Logan. By the way, aren't you going in to the office today?" she added, and seeing Sherida's faintly surprised look: "Logan is a fully-fledged solicitor in case you didn't know, though heaven knows how it happened. He goes in to the office at Polperrow every now and again, but generally more 'again' than 'now.' Were you saying something about work, Sherida?"

"Yes. I ought to get on and do something, oughtn't I?"

"Well, I don't think there's anything you can do till Leah gets back, unless you wade through some of this mail and sort it. I'm terrified of getting things mixed and bringing about some awful disaster in her engagement book."

"Oh, leave Leah's fan mail till she gets home," Logan said lazily. "You'll have enough to do in the future coping with her ecstatic correspondents without beginning today." He looked at Sherida, his eyebrows tilted half ironically. "By the way, did you know that Leah runs a stupendously successful literary career in the intervals of keeping the local Mothers' Union and Conservative Women and Rescue Home in good order?"

"No, I didn't know," Sherida said. "Does she write books?"

Christine answered eagerly before anyone else.

"No, not books, but poems. She's 'Faith Hope'—you must have read lots of those prose lyrics that she writes every day for the *Daily Matins*. They've been published in volume form too; the fourth one came out last Christmas and did terrifically well. You have read them, haven't you?"

She looked so shocked and astounded at the idea of anyone not being familiar with "Faith Hope's" lyrical sentimentalizings that Sherida said hastily:

"Yes, of course I have. She writes for *Women in the Home* too, doesn't she? They're—they're very sweet."

It seemed a lame and inadequate word in the face of the family's expectant silence, and she felt herself flushing a little, but Christine didn't notice.

"And an enormous help to people," she went on in a faintly reverential tone. "She's had letters from people all over the world saying how much her messages mean to them and what a comfort they are if they're in trouble or sad. Leah treasures all those letters. Andrew, if you want me to darn your bathing suit you'd better give it to me now and let me get on with it."

When she and Andrew had gone—Mallory had strolled off into the garden before the subject of "Faith Hope" came up—Jane said quickly and a little uncertainly, Sherida thought:

"Christine makes Leah sound horribly pious and priggish when she talks about her poems like that, but really Leah laughs at herself for them, just a little bit. And of course she keeps it a dead secret; not a soul outside the house knows, not even Mrs. Brastock, and she'd hate it if they did. I think she began it as a sort of amusement after her accident when she was first an invalid and sent some of the poems up for fun to a newspaper, and they took them, and people seemed to like them, so she went on. She's so frightfully interested in other people and their problems and lives—interested in a nice, human way, I mean. And that's why she runs a problem corner in one of the women's magazines too, because she really does want to help girls with their difficulties. And I'm sure she must have given a lot of them frightfully good advice."

"So that," Logan put in casually, "is why she needs a trained secretary, though locally it's thought rather odd and affected of her. It's going to be really hot presently."

He got up and went to the window, and Sherida felt that the conversation had been switched over abruptly from the subject of Leah's literary activities, that neither he nor Jane wanted to continue it.

"Are you going for a walk, Logan?" Jane asked, lighting a cigarette. "If you are you can leave a note at the farm for me."

"Yes, I'm going along the cliffs, and Sherida is coming with me." He waved a hand peremptorily before she could interrupt. "With all this spate of secretarial work launched on your head you won't have much time for sight-seeing after today, so you'd better make the most of it now. I'll meet you at the door in ten minutes."

It didn't seem much use protesting in the face of such concerted determination, so Sherida nodded. Jane with a sigh took herself off to attend to some housekeeping, and Mallory came in from the garden with the morning paper in his hand and his pipe in his mouth and propped himself against the mantelpiece. It struck Sherida suddenly that he looked very young to be Logan's and Jane's father; there was no grey yet in his thick brown hair, and his face had only a very few lines on it, finely etched about the eyes.

"Is it all right, Major St. Aubyn, if I go for a walk this morning?" she asked, and he looked up quickly, as though he had half forgotten her presence in the room.

"Good lord, yes! Stay out as long as you like and don't feel that you've—well, that you're tied to the house or anything like that. Have the family been telling you about Leah's writing?" She nodded, and he went on abruptly: "I hope they haven't put you off the job by too much chatter about toil and turmoil and work. You won't find my wife difficult or temperamental;

she's about the sanest and most even-tempered woman I've ever met, I can promise you that." He smiled suddenly, looking past her out of the window at the hyacinth-blue, cloud-scrolled sky. "I'm glad it's fine for your first day here, after last night's inhospitable Cornish welcome. It makes such a difference to one's first impressions of a place to see it in the sunshine, and first impressions are pretty important. We want yours to be pleasant ones."

"But they were last night," she answered quietly and wouldn't remember that odd, melodramatic sense of reluctance she had felt when it came to stepping out of the car into the house. "You're all so kind and it's such a lovely place. I'd better get ready to go out."

She put on a short rust-red suède jacket and tucked her hair into a dull yellow scarf and wondered a little if this mightn't all be a dream. Mallory had talked about first impressions, and hers were almost too unbelievably pleasant. In a way it made her a little watchful, as though she couldn't quite believe in it, as though she were determined to find a snag somewhere. But at the moment she couldn't find a single one; the friendliness of her room was like something she had known all her life, the sea air was strong and vitalizing against her face, and Logan was shouting to her down in the hall.

"All right, I'm coming!"

She ran downstairs, finding her way now unerringly and without thinking, as though her feet had trodden these complicated corridors for weeks instead of hours. Mallory St. Aubyn stood at the dining-room window and watched them walk down the garden and out of the gate on to the cliff. His pipe was out, but he still sucked at it unthinkingly.

"I can't imagine," Sherida said, an hour later, "why I imagined Cornwall was a sinister, gloomy sort of county. I suppose I was tired last night after the journey and in a silly mood. You couldn't imagine anything less sinister than this."

They were standing out on the headland. The rough, tussocky grass was springy under their feet and bloomed with a suggestion of uprising green plant life, and the sea, curling lazily round the foot of the jagged rocks, had lost its greyness and was cobalt blue.

The gulls swung just above their heads and down in the brilliant void below them, their bodies balancing against the wind on clean-lined white pinions that quivered with delicate flexibility as the golden yellow eyes watched intensely for any chance scrap of food drifting on the water. A few sheep nibbled at the coarse grass, and the sun was warm on Sherida's shoulders.

"Tell me," she went on suddenly, "why did you say yesterday that you wondered if I could 'stick it' here? It seemed—well, rather a curious word to use."

"Did it?" Logan struck a match reflectively. "Perhaps as a supposedly legal man I should be more careful of my phraseology. But—you haven't been here very long yet, Sherida, and you don't know much about us, do you?"

"No, I suppose not. But I like you. I did at once, and first impressions are generally right, aren't they? And I think Cornwall is beautiful."

"Yes, it is." He stood very close to the sheer cliff edge, looking down at the rainbow-patterned clouds of spray that were breaking in lazy showers over the black-toothed rocks. "But somehow it rather reminds me of one of those black leopards in the Zoo; it flatly refuses to play up to its admiring public. It won't make friends, it won't give up its independence. And it treats its visitors pretty roughly. It hammers them with gales and smothers them with fog and drenches them with rain and spits at them with sea spray, and the moors and cromlechs make ugly faces at them to scare them away. Last night's effort was nothing to what Cornwall can do in the way of telling tourists that it doesn't like them. Doesn't that put you off?" He looked at her, half curiously. "I hope not, but you ought to know the worst about Cornwall as well as about us, to start off with."

"But what is the worst about you?" Sherida murmured. They were sitting down now, and the turf was as springy as a mattress underneath them.

"Our sublime self-sufficiency," Logan answered calmly. "Our utterly selfish self-centredness. I believe if the rest of the universe were to disappear in the night and we were left untouched, we'd get along perfectly happily without them."

"But your—Mrs. St. Aubyn doesn't sound like that," Sherida protested, and he grinned.

"Lord, no, she isn't! For years poor Leah has been trying to instil some Christian charity and friendliness into us, and I don't believe she'd admit she's beaten even yet. But then Leah isn't pure Cornish-bred, as we are. Our mother came from Zennor Church-town—that's just about the wildest village in all Cornwall, right up on the moors. Her father was vicar there for thirty-eight years, and if she'd lived a couple of hundred years ago she'd have been ducked as a witch. She used to sit up under the Polar Bear Rock on Zennor Hill and whistle, and the foxes and badgers came out to eat biscuits out of her hand. I believe Jane could do that if she tried, but she's scared of the moors, and Leah doesn't encourage bogeyfied Cornish goings on of that kind, for which I don't blame her. We've just got time to get over to the Plume before we start back for lunch. Come on."

Sherida followed him, her eyes thoughtful. A curious young man, with his untidy, tow fair hair and slanting greenish-blue eyes. There was something faunlike about him, something faintly mystical, and yet within the space of a second he could turn himself into a typical, languid, bored young Englishman with a pipe in his mouth and a drawl in his voice.

"There you are, there's the Plume," he said over his shoulder, and they paused on the edge of the steep slope that ended in a precipice wildly tangled with a matting of bramble and thrift and hemlock.

Across the narrow gorge another precipice rose nakedly toward the sky, the slate-blue rock glittering as though it were powdered with crushed diamonds, and down the centre of it a narrow, silver white line was ruled, so straight and rigid that it was almost impossible to believe that it was formed of water falling sheer from the top of the gorge to the little cove at its foot.

"Locally," Logan said, "they tell you that the Plume is the spirit of a beautiful village damsel who was pursued dishonour-ably by a reprobate young squire and, rather than submit to him, flung herself over the cliff one stormy night. And the Plume is still so chaste that she won't allow any man to climb up the cliff to reach her. It doesn't look a difficult business from here, but it's impossible to get up there. I know, because I've tried it myself twice and I've always been defeated, and that's enough of local folklore and legend for one morning, and I'm feeling ready for lunch, so come along."

3

IT WAS JUST before lunchtime that Sherida was conscious of the atmosphere of the house changing subtly, of a vibration like an electric current of excitement and expectancy running through it.

The dogs were noisy and rampageous, the maids bustled about with more than their usual energy, the gnarled old gardener came up to the house with a great armful of early daffodils and pheasant-eyed narcissi for the drawing-room vases, Christine's cheeks were delicately flushed, and even Andrew retired of his own free will to the bathroom and put in some strenuous work on his grubby hands with a nailbrush.

Sherida, finishing her own unpacking and listening to the sounds of preparation about the house, was suddenly aware of the fact that her own heart was stupidly beating a little faster in a nervous fashion, as though she were about to face something that might be an ordeal. It would have been easier, she thought, if, during the time she had been at Bastions, the family hadn't set themselves out to drawing for her benefit such a complete and detailed portrait of Leah. But they had said so much, elaborated it so carefully that it seemed to Sherida that when she really did meet Leah St. Aubyn there would be nothing left for her to find out for herself. She had been presented with a ready-made conception of her character, a sort of predigested opinion, and the spirit of independence in her rebelled a little against the method.

Not that she wasn't still faintly bewildered by the surprises of the portrait that had been drawn in front of her eyes. Leah St.

Aubyn was "Faith Hope," whom she had vaguely visualized after
reading some of her "poems" as a little white-haired, lavender-
scented old lady, probably a spinster, who lived in an atmosphere
of potpourri and old lace and faded family snapshot albums. To
discover that she was a moderately young woman, mother and
stepmother to a large family, full of brisk competence and modern
efficiency, was something of a shock. Were the St. Aubyn family,
excluding Christine, faintly ashamed of the "Faith Hope" side of
Leah's activities?

Down below there was a sudden commotion of sound, a running of feet, a raising of voices.

"Ja-ane! She's come . . . she's arrived . . . much earlier
than we expected. . . . Daddy! It's Leah!"

Sherida went along the passage and stood for a moment on the
landing by herself, letting the family have their excitement and
pleasure to themselves. The hall door was open and suitcases
were being brought in, while the dogs barked and plunged about
on the polished floor and the St. Aubyns clustered outside, talking.

"What sort of a journey did you have, darling? . . . You
aren't looking a bit tired. . . . How was Granny? . . . It's
lovely you had such a fine day for the drive back. Was that new
seat really comfortable? It seems ages since you went away."

Nobody had mentioned yet that Sherida Binyon had arrived.
The hall was full of the scent of narcissi and wallflowers, and
now Mallory and Logan were lifting in a light wheel chair over
the threshold of the front door. Looking down from the landing
Sherida saw the top of a rather untidy, bright golden head and
a foreshortened face below it, unexpectedly rosy-cheeked and
sun-tanned. The body that sat in the chair was larger than she
had expected; in fact there was nothing frail about it, it looked
big-boned and strong and tall.

"Come over by the fire, Leah. You aren't cold, are you?"

Mallory was pushing the chair up to the hearth rug, and she
turned her head to look at him and to say:

"Darling, not in the least. Badger huddled me up so in rugs
and cushions and foot muffs that I was nearly stifled. I'm longing
for a good blow of sea air—you know what Mother's house is

like, practically hermetically sealed from October till May. Are
you all all right?"

It was an attractive voice, Sherida thought, rather low-pitched,
crisp, a voice that would carry without any effort in a big hall.

"We're all fine, only we missed you—just a tiny bit," Christine
said in her rather yearning brand of voice, and from the hall
door that he was closing Logan said almost casually: "Sherida
Binyon, your new secretary, arrived all right yesterday evening,
after the devil of a journey."

"Sherida Binyon? Good gracious, why on earth didn't you tell
me she was here? Where is she?" Leah said quickly. "Go and call
her, Christine darling, I don't want her to feel out of things. Go
on, Christine."

"Oh, all right, only I expect she's busy in her room." There
was a note of sulkiness in Christine's tone at being ordered away
for a few seconds from the side of her adored, and Sherida made
a rapid and silent retreat down the passage again and seemed
to be just coming out of her room when Christine put her head
round the landing and called to her: "Sherida, Leah's arrived,
so will you come downstairs?"

She scarcely paused to gabble out her slightly peremptory
message and then she was gone, flying downstairs again. By the
time Sherida followed her she was back beside Leah, sitting on
a leather pouffe, the fine auburn silk of her hair swinging loose
against flushed cheeks, her attention demanding Leah's so posses-
sively that for the moment everyone else was excluded from it. It
was Mallory who, looking up over Christine's head, saw Sherida
coming down the stairs and said quickly:

"Here she is. My wife arrived home sooner than we expected,
Sherida."

With an energetic and skilful movement Leah St. Aubyn
swung her wheel chair round and away from Christine toward
Sherida and held out her hand.

"I'm so sorry I was away when you arrived," she said easily.
"But I hope the family looked after you all right and that you
think you're going to like it here. Welcome again to Bastions any-

way—Sherida. Nobody seems to be calling you 'Miss Binyon,' so I'm certainly not going to."

Seen face to face she looked even healthier than she had from above, so glowingly healthy in fact that it seemed fantastic that she should be sitting there in that invalid chair, that she couldn't leap out of it and run up the long stairs as vigorously as Andrew himself. Her face was softly, almost childishly rounded and full-lipped, with the untidy gold of her hair waving across her forehead and round her ears, and her eyes were vividly blue against the peach-bloom warmth of her skin. The hand that she gave to Sherida had a cool, strong grip, and when she smiled there was a dimple in one cheek and her very white, square front teeth showed a tiny gap between them.

"I think it's beautiful here," Sherida said, and from behind her Logan put in lazily:

"In spite of a typical Atlantic gale as a Cornish welcome, and being left stranded on the station platform by me while I struggled with a puncture. But I tried to make up for it by taking her for a long walk this morning and showing her the Plume, by which she was duly impressed."

"Oh, did you?" Leah's limpid blue gaze flickered from Logan's face to Sherida's. "I'm very glad you made good use of a fine day and didn't waste it trying to wrestle with the mess I left behind me on my desk. Which reminds me that I ought to go and make some effort to find out what it's all about. Sherida, will you come and give me a hand?"

"Oh, can't I?" Christine said eagerly. "I'm awfully good at sorting and filing letters."

"Yes, darling, so good that I find unpaid bills put carefully away with receipts and unanswered invitations with answered ones," Leah said dryly, but with a little squeeze of Christine's thin arm. "I think Sherida and I ought to be able to cope with it. Come along."

Logan and Andrew pushed her chair across the hall, down a short corridor and through a doorway into a big room that looked out over the cliff and was swimming in red-gold afternoon sunlight. It might have been a sitting room or a study or a library; there were comfortable chintz-covered armchairs and a big settee, there was a businesslike roll-top desk in the window bay, and along two walls there were tall bookshelves, crammed rather untidily with books. There was a big filing cabinet in one corner, and the seventeenth-century fireplace was framed in fine plasterwork, but apart from that everything in the room was almost defiantly modern. A vividly coloured Gauguin looked oddly out of place hanging on a cream washed wall below a low oak ceiling beam.

There was a bedroom opening into it, and a bathroom beyond. The suite was complete, and the little steps up and down between the rooms had been levelled so that the wheel chair could pass through easily. Christine had done the flowers in here after lunch, massing jonquils and wallflowers so heavily in the green Lalique jars that the scent of them, thickened by the warmth of the fire, was almost overpowering.

"Thanks, darlings," Leah said as they pushed her chair up to the desk. "And for heaven's sake somebody open a window as wide as it will go, this room smells like a hospital ward on visiting day. And then remove Andrew, will you, Logan? Yes, I want to get rid of you, Andrew, and that's flat. Buzz off and go and see if you've got any more spots."

The reluctant Andrew departed with Logan, and Leah relaxed in the chair, running her fingers through her flyaway hair and lifting it away from her smooth forehead.

"Peace at last," she murmured. "You'd think I'd been away two years instead of two days, wouldn't you? But they're rather sweet. And as a matter of fact time drags horribly for me too when I'm away and I get in a ridiculous panic about everything and wonder what possessed us to live in a house poised in such a dangerous position on the edge of a cliff. I have visions of it collapsing in a gale and hurling the whole place into the sea, or of Andrew falling head first over it, or of Logan being silly and bathing when it's too cold and getting cramp." Her face changed a little suddenly, lost some of its gaiety and glow. "But I think Logan has learnt to be careful with the sea round here," she added quietly, and Sherida knew what she was thinking of, though Leah wouldn't realize that she did. She reached for a cigarette from a little green agate box on the desk and smiled. "In fact I degenerate into a silly, fussy, self-opinionated mamma of a large family when I'm away in spite of all my stern modern resolutions. Have a cigarette and tell me how you really like it here."

"I think it's lovely, Mrs. St. Aubyn." Sherida struck a match for their cigarettes. "And I hadn't realized it was such a wonderful old house."

"Bastions? Yes, it's old, and I suppose it is wonderful," Leah said thoughtfully. "But, as I expect you've noticed by the way this room is furnished, I've got the most shocking taste in the things I like to have round me. I can't stand ye olde spinning wheel and great-great-grandma's-samplers sort of atmosphere that goes with this kind of house. I couldn't do anything about the rest of it, but in here I was quite firm about what I wanted and meant to have. Is your room all right?"

"Yes, it's charming and so—friendly. The whole house is."

"Is it?" Her eyes narrowed a little. "And yet on the whole Bastions hasn't been a terribly happy house. Sad and rather tragic things have happened here, and I used to hate that sinister-looking gentleman hung on the landing, but thank goodness I never have to see him now. Sometimes I do wonder if it's been a lucky house for the St. Aubyns, though they cling to it like a limpet to its bit of comfortable rock. But I'm glad it's been friendly to you, Sherida. By the way, what an uncommon name for a girl. When I got your first letter I read it as 'Sheridon' and visualized you as a lanky, terribly highbrow young man with hair flapping in your eyes and a pink tie flapping on a pea-green shirt front."

"It's a kind of family name," Sherida explained. "But I get tired of spelling it for people. Would you like me to start going through some of this mail, Mrs. St. Aubyn?"

"Yes, I suppose we'd better tackle some of it." She drew her chair nearer to the desk. "Incidentally," she went on quickly, "have any of the family been trying to explain my work to you? I mean—have they divulged any of my literary secrets?"

"Well—yes, I suppose they have," Sherida said, a little puzzled by Leah's tone, half mocking, half anxious. "Christine told me that you are 'Faith Hope'."

"She would!" Leah groaned. "That child's heroine worship for me is becoming a subject for one of those turgid German psychological films. But of course you had to know if you're going to be my secretary. Well, what do you think of it—my 'poetry' I mean."

"I think it's very clever," Sherida answered quietly. "And it's enormously popular."

"Yes, just as strawberry jam piled on Devonshire cream is popular with greedy small boys." Leah wrinkled her nose a little. "That's what I feel about 'Faith Hope' and her yearning outpourings, Sherida, so for heaven's sake don't think you've got to pretend, or live in dread that I'll present you on your birthday with a complete set of my works bound in forget-me-not crushed morocco. Just pass me that bunch, will you, I think they're personal."

Sherida handed her a small stack of envelopes and bent her head over another one. She was feeling a trifle confused within herself over Leah's attitude toward her own work. A clever woman—yes, she must be cleverer than anyone gave her credit for if she could turn out a constant spate of the stuff without a single drop of sincerity to oil the wheels. This cynical, mocking estimation of herself was at least something that the family hadn't prepared the new secretary for.

The little white-haired, lavender-scented old lady that Sherida had imagined "Faith Hope" to be would at least have sat down to write her prose lyrics with a gentle light in her faded eyes—but would that have made them any the less cloying and banal? It was difficult to make up one's mind about that, but Leah's breezy contempt seemed to touch "Faith Hope" and her writing with a taint of fraud, to make it cheaper than it need be.

"I know what you're thinking, Sherida," Leah said, her head still bent over her letters. "You're thinking, 'If she feels like that about her stuff why on earth does she grind it out? It can't be for money.' Am I right?"

She looked up suddenly, meeting Sherida's eyes, and Sherida answered steadily.

"I'm afraid I'm too interested in people, Mrs. St. Aubyn, and—well, in what makes the wheels go round. I'm sorry."

"But there's no need to be. I understand exactly how you feel, but I don't know if I can explain." She took another cigarette and lit it restlessly. "You see, my life has been rather different since I found myself in this chair. Oh, I was lucky, I had everything and everyone to make it as easy as possible, but even so I felt I had to find some resources in myself. I don't say what I produced was much of an effort, but it was something. I suppose I started it as a sort of joke, and then it got a grip on me and gave life a kind of personal excitement. All the money I get I send to charities, and I'd honestly murder anyone who let the secret out. That all sounds very lame, doesn't it?"

"But I can understand it," Sherida said quickly. "I'm sorry, Mrs. St. Aubyn. There isn't any reason why you should explain anything to me."

"No, I don't agree with you." A curl of smoke drifted round Leah's bright head, and she smiled. "If a girl has to come and live in a house with a swarm of people, bang in the middle of their lives, she ought to know something more about them than just the surface things. I hope you're going to stay, Sherida. . . . Hullo, Jane! Are you going to unpack for me?"

Jane put another small log on the fire and answered with her back turned.

"Yes, I'll do it now. Simon Crowdy is here, Leah. Shall I ask him to come in?"

"Simon? Yes, of course, Jane, why didn't you bring him in at once? Sherida and I are only gossiping. How nice of him to drop in." Jane went out into the passage, and Leah added briefly: "Simon Crowdy is our doctor, and he's so kind about keeping an eye on me, though it isn't in the least necessary—as you can guess by looking at me. Simon, this is good of you. Come in."

With a mental picture in her mind of a typical country family doctor, Sherida had expected someone grey-haired and paternal in appearance. But the man who came in with Jane was certainly neither.

He didn't look more than thirty-eight, very tall and wide-shouldered, with a thin, humorous face, thick blue-black hair that was inclined to curl on top, and eyes of a sharp, clear hazel brown, as thickly lashed as a girl's.

"How are you, Leah?" He took the hand she held out. "I was passing, so I thought I'd just drop in and see if you'd survived the journey all right, and I see you have. Not too tired?"

"Of course not! You're a bigger fusser even than Mallory, Simon. As a matter of fact the trip did me a lot of good. One night's stay in the antimacassar-plaited-bulrush-Japanese-paper-fan atmosphere of my dear mother-in-law's house in Truro makes me quite appreciative of the Tudor period. At least it wasn't so brittle and fiddle-faddley, was it? Sit down."

"Mrs. St. Aubyn, shall I finish these letters up in my room?" Sherida asked, collecting the rest of the envelopes. "It won't take more than a few minutes."

"Oh! . . . Simon, this is Sherida Binyon, my new secretary-companion, Dr. Crowdy." She brushed over the introduction in a slightly perfunctory way. "There's no need to bother about them any more, now, Sherida. Go and have a breath of air till teatime. And Jane darling, have you remembered to ring up poor Mabel? Because if you don't do it soon she'll be over in a few moments expecting to find my corpse neatly laid out on the bed."

"No, I forgot. I'll do it now." Jane had been bending over the fire, and her face was flushed. "Come along, Sherida." And over her shoulder she added abruptly: "Are you staying to tea, Simon?"

"Well, I shouldn't really," he answered lightly. "But if there's one thing that leads me astray from the path of duty it's the thought of your chocolate walnut cake. Or do you want a quiet afternoon in the bosom of your family, Leah?"

"The bosom of the family is always available, Simon. We'll have tea ten minutes earlier so that you needn't feel too guilty about being late to inspect Mrs. Abbot's bad leg. Tell Emma, Jane."

Jane closed the door with a curious softness and didn't speak as they went into the hall. Then she said, still in that odd, almost gruff tone, "I'll ring up Mrs. Brastock now. Don't wait for me, Sherida. I'll come out and join you in the garden. You haven't seen it properly yet, have you? Logan's out there somewhere."

She went to the telephone, and Sherida pulled on the yellow cardigan she had left on the hall table and went outside. Something had upset Jane a little; she could see it in the nervous colour in her face and the way her small mouth shut so tightly that the lips were almost invisible. And Leah had been neatly skilful in the way she had got rid of them both from the room— Sherida pulled her thoughts up with a jerk. There she was dabbling her fingers in the pool of melodrama again, simply because Leah St. Aubyn's doctor had dropped in to see her professionally and wasn't as old-fashioned and middle-aged as he might have been.

She hadn't really explored the garden side of the house yet, and she walked slowly, admiringly. The contrast between the austere cliff front and the sheltered grounds sloping down to the little river was startling. Behind the fifteen-foot-high elder hedges that raised a sturdy barrier against the wind and sea spray, the hollow was like a sun trap, warm and golden-aired.

The garden was built in shallow terraces, the top one occupied by a smoothly sloping lawn, clumps of silvery-leaved palm trees, and banked flower beds showing already the boldly coloured motifs of the spring heraldry of tulip and daffodil and crocus.

Below there were two tennis courts, grass and hard, and a big square pool fringed in rose-red brick, with dark lily pads mantling the clear surface. A steep-banked grass alleyway was massed with wallflowers, honey-scented. On the lowest terrace, bordering on the road, there were greenhouses and strawberry beds and a wide strip of feathery whiteness where a cherry orchard was just breaking into blossom.

Sherida was standing on the edge of the pool, watching the darting brightness of goldfish amongst the twining lily stems, when Logan joined her and smiled.

"Hullo, have you had to come up for air already from the incense-saturated atmosphere of 'Faith Hope's' fan mail?" he asked her, and she shook her head.

"No, but Dr. Crowdy came in to see Mrs. St. Aubyn."

"Oh!" He struck a match for his rather foul-looking pipe before he asked casually: "What do you think of our local medico?"

"Well, I only saw him for about half a minute, but I should thinks he's extremely clever."

"He's that all right. He saved Leah's life practically single-handed after the—accident. She was too ill to be moved to hospital."

"He must have been very young then."

"Yes, he was. He was doing locum for Dr. Garstang while he was on holiday, and when the old boy took a purler over a Tyrolese precipice and had to retire, Simon took over the practice. It was the luckiest thing in the world for Leah that he stayed on. Of course Father had specialists down, but Simon really did the job, and Leah seemed to have such confidence in him from the first, in spite of his youth. That helped a lot. Now of course he's frightfully proud of her because she's his star patient."

"He must be. I should think he would give his patients confidence."

They were strolling down the shallow flights of stone steps that led from terrace to terrace.

"Well, what do you think of Leah?" Logan asked her suddenly, almost as though he were trying to catch her out. "I can guess what you felt about her before you met her. It's fatal to be told beforehand how utterly charming and wonderful and attractive a person is—you make up your mind instantly that you're going to dislike her, that you at any rate aren't going to fall for that charm. And I don't mind betting that was what you were thinking this afternoon when you came downstairs."

"You're a psychologist as well as a lawyer, apparently," she answered lightly. "But it's rather a waste of time doing that where Mrs. St. Aubyn is concerned, isn't it? I mean—you were all quite right about her. She is a wonderful person."

"We needn't have dinned it into you so thoroughly that she

is; you'd have found it out for yourself." He looked at her and smiled. "So you think you'll stay here, Sherida? You don't know how glad we all are about that. But somehow, when you came into the house, I think we all had a feeling that you would stay because you—well—you seemed to belong. Come and look at the greenhouses."

4

JANE BROUGHT TO AN END an interminable telephone conversation with Mrs. Brastock by the simple and drastic method of hanging up on her while she was still in the middle of an effusion of thanks and affectionate messages to Leah.

The receiver clicked into place, but Jane leaned back for a moment in the chair, listening. The house was very quiet, and in the quietness she could just catch the distant murmur of voices from Leah's sitting room, the sound of a man laughing. Her young face suddenly went so tight and strained that it looked as gaunt as the face of a primitive Madonna, with the delicate bonework of the temples and cheeks standing out sharply.

"I'm such a fool," she thought flatly. "Why am I like this when he comes here? He's known me for ages and he doesn't expect me to be as beautiful as Norma Shearer or as witty as Gertrude Lawrence or as full of sex appeal as Marlene Dietrich. But when he comes to the house I can feel myself turning into a poker, I can't even be myself."

She was so lost in her thoughts that she didn't notice Mallory coming out of the study and crossing the hall to her, and his voice made her give a startled movement.

"Were you ringing up Mabel, Jane? I'd forgotten about it."

"Yes, but I think she's coming over to see Leah after tea, just to make sure we're telling her the truth. Are you coming out? Sherida and Logan are in the garden."

"Yes, it's too nice to stay indoors." She moved past him to

pick up the woolly cardigan she had thrown on an armchair, and Mallory slid a hand through her arm and said quietly: "What's wrong, Jenny? Aren't you feeling well? You're looking rather what Rosanna used to call 'peeksome'—and you're much too thin. I've a good mind to ask Simon to prescribe large doses of cod-liver oil and malt for you."

"Daddy! That's nonsense." Her eyes were suddenly frightened and too bright. "There's nothing the matter with me. It's the spring, darling, when young ladies are inclined to indulge in spots and tantrums, that's all."

He was still holding her arm, and he looked down into her eyes with a faintly puzzled and troubled look in his own, as though he were trying to probe behind the defensive expression on her face.

"Are you sure? Simon's pretty good at tonics."

"Daddy, you might have more consideration for poor over-worked Simon's time and attention than to bother him with anything so silly. And you know I hate tonics; they make my eyes pop out of my head and bring me out in rashes. Promise you won't?"

He let her arm go with a reassuring little pat, but his eyes were still watchful.

"All right. . . . Oh, here is Simon! Well, she's none the worse for the trip to Truro, is she?"

Simon shook his head and smiled.

"No, but all the same I should make her take things quietly for a day or two—if you can. Do you mind if I ring up the chemist about something? I've been lured into staying to tea instead of going on to see him."

"Of course, go ahead," Mallory said and turned towards the garden, but Simon spoke again, a shade abruptly.

"By the way, Major, what's this Leah was saying about taking in evacuee slum children if this war business comes to a head? She's not really serious, is she?"

"Yes, she is," Jane said as she pulled on the red cardigan. "Mrs. Gale was ringing up about it this morning. We're going to have ten."

"Ten!" Simon's black brows drew together violently. "But good heavens, are you agreeing to that, Major? It's absolutely impossible for your wife to undertake anything like that."

"Well, it's a little difficult," Mallory said mildly. "Leah feels we ought to do what we can."

"But nobody in their sane senses can expect anything like that of Leah," Simon said. "You know that if it's necessary I'll give a medical certificate that would exempt Bastions from any sort of billeting."

"But have you asked Leah if she'd like that?" Mallory said dryly. "After all, Bastions is a pretty big house."

"And there are other people in it besides Leah," Jane broke into the conversation again in that curiously aggressive way. "I shall be here, and I ought to be capable of looking after a few children without bothering Leah, and there's Sherida too. I should think she's extremely capable at anything like that. If there's a war we've got to do something to help."

"Not, I hope, at the cost of Leah's health." Simon was almost glaring at her. "However, it's for you to settle these things, Major. I'm only warning you that your wife isn't quite so strong and vigorous as she sometimes seems to be. I'll telephone if I may."

He jerked the receiver off the telephone and asked for his number in a voice that rasped a little with impatience. Jane slid away from Mallory and went out into the garden, conscious of a tight headache and a dryness in her mouth.

"I know what he thinks of me, that I'm a callous, selfish little brute," she thought wearily. "That I don't care twopence about Leah—and I seem to set out to make him believe that more and more. Oh God! I almost wish there would be a war. Perhaps he'd be called up and have to go away, he's young enough. I couldn't go because of Leah."

She didn't go down into the lower garden, but went out onto the cliff and stood on the dizzy path looking over the edge at the rocks. Sheer below her, clinging almost impossibly to the face of the cliffs, were the ruins of some of the old Cornish mines whose workings had stretched out far under the bed of the sea. Abandoned long ago, the buildings still hung on to their precarious footholds, their sturdy brickwork stubbornly defying the incessant onslaughts of wind and sea, but inch by inch they were crumbling now. They made Jane think of shipwrecked sailors clutching desperately to a tiny jag of rock, knowing that one day they must give in and be swept away to annihilation, and yet obstinately keeping that moment at bay till the last possible minute. Why couldn't the sea let them alone and allow them to go on living?

Her eyes followed the soap-sudsy white line of breakers below the gaunt and roofless ruins of the mills. The wind had dropped still more, and beyond the rocks there was only a slow, opalescent swell, satin bright, unthreatening. But she was remembering that day a long time ago now, when she had felt that bright water close over her wet head, felt it take her childish body into a grip of such gigantic force and determination that it had been almost comforting.

If it hadn't been for Leah . . . How could Simon Crowdy not realize that she would be willing to die in a hundred tortured and lingering ways to save Leah one moment more of pain? Perhaps she hadn't got Christine's emotional way of displaying affection, perhaps she was woodenly inarticulate and too reserved, but if he had possessed any spark of understanding or intuition he would have known.

What a strange and lovely colour the sea was this afternoon, like the inside of a delicate shell, shot with faint rose and gold and turquoise, eternally fluid and restless and yet giving an impression of solidity. It was queer that, in spite of what had happened that windy summer's day, she had never had any fear of the sea, no sense of its enmity. She had gone in to bathe a week after her escape and had swum just as far out without a thought in her head but tingling enjoyment.

"Jane! . . . Jane! Tea's ready."

"Coming!" She dragged her mind away from the view and scrambled back up the twisty, breakneck little path that dangled like a spider's thread over the cliff face.

5

MALLORY WENT INTO Leah's sitting room late that night after the rest of the family had gone to bed and with a fresh pipe filled and lit stretched himself comfortably in one of the cushiony armchairs by the fire. She always went to bed very late and seemed to need very little sleep; it was as though the pent-up and chained vitality in her body could never be used up. It had taken him a long time to get used to the thought of her lying there hour after hour in the darkness, struggling to subdue the feverish strength of her mind and untired body, but from the first she had flatly refused to let anyone share those night vigils with her.

"I'm nursed and fussed over all day, darling," she had said to him. "Let me at least have the nights to myself. Let me feel enough of a human being for that."

He had understood what she meant, and as soon as the doctor allowed it the trained nurse left. She was very quick at learning to manage things for herself. Jane or Emma, the grey-haired housemaid who had been fourteen years at Bastions, would come in at midnight to help her to bed, and then she was left alone with the bell on her pillow.

"Sure you aren't tired?" Mallory asked her, and she shook her head. She was brushing out the thick, vivid hair about her shoulders, and at every stroke it rose like a live thing, crackling with red-gold sparks.

"Not a scrap. It's exhilarating to be home, and I suppose it's silly but I feel as though I've been away ages. What's been happening since yesterday?"

"Nothing much, except Sherida's arrival. How do you like her?"

"Very much," Leah said. "She seems a nice, practical, down-

right girl, the sort one can treat as a human being and a friend."
She shook her hair over her face. "But I was surprised to find that
she's quite so attractive. I suppose it's contrary of me to worry
about that, considering I never stopped moaning about Miss
Miffity's extreme unattractiveness."

"Sherida certainly is pleasanter to look at. But is there anything to worry about in that?"

"Of course not—not really," Leah put the ivory brush down
and tied a wide brown ribbon round her head. It gave her a
round-faced, schoolgirl look. "Light a cigarette for me, will you,
darling? I was only thinking of Logan when I said that."

"Logan?" Mallory gave her the cigarette. "Why?"

His questions were always very much to the point and un-
garnished by unnecessary words.

"Well—he's inclined to be susceptible, isn't he?" Leah said.

"Is he? I hadn't noticed that particularly."

"Darling!" Leah blew a neat smoke ring and watched it float
away across the room. "You're like most fathers. Logan's a
grownup young man now to you, and you don't feel you ought
to concern yourself too much with his affairs. But I'm a woman
and practically Logan's mother, and I can't quell a natural interest in him. He's inclined to be a heartbreaker—in a very mild
way, of course. But there was Patricia Mond and then Bette
Francis and that girl who stayed at the Rectory last summer.
I'm afraid they all went away with lumps in their throats, though
it never occurred to him. I don't blame him; they were all pretty
and amusing and he's much too young to settle down seriously
yet. But I can't help wishing that Sherida hadn't got quite such
big brown eyes and such an attractive profile. I want her to stay
on."

"She will," Mallory said a shade dryly. "And Leah, if you've
been watching Logan, I've been watching Jane. I'm a bit worried
about her."

"Her health, do you mean? Yes, she is too thin, but I think
she's a wiry child and she never seems to get tired."

"No, I didn't mean her health exactly," Mallory prodded at
his pipe with a match. "I think she's unhappy, Leah, and rather

on edge. And I'm not so stupid that I can't guess the reason. You must have too, ages ago. It's Simon."

He put the pipe back in his mouth, and Leah didn't make any movement except to tilt her head back a little and blow another smoke ring.

"Yes, I did guess some time ago," she said quietly. "And I've been trying to do something about it, though perhaps you haven't noticed."

"You mean you try to keep them from seeing too much of each other? Yes, I had noticed that. Is that the best thing to do?"

"Good heavens, Mallory!" She looked at him sharply. "You surely don't want to encourage anything like that for Jane? Simon's been married and divorced."

"Well, a good many people are nowadays," he said, and she made an impatient gesture.

"Yes, but it still has some significance, you know. It means that Simon didn't make his wife particularly happy. Don't you feel that Jane is too young to embark on a secondhand marriage—you know she's the type of girl who is going to take any sort of love affair desperately seriously. I have a great respect for Simon's cleverness and I like him as a person, but he's too deep water for Jane yet."

"I expect you're right," Mallory said slowly and stretched his legs closer to the fire. "She doesn't meet many young men here, and she's always had rather a mature taste."

"She ought to go away more often," Leah said. "For holidays in London and cruises and things like that. I wish she would, Mallory. I hate the feeling that she thinks she's bound to Bastions—and me, because of the—accident. It might have happened in a dozen different ways without any responsibility on her, and she was only a child anyway. Try and get her out of that feeling. I've tried, but she's obstinate about that sort of thing, bless her."

"I don't think she feels tied in that way," Mallory said thoughtfully. "She loves it here, and she isn't a London lover. She's too much like Rosanna for that."

"Yes, of course," Leah said quickly. "Rosanna was miserable in a town, wasn't she? I think perhaps I will go to bed now, darling, if you'll ring for Emma. Good night—and it's lovely to be home."

"Good night, Leah. Sleep well. Shall I send Jane down too?"

"No, don't bother her. I hope she's gone to bed, she looked tired."

When he had gone she pulled her chair a little nearer to the fire and sat staring into it, her body slumping a little as though it were weary at last, her hands relaxed. When she tilted her head back at that angle against the cushion the light fell differently on her face and it looked less young and rounded, almost drawn, with a little furrow cut between the straight golden eyebrows.

6

SHERIDA AND LEAH had just settled themselves, one on each side of the big desk, to deal with the heaped-up correspondence, when Mabel Brastock announced her arrival by a high-pitched "Coo-ee!" out in the hall.

"Oh dear!" Leah murmured faintly. "We don't seem to get much time to work, do we? Just push those letters into a drawer, will you, Sherida? Mabel's one of my greatest friends, but 'Faith Hope' is the one secret in my life I don't intend to divulge to her. Oh, come in, Mabel dear! This is nice of you."

"Good morning, Leah. I dropped in just to make sure you're really all right."

"Of course I'm all right. You met Sherida yesterday, didn't you?"

"Yes. Good morning." Mrs. Brastock vouchsafed Sherida a very casual nod before she plumped herself heavily into a chair. She was wearing the same yellowish-green tweed suit, but today her head was swathed in a voluminous and very loosely knitted lemon-yellow wool turban that threatened to descend in folds over her face at any moment.

"I'm on my way to the billeting-committee meeting," she went on with a worried sigh. "And I suppose that means a whole morning wasted. Poor Ethel McReady hasn't the faintest idea how to hold a meeting together as chairwoman, and we discuss everything under the sun except billeting until about five minutes to one, when she says feebly, 'Well, we don't seem to have decided anything very much. Has anyone any ideas—or shall we leave it till our next meeting?'—which we invariably do. Sometimes I simply itch to take charge of things myself, but I suppose as poor Ethel was invited to be chairwoman, she'll have to be left to muddle along. By the way, Leah, I heard an extraordinary rumour in the village that you've offered to take in ten slum children. It's not true, is it?"

"Of course it's true, why shouldn't it be?" Leah said decidedly. "As a matter of fact we're prepared for fifteen."

"Fifteen!" Mabel's jaw fell open a little. "But Leah, darling —you of all people! It's outrageous that you should even be asked. Good heavens, it's going to be bad enough for the rest of us, and Keith is getting quite worked up over my attacks of palpitation, though I don't let him know how bad they are sometimes. But to expect you—but of course Dr. Crowdy has got a medical certificate exempting you from anything like that simply waiting to be signed."

"Well, it isn't going to be signed," Leah said abruptly. "I should be ashamed even to suggest it, Mabel. When it's a question of war and the safety of children, what on earth does my health matter? Or the health of any of us old women, for that matter."

"Oh—quite! We all feel like that about it," Mabel said hastily. "I've offered to take in expectant mothers, and nobody can do more than that. But of course what I'd really like," she went on dreamily, "would be a batch of nice young Colonials. We had numbers of them in the last war, and they always used to say that our house was the only one in England where they felt really at home. Of course the atmosphere is much more free and easy and unconventional in a family that has connections, as we have, with Australia. Somehow it makes a difference in one's mental outlook."

"Does it? Personally I shouldn't have thought that having had one great-great-uncle sheep farming in Australia about a hundred years ago would make much difference to anyone's mental outlook. And don't they dislike being called Colonials?"

"By strangers—yes. But if you belong you can call them anything you like." Her indignation was interrupted by the sudden collapse of her woollen turban in folds over her face. "Oh dear, I didn't put enough hairpins in. Have you any handy, Leah?"

"Yes, in the little silver tray on my dressing table. Sherida, would you mind bringing it out for Mrs. Brastock?"

It was the first time Sherida had been into Leah's bedroom. She moved across it quickly to the triple-mirrored dressing table, conscious of a faint, clean fragrance that hung in the air and of a vigorous breeze sweeping in at the open windows. It was the sort of room that suited Leah's personality, rather unfemininely severe in its furnishing and decoration, rather austere in its wide bareness. The bed was especially high, with an adjustable head-rest, and nothing could disguise its air of hospital efficiency, though the heavy amber-gold flower-embroidered Spanish shawl that was used as a bedspread did its best.

There were only three pictures on the walls, and they were modernistic seascapes, but standing on the dressing table there was a silver-framed photograph, and as she glanced at it casually as she looked for the hairpin tray, Sherida felt a shock of surprise. It was a slightly faded and old-fashioned portrait of a young woman who wore her dark hair looped up from a centre parting, under a velvet ribbon, and her narrow, bare shoulders rose slantingly from a beaded evening dress, but the pointed, serious face was Jane's, so vividly Jane's that for a moment Sherida was bewildered.

Then she realized that this was Jane's mother, the Cornish-born girl from Zennor Churchtown who used to sit out alone on the moors, coaxing the badgers and foxes to come out and play in answer to her whistle. She looked as young as Jane here, with the same brilliantly light grey eyes, the same narrow temples and restless mouth, the same look of suppressed, urgent vitality. There were no other photographs in the bedroom, and it seemed curious to Sherida that a woman should ornament her dressing table with a portrait of her predecessor in the house.

She picked up the silver pin tray and went back to the sitting room, where Mrs. Brastock was struggling with the unruly turban and a quantity of flyaway wisps of pale hair.

"Oh, I suppose you've heard the news from the Rectory?" she was saying as Sherida came in. "That Catherine is coming back? But of course Logan must have told you."

"Logan?" Leah's voice had a cool surface of indifference. "No, I don't suppose he knows. I thought Catherine was settled now in London."

"Yes, but she's had an appendix or something, and she's got to give it up. Or at any rate that's what the Maitlands say, but my private opinion is that independence and the life of an artist woman on her own in London hasn't turned out as amusing as Catherine expected, so she's coming home. I wonder Logan hasn't heard. He'll be pleased."

"We'll all be pleased to have Catherine back," Leah said.

"Yes, of course. She's a nice child, and of course she's extraordinarily interesting—at any rate to a mild student of psychology like myself."

She clutched at a strand of hair that insisted on floating out over the top of the turban and rammed it into place.

"Interesting?" Leah said, and her eyebrows went up a trifle, so that Mrs. Brastock made an impatient gesture.

"Yes, that's what I said. It's intensely interesting to watch a baby whose origin and antecedents and family history are completely unknown grow up from babyhood. Of course sometimes the results of an experiment like the Maitlands' can turn out to be tragic or disastrous, but they've been lucky. Though I must say I think it ungrateful of Catherine to have wanted to rush off to London as soon as the Maitlands had finished bringing her up and paying for everything for her."

"But I don't really see why she should be so terribly grateful," Leah murmured. "Society owes something to girls like Catherine, and I don't imagine the Maitlands adopted a baby entirely for their own amusement. Aren't you going to be late for your committee, Mabel?"

"Oh dear! I suppose I am, though there isn't much point in getting there too punctually, since for about the first hour we don't discuss anything except Mrs. Folliot's bridge hands last night and why Doreen Bardon just didn't win the last golf-club competition. Is my hair all right now, Leah?"

"There's still a bit of the scarf end sticking out at the back," Leah informed her, and Mrs. Brastock rammed in another hairpin.

"That's better. I can't think why you don't wear a turban, Leah, it's such a comfortable fashion, especially for a windy day, and not too hideously unbecoming. I think I'll get along now because if I'm early I may be able, in a tactful way, to help poor Ethel keep things together and get to the point."

As she embarked upon this monologue she was hovering vaguely round the edge of the desk, and her eyes came casually to rest upon a little pile of letters Sherida had been sorting. With equal casualness Sherida slid a sheet of blotting paper over them, and Mrs. Brastock made a jerky, thwarted movement.

"Well, I must be going. See you at the Red Cross meeting on Tuesday if I don't pop in before, but I expect I shall. And do remember to tell Logan about Catherine coming back; I know he'll be especially pleased. Take care of yourself, my dear."

She didn't vouchsafe Sherida even a nod of farewell as she departed, and Leah leaned back in her chair and said thoughtfully:

"I wonder why it is that sometimes one's friends' best qualities seem to be the most maddening things about them. Mabel Brastock is thoroughly kind and efficient and warmhearted—but on occasions I could willingly wring her neck just because she is. Did you think we sounded very gossipy and catty talking about Catherine Maitland like that? But it's never been any secret here that the Maitlands adopted her when she was six months old from an orphanage. She was found wrapped in a shawl in the waiting room at Truro station, and she was the most delicious baby. And she's grown up into a thoroughly nice girl; one would never imagine that she isn't a real Maitland. . . . Shall we get on with these letters, Sherida, before anyone else bursts in on us?"

There were only two further interruptions during the morning, one by Christine, who hung yearningly over the back of Leah's chair, offering to darn her stockings or sharpen her pencils or do anything that needed doing and would keep her in the sitting room; an offer that was refused by Leah so firmly that Christine departed sullenly, her fine auburn hair spraying out like silk against her narrow cheeks and temples, her thin shoulders hunched.

The other interruption came just before lunchtime when Mrs. McReady, short and plump and innocently blue-eyed, looked in to report on the result of the billeting-committee meeting.

"We managed to collect a list of volunteers who are ready to take in the children at very short notice," she said. "But I haven't put your name down for that, my dear; it wouldn't be fair until we've used up everyone else possible. We managed to get as far as that at any rate, but it wasn't too easy with poor Mabel in full spate. I know she's a great friend of yours, Leah, but really —by the time we'd heard about her last year's prize begonias and how dreadfully darling Keith spoils her and how all the Heidelberg students were prostrate at her feet with admiration when she stayed there for three weeks in nineteen hundred so that she simply can't believe the Germans aren't still at heart just simple, gentle sentimentalists, there isn't much time for anything else." She looked at Leah with a twinkle in her eyes. "Didn't she come scurrying to the meeting especially early so that she could very tactfully, of course, help me run the whole thing and keep to the point?"

Leah looked back and laughed and shook her head.

"You know Mabel as well as I do, Ethel. Enough said. Have you met Sherida Binyon, my new secretary? This is Mrs. McReady, Sherida."

"How do you do?" Mrs. McReady's smile was quick and

warmly friendly, like a child's. "Have you really got rid of Miss
Miffity and the creaking corsets and the smell of moth balls?
By the way, Leah, is Christine all right? I passed her in the garden just now, and she looked so white and drawn and hardly
answered when I spoke to her. I wondered if she wasn't well."

"Oh dear!" Leah said, and her smooth forehead puckered a
little. "Yes, she's perfectly well, but she wanted to stay in here
all the morning and do odd jobs for me and I wouldn't let her,
so I suppose she's feeling wounded and desolate. You know I
rather wish I'd taken your advice, Ethel, and sent her to boarding school with Meg, but she worked herself up into such a state
at the idea of being away from me and Bastions that I was quite
scared about her. It's too late now, one can't send a girl of sixteen to boarding school for the first time."

"I think it would have been better for her if she had gone,"
Mrs. McReady said. "And she could still easily go to Merrion
Towers; it's a finishing school more than a boarding school."

"Yes I know. But honestly, Ethel, you don't know how
frightening Christine can be when she works herself up into one
of her emotional storms, and I think she'd be utterly miserable
there. Oh, I know I'm silly and too soft with her, but I suppose
one tends to be toward stepchildren. They seem much more of
a responsibility and a weight on one's conscience than one's own
children. If Andrew went into an emotional storm I'd give him
a good wallop and stop his jam for a week, but Christine's
different. Can you stay to lunch?"

"No, I'm afraid not." Mrs. McReady pulled on her gloves.
"It's nice to see you looking so well, Leah. And if Christine is
still moping this afternoon send her over to help me paint the
Scout sale posters. Good-bye, Miss Binyon and I hope you're
liking Cornwall."

"I'm loving it," Sherida said, but it seemed to her that there
was a faintly reflective, speculative look in Mrs. McReady's sea-
blue eyes as she smiled and went out.

7

CATHERINE MAITLAND sat in a corner of a first-class smoker with her hat on her lap and her eyes on the racing landscape as the Penzance express ate up the miles.

It was one of those exquisite, sunglass days of spring when the frail air seems to vibrate like harpstrings to the touch of the wind and the trees have no solidity, only a fluent, tremulous loveliness. They were well over the Cornish border now, and the afternoon was cloudless, but still the country seemed to give out something of its own mysterious darkness into whose heart the sunlight never quite penetrated. Against the eggshell sky the moors and hills were painted stiffly in grape-blue and plum-coloured folds; an unexpected pool shone brilliant amethyst, and along a hilltop a wood of slim larches was pencilled delicately in violet.

"I'm happy," Catherine thought. "Or at any rate I ought to be happy, because I'm going home and I really hated it in London. I wonder why I'm not."

She had a small, compact face framed in cloudy dark hair, burnished faintly with red. Her nose turned up a little, and her eyes were almost the green of old Bristol glass, and they had an upward tilt like the corners of her mouth. She was wearing a dark green tweed suit and coat with a coral-red blouse, and her nail varnish and lipstick matched it exactly. Her hands were small, square, and neat like her face and figure, and she used them a good deal, especially when she talked, sketching vigorous and expressive little gestures in the air in front of her, so that people sometimes thought she was French. Hand waving is always considered rather a foreign characteristic in England, where hands are used for the doing of such sensible things as pouring out tea or knitting, but not as a help to self-expression.

They were running across a stretch of moorland now. Three cromlechs squatted malevolently upon a small tor. They looked like petrified toads, and their shadows were smeared darkly across the pale gold earth, but Catherine waved to them in greeting, quite oblivious of the surprised and faintly alarmed watchfulness of an elderly woman in the other corner of the compartment. She wasn't used to travelling in the company of a young woman who waved to pieces of the landscape and hummed bits of Sibelius' second symphony under her breath. Her train-journey technique was an inflexible affair of barricading herself in behind a rampart of *Country Life,* the *Queen,* the *Gentlewoman,* and *Good Housekeeping* and remaining there whatever happened short of a train wreck.

Jerking her attention away from Catherine's odd behaviour —though she did shift herself just a fraction of an inch nearer to an easier grasp on the communication cord—she returned to the *Queen's* social-doings page.

"Young artist's interesting contributions to the Manvers Gallery water-colour show," she read. "Miss Catherine Maitland's Cornish seascapes have been attracting a good deal of attention in the spring exhibition, and critics are praising them for their bold and limpid colour sense. Miss Maitland is the daughter of the Rev. and Mrs. Talbot Maitland of Bravizor Rectory, Cornwall, and she is also achieving success as a portrait painter, though she has not exhibited any portraits yet."

The elderly woman sniffed a little. A woman portrait painter —she disapproved of them on principle just as she disapproved of women doctors and engineers. When her daughter Felicity had her portrait painted in her Presentation gown and feathers, it would be by someone dependable and confidence-inspiring. Catherine Maitland, whoever she might be, would probably paint poor Felicity with a grey face and hair like seaweed.

Catherine looked at her watch and thought: "In twenty minutes I shall be there. Yes, I'll be there—but where shall I be really? In the same old muddle, I suppose. I wonder—no, I'd better not do that. It's no good thinking about anything till I've seen him again—and seen her. After all I've been away nearly three months. Not that three months will have changed her, but it might—it just might have changed him. Logan—I wonder why it's such a nice, burnished name. When I say 'Logan' I can see a lovely bit of old oakwood with a smooth grain and rich, goldy-brown lights underneath the surface and a sort of warm feeling when you touch it. Logan. . . ."

She loved the name so much that she whispered it aloud, her lips moving, her eyes fixed on the views of Newquay and St. Ives fitted into the mirror opposite. The elderly lady rustled the pages of the *Queen* indignantly and whisked her thin hand peevishly through the air in order to disperse a faint streamer of smoke from Catherine's cigarette that lingered on the air. Catherine looked at her, tilted back her head, and blew two large and perfect smoke rings and then tranquilly pulled on the little green felt hat that had a coral feather slanting up the front. The elderly woman glowered but said nothing.

"She'd tick me off for that," Catherine thought, "if my suitcases weren't pigskin and my shoes handmade." She sat still suddenly, staring at them and thinking. "And the funny thing is that they aren't really. My suitcases are made of cardboard and my shoes are those eight-and-elevenpenny things made of patent leather that cracks across the toes, and I bought this suit on the instalment system, a shilling a week and a present of an artificial silk hankie thrown in because it cost more than a pound. That's what I am really, my dear, and I'm sorry."

The train was slowing down at the station now, and there was Perowen waiting to meet it and looking as though, if he could have his way, he would gladly rush off and alter the points so that the entire train and its passengers would go hurtling into the sea. However, when Catherine leaned out of the window to wave to him, he answered her summons and came to take out her cases, trampling heavily and indifferently over the legs of the elderly woman in the process.

Catherine followed him, but at the carriage door she stopped suddenly and spoke.

"You know you could have been as rude to me as you liked," she said sweetly. "Because I'm not quite what I look. I'm only an orphanage foundling really, and these clothes are just a fraud. It's rather a shame to be so deceptive, isn't it? Good afternoon."

"Catherine!" a voice said behind her. "Hullo, Catherine! I believe you're behaving in a nutty way again. Now own up."

"Logan!" The wild-geranium pink came running into her face. "I—well, yes, I'm afraid I am. I didn't know you were here."

"So I imagine. What on earth were you saying to that old dame? She looked completely petrified."

The train, gathering speed, swept past them, and they had a glimpse of an agitated and open-mouthed face peering out of the window, for the elderly woman traveller's dignity had been shattered once and for all. Catherine laughed and tucked her arm into Logan's.

"I was just telling the truth, but people always seem to think you're stark, staring mad when you do that. What are you doing here, Logan?"

"Oh—looking for some parcels Father expects," he said casually. "But they don't seem to have turned up. All right, Perowen, you can put Miss Maitland's luggage into my car."

"Isn't there anyone from home to meet me?" Catherine asked innocently, her eyes scanning the empty road. "How unkind of them."

"Well, I mentioned I was coming to the station and could bring you back, to save the Reverend a journey," Logan murmured and then gave her arm a little shake. "You little fool, you know perfectly well I came to meet you. Get in."

Whenever Logan approached any car the engine seemed to spring into palpitating life of its own accord, so that there was a scramble to get into it before it hurled itself at the hill. Catherine pulled off the feathered hat and flung it into the back, and Logan smiled at her.

"All set? How are you, Catherine? Is there any difference?"

"Difference? What do you mean?"

"Well, when the train pulled in I rather wondered who I'd be driving back—Miss Catherine Maitland, the suddenly successful and much-fussed-over young artist, or——"

He looked at her again, but she didn't quite meet his eyes. "Well?" she said softly. "Which is it?"

He changed gear for the hill before he answered, and then it was in a roundabout way.

"You were wearing that green coat and skirt when you went away," he said. "And that pink jumper."

"Pink! Logan, it's coral. I've never worn pink in my life."

"It's pink," he said calmly. "And pink is pink, however many peculiar-looking water colours you get hung on a gallery wall."

"All right," she said meekly, "it's coral—pink. I can smell the seaweed. Has it been rough down here?"

"Tempestuous. A bit of one of the old mill houses fell over the cliff night before last. How are you, Catherine?"

"Grand. How is everyone down here?"

"Equally grand. By the way, how is your appendix?"

"Oh, it isn't going to explode in the car before we get home," she murmured. "It only let out a squeak when one of those old doctors prodded it too hard. Personally I don't even know it's there, but it was a good excuse to come home. I got so sick of living on prawn snacks and celery straws and gin. How is Leah?"

She dropped that onto the end of her sentence so casually and easily that she surprised herself.

"She's wonderful. And she's got a new secretary-companion, a girl called Sherida Binyon. She's tall and slim, with brown hair and eyes the colour of those dark wallflowers, and she thinks we're rather a dramatic sort of family, I don't quite know why. But she'll get used to us. Lord, that seaweed is a bit overpowering. Shall we drive along the cliff?"

"Yes. Have you fallen in love with the new secretary-companion, Logan?"

"No," he answered carelessly. "I don't like brown eyes very much; they look too much like toffee by candlelight. Besides, I'm in love with you, Catherine."

She didn't make any answer but turned her head away a little. The afternoon sky was still pale blue, but there was a peach-coloured glaze creeping over it, and the wings of the sea gulls looked like tossed-up rose petals. Under the headland the sea was damson blue, but further out it was still peacock bright. She spoke at last, in a low voice.

"Logan, I don't think that's wildly funny," she said, and the car slowed down with a jerk.

"Well, I wasn't exactly trying to rival Arthur Askey as a comic," he answered abruptly, and stopped the car altogether on a wide sweep of short turf beside the empty road. "We'll stop here for five minutes, Catherine, and talk," he added quietly.

"Yes, but—not about that. Not yet, Logan, please. If you'd only try and understand how I feel——"

"You know, my sweet," he said patiently, "this orphanage-foundling complex of yours gets a tiny bit monotonous after a time. That's what it is really, isn't it?"

She couldn't say that the complex wasn't hers but someone else's; she couldn't ask him frankly, "Have you asked Leah what she thinks about it?" She clasped her hands round her knees and stared at the sea and wondered why she had left London. And yet she could feel the reluctant happiness of being back seeping through her whole body.

To look down on the sea again, to feel the wind through her hair and the salt dryness on her lips gave her a queer, emotional satisfaction that had something physical about it. It was as richly stirring as the feel of a lover's arms round her.

"It's so lovely to be back," she said, ignoring his question. "I don't feel I can take in anything else just yet. I want to sit quiet and feel it. You know how silly I am, Logan."

"I know." He looked at her and smiled. "I remember you at parties when you were small, suddenly going off by yourself into a lonely corner and sitting very still, and when anyone asked you if anything was wrong, if you felt sick, you simply said reprovingly, 'I'm only feeling happy. Go away and don't talk.' All right—and I'm sorry for being such a clumsy idiot about the way I blurt things out. Look here, come home and have a sherry and see the family before I take you home; there's heaps of time. They're all dying of curiosity about you in your new rôle of brilliant young artist."

"Good heavens, why! What do they think I'm going to look like now?"

"I'm not sure, but I think Christine expects you to come floating in wearing Chinese pyjamas and sandals, with your hair dangling over your forehead in a fringe and your eyelids painted emerald. You'll be a sad disappointment in your tweeds and pink —sorry—coral jumper."

He started up the car again, and they drove along the cliff road towards the dip of the valley. Up the coast a small tramp steamer was bucketing, the smoke from its little funnel streaming wildly like a bit of dirty rag, the ploughed wake behind it shining vermilion.

Sherida was sitting in the hall, going over some shorthand notes for Leah, when they came in, and she looked up at the sound of a girl's voice with Logan's.

"Sherida, this is Catherine Maitland," he said, and as they came across the lounge Sherida found herself thinking, in surprise: "But I didn't know Logan was like this, so young and spontaneous. He's always seemed rather cynical and cold."

But there was nothing cynical or cold in his shining face now, and Sherida looked quickly at the girl with him, remembering that scrappy and faintly sinister conversation concerning her that she had heard between Leah and Mrs. Brastock. There was nothing to suggest possible danger or tragedy for the Maitlands in this face with its boldly squared forehead under the dark hair, nothing even to suggest mystery. This was completely Catherine Maitland, the daughter of a country rector and his wife, with a tradition of good family and breeding behind them, and Sherida suddenly hated Mabel Brastock for her glib insinuations.

"Is that Catherine's voice I hear?" Mallory came out of his study, with Jane, and there was a chorus of voices and greetings between them, and Sherida, watching Mallory now, saw that his enthusiasm about Catherine's return was as real as Logan's. "Come in and have a sherry," he said, his arm through hers. "Come along, Sherida, it's in my study. We must toast our local celebrity."

She had only been once into Mallory's study since she came
to Bastions, and then only for a moment. Like Leah's sitting room,
it was very much his domain and as typical of him, Sherida
thought, as Leah's sanctum was of her. Built onto the side of the
house in a wing that had been added in Regency days, it was a
much loftier and more spacious room than any of the others, with
a fine old Adams fireplace and walnut bookcases going up to the
cornice. There was a faintly heathery, leathery scent in the air,
but apart from that the atmosphere of the room wasn't aggressively masculine; the few pieces of old Georgian furniture and the
pictures along the one clear wall had been chosen too fastidiously
for that. The deep armchairs were covered with velvet-smooth
Persian saddle bags, and one small cabinet by the door displayed
Chelsea china figures and old enamelled snuffboxes, delicately
elegant.

"Well, here's to greater success, Catherine," Mallory said. "But
we're all glad London hasn't got into your blood too violently.
How long are you home for?"

"Oh, ages, perhaps for good," she answered. "It wasn't my
appendix that was wrong, it was my lungs gasping for Cornish
sea air, and I knew it the moment I stepped out of the train.
Mallory, you've got another French snuffbox, show it to me."

"You're observant," he said with a smile as he opened the
cabinet door and brought it out, a fragile square of chased gold
with an azure-blue and petal-pink enamel lid. "I picked it up in
Cheltenham last month. You know you're a contradiction, Catherine," he went on as she held the box in her hand, running one
finger lovingly over the glossy surface. "You're one of our most
oncoming young modern artists. You ought to despise old stuff for
its gimcrackery. Why don't you?"

She didn't answer him directly, but said slowly:

"We're rather a dreary generation on the whole, aren't we?
We don't create much beauty of our own, and our one idea seems
to be to smash up everybody else's creations. Jane, I haven't seen
those new photographs you had done when you were in town
last. You said you'd give me one if I approved of them."

"Well, if you don't approve of these you'll never be able to stand any photograph of me. Not that it's in the least like me, but still—that's rather pleasing. Here they are."

They moved over to the big window bay to inspect the photographs and stood there together talking and laughing, and so none of them heard the library door open quietly and the wheel chair slide over the Persian rugs. The voice startled them, so smooth and soft behind them.

"So this is where you've all got to! The house was so quiet I wondered." She saw Catherine then and gave a sharp little exclamation. "Why, Catherine! . . . Why didn't somebody tell me you were here? This is lovely, my dear, and how nice of you to come in and see us so soon. How are you?"

Her hand was outstretched, and Catherine had to take it, feeling the warm, unexpectedly strong fingers close firmly round hers. An odd little moment of silence had fallen upon them by the window, as though Leah's arrival had done more than interrupt a conversation: as though she had startled and jarred them; but Logan broke it abruptly.

"I was giving Catherine a lift home from the station, Leah, so I brought her in for a quick sherry. I thought you were out to tea with Mrs. McReady."

"I was, but I got home ages ago." Leah let go of Catherine's hand with a final little pat. "I saw your mother this morning, Catherine, and they're so excited about you coming home. I don't think they expected to see you back here for a long time, since you made such a success of your London venture and found life so exciting there." Her blue eyes met Catherine's bronze-green ones innocently. "But of course you're down here under doctor's orders, aren't you? I hope it isn't anything very serious."

"No, it's nothing at all," Catherine said coolly. "I was coming home in any case, because life in London isn't so fascinating that it's driven Cornwall right out of my head. I must be getting along home now, but don't bother about driving me over, Logan, I can walk across to the Rectory in two minutes."

He didn't bother to answer her but slipped a hand through her arm and said to the others in general:

"I'll go on and collect Christine from the Brastocks while I'm that way. Come on, Catherine."

Sherida put down her empty glass softly as the door closed and said: "I've nearly finished those notes, Mrs. St. Aubyn. I'll just get them in order for you." She went out of the room quickly, but before the door quite closed behind her she heard Leah say lightly:

"It's nice to see Catherine again after such a long time, and I'm glad she's come home, even if it's only for a visit. The Maitlands are lonely without her." Sherida didn't hear any more, but in the room behind her Leah went on, after a little pause, "I think London has changed her though."

Mallory, putting the French snuffbox away in the cabinet, answered casually:

"I didn't notice that she changed much; in fact she seemed to me to be exactly the same as when she went away. I never did believe that a mild success as an artist would go to Catherine's head as everyone seemed to expect it would."

"Did I say anything about it going to her head? I wouldn't mind a sherry, darling, as I wasn't in on the celebration party." There was a faint note of reproach in her voice, and Mallory went to the sherry table quickly and filled a glass for her. "Thanks. What I meant was that Catherine has learned to be clever while she's been away."

"Clever?"

"Yes. Didn't it strike you, darling, that it was a tiny bit odd that she was so unchanged, even to coming home in the same suit and hat that she went away in? After all, in four months of living in rather dashing artistic circles in London one might expect her to gather a little sophistication—and some new clothes. It all seemed to me to be just the tiniest bit too studied—but perhaps I'm being too clever myself."

"I think you've been reading too many clever analytical modern novels, my dear," Mallory said lightly. "Catherine's always been completely natural and always will be. Do you think this sherry is as mellow as the last lot? I'm rather doubtful."

Leah took a reflective sip and shook her fair head.

"No, I don't think it is, if one considers it. Mallory, are you annoyed with me for what I said about Catherine? I didn't mean it unkindly, but one can't help being—well, interested in her reactions to things."

"And we all know that you've got a passion for studying human nature," Mallory said rather quietly. "Wouldn't you like a breath of air in the garden? It's a lovely evening."

At the old grey stone porch of the Rectory, Logan was lifting Catherine's suitcases out of the car, but he shook his head when she invited him in for a moment.

"No, I'll be buzzing along to fetch Christine. Catherine, you aren't angry with me for what I said on the way back, are you? I didn't mean to spring things on you so violently and—well, unromantically. It's like me to tell a girl I'm in love with her just when she's come off a long train journey and is feeling tired and empty."

"And dishevelled and decidedly unattractive—that was why it was rather a nice moment to do it, Logan." She smiled at him, but there wasn't much laughter in her eyes. "I'll be seeing you again soon, shan't I?"

"Of course. Come over and have dinner tomorrow and regale the family with stories of the wild life you artists lead in Chelsea. I'll fetch you. And Catherine—you know why I made you come in for that drink, don't you? Well, I was right, wasn't I? We were all so glad to see you."

She knew what he meant by "all," but for an instant her eyes avoided his.

"Yes, of course you were right, Logan. I'll be over tomorrow. Good night and thanks for the lift."

The Brastocks had no family of their own, but for years past they had built themselves up a reputation for "getting on" well with young people and for entertaining them on a lavish scale. Lavishness was certainly the keynote of their efforts, which always had a curious tendency to get slightly out of hand.

Children came home from other parties in the Christmas holidays in a state of happy jubilation, but from the Cliff End parties they invariably came home in a state of flushed and rowdy obstreperousness and ended the evening by being sick and going to bed with a temperature. There was always too much of everything at the Brastock parties, too much to eat and drink, too many presents and noisy games, too many squabbles and tears.

The days of children's parties were nearly over now, but the Brastocks still exerted themselves to amuse the young people in the same style, and Logan, coming in to collect Christine, found the big drawing room full of noise and cigarette smoke and the strains of a wireless dance band. A dishevelled table at one end staggered a little under the weight of plates of food and empty glasses, and Logan frowned at the sight of the drained jugs down its length. Mabel Brastock's idea of a "harmless" cider cup suitable for her "young" parties was inclined to be too strongly flavoured with gin to meet with Logan's approval, and when he saw Christine come into the room from the conservatory that opened old-fashionedly out of it, he scowled again.

Her silky fine hair was ruffled and her face flushed, the delicate skin stained so sharply with red that it looked unnatural and faintly grotesque. He spoke sharply, ignoring her companion, young Maurice Murdo, whose tousled exuberance wilted a little under his senior's cold stare.

"Are you ready to come along home, Christine? I said I'd fetch you as I was driving this way."

"Good heavens, already?" Christine's lower lip came out in a childish pout. "It's frightfully early and nobody's going yet."

"You're expected home for dinner," Logan said briefly. "Come on."

She gave him a sullen look and then hunched her thin shoulders rebelliously.

"Oh, all right! This is the heavy big-brother stuff I have to put up with, Maurice. See you tomorrow for tennis."

She collected her coat and after effusive and long-drawn-out farewells got into the car at last and sat with one shoulder turned toward Logan to show that she was still angry with him.

"Whew!" he said. "You'd better do some deep breathing exercises, Christine, if you want to get rid of the fumes hanging round you. How many cigarettes have you smoked—and what was in that revolting-looking cup you were swigging down with such gusto? You'd better not go too near Leah till you've sucked a jujube or something."

"Logan, you are beastly!" She flung her head back defiantly. "You talk as though I'd been to some awful debauch instead of to a perfectly ordinary party given by Aunt Mabel. What do you expect us to do there—eat pink jellies and play Blind Man's Buff? After all I'm nearly seventeen. What are you doing coming to fetch me anyway? You aren't generally so thoughtful about your little sister."

"I was out this way in the car, taking Catherine home," Logan said shortly. "So I thought I'd better collect you before the party got too out of hand. Catherine arrived back this evening."

"Oh!" There was a queer, heavily dramatic note in Christine's voice. "Well, I'm sorry I wasn't at home to add to the general rejoicings, but I suppose I'll be seeing her."

"She's coming to dinner tomorrow," Logan said, and Christine made a restless movement, pushing the blown hair back from her hot face.

"Does she have to come over to see us every five minutes?" she said sharply. "You're so selfish, Logan, you never think of anybody but yourself, least of all Leah. You know Leah's unhappy about you and Catherine, and I think it's beastly of you not to care."

The car jerked a little as Logan changed gear at the bottom of a hill, and his voice was rough.

"If I were you, Christine, I'd keep quiet and try and collect yourself a bit before you get home. You're as fuzzy in the head as an owl, and you're talking nonsense."

"No, I'm not!" Christine said shrilly. "I know more about what Leah feels than any of you, because I'm closest to her, she's said so often. And I know how she feels about Catherine. I heard her talking to Aunt Mabel about her. She said she could never trust her because—because what she seems to be is all artificial, because nobody will know what the real Catherine is like underneath until it bursts out one of these days from her subconscious self. She said she was frightened for you . . ."

Her voice died away abruptly as Logan slowed the car down and turned to look at her with such a tight-lipped expression of anger on his face that she shrank a little.

"I wasn't listening, truly, Logan," she stammered. "I just happened to overhear a bit of what they were talking about in the garden one day. I can't bear Leah to be unhappy about anything, and I thought you'd feel the same. I didn't . . ."

The car stopped altogether, and Logan opened the door and said briefly:

"I think you'd better get out and walk the rest of the way home if you want to appear at dinner in a presentable state. The fresh air and exercise may pull you together. Go on."

"Logan, I didn't mean . . . I only wanted . . ." Her voice trailed into silence, and she got out of the car and, with her hands dug deep into the pockets of her white coat, began to walk up the hill. Logan lit a cigarette with a savage gesture and sat watching her, not starting the car. His face was rather white, and when he was angry the light greenish blue of his eyes turned almost black. He was angry, so angry that he could have shaken Christine until her teeth rattled, and yet in justice he had to admit that his fury reached beyond her to something else. It wasn't simply that she had eavesdropped and turned the results into childishly malicious gossip; it was that her eavesdropping had suddenly forced him up against a truth, a cold, hard fact that he had been determinedly refusing to see or admit existed.

Leah didn't like Catherine, and Catherine had tried to make him understand that, as tactfully as she could. Well, now he had to face the blunt truth, and suddenly his depression vanished. All this mystery and silence had simply added to the misunderstanding. Knowing Leah, it was impossible to believe that she wouldn't, when she knew how much he cared for Catherine, change her point of view and forget her fantastic fears and misgivings about her.

Christine was nearly at the top of the hill. He started up the car, caught her up, and slowed down to walking pace.

"You'd better get in now," he said. "We'll be late for dinner."

For a moment she looked as though she were going to cling to her dignified sulkiness, and then her face crumpled childishly with a threat of tears.

"I'm terribly sorry, Logan, honestly. I didn't mean . . ."

"It doesn't matter," he said quietly. "I lost my temper a bit. But don't spread gossip, even amongst the family, Chris; it's a dangerous thing to do. Hop in, I'm getting cold."

8

CATHERINE DIDN'T COME to dinner the next evening, because Jane rang her up to say that Leah wasn't well and they wanted to keep the house very quiet.

"Oh, I'm so sorry!" Catherine said. "It's nothing serious, is it?"

"No, I don't think so. Only you know how it is with Leah— we're always rather scared. I'll ring you up tomorrow, Catherine."

Leah had been working with Sherida at some proof correcting in the morning, when the queerness came over her. Sherida noticed for a few moments, when they first started, that she seemed oddly restless in her chair, fidgeting it backward and forward and pulling at the cushions behind her as though she couldn't get them comfortable. Then she settled down with a cigarette in her hand and they worked for half an hour in preoccupied silence, and then suddenly Sherida, glancing across at Leah, saw that her face was an odd greyish-white colour, tight-drawn round the mouth, and that she had put down her pen. Before Sherida could speak she said in a low, strained voice:

"I don't think I'll do any more this morning, Sherida. And I wonder if you could call Jane. I'm not feeling very grand, and I think I'll lie down for a little while."

Jane, summoned from the garden, came hurrying in, her eyes

frightened, and Sherida was conscious of an atmosphere of nervous tension filling the house within five minutes of the message being sent out by Emma. She went on with her work because there didn't seem anything else to do, and in the hall she heard Emma's agitated whispering to somebody and Andrew's voice, hushed and scared. Jane came out of the bedroom a moment later, her face white, and Sherida asked quickly: "Can I do anything, Jane? Is she ill?"

"It's one of her attacks." Jane kept her voice low as she closed the door softly behind her. "Pain and sickness and a dreadful headache—she gets them sometimes. Father's up at the golf club, isn't he? I don't suppose I could get hold of him, so I'll ring up Simon on my own, though Leah doesn't want me to; she says she'll be all right in a little while. But I can't leave her like that, in such pain. Sherida, would you ring him up for me, while I'm getting hot bottles and things? Do it from the hall so that she won't hear; the number is 31. And ask him to come as soon as he can."

Sherida put the call through while Jane vanished into the kitchen regions, and she recognized Simon Crowdy's voice answering her.

"Dr. Crowdy? This is Sherida Binyon speaking from Bastions. Can you come over and see Mrs. St. Aubyn as soon as possible? She isn't well."

"Leah?" His voice had a sudden sharpness. "What's wrong?"

"Jane says it's one of her attacks of pain and . . ."

"All right, I know," he interrupted curtly. "I'll be over in ten minutes."

He hung up as Jane came back with an armful of hot-water bottles and a wineglass full of brandy.

"He'll be over in ten minutes. Is there anything else I can do?"

"No, thanks, Sherida. It's good of him to come so soon. I expect she'll be all right."

But the strained whiteness of her thin face didn't match the confidence of her words as she went into the bedroom. Sherida went back to her work, and within two minutes Christine came in with such a wild look in her silver-blue eyes that Sherida was startled.

"Why didn't somebody tell me sooner that Leah's ill?" she said with a rising note in her voice. "I didn't know till I came in just now. Can I go in to her?"

Her hand was on Leah's bedroom door when Jane came out and stood blocking it with a curious determination.

"Jane! How is she? I want to go in and be with her."

"Well, you can't," Jane said quietly. "She's half asleep, and Simon will be here in a moment. It's nothing very terrible, Christine."

"You're not telling me the truth," Christine said, and her thin hands were clenched. "You're trying to keep me out of there—and I won't be kept out when Leah's ill. I can help and she needs me, I know she does—but you're jealous of what I can do for her. I hate you, Jane! Let me go in."

She pushed violently against Jane, her red hair falling over her face, her fingers curving suddenly like claws, but Jane stood her ground, her mouth tight.

"Christine, don't behave like a child. Do you want to disturb her and make her head worse? She isn't . . ."

"I don't believe you!" Christine's voice was a scream that shrilled against the quietness of the house. "I won't be treated . . ."

It was Sherida who acted swiftly, almost without thinking, because Jane looked stunned and bewildered. She was over to Christine in one smooth stride, and, gripping her by the shoulders, she shook her till her slender neck jerked backwards and forwards.

"Be quiet and pull yourself together," she said under her breath. "This isn't much of a way to help, is it?"

Christine's tense body went suddenly limp between her hands, and her rising voice clicked into silence as abruptly as though it had been physically broken. Without a word she drew herself away from Sherida and went out of the room, her shoulders hunched and her face hidden.

"I shouldn't have done that," Sherida said, "but she was on the verge of hysterics, Jane."

"I know. I'm glad you were here, Sherida. I get scared of Christine when she's like that, and I don't know what to do. Oh, here's Simon at last, thank heavens."

He didn't stop to speak to either Jane or Sherida; he pushed past them into the bedroom with his bag in his hand and closed the door behind him as though he didn't want anyone to follow him in.

Sherida was in the hall talking to Mallory half an hour later when Simon came out. Jane had rung up the golf club and sent a message out to him on the links, and he had come back at once, but there was nothing very disturbed about his manner when he came in, and the brown quietness of his face was unagitated.

"I expect she's been overdoing things," he said. "She feels so strong in herself that she doesn't realize her own weaknesses. Well, Crowdy?"

"It's not serious," Simon said rather abruptly. "Not at present, anyway; but you know how careful we have to be. I've given her an injection, and she ought to sleep as much as she can, so keep things quiet. I'll be in after tea. By the way"—he turned and looked at Sherida, his dark, heavy eyebrows drawn together into a bar, his eyes intent—"Jane tells me that you dealt with Christine when she began to work herself up into one of her overwrought moods."

"I—yes, I did, because I thought someone should. She seemed to be getting hysterical, and I was afraid Mrs. St. Aubyn would be disturbed. I hope I wasn't too drastic."

"No, you did exactly the right thing. Christine ought to be shaken periodically till her teeth rattle in her head, but Jane's never had the courage to do it; she isn't exactly the sort of person who can be drastic—are you, Jane?" She had come down the stairs behind him quietly, and he turned round and smiled at her. "Don't look so woebegone. I know how you all feel when Leah's ill, as though the mainspring of the house has run down, but she'll be all right. And I think some relaxation would be good for you, Jane. What about the opening Saturday-night dance at the Avalon Castle Hotel? Would you like to come to it with me—if I can get away?"

Swiftly and almost painfully the smooth, egg-brown fineness of Jane's skin was flushed with colour, and Sherida knew that she was completely unconscious of anyone being in the hall but Simon, looking at her with a faint smile.

"Oh, I'd love it!" she said. "But—will it be all right leaving Leah?"

"I should imagine so," Simon said casually. "There are other people in the house, aren't there? There's Christine, and Emma and Miss—er—Binyon. I'll call for you at eight o'clock, Jane, and we can have dinner there, unless I get hung up somehow, but I'll try not to be. See that Leah sleeps as much as possible this afternoon."

His intense, alarmed preoccupation with Leah and her illness seemed to have dissolved suddenly into professional impersonalness, and with his change of mood the house's strained tension relaxed too. Jane bent to pat one of the dogs, and Sherida guessed that the gesture was because she had become conscious abruptly of the colour flaming in her face.

"That's going to be rather fun," she said. "You think it's all right to go out, don't you, Father, if Leah's still in bed?"

For just an instant Mallory hesitated before he replied, his eyes going to Leah's sitting-room door, the corners of them crinkling a trifle. Then he knocked his pipe out against the fireplace and said tranquilly: "Of course it is. Leah doesn't expect you to stay cooped up in the house just because she's in bed for a few days. I'm going down to the cove to look at this driftwood that's been washed up. Would you like to come, Sherida, for a blow?"

There were two paths down from the cliff to the cove, one by way of the old mine buildings, the other, less precipitously, down the milder slant beyond. Sherida had been down that way several times, but not down by the mines, and Mallory paused at the top of the path.

"This is the quicker way down, but—are you all right for heights, Sherida? Not that it's bad at all, but I took Miss Miffity down here one day and she suddenly threw her arms round a boulder and went into hysterics, and I had to lug her back bodily and ply her with large quantities of brandy at the summit."

"You won't have to do that to me," Sherida said. "I promise."

"I think really it was the lure of the brandy bottle in the dining-room sideboard," Mallory said. "Come on then."

The path was steep and twisty but not too alarmingly narrow, and here and there there were little scooped-out flatnesses where one could lean against a rock and look at the view and shelter from the wind. After a night of rain the air was diamond bright, dazzling, so that the landscape was like something a too faithful and zealous artist had painted, overloaded with detail. You could see the tufts of sea grass clinging to the headland across the cove, and every crack in the blue-grey face was carefully etched in violet, and each pebble on the beach below sharply separate.

One of the latest storms had managed at last to make an impression on the lower mill ruin; part of a wall had collapsed, and the crumbled brickwork had a raw, suffering look that didn't match the rest of the weathered stones.

"The mine goes right out under the sea," Mallory said over his shoulder. "We had a terrible job in the old days stopping the children from exploring it on their own. Logan and Jane did get halfway down one of the shafts one day before we hauled them up again. I suppose it's really rather surprising that the family has survived intact, and I don't feel that it's been due to my care that they have. It was Leah who did all the worrying—and acting." They had stopped for a moment on the ledge where the cliff dropped sheer to the breakers bounding and spraying forty feet below in a whirl of rainbows. "When I see her ill as she is today," he went on abruptly, "I can't help feeling that I've made a pretty miserable thing of my share of the responsibility in looking after them."

"But you couldn't help it," Sherida said. "Accidents like that can happen to any children anywhere. Especially when none of them was ever afraid to take risks."

"I suppose so. It was Leah's sense of responsibility, though, that made it as bad as it was. She could have gone for help, and I think it would have been in time, but she didn't stop to do that; her one thought was to get to Logan and Jane herself. I wish you'd known her before, Sherida. . . . The wind's cold here, isn't it? Let's get down to the cove."

It was the first time he had spoken to her about the tragedy of Leah's crippledom, and as she followed him down the path Sherida wondered a little what the pre-tragedy Leah really had been like. Had her ardent vitality been less obtrusive, or was it only because it was brutally pent up and imprisoned now that it thrust itself upon one's notice? Somehow she couldn't quite picture Mallory keeping pace with the activities of a feverishly energetic wife; the air of dreaminess, even of faint remoteness, that surrounded him suggested rather that the measure of his life was set to a very personal rhythm.

She wondered too, suddenly, what life was really like for a man married to a cripple, especially for a man as young in body and spirit as Mallory was. But that side of the St. Aubyns' private life had nothing to do with her, and she was a little ashamed of her own curiosity that seemed to abuse the friendliness they had all offered her.

The driftwood had been hauled up the silver-sanded beach and stacked tidily above high-tide mark against the wall of the cliff. It took a long time for the sun to penetrate to the Bastions cove that was cut so sharply and deeply from the face of the coast, and the air was very cold and the turquoise water had an icy look.

"It doesn't look very exciting," Mallory said, kicking at a spar with his foot. "But it will come in useful for firewood. Have you ever seen salty wood burning, Sherida? It isn't red, it's blue and gold and emerald green. . . . I'm glad Crowdy is taking Jane out to the dance on Saturday; it will do her good."

The abrupt change of conversation startled Sherida, and she realized that Jane and the invitation to the dance had been in Mallory's mind ever since they left the house.

"Yes, it will," she said, and Mallory looked at her.

"Do you think Jane leads rather an unnatural sort of life for a young girl?" he asked slowly. "I mean a life that's too quiet and bound up in the house and family? She's very young, and sometimes I feel it's unfair to her. She ought to be having a good time in London, and I've often thought about taking a flat there so that she could go and stay and enjoy herself."

"But Jane doesn't want anything like that. She loves everything

here, and I don't think she yearns at all for a lot of gaiety and
excitement in London."

"But my point is that she ought to." Mallory kicked at a hunk
of timber thoughtfully. "Sherida, would you help me a little? I
suppose it's a queer thing to admit, but—frankly, though I get
on very well with all my family, I can't say that I know them intimately. You and Jane are friends, and I expect she talks to you
as she wouldn't to me, and I'm not asking you to spy on her. But
if you could find out just how deep her apparent happiness and
contentment with things as they are really goes, I'd be very grateful."

"Don't you believe she's happy?" Sherida asked, and he
hunched his square shoulders.

"There's one thing I do know about Jane, and that is that she's
burdened with a too sensitive conscience. I get the feeling sometimes that she's dedicated herself to what she thinks ought to be
her purpose in life—looking after Leah and Bastions, because of
the way Leah was injured." He hesitated, fished in his pocket for
his pipe, and went on quickly: "Of course Leah doesn't imagine
that for a moment, and it would make her very unhappy if she
did. The one thing she's always struggled to do all these years is
to make herself independent; in a way it's rather a mania with
her. But talk to Jane about the future, Sherida, and her ideas on
the subject; every girl must have some hidden away at the back
of her mind. Or would you hate doing that?"

"No, of course not. But Jane doesn't talk much about that sort
of thing, Major St. Aubyn."

"I know." He sighed. "I expect you've been here long enough
to realize by this time that we're rather a queer family. All our
personal emotions are inclined to eat their way backward into
our minds instead of rising to the surface. That's dangerous." They
were going back up the wider path that curved easily above the
river, and he asked abruptly: "What do you think of Simon
Crowdy?"

"I should think he's a very clever doctor," Sherida answered
and was aware of Mallory's impatient gesture sketched in the air
with his pipe.

"I don't mean that. How do you feel about him as a person?"

"I like him." She was surprised at the readiness of her reply and to find that she really meant it. She did like that lowering-browed, inscrutable, and yet rather emotional young man. "Of course I've only spoken to him about twice; I don't know him at all. But I do like him."

It seemed to her that Mallory's face relaxed a little as though he were pleased and relieved about something, but before he could say anything more, Catherine's voice hailed them from the bend in the path where it curved above the boisterous rush and tumble of the stream. Here the waters seemed to become conscious of the nearness of the sea, of the nearness of their escape from the con-fines of bank and ravine, and to fling themselves forward in sudden eagerness. The rounded, brown-stained stones were almost hidden under flurries of impetuous foam and the golden haste of shallow waterfalls. It was as though the water knew that its free-dom from restraining banks and channels was at hand, as though it could sense the wider liberty of the sea's offering and couldn't wait to get there. The whirlpools round the rocks spun like rou-lette wheels, faster and faster in a rapture of speed.

"Hullo, Catherine!" Mallory called to her as she came down the path. "Have you been up to the house? Logan's in town today."

"Yes, I know. I'm terribly sorry Leah is ill, Mallory. Is she bad?"

"Oh no, it isn't anything much," he said, and it struck Sherida that his air of unconcern was oddly out of tune with the general panic that had seized the house during the morning. "I expect she'll be all right in a day or two. You're coming over to dinner tonight, aren't you?"

"No, I don't think I'd better come," Catherine said quickly. "Leah will want to rest, and it might worry her to have people in. I'll come when she's better, Mallory." And again Sherida, listen-ing and taking no part in the conversation, gathered another impression that Catherine was glad of an excuse to put off the invitation. "By the way, the Brastocks were up at the house looking for you, and I think they're coming down."

There was no need to announce the fact; Mrs. Brastock's voice rising in spirals of sound could be heard on the cliff top.

"Did I tell you, darling, that I ran into Barbara Kane, or rather Duggan, in town yesterday? We had a cup of coffee together at Fuller's, and though I expected that queer marriage of hers to have changed her a bit, I didn't expect anything quite so startling. Make-up plastered on and a demented sort of hat on her head. Well, when she asked me how I thought she looked, I said, 'Well, my dear, if you want the absolute truth you look like a rag and a bone and a hank of hair with a very idiotic hat stuck on top, but of course it's terribly smart, so I suppose you're satisfied.' "

Sherida didn't look at Mallory or Catherine. She had been long enough at Bastions to realize that Mrs. Brastock's familiar, "Well, if you want the absolute truth" was always the herald of some particularly unpleasant comment.

"Well, my dear, if you want the absolute truth" she would say, and then she would tell you that your new coat and skirt were quite well cut but wasn't it a mistake for thin people to wear suits that made them look like lampposts; or that she did hope you would make a success of the raffles at the church bazaar, because poor Mrs. Maitland had asked six other people first to take them on and they'd all refused; or that she was surprised your husband played golf so often with that pretty Styles girl, because she was so bad that it must spoil his game, but perhaps he didn't worry about that.

She caught sight of the three of them coming up the path and swept down upon Mallory in a state of dishevelled agitation.

"Mallory! I couldn't think where you'd got to; nobody seemed to know, but I couldn't imagine you'd gone very far with poor Leah so ill. I couldn't even find Jane up at the house, and I was so worried in case Leah woke up and wanted one of you and I'd have to say I couldn't find you. Good morning, Catherine."

Her gooseberry eyes accused Mallory of philandering down cliff paths with two attractive young women while his wife lay at death's door, but Mallory took his pipe out of his mouth and said calmly:

"Good morning, Mabel. It was nice of you to come over, but Leah isn't bad. Simon's been over and says there's nothing to worry about. I expect Jane went down to the village, as she's comfortably asleep. By the way, Catherine, are you going to the Avalon Castle dance on Saturday? Simon is taking Jane."

"Oh, good!" Catherine said. "I was going to ask her if she'd fixed anything up for it. We'll all join up, and it ought to be fun."

"I didn't know Simon Crowdy was keen on dancing," Mabel put in sharply, "or that he had time for that sort of thing. Still, it will be nice for Jane, so I hope he won't fail her at the last moment. The poor child would be so disappointed. So if Leah isn't better by then, Mallory, just let me know and I'll come over and be with her so that Jane can go to her dance and not miss the fun. Do you think Leah is awake yet? I'd like to peep in and see her for a moment."

"I don't think you'd better go in this morning," Mallory said firmly. "I'll tell her you came over to inquire, Mabel. Good-bye, Catherine, and come over again soon."

The Brastocks and Catherine departed along the cliff toward the Rectory, and Mallory and Sherida went on to the house. He looked suddenly tired and drawn, she thought, as though there had been undercurrents in that conversation with Mabel Brastock that had worried him.

9

Jane didn't go to the dance on Saturday night with Simon Crowdy. But Leah was much better on the day after her attack, though her face was still a little haggard and sharp round the cheekbones. Simon's report to Mallory was very satisfactory when he came out of her room.

"Keep her quiet for a few days and don't let her get up till tomorrow. She's been overdoing it, that's all."

Sherida, watching Jane, saw her spirits taking an almost dizzying swoop upwards, so that her narrow face glowed and there was a light behind the bright grey of her eyes.

"Sherida," she said, "I'm sick of the way I do my stupid hair. I mean I'd like to do something different with it for the dance. Come and suggest something."

They spent an hour in Jane's low-ceilinged bedroom, experimenting with combs and hairpins until Sherida was satisfied and stepped back.

"There you are, Jane. How do you feel about that?"

Jane looked in the mirror. Her dark hair was brushed up from her delicate forehead and ears and curled on top of her head, and now one could see the rather startling beauty of that line from temple to jaw and down to the pointed chin that the loosely swinging hair about her cheeks had blurred.

"Oh!" she said. "But I'll never be able to live up to it, Sherida. It's like a child dressing up; everybody will be able to see at once that it's only a pretence."

That was the curious complex that was at the root of all Jane's moodiness, Sherida thought. She couldn't believe that anything about herself was real, not even her own profile; she had always been told that she was a dreamer, too imaginative, too imitative. She had never grown to feel that there was any solidity under her feet, the solidity of her own personality.

Sherida remembered Leah talking about Jane one day, in a gentle, amused fashion, saying, "Jane is still the little girl who spends her time in the middle of a fairy story of her own invention, and it's not much use trying to change her, though I'm afraid one day she'll have to come to earth with a thump." But when would that day be allowed to come? Leah would look at Jane's upswept dark hair and would say with a note of tender mockery in her voice, "Darling, you look sweet, but what are you pretending to be now, a Mayfair glamour girl out of a Noel Coward comedy? Your name isn't Amanda, you know."

Sherida could see the realization of all that in Jane's eyes as she stared at herself in the square, walnut-framed mirror that stood on her chintz-petticoated dressing table.

"Well, aren't we all pretending something most of the time, Jane?" she said lightly. "You'll pretend that you're glamorous and gay and that you're having a wonderful time and suddenly it will all be perfectly true. Are you going to keep your hair like that for lunch?"

"Heavens, no!" Jane murmured and drew out a hairpin carefully, so that a dark strand of hair fell across her forehead. "But I think I can remember how you did it. Sherida, do you think that it matters if a person has been divorced?"

"How do you mean exactly?" Sherida asked, realizing that this was very nearly becoming the sort of conversation Mallory had suggested she should have with Jane.

"Well, I mean—Simon Crowdy's been divorced. Did you know that?"

"Yes, I heard someone mention it. Did you know his wife?"

"No, it was before he came here in partnership." Jane's hair was all down now, and she brushed it back loosely. "He got married while he was still a medical student to an actress, and it didn't turn out very well, and she divorced him about ten years ago. Simon's never made any secret about it, but some people seem to think that there's something horrible and sinister about him because of it. How do you feel about it?"

"I can't say much about Simon Crowdy because I hardly know him," Sherida answered cautiously. "But it happened a long time ago, and he must have been very young when he got married. I certainly don't see anything horrible about it, and I shouldn't think you need feel guilty about going to a dance with him. After all, he's a great friend of the family, isn't he?"

"We couldn't do without him," Jane said slowly. "He's never asked me to a dance before, and I'm going, Sherida, whatever happens."

But all the same she didn't go to the dance.

10

LEAH WAS MUCH BETTER by Saturday morning, so much better that she insisted on getting up directly after breakfast and going out on the cliff in her chair to get some fresh air.

There had been rain in the night with a little wind, but by sunrise a tremendous and astonishing quietness fell upon the coast, such a quietness that it was almost uncanny. It was the mist blanketing the sea that hushed everything, even the slap and splash of the breakers, but as the morning lengthened the fog banks broke up.

On the cliff top the world was pearl-coloured, shot with dim flashes of opal brightness where the mist thinned, showing a sudden patch of blue sea or golden turf or violet cliff. It reminded Sherida of some curious, dreamlike landscapes painted by a young Hungarian artist that she had seen once in London. One woodland scene had always stayed vividly in her memory. It showed a forest of trees ranging through every shade of blue from azure to pale forget-me-not, etched delicately against the same sort of pearl-coloured air, and the grass was primrose yellow and the leaves silver. One couldn't have believed that Cornwall could ever be so quiet and wistful in its mood.

Mallory and Jane pushed Leah's chair while the dogs scrambled round it.

"Let's go right to the edge," Leah said. "I still feel half stifled with the heat of that bedroom."

The edge was dangerous today, for there was no marking line, only a chasm of faintly gold-shot vapour swirling over the cove, through which the disembodied voices of the gulls cried plaintively.

"I think it's going to clear later on," Jane said. "I do hope it does by tonight; I hate driving in fog at night."

"It will be all gone by lunchtime," Mallory said. "If you're all right, Leah, I'll go along and have a look at that path; I think it needs clearing."

The sun broke through before he reached the path, and the brightness touched Leah's hair, for she never wore a hat unless she could help it.

"I think he's right," she said, but there was a curiously forced note of cheerfulness in her voice. "At any rate I hope he is, because I'd hate there to be any fog at all tonight of all nights, when you're out late."

"Oh, I expect Simon is used to it anyway," Jane said carelessly. "He must know every inch of these roads round here."

"I daresay he is, but that's not a thing I'd like to rely on—not tonight." The oddness of her voice was so noticeable now that Jane looked at her and asked quickly, uneasily:

"There's nothing wrong, is there, Leah? I mean—you don't mind my going out tonight? You're feeling all right, aren't you?"

"Yes, I'm feeling all right—physically, and my other feelings don't matter, I'm not going to let them matter. Give me a cigarette out of my pocket, Jane."

Jane lit it for her, and her eyes were watchful, wary.

"What do you mean by your 'other feelings'?" she asked, and Leah made an impatient gesture, waving the smoke away from her face.

"My stupid, overimaginative ones, which I said don't matter. It's simply the effect of the fog and the quietness—I hate the cliffs and the sea when they're very quiet—and of being ill, I suppose. I wish it were tomorrow, that's all, and that you were safely home from this dance."

"But why? What do you mean by 'safely'?" Jane's face looked pinched and sharp.

"Darling, not what you're imagining. Good heavens, I'd trust you with Simon anywhere and in any circumstances. It isn't that at all. It's—Jane, do you remember the day of the accident? Do you remember breakfast that morning? You weren't very old, but perhaps it stuck in your mind a little. I wonder if you can remember what I said, just as you were finishing your last piece of toast."

"Yes, I can remember." Jane's voice was very low. "You said,

'It's a perfectly gorgeous day, but somehow I wish it were to-morrow.' " She took a cigarette from Leah's case too and struck a match, and surprisingly her hand was quite steady. "Leah, do you mean that you feel like that now, about today, or rather tonight?"

"It's because I'm not really well yet," Leah said almost plead-ingly. "I'm trying hard not to be idiotic. Only it frightened me when that thought flashed into my mind, exactly the same thought and the same feeling. It's only the fog. But—ask Simon to drive very slowly all the way, darling, and perhaps you could give us a ring when you get there and when you're starting home. I'm a tiresome, fussy old fool of a stepmother, and I know it—how I know it! That's all I want you to do, just to ring up. I'll take some aspirin and be perfectly all right afterwards, except that I'll be furious with myself for being such a nuisance. There's the sun properly through at last, and it's going to be a gorgeous day. Has the path fallen into the sea altogether, darling?"

"No, it's still there." Mallory strolled back with the dogs at his heels. "It's going to be quite warm presently. Are you going in, Jane?"

"Yes, I've got some odds and ends to do." She threw the ciga-rette over the cliff edge and watched a trail of tiny red sparks fly upwards and lose themselves in the blue air. "Don't catch cold, Leah."

Sherida was in the hall when she came in, stamping some letters for the post, and she said over her shoulder:

"Oh, Jane, would you like me to sew on that hook and eye now? It will be easier if you put the frock on while I do it, because it's in a tricky place."

There was one second of silence before Jane answered, in a perfectly cool and level voice.

"No, don't bother, Sherida. I'm not going to wear that frock. I'm not going to the dance tonight."

Sherida dropped the envelopes in a heap on the table and faced her abruptly.

"Not going . . . what on earth do you mean, Jane? Mrs. St. Aubyn hasn't been taken ill again, has she?"

"Oh no, she's perfectly all right, and she's having a good

blow of fresh air and sunshine outside. I suppose if Simon isn't in I can leave a message."

She moved mechanically toward the telephone, but Sherida, moving sharply, caught at her thin arm that felt as boneless and unformed under the jersey as a child's.

"Jane, you and I are friends, aren't we? Tell me what's happened. Why aren't you going to the dance with Simon Crowdy?"

"Because it wouldn't be fair to go." Jane's fingers curled round the receiver, but she didn't lift it. "It's Leah . . . oh, it isn't anything to do with Simon! It's simply that she's got exactly the same sort of frightened feeling that she had on the day of the accident, a feeling of something horrible in the air. She's like that, you know; that morning she felt that something awful was going to happen, and she said so at breakfast, we all heard her. She's got it again today, and I can't go to the dance and leave her to spend the evening waiting for me to get back. She wouldn't say anything, but it would nearly kill her, the strain and horror of it. Simon won't mind; he can go and join up with Catherine's party."

"But, Jane," Sherida said, but it was too late; she had taken up the receiver and dialled Simon's number, and her voice was still cool and steady.

"Is Dr. Crowdy in? . . . Is that you, Mrs. Keats? I want to leave a message for him, it's Miss Jane speaking. Will you tell him that I'm terribly sorry I shan't be able to go to the dance tonight. I've got bad toothache and I'll have to go see a dentist this afternoon and probably have a tooth out. Tell him I'm frightfully sorry. . . . Thank you."

The receiver clicked back into place, and still her face had that hard, blank look and her eyes a piercing brightness.

"Jane," Sherida said gently, "I honestly don't think that was necessary."

"It wouldn't have been any use going," Jane said. "I'd have been thinking about Leah all the time. It's not much to give up, is it? As a matter of fact I have got a hole somewhere at the back, so I'll go and have it seen to this afternoon before it gets any worse. If Simon should ring up—but he won't—say I'm lying down, will you? Thank you, Sherida."

She had gone upstairs before Mallory came in, and it seemed to Sherida that there was a faintly anxious look in his eyes when he asked casually where Jane was.

"I suppose she's busy making preparations for the dance to-night," he added, but there was still an inquiry in his voice.

"N-o," Sherida answered quietly. "She isn't going to the dance, Major. She's just rung Dr. Crowdy up to tell him."

"Not going! But good lord, why not?"

"She says she's got toothache."

And suddenly he knew by Sherida's face that she wasn't going to say any more, in spite of the half-promise she had made to him, and he went across the hall without speaking and out into the garden.

Leah had come in from the cliff top, and her chair was standing on the edge of one of the shallow terraces in a patch of sunlight that played like a fine spray of golden water upon a thick border of newly opened daffodils. Leah was looking at them, and Mallory stood still and watched her, feeling pity strike at his heart with a dull blow. The spring was a hard time for Leah— for both of them. The ardent restlessness of the wind, the changing cloud patterns above the headlands, the impetuous burgeoning of flower and leaf and moorland grass demanded some kind of human response. But neither of them could give it; they had to sit as it were outside the spring, looking at it through the windows of their helplessness and, in the secret depths of their hearts, hating it.

He went down the steps and joined Leah, and she turned her head quickly and smiled.

"I suppose I ought to go in and do some work. Poor Sherida must be desperate about getting anything done while I'm in this idle mood. Shall we go?"

"There's no hurry, is there? The sunshine is doing you good." He bent to pull a burr out of one of the dogs' ears and added in a curiously offhand way: "Jane isn't going to the dance to-night. She told Sherida she had toothache."

"What!" Leah's eyes were dismayed, frightened. "But that's ridiculous, she hadn't a sign of toothache five minutes ago. Oh, why is she so silly?" She beat one hand against the arm of her chair. "But of course it's my fault, I said something very stupid to her when we were on the cliff. No, it wasn't about Simon." She met Mallory's look defiantly. "You're right about that, she's old enough to decide things for herself in that way. It was only that— I had such a queer feeling about today, a sort of sense of foreboding and dread, and I haven't had it since the day she and Logan were nearly drowned."

"And you told her about your feeling?" Mallory said softly, his head bent again over the dog.

"I—it slipped out, Mallory. When she talked about driving in the fog, I told her to ask Simon to be very careful, that was all. But I never dreamed that she'd do anything so absurd as put the whole thing off. She must go; I'll ring up Simon."

"I don't think you'd better do that, Leah. She's rung up already to say she can't go because of her toothache, and there's no need to make her look a fool to him. She's old enough too to decide whether she wants to go or not. Would you like to go back now? The sun's gone in."

He turned the chair and pushed it up the gently slanting path that had been especially built down the terraces so that Leah could get all over the garden.

"Mallory, you're angry with me about this," Leah said. "Well, you can't be more angry than I am with myself. If only Jane would get over this terrible sensitiveness about me. I keep hoping that she's grown out of it, that her horizons have widened a little, but it's always the same, I have to be so careful about what I say to her. I'll remember that in future. It's a little awkward about this, because Simon is coming over some time this afternoon to see me and he'll ask about Jane."

"I'd leave things alone now if I were you, Leah. Jane's made up her mind she doesn't want to go."

"I wish you'd talk to her and make her see a little sense, Mallory." Leah's voice shook angrily. "After all, it's pretty difficult for me. If she were my own child I'd simply say, 'Don't dramatize things so much, darling, and stop seeing yourself as the heroine of a Victorian self-sacrifice novel.' But because she isn't my own daughter I can't say it, but you could. Oh, I admit it was thoroughly stupid of me to mention that idiotic premonition of something going wrong that I woke up with."

"Was it entirely connected with Jane driving to a dance?" Mallory said mildly. "There are other members of the family who could get into trouble during the length of a day. If Simon asks about Jane I should say she's gone to the dentist; that's what she wants us to say. You'll be all right now, won't you? I don't want to go in yet; I've got to get down to the A.R.P. meeting."

Jane stood at her window behind the half-drawn curtain and, looking out, she saw Simon Crowdy drive away. The car had been standing outside the deep stone porch for three quarters of an hour, for far longer than was necessary for a professional visit to a patient well on the way to recovery. Jane, penned up in her room and afraid to venture down in case she ran into him, felt that three quarters of an hour pass as slowly as a lifetime. What were Leah and Simon talking about? For that matter, what did they ever talk about at such length in the privacy of Leah's sitting room?

He came out at last and started up the car before he put his hat on. He had a habit of always taking off his hat and flinging it onto the seat before he went into a house. The car swung round the curve of the drive. Jane powdered her nose and hung up the frock she should have worn that night, that had been spread out on the bed. It was a frock Mallory had given her, choosing it unexpectedly himself one day in London, but Leah didn't like it. It was made of coral-red taffeta, finely striped with amber gold and cut on Empire lines with a high waistline and a wide flounce round the hem. Leah said it was too sophisticated and in rather bad taste for a girl of Jane's age, but Jane wouldn't have it dyed or altered, and she had meant to wear it tonight, though Leah had tried to persuade her to decide on the shell-pink chiffon with the smocked coatee. For some reason that she couldn't explain, Jane had begun to hate that frock with its insipid flutteriness and nightgownlike innocence.

She closed the enormous wardrobe gently upon the crisp shape of the taffeta frock and went downstairs, moving lightly, but though her footsteps were almost inaudible, Leah's voice called to her from her sitting room.

"Is that you, Jane? Come in here a moment, darling."

Leah was sitting at the desk as though she had been trying to concentrate on some work, but there was a tired, heavy look about her eyes, and even the bright gold of her hair looked lifeless and listless. She met Jane's eyes with an expression that had a kind of pleading and pathos in it, and Jane felt a warm thickening in her throat that always came there when Leah looked like this.

"Jane . . . Jane, why are you such a silly child about things? I can't forgive myself for this morning, but I never thought you'd take it seriously. I think I hoped that you'd laugh me out of the whole stupid mood."

"Oh!" Jane said flatly and felt her own inefficiency pressing against her shoulders like a weight. There didn't seem to be any hope that she would ever develop intuition or quickness of mind; the processes of her thoughts were still infinitely childish and laborious. In a flash she understood Leah's mood of the morning, of the impulse that had made her talk about it. But there had been no comfort for Leah, only a deepening of the sense of unease. "Oh, I'm sorry, Leah!" she went on in a low voice. "I didn't think you could be laughed out of it, and I imagined you worrying yourself sick tonight if I went to the dance. I'm so dense about that sort of thing."

"Well, perhaps it was asking too much of your sense of psychology," Leah said ruefully. "That part of it doesn't matter; I'm only feeling so desperately guilty about having spoiled your lovely evening out with Simon." She took one of Jane's thin hands and rubbed it against her cheek gently, and a curious little electric shiver ran through Jane's arm. "Well, at any rate, having made such a mess of things for you, I did my best to put them a little bit right for you with Simon."

The sense of warmth ran suddenly out of Jane's hand, and she made a slight movement to draw it away.

"With Simon? But how? I mean, there wasn't anything to put right."

"Jane darling, you've a lot to learn about young men." Leah smiled at her and casually let go of her hand. "Simon was bound to find out that your toothache excuse was simply trumped up, and he wouldn't feel very flattered at the idea of being let down at the last moment on a flimsy lie like that. I told him the real reason why you had backed out, and I'm sure he understood."

"Oh!" Jane said and she moved away to the window and mechanically poked a finger through the wires of the parakeets' cage that hung there. She felt angry in a cold, helpless way. She could clearly hear Leah talking to Simon, explaining the whole business gently and tenderly so that when he left the house he would be thinking of Jane not as a grownup young woman but as a ridiculously sensitive and imaginative child whose queer little moods had to be humoured and handled gently. Probably he would be thankful that he had escaped the boredom of spending an evening with this undeveloped and fey creature.

"Jane, what do you mean by that very inexpressive 'oh'? Are you annoyed with me for telling Simon the truth?"

"I—there wasn't any real need to," Jane said. "It makes it complicated for me afterwards." What she really wanted to say was, "Why can't you leave my affairs alone? Why can't you let me settle something for myself, even if I do it in a clumsy, stupid way? Why can't you let me have a definite personality? I'd rather Simon Crowdy thought I was rude and casual because of something I did myself than he should think I'm childish and whimsical because of what you tell him about me."

"Darling, I can't see anything complicated about all this." Leah was speaking reasonably, anxiously. "Simon's a very understanding person, and he knows exactly how you felt. He certainly won't be tactless enough to say anything about it to you."

"I expect you asked him not to, didn't you?" Jane said in a tone that made Leah stare at her, her eyebrows drawn together a little. "Oh well, it doesn't matter, does it? Shall I bring you in some fresh daffodils? I'm going down to cut some for the dining room."

Sherida came in with a sheaf of afternoon letters and laid them on the desk in front of Leah.

"There doesn't seem to be anything urgent, Mrs. St. Aubyn, but the 'Faith Hope' poems for next month ought to go out tomorrow if possible. I can type them tonight if you have them ready. And I've picked out the most interesting questions for your corner for the answers to be dictated. Unless you'd rather go through them yourself, only they'll want to go to press on Tuesday."

"What? Oh yes!" Leah made a distracted movement. "I've got two poems scribbled down somewhere, and that will have to do to go on with. Tell them I'll send the others during the week. And the answers . . . did you call them 'interesting,' Sherida?" Her eye ran down the page of neatly printed type in blocks with a wide space to one side. "It seems to me I could write out about six stock answers and leave you to send them to the appropriate inquirers. If my readers read my columns every week as they say they do, you'd think they'd know the answers by heart without wasting stamps on me. Sometimes . . ." She stopped short suddenly, a pencil twisting between her strong fingers, the colour rising a trifle into her face. "Heavens," she said with an uneasy little laugh, "it's a good thing they can't hear me, isn't it, or else their illusions of me as a honey-sweet, mellow-tempered confidante would vanish into thin air. It's not really that I'm bored by them, Sherida, it's just that I still seem to get tired rather quickly, and I've been thinking about other things today. I've really got quite enough problems in my own family to cope with without offering to shoulder a thousand and one strangers' difficulties for them. Not that they ever take my motherly and horribly sensible advice, I'm sure. You know sometimes I'm tempted to send out just one bit of advice that isn't sensible and sweetly maternal; I'd like to tell just one neglected little wife not to sit patiently at home dishing out loving understanding and kindness, but to blow all the housekeeping money on a new frock and a matched make-up and what's left over on an evening at the Hammersmith Palais de Danse. That's the effect continual reasonableness has on me, I'm afraid. Have a cigarette, Sherida and tell me, is Jane very miserable about not going to this dance tonight?"

The abrupt change of conversation didn't surprise Sherida; she had felt that it was being led up to skilfully, and she was ready for it. Discussing Jane with Mallory was one thing, but with Leah it was quite another.

"I expect she's disappointed," she said casually. "But it's not much fun to go to a dance with a violent toothache. Are these the poems, Mrs. St. Aubyn?"

She pointed to a sheet of pencil-scrawled paper, and Leah nodded and stubbed out the barely lighted cigarette wearily.

"Yes. The first one is on daffodils and the second on the arrival of two little blessings instead of one, in the shape of twins. Not very original, are they, but mercifully in the spring everyone's mind runs stolidly on daffodils and babies. The rigid mental habits of the public are helpful sometimes. But what do you think of them, Sherida? Do you think I'm slipping a little?"

Sherida ran her eye down the scribbled lines, and her expression was completely noncommittal.

"They seem to be quite up to standard," she said, a shade dryly, and Leah laughed without any resentment.

"That's an eminently safe and tactful comment to make, Sherida, and you're becoming the perfect secretary. Besides you're right, they are quite up to my particular standard of poetic inspiration. Take them away and type them while I wade through these letters."

"She's an extraordinary woman," Sherida thought as she fitted paper into her machine and began copying the first "prose-lyric." "What possible satisfaction does she get out of despising her work like this, or out of the work itself? She can't do it for money; Mallory can give her everything she wants. I suppose it's a kind of clinging to personal power and importance."

She thought suddenly of Leah's hands, broad-palmed, square-fingered, sun-browned, and almost violently strong and unlike the hands of an invalid. Everything that was thwarted and pent up betrayed itself in Leah's hands, and the rest of her body must hate them because they were the only things belonging to her that were free and normal. Sherida shivered a little. Those healthy, warmly tanned hands were somehow more disturbing and frightening than the most ghostly and porcelain fragile ones that had ever belonged to a wasted body.

I I

CATHERINE DIDN'T have her appendix out, but she didn't go back to London. She stayed on at home at the Rectory, and on every possible day she loaded easels and palettes and a lunch packet into her own battered little Baby Austin and went up alone onto the moors to paint. The days she chose were unexpected, not those of limpid clearness and flawless sunshine but rather those of wayward weather, with a threat of storm hanging along the sky line; days when the wind flowed in visible silver waves across the amethyst hills, and the cromlechs had a black and dour aliveness of their own as they crouched in the middle of the heather.

Jane went up with her sometimes, not at Catherine's invitation but at her own suggestion. Catherine knew she had a curious dislike of the moorland, and the mood she came in was half one of nervous awe, half of forced gaiety. But it was as though she were trying to tackle something and conquer it.

She sat on a rug with her back against one of the giant stones while Catherine painted the view that was a study in smoke grey and petunia and pewter, with one sharp bar of lemon-yellow sunlight drawn across the horizon with an oddly sinister effect, as though it were goblin light shining from some unnatural source.

They hadn't talked much, and Catherine was frowning over her brushwork. She hadn't tackled a subject like this before, and it surprised her to find that even Nature herself could veer suddenly towards a modernistic effect of harshness and grotesqueness. It wasn't possible to make this landscape pretty and harmonious; it had to be painted boldly and discordantly, and she refused to be defeated by her own instinctive artistry. If Cornwall under a lowering, windy sky looked grim and unkind, she wouldn't soften the portrait, and she wasn't feeling particularly kind to anyone these days. Her nerves felt as though they had been sand-papered, and there was a perpetual blind anger pressing against her brain, tiring it.

She had had dinner at Bastions the evening before, on Logan's invitation that had suggested a pot-luck family party, but when she arrived, not having bothered to do more than change into an afternoon frock, she found the Brastocks and the McReadys and Simon Crowdy and John Hayes all there in full evening dress, and Leah full of apologies for not having let her know that the evening had been developed into a full-blown dinner party solely for her entertainment.

"You're working too hard," she said affectionately. "You need a little gaiety, Catherine, and we can't have you turning into one of these solitary artist women who don't care what they eat or wear. Not that you've got far along that line yet, but you mustn't be encouraged."

Her smile was sweet and bantering, but Catherine felt that she had been quietly and firmly pigeonholed as one of those eccentric artist people who couldn't be bothered with social conventions, who arrived at a big dinner party in a rather shabby afternoon frock and didn't quite know how to behave. And was it altogether the artist in her that was held responsible for these failings?

"Catherine, do you like Simon Crowdy?" Jane's voice startled her a little, breaking into the sharp stillness of the air as though a pebble had been flung against a pane of glass. The Cornish quietness always had that quality of echo and resentment. A gull swinging far inland over their heads screeched angrily and cocked a malevolent yellow eye down towards them.

"Do I like Simon? Yes, I suppose so. I don't know him well enough to know whether I do or not."

"But you've known him for ages, Catherine, as long as we have."

"Only as the family doctor. I don't know him as a person."

It was curious, Jane thought, how many people said that when they were asked about Simon. He seemed to have lived for years amongst them without allowing anyone to know him intimately —except Leah.

"Well—I wondered whether he said anything to you at the dance at the hotel about my letting him down. He joined your party, didn't he?"

"For a few dances, but he left very early, and I think he was bored with us. No, he didn't say anything except that you couldn't come because you'd got toothache."

"And I suppose," Jane said defiantly, "that you all thought that Leah had stopped me from going."

"Well, didn't she?"

Catherine said it casually, as though it wasn't of much importance and all her attention was concentrated on putting in that lurid streak of sunlight with the right effect of storm.

"No. At least not directly; I mean she didn't intend to stop me from going. I think she was angry with me about it. She did her best to apologize to Simon for me, but I rather wish she hadn't done that."

Catherine had heard details of the episode of Leah's psychic "feeling" on the morning of the dance from Logan, who had spoken of it in a puzzled way.

"I don't suppose for a moment she wanted Jane to stay at home," he had said. "But I can't help being glad she did. Leah's an extraordinary person, and she certainly has an uncanny sixth sense in spite of looking so practical. We all know she had that queer sense of foreboding and dread on the day of the bathing accident. I don't think Jane would have enjoyed the dance even if she had gone."

Catherine had restrained herself from remarking that a foreboding of tragedy generally meant something inevitable, something not to be turned aside by precautions.

"Well, let's hope that next time Simon asks you to go to a dance," Catherine said dryly, "Leah won't have any psychic glimpses into the future. Shall we have our sandwiches now? The light's gone and I can't do any more."

They unpacked their sandwiches and got down in a more

sheltered corner behind the leaning angle of the purple-blue stone
that looked like some gigantic fungus sprouting out of the dark
earth. Catherine noticed that Jane didn't lean comfortably back
against it as she did, and that once when her bare arm brushed it
she gave a sharp, startled movement as though the contact burnt
her. Jane saw that she noticed that, and she laughed a little
awkwardly.

"I know everybody thinks I'm idiotic about the cromlechs,
Catherine, but I can't help it. I feel as though they were watching us all the time. It's funny, isn't it, when Mother loved them
so?"

She so rarely spoke of the real mother who was dead that
Catherine was startled. She sometimes wondered how much
Jane remembered of the mother who had died when she was only
six. Catherine could remember her; could remember coming
over to play with the little St. Aubyns and being welcomed in
the hall by a thin, swiftly moving young woman who always
wore soft, warm autumnal colours, dull orange and maize gold
and russet red, who could invent the most entrancing games with
sea shells and the goblin faces of snapdragon, who used to make
the children hide behind the dining-room curtains while she stood
on the lawn with crusts in her hands and whistled to the sea
gulls, who came down in beating white clouds to take them
from her.

Catherine remembered Mrs. Maitland telling her gently that
Mrs. St. Aubyn was dead and herself crying unbelievingly: "But
she can't be! She couldn't ever keep still long enough to be dead,
and there aren't any birds or animals up in heaven. She'll be so
unhappy."

Mallory, for all his brown solidness, had a curious taste in
women, choosing first Rosanna Jane Penruddock and then Leah
Benson, the one so shadowy and in tune with all the Cornish
strangeness, the other so violently alive and passionately resentful of it. And sometimes Catherine wondered if Leah were trying not so much to subdue the personality of Jane as the personality of that other Rosanna Jane that had been reproduced so
exactly in her daughter.

And yet Leah and Rosanna had been intimate friends. Catherine remembered Leah's first coming to Cornwall on a summer visit to the Brastocks the year before Rosanna died, at the start in fact of that long-drawn-out and relentless illness that wore her away until her face was as transparent and colourless as a communion wafer. Leah had only come for August and September, but the beach picnic parties, the cliff hikers, the motor coaches vanished, the fog swirled in in autumnal thickness, the sea spray was blown far inland by the early winter gales, and still she stayed, spending hours every day in Rosanna's room. When she left, Rosanna had always looked more full of life and resistance, with a faint shadow of colour in her narrow face, and the children had gone with her as far as they were allowed to see her on her way home.

Catherine had overheard Mallory, two years after Rosanna died, talking to Mr. Maitland about Leah when he heard she was coming down to Cornwall again.

"I shall never forget how she tried to save Rosanna by sheer will power and determination," he said. "I think she kept her going for months by it. And sometimes when she left her, Leah used to look as white and exhausted as though she were physically ill herself. I believe she drained her own vitality somehow into Rosanna until she had hardly any left for herself."

It had been another two years before he married Leah, and it had seemed to everyone such a right and happy thing for him and for the children. But within two years Leah was dragged out of the anger of the sea with her back broken, and it was difficult to say how happy things were now for Mallory. Not that anyone could judge, or even had the right to try to.

"By the way," Catherine said lightly, reaching for a cigarette, "be an angel and next time I'm coming over to dinner with you, give me a ring and let me know what I ought to wear. I didn't seem to hit on the right thing at all last night, but Logan didn't tell me and I could have wrung his neck."

"But it wasn't his fault," Jane said sleepily. "Leah didn't make up her mind to have more people in until after he went off yesterday morning. Then she suddenly said—and I'm afraid we all thought it rather funny—that we must realize that you're quite a celebrity now and that we oughtn't to ask you in to any old meal in that casual way. Hence the grand dinner party in your honour."

"I see," Catherine flung a crust of sandwich out to one of the watchfully swooping sea gulls. "But she wasn't trying to be funny, was she?"

"No. As a matter of fact she was quite serious about it. I don't suppose you realize it, Catherine, but Leah's quite awed by your success, and she feels people down here aren't taking enough notice of it. She thinks you ought to be treated with more respect and given a gayer time, and she gets annoyed because Logan and I can't get hold of the idea."

"I'm grateful to Leah," Catherine said slowly, "but I think she's exaggerating my importance and fame just a bit."

And how clearly she could hear Leah doing that, especially to Logan. "We must think of Catherine in a different way," she would say anxiously. "She's going to have a big career that matters tremendously to her, perhaps more than it would to—someone else. We can't expect things to be exactly the same between her and us."

"It's getting chilly," Catherine said abruptly. "Let's pack up, shall we? I've finished painting anyway."

Jane, on her knees as she collected the remnants of the picnic, glanced across at the canvas Catherine was taking down, and she put her head on one side a little and said thoughtfully:

"Are you trying a new style of painting, Catherine? That doesn't look much like anything you've done before."

"Doesn't it? What's the difference?"

"I can't quite explain. I think—well, if you don't mind my saying so, it's rather grim and ugly, and you've never painted anything like that before."

"Perhaps it's part of my artistic development," Catherine said. "And there are times when even your beloved Cornwall looks distinctly grim and ugly, Jane darling. Come along, it's going to rain."

That lurid sulphur yellow streak of light had vanished from the sky and all brightness of air with it. The early spring afternoon lay as sombre and sullen as November along the rough hills, and the sky looked bruised and swollen with the buffeting of the wind. Jane gave a sudden shiver and dug her hands into her coat pockets.

"I don't wonder it gives you the creeps up here; it always gives them to me, even on a sunny day. That's one thing I haven't inherited from Mother, isn't it? I'll bring the baskets."

1 2

JUDY, THE GOLDEN SETTER, was going to have her first litter of puppies, and Mallory, taking her for a gentle walk round the gardens, frowned over her listless meanderings in uneasy circles across the lawn. Sherida watched too, but from the terrace Leah laughed and called down to them.

"Mallory darling, you're exactly like that old nurse I had before Andrew was born, who hovered round me every moment of the day as though she expected me to produce him under the cedar tree. I thought animals like to manage these affairs for themselves in privacy."

"Animals can have things go wrong too," Mallory said briefly. "Come on, Judy."

She came up to him wearily and rested a silky golden head on his knee, her chestnut-brown eyes full of bewilderment and appeal. Sherida didn't find his gentleness with her comic or cranky. From the terrace Leah watched them and suddenly turned her eyes away sharply, feeling a queer, stifled feeling tighten against her chest. Mallory was down there expending his solicitude and care upon a dog who was going to have puppies. His wife would never see him looking like that at her, never again. And the mournful-eyed bitch was living more fully and deeply than she, a human woman, could ever live again.

It wasn't precisely a maternal instinct that strained and clamoured mutely within her, though she was fond enough of children. It was rather the instinct for creation and power and perfection that had always been part of her scheme of life. When she married Mallory she had made up her mind that she would have three or four children, beautiful and superbly healthy, with finer, firmer bodies and more vivid personalities than Logan and Jane and Christine possessed. She hadn't thought of them very personally, but as achievements she would set her mind and body to, and Andrew had been a good start.

He had been a far sturdier baby than any of the others, she knew; she had seen surprise and pride in Mallory's eyes when he first saw him. He had grown used to the tiny, fretful creatures Rosanna had mothered; he had been astonished at the easiness of the whole business for Leah, after Rosanna's illnesses and struggles.

Leah wondered sometimes if Mallory remembered that morning he had first seen Andrew, if he remembered how she had looked, sitting up against the pillows with her golden hair swinging in thick plaits over her shoulders and her cheeks glowing with colour. She had felt and knew she looked as though she were perfectly capable of getting up and playing a hard round of golf then and there.

Now that look of anxiety and concentrated attention in Mallory's eyes had to be for a dog who was going to have puppies.

"I'm going in," Leah called down to them. "Simon's coming over to tea. Perhaps he'll come in useful for Judy if she needs expert attention. Don't come in yet, Sherida, I haven't finished those letters yet."

The edge of sarcasm in her voice went over Mallory's head as he quieted Judy's nervous tremblings and coaxed her back toward the garage, where her bed was made up in a comfortable and undraughty corner. Sherida went on strolling, down towards the orchard. The blossom was just trembling into white and rose-tinted foam along the dark branches, and the first bee of spring boomed and bumbled drowsily against the breeze. Under the trees the grass was thick and deep, tasselled with cowslips and cone-shaped grape hyacinths, and her footsteps made no sound as she moved.

She heard the voices beyond the old stone wall that bounded it before she realized it, before her brain took in the fact that she was eavesdropping. It was Logan's voice, with a queer note of grimness in it.

"We can't go on like this, Catherine. Good God! I'm tired of saying that to you, and I expect you're tired of hearing it. But I mean it this time. You must have made up your mind."

"But one's mind changes from day to day, Logan, as things change. And they have changed since I was down here last. I— I've got started on a career——"

"Yes, I've heard that from someone else," Logan said. "Leah's been dinning it into my ears, only I thought she was talking rubbish. Perhaps she wasn't though?"

"No, perhaps she wasn't." Catherine's voice was so cold and empty of expression that it was hardly hers. "I think Leah understands——"

Within that moment Sherida realized what she was doing, and she went on tiptoe back through the orchard, stooping low under the branches of the old cherry and pear trees. It was queer, but during these past few days all the happiness seemed to have flowed away out of Bastions, as the moody sunshine flowed away abruptly out of the Cornish sky on a change of wind. And it was difficult to understand why it should happen. It seemed to Sherida as though this afternoon the figures of the St. Aubyn family had been dotted about in mysterious isolation, each one almost stereoscopic in its apartness.

Mallory quieting the uneasy dog, Leah silent and watchful in her wheel chair on the terrace, Jane sitting alone at her bedroom window with her dark head bent over some hidden letter writing, Logan and Catherine saying bitter, hard-voiced things to each other, herself wandering aimlessly through the orchard —on the surface they looked ordinary, but in the vicinity of each one of them there was a vague stir of unrest.

Yet everyone was perfectly natural again when they met for tea in the long drawing room and sat dawdling over hot buttered toast and saffron cake. She almost believed that she had imagined that overheard scrap of conversation between Logan and Catherine, for he looked so entirely unruffled and Catherine was so gay. And yet—wasn't there a quiet purposefulness in the way she kept the conversation upon her doings in London, the odd, interesting people she had met, the exciting contacts she had made, the possibilities they opened up? She had never enlarged much on the subject before, but today she was full of stories and even of a faint, childish boastfulness that made Leah smile and tease her a little.

Simon Crowdy was late arriving and came in when they had nearly finished, and as he came in Jane murmured, "Hullo, Simon! I've got to go along to the post office. See you sometime again," and slid out of the room so unobtrusively that Leah didn't notice her going. Catherine went too, and Logan lit his pipe and strolled out into the garden, and Mallory said something about having a look at Judy and departed too, and only Sherida and Leah and Simon were left in the drawing room, where the ruddy gold afternoon light slanted in theatrically from the big windows.

For the first time since she had come to Bastions, Sherida felt awkward, uncertain what to do. It would be tactful to go, and yet it might be tactless too, and she felt Simon watching her with a faint smile, as though he found an ironical amusement in her dilemma and in discovering how she would handle it. But it was Leah who did that, easily and simply.

"Sherida, I've been a lazy slug all day," she said. "And I haven't even looked at those letters that came this morning. Would you rush away and appeal to your trades union for protection if I were to ask you to be an angel and start on some of them? You know better than I do what to answer."

"Of course I'll do them, Mrs. St. Aubyn. I've finished the others."

She was almost grateful to Leah for having got her out of the room so naturally, for there was nothing she wanted less than to stay. As the door closed behind her Simon said casually:

"She seems to have settled herself down here very well. You were afraid she'd find it dull, weren't you? But she doesn't seem to."

"No, she doesn't complain of the dullness, and she's settled herself down completely," Leah said with a hint of dryness in her tone. "And perhaps it isn't quite as dull from a girl's point of view as I imagined it might be. Simon, you aren't still annoyed with poor Jane over that stupid business about the dance? She seems to avoid you. But I explained it was all my fault, and she's such a sensitive child she'll be miserable if she thinks you're still fed up with her."

"But I'm not. And why should Jane bother very much about my annoyance, if I were annoyed? Perhaps she didn't want to come to the dance at all."

"Now, Simon, that's exactly what I was afraid you'd think, and it isn't fair. Jane was as excited as a child at the idea of the dance; in fact she was looking forward to it almost too much in the way she does. As a little thing she always used to feel sick long before she arrived at anything. It cost her something to give it up because of my idiotic nonsense, and I'm trying to think of something to do to make it up to her. I suppose—isn't there going to be a golf-club dance next month? Couldn't you take her to that? I'll see that she doesn't develop 'toothache' at the last moment this time. Oh dear," she sighed faintly, "it's no joke handling a temperamental family that belongs to someone else really. I suppose if I were older, nearer the age Rosanna would have been, I wouldn't find it so difficult, my point of view would be more sensible. The trouble is that I sympathize too much with them. By the way, I wonder if Christine is anywhere about. She's been complaining of headaches again, and I thought you might run your eye over her. I get so worried about her."

"She doesn't need my ministrations," Simon said. "Sherida's shaking the last time she started hysteria did her far more good than any of my tonics and vitamins. I must go. Take care of yourself, Leah, and don't let the family tantrums turn your hair white. They're getting old enough to manage them for themselves."

She held out her hand, and it lay in his for a second, and he could feel the warm strength of her palm, the tautness of her wrist. Jane was crossing the hall toward the garden as he came across it, and she flushed a little, because it was obvious that she was only just going out, though she had departed from the drawing room a good half-hour before.

"Hullo! Can I give you a lift down?" Simon asked her, and she shook her head.

"I'm afraid not, thanks. I've got to take all the dogs, and they'd make such a mess of your car. They need exercise anyway. How do you think Leah is looking?"

"Very well indeed. I feel my visits are rather superfluous, you all look after her so efficiently." He paused on the doorstep, hatless as usual, and she kept her eyes determinedly away from him. "By the way, what about the golf-club dance next month, Jane, are you booked for that? If not, shall we ornament it together?"

She did look at him then, the grey of her eyes piercingly bright and angry.

"Did Leah suggest you should ask me, to 'make up' for my disappointment over the Avalon Castle dance?"

She shot the question at him so abruptly, with such unexpected directness, that he was taken aback.

"Well, she didn't exactly . . . we thought . . . I mean I thought . . ."

"With a little prompting from her." Jane's thin face was flushed a queer, dull red. "It's kind of you, Simon, but I'm not an infant who wants special treats thought up for it because it's had a supposed disappointment. It's kind of you, but I know you don't care for the club dances, and I don't either."

She knew she was achieving a greater childishness than ever before and that now nobody was to blame but herself, but something had got out of hand inside her. And yet Simon didn't smile with his usual tolerant and faintly ironic amusement at her outburst; he looked at her thoughtfully, consideringly, with a hint of surprise, and said quietly: "Well, I'm sorry. But if you do go, Jane, and if I manage to get there, keep a few dances for me. Good-bye."

The wind rose in the evening, and by the time Sherida went to bed it was a full gale, thundering round the house and clawing at its stones like a marauding wild beast. The house set its sturdy shoulders against it defiantly, but everything in it trembled and vibrated a little with the force of its resistance.

There was moonlight, not shining steadily but in dramatic bursts and flickers, as though amateur hands were fumbling with the complexities of theatre lime and spot lights. Bits of the landscape—the headland, the twisted old blackthorn near the cliff edge, a clump of furze bushes, the church tower—would leap into sudden and urgent life, piercingly bright in black and silver, and then in a second would be gone again as the black cloud shadows ran like a millrace across the sky.

She sat up late, reading, sleep driven from her by a persistent little itch of restlessness that made it difficult even to concentrate on a book, and presently, just before midnight, when she was thinking of taking aspirin and forcing herself to relax, she heard doors open in the hall and footsteps cross it and come hurrying up the stairs. Because of that feeling of uneasy expectancy she opened her door and saw Mallory coming down the passage to his room with a torch in his hand and a mackintosh over his arm.

"Is anything wrong?" she asked softly. "Mrs. St. Aubyn isn't ill, is she?"

He switched the light of the torch onto her, but she was quite unconscious of her hair tied up carelessly with a green ribbon, of her unpowdered nose and unlipsticked mouth.

"No," he said, "it isn't Leah. I'm sorry if I disturbed you, Sherida. I'm just going to Judy, she's having rather a tough time. I came up to fetch some cigarettes and a rug. I may be down in the garage some time."

"Poor Judy!" Sherida said and she didn't smile. "Can I do anything to help? I'd like to if I can. I can't sleep with all this wind, so I might as well be doing something useful. Do you want anything else that I could bring down?"

"Well, I'd be glad of some hot water in a thermos. But look here, it's a wild night and I can manage alone. Why should you come out?"

"But I want to. I'll bring the hot water down in about ten minutes if you want to go on."

He hesitated for a moment, his eyes still studying her above the white shaft of light from the torch, and then he nodded.

"Thanks, Sherida. It's good of you to bother. Put a waterproof on, it's raining hard now. Can you find your way to the garage?"

"Yes, I've got a torch."

She closed the door and hauled on some clothes, slacks and a high-necked red jersey and an oilskin. It was ridiculous to feel this tingle of conspiratorial excitement vibrating through her; there was nothing particularly adventurous in going down to a draughty garage to look after a sick dog. But it was giving her an excuse to go outside late at night in a gale, and she realized suddenly that for weeks she had been longing to do that but had never quite summoned up enough courage to wander out at midnight, even in such an unconventional household as Bastions.

She didn't turn on any lights but used the torch and went downstairs lightly and into the kitchen to boil a kettle. There was a big thermos on a shelf, and she filled it and on an impulse cut a wedge of plum cake and put it with some biscuits into a paper bag in her pocket. The front door with all its ancient bolts and chains was too much to tackle if she didn't want to disturb the whole house with her clankings and rattlings, so she went out by the back door, wrestling for a moment to close it behind her as the wind clung to it jubilantly.

Downstairs, in the specially built, adjustable high bed that stood stiff and white in the middle of her room, Leah lay breathing quietly, but in a slow, dragging way, and her hands were clenched as they rested on the satin eiderdown. The curtains and blinds were drawn well back, and her room was full of flying shadow and moonlight, but the wind wasn't as noisy down here as it was upstairs. She hadn't been able to sleep though, and she had needed all her self-control to hold herself back from taking another of her sleeping tablets.

But now she didn't want one, she didn't want to go to sleep; she wanted only to lie awake listening, straining her ears for a recurrence of those footsteps, those soft, separate closings of doors and hushed, secret movements against the resentful, surprised quiet of the house. Not a board could creak in the house but she knew its origin. Mallory had been moving about restlessly for some time; she had heard him go out of the house and then come in and go upstairs, and then go out again. And then ten minutes later she had heard another door open and close and those lighter, cautious footsteps come down the stairs and pass through into the kitchen regions, and then, faint above the whine of the wind, the quiet closing of the side door.

Sherida had gone out, at half past eleven, after everyone else was in bed. Leah dragged herself upright on her elbows and stretched out a hand toward the bedside table. There was always a plate there with an apple and some biscuits on it in case she wanted to nibble something during the night, and in the blackest darkness she could put her hand on it unerringly. But tonight she was clumsy or careless, her hand knocked the edge of the plate and she felt it shoot away from her and heard it land on the floor with a dull thud and the bouncing of the apple.

She was trembling so with fury that she felt sick and stiff. That was one of the hardest things to bear, the blind, stubborn animosity of all inanimate things: the fountain pen that spat ink all over a clean sheet, the last match that broke in half as she struck it, the ball of wool that leapt out of her hand and rolled under the farthest chair, the pencil point that broke off, the hair curler that tangled itself with slow deliberation in the depths of her hair so that it was torture to drag it out, the torch battery that flickered out without any warning. She was helpless and at the mercy of all these things, and they knew it, they revelled in tormenting her with their dumb hostility.

She thought of the look in Mallory's eyes as he stroked Judy's weary head and she thought of the light, quick sound of Sherida's footsteps passing out of the back door into the windy night. She would brace her tall, slender body strongly against it, and her hair would fly back from her face, and she would have a living companionship with the vigorous air, the sweeping shadows, the ardent bend of the trees.

There was another sound, close at hand, that made her move

nervously, looking toward her door. It opened noiselessly, and a dressing-gowned figure stood there with moonlight touching with ghostly luminosity a narrow pale face framed in fine, bright hair.

"Christine! Darling, what on earth are you doing down here?"

"I didn't wake you up, did I?" Christine asked in a conspiratorial whisper. "I had a feeling somehow that you couldn't get to sleep and wanted something. And I thought I heard a sort of bump in your room."

"It was only my plate of biscuits and the apple shooting onto the floor—I knocked it off the table. You've got sharp ears, Chris."

"I think I would hear upstairs if you even dropped your hankie off the bed. I'll pick them up." She grovelled under the bed and emerged with a handful of biscuits and the truant apple. "They're all crumbly. I'll get you some fresh ones."

"No, don't bother about the biscuits, I don't really want them, but I'd like the apple. I'm thirsty."

She took it from Christine and bit into it with a kind of vicious pleasure in the feeling of her strong teeth crunching into the crisp flesh. The apple had had its tiny moment of triumph, but now she was having hers. Christine sat on the edge of the high bed, her pyjamaed legs swinging, her eyes on Leah's face.

"You ought to have got to sleep ages ago," she said abruptly. "Didn't you take your sleeping stuff, or did the wind keep you awake?"

"No, not particularly, but the house seems to be in one of its noisy moods tonight; everything is creaking and groaning and fidgeting."

She wondered if Christine had heard the opening and shutting of the various doors and those cautious footsteps. She ought not to be encouraged either in these nocturnal wanderings or in the slightly melodramatic tone she was indulging in, but for the moment Leah felt oddly unwilling to behave like a sensible and briskly reproving stepmother.

It was comforting to have Christine sitting here beside her with all her emotional attention fixed upon her. The bedside lamp was on, and its light shone slantwise under the tilted shade upon Christine's smooth head. The brilliant red-gold of her hair was neither a St. Aubyn nor a Rosanna colour, and she was really only like Rosanna in the smallness of her bones. Perhaps that was why, secretly, Leah was drawn more toward her than toward the other two. If she had more children one of them might easily have been like Christine, with the same vivid colouring.

"Leah," Christine said abruptly, "were you lying awake because you're—unhappy about something or someone? I could feel you were unhappy, right away upstairs. I thought of you lying all by yourself in the dark, feeling miserable, and I couldn't stand it. I wish—Leah, why won't you let me move my room down to the old day nursery? I'd be near you then at night, but I wouldn't be a nuisance, I promise. It's just that I could slip in sometimes when you're awake like this, without disturbing anyone else. Can't I do that?"

Her arms were linked round her thin, hunched knees, and she was staring at Leah with such intensity that her face seemed to be all eyes. This was a subject that had been brought up several times before and dealt with firmly and sensibly, but tonight Leah's determination wavered. It was absurd to say that it was unhealthy to encourage a girl of Christine's age in a natural show of affection and consideration. She was old enough to think about these things, and she had thought about it. She loved her bedroom upstairs with the low oak beams and the chintz-befrilled furniture and the long view down the valley. She would find the day nursery stuffy, and there was no view at all except over a corner of the lawn, and so the offer cost her something to make, and it would be cruel to sneer at it as something childish and hysterical.

"Darling, it's very sweet of you," Leah said slowly. "I think I would like to have you near me at night, though I don't intend to be a bother to anybody after all this time. We'll see about it tomorrow."

"But don't talk it over with everyone else in the house," Christine said. "After all, it's my affair if I want to move my room, it hasn't anything to do with anybody else. Don't let them all interfere, Leah, because why should they? I'm not a baby, and I—I feel differently about things, and I've got a right to. Leah, are you worrying about Catherine and Logan? Or is it somebody else?"

But Leah was suddenly tired, not sleepy but tired mentally. She wanted to be left alone in the dark to lie and listen for the return of those footsteps, and she wanted to think. Besides it wouldn't do to let this conversation run away with her, and she pulled a pillow into position and yawned a trifle ostentatiously.

"Of course not, Chris. I'm not worried about anything really. If you can't get to sleep you begin to see life in rather a drab light, but I am sleepy now and the wind is much quieter. Run along to bed, darling, and don't catch cold. But thank you for coming down."

Christine kissed her quickly and went out, shutting the door as softly as she had opened it. The wind had dropped a good deal, and it was quiet outside too, so quiet that Leah couldn't miss the sound of doors opening, the sound of returning footsteps, but the house lay wrapped in silence.

13

JUDY LIFTED HER HEAD lethargically to glance along her flank at the three shapeless golden brown balls that squirmed beside her, and then she dropped it back on the straw with a blissful sigh and went to sleep. Mallory patted her and straightened his back and smiled at Sherida across the storm lantern he had put on the ground between them.

"Well, that's a good job done. I'm glad we came down. You must be frozen, Sherida. We'll have something hot in the house, and we can go along now."

"I'm not a bit cold," Sherida said. She collected the kettle

and the thermos and stood up, and her shadow sprawled waver-
ingly across the garage's whitewashed wall. Mallory was still
kneeling beside Judy, arranging a piece of sacking on a string to
keep the draught off her and her puppies, and suddenly, almost
as though he had spoken, Sherida knew with piercing clearness
and certainty that there was a curious lack of fulfilment in his
life, a deep-down core of emptiness that had never been filled by
either of the women he had married.

Mrs. Maitland had talked to her one day about Rosanna.
Mallory, home on a few days' leave from France as a twenty-
year-old subaltern, had met her at Bastions and married her on
his next leave. Sherida could well imagine the effect her strange,
remote personality must have had on a boy transplanted suddenly from the mud and blood and filth of Flanders trenches to
the pure, cold austerity of a Cornish spring. Rosanna had
symbolized something for him, but after the war when they
settled down to married life her symbolism might have grown
a little dim and unsatisfying.

And then Leah? That was easier still to understand. After
Rosanna's wind-blown elusiveness the richness of Leah's vitality
and reality must have been like a warm fire to him—and he had
had three young children left on his helpless hands. Everything
had always been too easy and too swift for Mallory. He looked
up at her with a faint smile.

"I expect you think I'm like a fussy old spinster with an over-
fed cat. Leah does. Let's go along and get that hot drink for you."

He turned out the storm lantern and drew the garage door to
behind him, and from that cramped little world of whitewashed
walls and sacking and flickering light they stepped into the limit-
less world of broken darkness and flying moonlight and a wind
that now only sighed plaintively, like a child tired out after a
fit of furious raging, amongst the trees and the cliff grasses.

"What is it?" Mallory asked her as she hesitated where the
path to the house and the path to the cliff separated at right
angles. "Have you forgotten something?"

"No. It's only that it's such a lovely night, and I've been wanting ever since I've been here to walk along the cliff in the moon-

light. But do you want to get back to the house? I can stroll round alone."

"And fall straight down one of the old chimneys? No, I don't think that's a good arrangement. I think I'd like a stroll myself before I turn in. Mind the step."

They went through the belt of sturdy trees and out onto the cliff path, their bodies bending a little against the rush of wind that still swung in from the sea, like a boy vaulting a high gate. Now she could see the whole panoramic view that she glimpsed in a section from her bedroom windows, and the complete thing caught her breath a little.

From one jutting, ink-black headland, far out on the right of the bold sweep of the bay, to the cliffs and scattered jags of rock on the left, the pattern of the night was woven with a hundred different threads of luminous colour. Midnight blue shading to bottle green and a strange, clouded sapphire, silver and tinsel and pewter, steel-bright greyness and amber tinged with faint pink, aquamarine, and bronze, and a patch of startling, unearthly whiteness where a high rampart of cloud caught the full moonlight; it was incredible that darkness could be so brilliant and vivid. The detail was as fine and sharp as in some old steel engraving, and yet the wind flowing across it softened and blended it and suddenly remoulded the whole design. It was difficult to hang on to reality in Cornwall, Sherida thought, where even the landscape had no fixed outline or shape but changed as swiftly as cinema shots upon a screen.

"Well, is it dramatic enough for you?" Mallory asked, and she nodded.

"It's the most exciting thing I've ever seen. The bit I see from my windows is fine enough, but this—it's incredible."

"It isn't often quite so spectacular as it is tonight. But you mustn't develop a taste for roaming about on your own after dark along the cliffs, Sherida. I should have been worried to death if I'd known you'd got the idea in your head. You won't try this sort of sight-seeing on your own, will you? Look out for that rabbit hole."

A gust of wind hit her across the back suddenly, throwing her

off her balance a little, and Mallory put out a hand to steady
her. She felt it grip her arm and then slip through it so that she
was held against the force of the wind beside him, and for a
moment she lost awareness of the view and was only conscious
of that firm hold on her arm, of the solid bulk of his shadow
standing between her and the cliff edge. She hadn't answered
his question, and he gave her a sudden urgent little shake.

"I know you're adventurous, Sherida, but it really wouldn't
be safe for you to come out here alone, even in broad moonlight. Are you going to promise you won't?"

"Yes, of course I promise. I certainly don't want to add to
your worries by falling over the cliff in the dark. And though
it is lovely out here, it might feel rather lonely and frightening
if one were alone. I'm not used to the bigness of Cornwall yet."

"It can be unfriendly," Mallory said in a low voice. "But are
you afraid of loneliness, Sherida? Perhaps you know what it's
like and you've conquered it, but I hope you haven't been
through that yet."

"Yes, I think I have," she said, and it seemed to her that his
hand tightened a little on her arm.

"Yes, of course you must have. You must have felt lonely
when you first came to Bastions. I think I saw that you were
when you came into the hall that evening and had to face us all,
complete strangers and unknown quantities. It must have been
a nerve-racking moment for you."

"But it didn't last long. You were all so kind, even the house
was."

"Did you feel that it was a friendly house?" he said. "I think
it is in spite of some dark patches in its history. Rosanna used to
say that it had never let unpleasant doings or people connected
with it sour it. The funny thing is that Leah has never felt that;
she says its atmosphere depresses her. That's why she's made her
rooms so violently modern, as a sort of gesture of defiance, I
suppose. I've always felt that it would have been fairer to her
to have left Bastions and gone to live somewhere else, but of
course she wouldn't hear of it. I don't like the feeling though
that she and the house are hostile to each other, but she isn't

Cornish born and bred as Rosanna was, and she doesn't let herself be too much influenced by our superstitious whims and fancies."

It was the first time he had ever spoken of Rosanna to Sherida, and she had the feeling that he was talking more to himself than to her as he stood looking out toward the sea and holding onto her arm. Suddenly he made an abrupt movement as though he were shaking something away from him.

"You must be getting cold. Let's go in and get that hot drink if we can manage it without waking the whole house."

Behind them the shape of the house was solid and compact, sturdily shouldering away the pressure of wind and darkness. But Sherida had a feeling that it wasn't completely asleep, that there was watchfulness and wakefulness somewhere behind those dark windows.

They tiptoed past Leah's silent rooms, made some hot malted milk in the kitchen, drank it quickly, and then made their careful way upstairs. Afterward, thinking about it, Sherida rather regretted that extreme caution that gave the whole trivial affair of looking after a sick dog a conspiratorial atmosphere, a sort of dramatic secrecy. In spite of their wary tread she heard the stairs creak here and there and the house stir faintly. There was nothing to suggest that Leah wasn't sound asleep, but Sherida knew she wasn't; there was something alert and listening behind her closed door.

"Good night, Sherida, and thanks for helping me. And I enjoyed our blow along the cliff. If anything particularly spectacular comes along that you want to see, tell me and I'll escort you to a grandstand seat again—but don't forget your promise. No roamings on your own. Sleep well."

He didn't touch her, but she felt as though his hand had gripped hers, as though something electric and powerful flowed between them.

"No, I won't forget," she said. "Good night."

14

ONE OF THE THINGS Leah had from the first been most stubborn in was her refusal to slip into the easy, invalidish habit of breakfast in bed, wearing a becoming dressing jacket and a ribbon round her hair.

In fact all the pretty-pretty disguises that popular sentiment wraps around illness were curiously repellent to her. Tight-lipped, she used to sit unwrapping the numerous parcels sent to her in the early days, bringing out from their depths elaborate lace bed jackets and shawls and snoods, sets of patience cards and jigsaw puzzles, complicated back and book and newspaper and arm rests, and to Mallory she said grimly: "It doesn't seem enough for them that my legs are paralyzed. Apparently I'm to be paralyzed all over, including my brain."

The bulk of the gifts went to church bazaars, Leah's bed remained the high, severely plain hospital model, and at eight o'clock punctually every morning she was in her place in the big red-cushioned chair at the head of the dining-room table with the heavy silver coffee and tea pots in front of her.

Sherida was down ahead of any of the family that morning and found Leah alone there, glancing through her usual stack of letters, humming a little under her breath and looking as fresh as the morning that lay golden along the coast line after the night's stress. She said "good morning" and went on opening letters, and Sherida stood by the window, breathing in the sharp, almost dizzyingly pure air.

"It's nice after the gale," she said. "The wind was terrific and the view from the cliff was wonderful. I had a look at it with Major St. Aubyn after we'd settled Judy comfortably with her puppies. She's got three, safely. I hope we didn't disturb you coming in and out, Mrs. St. Aubyn. I went out to help with hot water and things."

"Did you?" Leah said with a faint smile. "No, you didn't disturb me, though I did hear someone moving about and wondered a little if burglars had managed to get in after Mallory's miniatures."

"Oh, I'm sorry," Sherida said quickly. "Perhaps I should have come in and told you what we were doing, but we both thought you were asleep, as you didn't make any sound."

"I'm not in the habit of screaming the place down with fright if I hear somebody walking about the house after dark," Leah said dryly. "And it didn't matter anyway. I guessed Mallory had got Judy's confinement on his mind and was agitating about it. I hope he didn't keep you up too late. Good morning, darling."

Christine had a habit of slipping into a room very silently and waiting for her presence to be noticed before she said anything. She kissed Leah but to Sherida's good morning vouchsafed nothing more than a wordless scowl that startled Sherida by its concentrated ferocity. She looked pale this morning with faintly blue circles round her eyes, and Leah said with concern in her voice:

"My dear child, you do look peaky this morning. Have you got a headache?"

"No; at least I had, but it's going off. It isn't anything, darling, just that I didn't sleep very well. It seemed rather a noisy night, and I couldn't get settled down. You were kept awake late too, weren't you, Leah?"

"What's all this about bad nights?" Mallory said briskly from the garden door. "I should have thought you were used to a bit of wind about the place by this time, Christine."

"I am, but it wasn't only the wind," Christine said deliberately, her eyes on Sherida again. "I kept hearing footsteps and the stairs creaking, very late."

"Just after twelve o'clock," Mallory said quietly. "That was me going out to look after Judy, and Sherida very kindly came along with hot water in a thermos. We were your ghosts, Christine, and if you'd put your head out of your door you'd have seen us. I'm sorry if we kept you awake, Leah."

"But my dear, you didn't." She was perfectly placid and smiling again. "I wasn't in the least bit mystified, because I guessed exactly what and who it was. Do you think I don't know the sound of every single door in this house opening and shutting? I don't know why Christine should have got worried about it. Have some coffee while it's really hot, that will settle your headache thoroughly."

"I don't want any. I don't think I want any breakfast at all. I'll take my book out in the garden and have some milk later if I feel like it."

She picked up a cardigan from the arm of her chair and went precipitately out, and Leah said quickly, half apologetically:

"She's in one of her rather silly moods this morning, Mallory, so we'd better leave her alone. She's been worrying about me being alone downstairs again and keeps on about changing her room down to the old nursery. I think we'd better let her have her own way if we don't want too much fussing. And I think I would quite like having someone near me."

"Jane wanted to come downstairs," Mallory said, helping himself to eggs and bacon. "And Kate offered to move in there. Do you particularly want Christine on hand at night, Leah?"

Her lips tightened a little, and a faint redness came up under the smooth rosiness of her cheeks.

"With the others I've felt that it would be a nuisance moving downstairs, but I don't feel that with Christine. She really wants to do it, and one can't help being a little touched by it. But of course if you don't approve, Mallory, I daresay you're right. There isn't the slightest need for me to have anyone sleeping near me at night. Help yourself, Sherida, to anything you want. I'll leave all these letters to you; there isn't anything personal in any of them."

The extra touch of colour had faded out of her face again by the time Logan and Jane came in, and the tiny stir of uneasiness that had rippled across the room died away so swiftly that Sherida wondered if she had imagined it. She still couldn't feel in any way guilty about last night, or that she was responsible for a moment of friction between Mallory and Leah, and she certainly didn't regret such a harmless thing as a walk along the cliff in the moonlight with him.

She took the letters up to her room and sat at her typewriter, leaning on her elbows, remembering that immense and awesome loneliness and loveliness, remembering even more sharply the feel of Mallory's hand on her arm when he steadied her against the gust of wind. She could see him down below in the garden, strolling toward the orchard, pipe in mouth, and suddenly she picked up a sheet of paper, wound it crookedly into her machine and began typing.

Mallory found Christine curled up in a sunny corner behind the summerhouse, her cardigan tucked under her head, her book limp and unopened on her lap.

"Well, how's the headache?" he asked cheerfully.

"Oh, it's all right, it's nearly gone," she answered listlessly and opened the book deliberately, as though she wanted to read.

"That's good. You shouldn't have bad headaches at your age," Mallory was plodding on determinedly against her mute resistance. "I've been thinking, Chris, about you lately. It seems a dull sort of life here for a girl of your age, year in, year out. Besides every girl ought to be fitting herself out for something, some sort of work. Wouldn't you like to try that domestic-science college at Newquay? A year there would be rather fun for you."

Her fingers that had been restlessly turning the pages of the book were abruptly still, and she lifted her bent head slowly.

"You mean—go there as a boarder?"

"Yes. Pamela Sherborne has written that she loves it, and you'd know her to start off with. Of course I haven't done anything about it; I wanted to talk it over with you first. I do want you to think about it, Chris."

"But going away from here," she said slowly. "I don't know —I don't want to leave Leah, and I don't think she wants me to go."

"Leah wants you to live a life of your own," Mallory said dryly. "And I might point out that there are a few other people in the house besides yourself to look after her."

"I know." Christine's hair flopped over her cheeks again as she lowered her head, and her voice was faintly breathless. "But I was going to move down to sleep in the old nursery, to be near her at night. She oughtn't to be quite alone like that. Last night I came down to her, and I found her wide awake, lying in the dark and so unhappy. If I hadn't come down——"

"Christine, there's one thing you've got to get out of your head once and for all." Mallory's voice was suddenly changed, almost rough. "It's this melodramatic notion of yours that you're the only person in the house who understands or cares anything for Leah, that she's a martyr to everyone else's unkindness. I can assure you that Leah's life won't be desolated and unbearable if you go away to a domestic-science school for a year. Do you understand that?"

"Yes, Father." She looked at him, her eyes blank, and he recognized on her face exactly the same withdrawn, remote look that he had seen so often on Rosanna's when she was in one of her odd moods. Perhaps he was being clumsy and stupid over the whole business, but his nerves were curiously on edge today, after that vague scene at breakfast. He got up and said abruptly: "Well, think over the domestic-science-school idea, Chris. And if you want to move your room, that's something to arrange with Leah," and walked away from her. She curled her thin legs under her and watched him go, her mouth tight-drawn, so that it gave her face an old look, the pupils of her eyes so enlarged that they looked more black than silver-blue.

15

SIMON CROWDY came to tea that afternoon and found Leah alone in the drawing room when he arrived. For tea she was moved out of her chair into a corner of the deep sofa, with cushions propped behind her back. Strangers coming to the house for the first time to tea without knowing that she was a cripple went away still not knowing, because her movements as she poured out tea were so strong and graceful, her back so straight.

She smiled at Simon and held out a hand, but his quick eyes noticed something tired about her eyes, a faint, dry heat throbbing in her palm as he held it for a moment.

"You're tired," he said. "You've been doing too much," but she shook her head defiantly.

"Now, don't be professional for heaven's sake, Simon. You're a bad psychologist in some ways, you know; you never let me forget for a moment that I'm not quite normal. It was a windy night and I didn't sleep very well, and that's all about that. Sit down and tell me how you enjoyed London. We'll begin tea because I'm not sure when any of the others will be in. Jane and Logan and Mallory have got dates, and Christine had one of her peaky fits, so I sent her out for a good long walk with Catherine and a picnic tea. Don't fiddle with the kettle, I can do it perfectly well."

She talked to him sometimes as though he were one of the family instead of her doctor, and he admired her for it. There was nothing of the whining, sympathy-seeking invalid about her, and he liked watching the supple movements of her firm wrists as she lifted the heavy silver teapot and electric kettle. One of his regrets was that he had never known her before the accident, when she had all the rich bloom of her health and energy untouched. He had only been settled in the practice a few days when he had received that urgent telephone call up to Bastions and had arrived to find her stretched, incredibly broken and shattered, upon her bed. Yet even then her eyes had been brave and her chin tilted stubbornly and she had been ready to argue with him. She was a good actress too, but all the same she couldn't hide from him today that something was a little wrong. The blue of her eyes went a deeper shade, and there were the faintest smudges of shadow under them when that happened, and he was always watchful for the signs.

"I enjoyed it," he said, "but it's good to be back. After you've breathed this air for a few years you don't seem able to swallow and assimilate the London stuff. Don't you ever want to go up to London, Leah? It would do you good."

"London—for me?" She shook her head, refused the plate of hot scones he offered her, and lit a cigarette. "No, I don't think so. The last time I was there was the Wimbledon of 1927. Michael Gedge and I performed in a remote corner under the eye of one solitary spectator, an ancient lady in an Edwardian net collar and jet earrings, and the whole thing was over for us in seventeen and a half minutes. But still I enjoyed it, and I'm glad I got it in before all that came to an end."

He had heard from various people that if she had gone on, Leah might very well have achieved the honour of something at least very near to the centre court at Wimbledon, and he could imagine the strength and energy she had put into her efforts. Now he suddenly found himself remembering something that had happened five years ago, down in the next bay where the jagged teeth of the headland rocks bit savagely through the breaking foam.

One of the last of the old sailing ships had been wrecked there in a gale and for weeks had lain just offshore, impaled on those rocks, her torn canvases and broken masts and shattered timbers shaking and breaking helplessly under the last brutal onslaught of the sea. And yet beneath the mutilation the lovely grace and fleet, strong shape were still there, and it was the same with Leah St. Aubyn. Behind the wreckage one could still see the woman she had been, moving easily and swiftly across the green lawn of Wimbledon, swinging across the short turf of the golf course, bracing her body and shaking back her flying hair against the drive of the Cornish gales.

"What on earth are you looking at me like that for, Simon? Am I suddenly showing symptoms of some strange and interesting disease?"

He drew his eyes away from her face with a nervous jerk, and his cup clattered a little in the saucer.

"No, of course not. I'm sorry, my thoughts seem to be wandering a bit today. How's Jane?"

He asked the question because it was the first thing that came into his head to break this awkward silence, not because he was particularly interested in Jane's well-being. And yet, having asked it, he suddenly did find himself interested.

"She's not annoyed with me about something, is she? She seems to be avoiding me, even up at the golf club."

"Is she?" Leah smiled tolerantly. "I suppose, ever since that stupid business about not going to the dance with you, she's shy and awkward about talking to you. She's very young, and young people haven't much idea of carrying off these little contretemps. She'll get over it if you give her time. Here's Sherida. Come and have some tea. By the way, how is our proud new mother? Sherida was out till all hours last night helping Mallory act as midwife to Judy's confinement. Judy is the golden setter and the apple of Mallory's eye. He's been behaving exactly like a nervous father expecting his firstborn all this week, so I'm thankful it's safely over for both of them. I haven't seen the family yet."

"They're lovely," Sherida said. She could feel Simon Crowdy's eyes boring into her in that disconcertingly intense way, and she wondered whether he had caught the faintly ironic flavour of Leah's remarks. The curious thing was that he wasn't like this unless Leah was present. Several times Sherida, out with Jane or Catherine for a walk along the cliffs, or a round of golf, had run into him, and he had been perfectly natural and friendly. It was only when she was there that his face took on that fiercely watchful, half-suspicious expression, as though he were putting himself into an attitude of defence in front of her. But defence against what or whom?

"Well, now Mallory can relax," Leah said, pouring out more tea. "If he's like this when a bitch produces puppies, he must have been in a pretty state when Andrew was born. Weren't you frozen down in the garage all that time?"

"No, it wasn't cold, and the walk along the cliff afterward warmed us up. I'd been longing to look at the view by moonlight on a windy night, but I hadn't got the courage to venture out by myself."

Her eyes met Simon's again, defiantly, deliberately, and he said quickly:

"No, it certainly isn't safe to go roaming about at night unless you know your way extremely well. Leah, are you lunching with the Brastocks tomorrow? Cicely is here on her annual holiday."

"Don't we know it!" Leah said with a faint, resigned sigh. "Yes, and do for goodness' sake turn up, Simon. You're our only really eligible young man and if you fail poor Cicely on her first few days here a gloom will be cast over her entire visit. She always lives in hopes, you know. If you're going out, Sherida, will you post these three letters for me? And tell any of the others if you see them about that there's still some tea going."

Sherida went off to the post, and none of the others appeared, and presently Simon got up.

"I must be going. If you aren't sleeping well just now you can have an extra sleeping tablet at night, you know, for two or three nights anyway."

"Simon dear!" She smiled at him and brushed away a floating trail of cigarette smoke from in front of her eyes. "You doctors are so firmly convinced that there's nothing in the world that can't be cured by a sleeping tablet or an injection. Well, I wish you were right. See you tomorrow."

He ground his gears rather clumsily as he started up the car. There was something wrong with Leah, and he felt queerly angry because he didn't know what it was, couldn't help her. At least not yet, but perhaps later on. . . . .

16

THE COMING OF SPRING and early summer to Cornwall is like the slow turning up of the wick of a reluctant lamp that gutters a good deal before it burns with a steady flame. There were stretches of what Jane called mimosa days, and there were days when the headland and the rocks were blotted out behind the netted, driving weight of rain and the coves were hidden in

ghostly billows of fog that rose like the smoke from an unnatural
fire whose element was not heat but icy cold.

On one of those days, a Sunday, Logan and Catherine got
caught up on the moors in the mist. It was a silent and silvery
morning, as delicately coloured as the inside of a shell, when they
started off in the car and left it on the road to walk up to one
of the tors that squatted, purple and toadlike, in arrogant shape
against the sky line. The heather here was not thick enough to
cover the granite outcrops that burst through the tough black
earth, and for the last hundred feet up the boulders had it all
their own way, forming a sort of broken and blurred flight of
steps up to the crouching monolith on top.

There was still no wind at all, and the air was close-textured
and smooth against their faces, like fine plush. This was the
highest point of that stretch of heath, and they could see over
the grape-blue folds and hummocks down to the river that curled
through the valley with a feather-stitching of soft green along
its edges where the ferns were uncurling their elaborately toothed
and fretted fronds. Far down the valley it wound suddenly into
the shadow of a little wood of smooth-trunked beeches standing
so close-packed and straight and severely sculptured by the gales
into compactness that the wood had the startling effect of a
little silver-coloured Greek temple, threaded with bird song and
wrapped in an enchantment of its own.

The toad rock was ugly and malicious, but its rough purple
side offered a comfortable shelter against the draughts of rain-
scented air that wavered across the moor. They ate their sandwiches and smoked their cigarettes with their backs to the sea,
and when at last they moved sleepily to go home and looked
out from the other side of the rock, they both gave a startled exclamation. A bank of fog, thickly white and sagging, had come
in so silently that they had never noticed it, and now it was
pushing long, crawling fingers of obscurity up the two valleys
that led back to the coast.

"Bother it!" Logan said. "Now we'll be late for tea, and
Leah's got a party of sorts on. Come on."

They reached the car just as the first wave of fog lapped over it, filling the air with clinging wetness that settled in drops like a cloud of silver flies on Catherine's hair. They both knew every inch of the road back, but even so they were Cornish enough to know that familiarity was no safeguard against unexpected danger in these parts. The fog and the moor had a way of getting their revenge on people who treated them without sufficient respect.

The car nosed its way down the steep, rough road, and Catherine, leaning out of her side, watched for the deep drop on the left while Logan divided his attention between the road and the ditch on the right. Once or twice the fog thinned abruptly, letting in a queer, harsh light from the shrouded sky, and in one of the patches they just dodged a dog fox who was trotting quietly and purposefully across the track with his chestnut brush dragging heavily.

But for most of the time they drove through a world that was vague and formless and only two-thirds developed, as it might have been in primeval days when the great forces of earth, sky, and water were still inchoate. Against the thick white fabric of the mist, shapes were printed dimly: a stunted tree with twisted branches, a roofless and deserted cottage, two staring sheep.

And then suddenly there was a bang and a lurch and the car came to a wobbling standstill at a dangerous angle of nearness to the apparently bottomless abyss on the right, and Logan said resignedly:

"I wondered if that tire would last. Sorry, Catherine, I'm afraid we're going to miss Leah's tea party. You sit still and have a cigarette while I cope with this. Do you mind?"

"Of course not; I rather like it out here anyway." Catherine lit her cigarette. "It's sort of lost and weird. I'm going to paint a picture of a Cornish moor in fog or burst in the effort. Look at that light driving across the rocks; it might be a Russian setting for *Macbeth*. Don't you want a hand?"

"No, it's all right. Wrap the rug round you if you're cold."

He worked at the wheel while she sat smoking and feeling in the oddest way happier than she had for days. It was only a respite, this odd interlude in the heart of the fog, but it gave her a momentary feeling of escape, even of security. They were alone here, and Bastions was lost; one could almost pretend that it didn't exist at all.

"That's done." Logan got back into the car, slammed the door, and took a cigarette. "Are you frozen?"

"No, not a bit. Look, there's a break over there. Isn't it exciting when you get the feel of blue sky behind mist? There's a sort of reflection coming through."

"I don't care a hang about any blue sky or any of your artistic scenic effects," Logan said roughly. "I brought you out here to say something, Catherine, and it's taken me all this time to work up to it, but it's going to be said—for just about the last time. Will you marry me—and when?"

Her cigarette had gone out, but she didn't notice and went on pulling at it and then threw it away. Her face was veiled from him by thin layers of vapour, so that he couldn't see it very clearly, but he could see that she was very white, and he put a hand on hers.

"Listen, Catherine," he said. "There's something you've got to understand. I'm very fond of Leah, I respect and admire her and I love her. But I haven't the slightest intention of letting her rule my life for me. If she doesn't accept you as what I want you to be, I shan't have the slightest hesitation in leaving Bastions and never going near it again. I love you. But I've got to know. If you say no, I shall be going away, I think, but I'm not saying that to work up your emotions. It's simply that I can't stand this position, and I don't think you can either."

"No," she said, under her breath. "I can't either, Logan. If you really want to take the risk——"

"What risk?"

"The risk of what I am—what I may turn out to be. I can see Leah's point of view."

"Leah's point of view doesn't interest me, because I happen to have one of my own. Catherine, what do you honestly imagine can happen, just because you don't know exactly who or what your people were? Can't you think of yourself as an individual instead of as a lump of blind heredity? That's a habit I'm going to cure you of, if it takes me all my life. That's a warning, so you know what you're in for."

Under the grip of his hand he could feel her suddenly relax, go limp and acquiescent, and he knew he should have done this long ago. She had been waiting for him to settle the whole thing, and he had been fool enough, to let it drag along for senseless weeks. She laughed suddenly, and when he stared at her she said:

"I was thinking how typical this is of you, Logan. We've had all sorts of romantic days of sunshine and sunset and blue skies, but you have to wait for us to get well into the middle of a dank and impenetrable Cornish mist on the top of a particularly bleak bit of moor before you do the thing properly."

"Well, you said you liked the fog, and I hoped it had put you into a properly receptive mood. You're a queer person too; obvious things like sunset and starlight don't have the obvious effect on you." His arm came round her shoulders with a sudden pressure. "There isn't going to be any more shilly-shallying, is there? We're going to tell everyone about ourselves the instant we get home."

"Right in the middle of Leah's tea party? All right," she added quickly as he looked at her, his brows drawn together. "I'm not going to argue about anything again, Logan, not even with myself. And perhaps it is getting a trifle chilly here."

"Good lord, yes, we're both frozen!" He turned his attention back to the wheel, and the car backed cautiously away from the ditch and crawled onwards.

By the time they reached the main road down the valley a stir of wind was shredding the fog into finer strands, and up on the cliff road they left it suddenly behind as a grimy, soggy-edged smudge across a sky of wet forget-me-not blue that curved downwards to meet a sea of peacock green, dappled with silver.

Leah's tea party was over, and only one guest lingered with her in the drawing room, Simon Crowdy. Jane was there too, and Christine, but there was something stiff and uneasy in the atmosphere when Logan and Catherine came in, his hand through her arm, her hair still spangled with dew drops of moisture.

"Here we are at last," Logan said, "and I hope to goodness

there's some tea left, we're both cold. We got caught in the fog and had a puncture, and then we got ourselves engaged and so time went faster than we noticed."

There was one second of silence, and then Jane got up and held out both her hands to Catherine, her face flushed.

"You and Logan—! Oh, I am glad, and it's simply lovely."

She kissed Catherine, and because of her enthusiasm the rather hard quietness of the others went unnoticed for a moment. Christine was still holding her teacup, and her face had gone queerly pale; Leah was leaning back on the sofa, smiling, but the soft, rounded line of her jaw had become square; Simon was looking on with genuine interest, and Leah spoke at last.

"That's very happy news," she said. "I'm so glad for both of you. But it isn't wildly unexpected, you know, though I didn't think Logan would choose the heart of an icy spring fog for his great romantic moment. Come and sit here by me, Catherine dear."

She held out her hand, and Catherine had to take it. Her own hand was small, square-nailed, and cool, and it was almost lost in Leah's, so big and soft and vibrantly warm. For that instant when Leah held her, Catherine had a curious and frightening illusion that Leah's form, or at least the upper and visible half of it, was swelling up monstrously, so that the room was suffocatingly full of the brilliant, untidy gold of her hair, the strong curves of her shoulders, the clear ring of her voice. Then in a flash it was gone and she was sitting on the sofa, drinking hot tea.

Christine had taken her cup over to the window and was staring moodily out, and Logan and Jane and Simon were talking round the fire. For a second Leah and Catherine seemed to be alone, but Catherine couldn't think of anything to say; her tongue felt dry and the palms of her hands clammy still from the touch of the fog.

"Catherine, I really am very glad about this," Leah said softly. "I've been worrying a little lately, because I knew how Logan felt, and I was afraid something had gone wrong between you, since you didn't announce anything definite. He's been so patient and faithful that it would have been sad if you'd turned him down for some reason or other."

"But I haven't," Catherine said quietly, and she looked Leah straight in the eyes. "I had to think things over a little, that was all."

"And I'm glad you thought them over sensibly, my dear. You young people sometimes aren't altogether sensible, are you? We must have a celebration party this week, but you'll be over to-morrow and we can arrange it all. Hullo, here's Sherida! You're just in time to join in the congratulations, Sherida. Catherine and Logan have announced their engagement."

Sherida's eyes went from one face to another swiftly, and she could feel an undercurrent of vibrations in the atmosphere, although everyone, except Christine, looked suitably happy.

"I'm so glad," she said. "All the happiness in the world to both of you."

"Thank you, Sherida." Catherine gave her a look that was warm and grateful.

It all seemed very normal and cheerful, but Sherida couldn't get rid of that faint sensation of oppression in the air.

She was going upstairs to change out of her tweeds for dinner, when she met Jane coming out of Christine's room with such a worried look on her face that she stopped and asked involuntarily:

"Is anything wrong, Jane?"

"No, it isn't anything much. Christine's been very sick, but I think she's all right now."

"Sick? But is she really ill, Jane? Have you told Leah?"

"No." They were going along the corridor toward Sherida's room. "I don't think she need be bothered. Christine isn't ill, she's only upset, and that always seems to make the nerves of her inside behave queerly."

She followed Sherida into her room, and Sherida could see that Jane was still anxious and puzzled by something, that she wanted to talk about it.

"But what is there for her to be upset about?"

"It's Logan and Catherine," Jane said slowly.

"Their engagement! What on earth is there upsetting in that? Everybody is frightfully glad about it."

"I know. It's difficult to explain." Jane stood by the window and swung the tassel of the blind cord nervously to and fro. "Christine is a queer child, you know. I mean—about Leah. Of course we all love her, but there's something hysterical and over-emotional about the way Christine loves her. Leah has tried to stop it and discourage it, but she has to be careful."

"I wonder how much she has tried to stop it," Sherida thought, but she was interested in what Jane was so haltingly trying to say. "Do you mean," she asked quietly, "that Christine thinks that Leah isn't as pleased as she seems about Logan marrying Catherine?"

"Yes." Jane's words came out in a sudden rush. "And it is true, you know, up to a point. Leah likes Catherine, but she—she doesn't really want Logan to marry her. Oh, I suppose it's silly of her, but she's nervous about Catherine being a—a foundling and nobody knowing anything about who and what her people were."

"But that seems rather hard on Catherine," Sherida said slowly. "Does any of that matter, when she's such a fine person in herself?"

"Of course it doesn't matter to any of us. We all love Catherine, and I know Mallory would rather Logan married her than any other girl in the world. Leah's only got this idea into her head because—because she's so fond of Logan and so desperately anxious for everything to turn out all right for him." Sherida felt a pang of pity for Jane, struggling childishly in a morass of difficulty, but before she could say anything Jane went on hurriedly. "She won't say anything about it, I'm positive of that, but Chris is being silly. She says Leah is unhappy and that Logan is selfish in not thinking of her and—oh! I don't know. It's all rather worrying."

Her pointed face looked small and harassed and her brow furrowed with the complications of these divided loyalties, and Sherida slid a hand through her arm.

"Don't take Christine's melodramatic moods so seriously, Jane; that's the best way to treat them. Tell her she'll have to go to boarding school if she's going to behave like a hysterical fourth-former with a crush on the games mistress. If you laugh at her she'll pull herself together, but at the moment she thinks that she's acting as a tremendous influence in the family. That's the best way."

"Yes, I suppose it is, but it's difficult to laugh at her when I feel more like shaking her the way you did. I'll threaten to turn her over to you; she's got a very wholesome respect for you ever since that incident." Jane smoothed down the dark elf locks that she had ruffled up round her forehead in her perplexity. "I'd better go and get myself tidy. Catherine is coming over afterward." She hesitated. "You won't say anything to her about any of this, Sherida, will you? She hasn't the faintest idea that Leah feels anything like this, and she's always so sweet to her. But of course I know you won't. I must fly."

Sherida opened her long window and let in a wave of cold, fog-smeared evening air. The view was still faintly muffled and the sound of the sea muted, though in the higher sky there was a gleam of afterglow, a dull, tarnished brightness. She was thinking, not of Jane's problems but of Catherine's eyes when she looked across at Leah in that moment when she was telling Sherida about the engagement. They had been frightened, and Catherine wasn't a girl who would be easily frightened.

17

THE ENGAGEMENT celebration party, under discussion, sounded quite a festive affair, but when it came to the fact it didn't differ very much from any of the other small dinner parties Leah gave, though there was champagne and in honour of the occasion all the womenfolk wore more elaborate evening frocks than they usually bothered to produce.

The McReadys and the Maitlands came, also Simon Crowdy, John Norris, who was surgeon at the Cottage Hospital, the Brastocks and Cicely Burnham, still spending part of her annual fortnight's leave with them. There was very little family resemblance between the two sisters; Cicely was very small and thin and had the kind of body that looked as though it would sound like a plank if you rapped it. She had an oddly smooth, shiny, sallow skin, a mouth too full of teeth, grey eyes magnified enormously behind strong glasses and damply sleek, pale blonde hair coiled in a bun on her neck.

Nobody quite knew why she came so faithfully to stay with the Brastocks, since she made no secret of the fact that she hated Mabel, but it was a cold, impersonal sort of hatred not centred so much on her as on fate that had casually given her everything that it had denied Cicely. She was equally frank about her own single-minded aim and ambition in life which had been the acquiring of a husband, the status of a wedding ring, and the dignity of a home of her own.

Even now when she discussed the matter—and it was one of her favorite topics of conversation—her sallow cheeks would flush with anger at the blind stupidity of men in general who ignored the generous gifts she was prepared to shower upon them, and her attitude suggested that if she had the physical strength and the power, she would like to march out into the high road, knock out the first man she saw, and drag him to the altar before he had fully recovered consciousness.

Catherine was wearing a dull green frock, and Sherida noticed that she had used a little more make-up than usual—was that because underneath it she was rather pale? But there was nothing of that frightened, wary look in her eyes that Sherida had seen on that afternoon when the engagement was announced. Whatever she was afraid of, she had got it well in hand now.

Leah in azure blue and silver, with sapphire earrings swinging below the bright gold of her hair, took the head of the candle-lit table and smiled affectionately across at Catherine as she lifted her champagne glass.

"Here's wishing you and Logan all the happiness in the world, Catherine dear. I wish it were a more settled and safe world for all you young people, but I know none of you are afraid of taking risks with your eyes open, and I'm sure neither you nor Logan is afraid of the future, no matter how sinister it looks sometimes. Bless you both."

Everybody drank the toast, Cicely with her round eyes fixed with a sort of hungry fascination upon this girl who had captured a young man; Christine with a wan droop of her eyelashes, everyone else with genuine sincerity and affection in their murmured words of good wishes. There was a little pause afterwards, and across it Cicely's rising voice spiralled sharply, like a snapping spring.

"I know you're an adaptable person, Logan, but all the same I'd love to see you holding your own in London's artistic world in Chelsea or wherever its headquarters are. Are you learning up all the right jargon from Catherine?"

Logan, who had lifted his glass quietly toward Catherine for a moment, put it down and answered coolly:

"I don't know anything about Chelsea or artistic 'jargon' as you call it, Cicely, and Catherine doesn't seem to expect me to learn it up. We aren't going to live in London."

"But Catherine isn't going to give up her painting, surely?" Mrs. Brastock put in with a lift of her almost invisible eyebrows. "That would be too much self-sacrifice to expect even from a bride-to-be."

"No, of course I'm not going to give it up," Catherine said easily. "But there's no need to live in London, especially if one wants to paint pictures of Cornwall. And if I take up portrait painting seriously I'm sure I'll be able to find plenty of subjects down here. Perhaps you'd sit for me, Mrs. Brastock—if I'm really hard up. Sherida, you've never shown me those old prints of York yet, and I do want to see them."

There was a faint suggestion of angry shrimp pink in Mrs. Brastock's round cheeks as she took a quick gulp of champagne, and Mallory suppressed a smile behind his table napkin as he glanced at Leah, but she didn't respond.

"I suppose," Cicely said bitterly, "that there'll be a spate of semi-war weddings now, with all this talk of war in the air. And eighty per cent of them will be catastrophes because men have such appalling taste. The moment there's a question of getting married quickly they rush off and pick up the shoddiest bits of trash they can find, while all the decent girls who would make good wives are left to go into munitions."

Mrs. McReady coughed a little, and Mrs. Maitland's tranquil grey eyes darkened, but Logan said lightly:

"Never mind, Cicely. Surely a war will bring romance into a great many—er—unexciting lives. Think of all the Whitehall departments that will suddenly be flooded with ravishing young staff captains and naval officers."

"You mean old dug-ups with bald heads and bleary eyes," Cicely said acidly. "I had a friend who worked in one of those offices in the war, and she spent a lot of money buying herself smart tailor mades and good shoes and things, but she told me it was all a waste of money because there wasn't a man in the place who was worth dressing—or undressing—for."

There was a rather startled silence round the dinner table at this downright pronouncement, but Cicely without any embarrassment plunged her spoon into her grapefruit cocktail with a vicious splash, and Jane said hurriedly that she and Logan had made up their minds to bathe next day, whatever the weather might be, in order to break their last year's record for an early start.

They were dawdling over nuts and port when Leah, in a gap in the general conversation, asked casually:

"By the way, Logan, what's your professional opinion about the Falmouth murder case? I was reading it over in the morning paper, and it seemed rather interesting."

The Falmouth murder, of a middle-aged and highly respectable middle-class couple by their daughter, had been the centre of a great deal of local excitement and argument all that week, and there had been large, smudged photographs of the accused girl, a heavy-browed, sullen-eyed type, on all the front pages. The man and woman had been found dead at the foot of a notoriously dangerous cliff, and the first assumption had been that one of them had fallen over and the other, in an attempted rescue, had overbalanced too, but within a week of the affair Mary Bassett had been escorted to the local police station and charged

with murder. The doctors had discovered that both the victims
had been stunned first by heavy blows with the usual "blunt
instrument" and had then been flung over the cliff edge, probably
in the hope that the rocks and sea would obliterate traces of the
first stage of the proceedings.

"Well, I don't know much about it," Logan said modestly.
"But as a matter of fact Ralph Truscott knew the Bassetts quite
well; he spent some week ends on their farm last summer. He
rather seems to think that the girl did it."

"But why should she?" Jane said. "It seems too horrible to
imagine a girl murdering both her parents."

"But my dear, haven't you heard the latest development?"
Mrs. Brastock put in eagerly. "Keith was telling me—you know
he's been down to Falmouth on business, and the whole town
was agog with the news. Mary wasn't the Bassetts' daughter at
all, although they called her by their own name. It appears that
she was a foundling who was left on their doorstep as a baby,
before they came over to their Falmouth farm. She was only
about a month old, and the Bassetts had always longed for a
baby and hadn't got one, so when nothing could be found out
about the child they decided to keep her and bring her up as
their own. And that I call real Christian kindness, to keep a baby
that arrives out of the blue from goodness knows what parentage
and sources. They did everything in the world for the girl and
loved her dearly, and then she goes and murders them, apparently because she was sick of farm life and wanted to marry
some young man they didn't approve of and also wanted the
money she knew they'd left her. It only goes to show how terribly
careful you've got to be about the mysteries of hereditary and
inborn instincts and all that sort of thing, and that if you adopt
an unknown child you're quite likely to end up by being knocked
on the head and thrown over a cliff by it. I really don't think——"

She came to a sudden stop, her mouth open, her hand holding a port glass poised in mid-air, while the rest of the party sat
silent, looking not at her but at Logan, who had gone white
over the cheekbones.

"Have we finished, Leah?" he said abruptly, and Mrs. Brastock made a helpless, flapping motion with her white hands.

"Oh dear! Of course I never thought . . . I didn't mean
. . ." she gabbled, but nobody listened to her as Leah with a
quick gesture pulled her wheel chair up beside her and everyone
got up from the table.

"Come along," she said, "we'll leave the men to discuss air-
raid precautions while we concentrate on something more interesting. Catherine dear, will you help me?"

She smiled at Catherine as she came to put the cushions into
place, but Sherida, watching her, saw something secret and
triumphant lurking in that smile, and suddenly she knew without a shadow of doubt that Leah had known exactly what
Mabel Brastock was going to say and had deliberately brought
the subject up.

There was a fire burning in the drawing room, and the stiff,
pale blue brocade curtains, faded and cracked with age, shut
out the sound of falling rain and rising wind. Catherine pushed
Leah's chair up to the coffee table, and Mrs. Brastock hovered
round them, her olive-green satin evening frock trailing limply
round her legs, her pale hair sliding in wisps out of the bun on
her neck.

"Oh dear, I feel awful," she murmured. "About what I
said just now, only I simply didn't stop to think, Catherine. I
mean——"

"Don't be a fool and make it worse, Mabel," Leah said bluntly.
"As though anyone in their sane senses would imagine that you
were suggesting that Catherine might bash the Maitlands over
the head with a rock and throw them into the cove! If you
hadn't behaved so idiotically not one single person would have
even remembered that she isn't really a Maitland. Here's your
coffee, Catherine, and for goodness' sake tell Mabel it's all right
and stop her from flapping about in a state of apologetic agitation for the rest of the evening."

"Of course it's all right, Mrs. Brastock," Catherine said quietly.
"No sugar, thanks."

She took her coffee cup over to the window seat where Sherida
was sitting, and her hands were perfectly steady and she hadn't

even turned pale, but Sherida knew that she had a feeling that she wanted for the moment to get close to a window, even though it was closely curtained. But behind it she could hear the sound of the sea and the wind, and they were friendly sounds, more friendly than the easy, affectionate tone of Leah's voice and the soft swish of the rubber tires of her wheel chair across the polished floor.

The men didn't stay long over their masculine gossip; they followed in five minutes, and the bridge tables were made up in one corner of the room. Logan touched Catherine's bare arm and said in a low voice: "Come into the study for a moment, darling, away from all this chatter."

She followed him silently into Mallory's study, where the air was warm and flavoured with morocco leather and tobacco scents. Logan switched on only one light over the old oak-panelled fireplace, and then he put his arms round her and held her so tightly that she could feel his heart beating through his shirt front.

"Catherine, you aren't letting that blundering idiot of a woman's foul gossip upset you? You've got more sense than that, haven't you, Catherine?"

She seemed small when he held her like this within the circle of his arms, and she rested her square forehead, with the dark hair brushed away from it, against his chest for a moment.

"I don't know . . . Logan, if only there was some way of finding out, of knowing for certain about myself . . . about who and what I am."

She knew by the tightening of his arms that he was angry with her but was making a desperate effort to control himself and speak gently.

"Listen, Catherine, why can't you think of it this way? Suppose you were the child of a Mr. and Mrs. Jackson, who were both killed in an accident when you were only a few months old. Supposing you had grown up with the Maitlands not as their daughter but as Catherine Jackson, whose father and mother were respectably buried in the village churchyard, would you know any more about them really than you do now? Or about yourself? It's just a convention. You wouldn't know a thing more about your heredity."

"I think Father and Mother do know," Catherine said in a low voice. "They must have made some enquiries before they took me. Logan, can't you persuade them to tell me—whatever it is?"

Logan let her go violently and went over to the fireplace.

"I can't stand any more of this," he said. "Are you so afraid of life, Catherine, that you won't take any risks at all? Don't you trust me to protect you from whatever it is you're scared of?"

"Yes. But it isn't only that, Logan." All her senses and being shrank away violently from what she was going to say, but something was driving her on. "There's something else. It's—Leah. Tonight, when she started talking about the Bassett murder, she knew that Mrs. Brastock knew of the latest development and that she'd tell us."

Logan turned round slowly from the fireplace, his pipe in his hand, and stared at her. Behind him the small fire of logs burnt peacock blue and jade green with the salt that had crusted over them before they were picked up from the cove as flotsam.

"Catherine, you're crazy," he said in a low voice. "So you mean to say that you believe that Leah would deliberately plan anything so cruel and beastly?"

"I don't suppose she planned it beforehand. I mean she didn't ask Mrs. Brastock to tell us about Mary Bassett, but she knew she would. Logan, don't be angry with me. I know you love Leah and that she adores you. I can understand."

"And you think that Leah was trying to suggest to everyone at dinner tonight that you're on a level with this Mary Bassett, that you're quite likely to develop murderous instincts suddenly? Catherine, don't you see how preposterous it is? Even if Leah knew that Mabel Brastock was bursting to tell us the latest news, it only shows that in her mind she didn't even remotely connect you with such a thing. Come here." He pulled her forward again and looked down into her upturned face. "Darling, let's fight this obsession of yours together. You aren't putting up much of a fight against it yet, you know. Now let's go back to the drawing room and forget about it. Shall we?"

"Yes," she said under her breath. "Let's do that, Logan. And I'm sorry, I must bore you horribly with all this."

It wasn't any use, she thought dully. She had to face and fight this thing alone. They were quiet for a moment, standing together in the dim light, and across the hall Cicely's heels clicked sharply as she went upstairs with Jane to powder her nose, and she was still talking. Mallory once said that Cicely's voice reminded him of a clumsy person trying to dig out a splinter from his finger; he could feel all his nerves wincing away from the jab and jar of it.

"Of course nobody understands how I feel about coming down here to stay. Because I'm small and dress smartly and look rather Mayfairish they all think I'm a fish out of water, but really it's the other way about. I simply hate London and all the rush and turmoil and excitement of living there. Of course I don't mind a quiet supper at the Dorchester occasionally or a little evening at Quaglino's, but if I have too much of it I begin to feel and look about a hundred. On the other hand I do think it's a pity that Mabel has let herself go so completely. I know without being a bit conceited that I've got a basic attractiveness because of my figure and colouring, but poor Mabel shouldn't let herself slip beyond a certain point. I don't believe . . ."

Her voice died away round the bend of the upstairs corridor, and Logan laughed and with one finger brushed back a tiny curl of dark hair from Catherine's temples.

"Have you any 'basic attractiveness,' darling? It sounds a handy thing to have up your sleeve, but Cicely's is so far up it that nobody's noticed it yet. Come on, let's go back and see how the bridge party is getting on. Have you quite recovered from your attack of the morbid blues?"

"Quite," she said lightly, and they went back to the drawing room.

Sherida had a headache and didn't want to play bridge and, since there were quite enough without her, saw no reason why she shouldn't slip quietly away to bed. She murmured an explanation to Jane, who said she'd tell Leah, and then went unobtrusively out into the hall and felt sweep over her a violent longing to escape from the pressure of people chattering in the drawing room and from painted eyes watching her from the family portraits. A stroll down the garden wouldn't be breaking her promise to Mallory not to go wandering along the cliffs in the dark. She let herself out of the unlatched front door softly.

The brief shower had passed over, and though the wind was still strong the air was mellow and faintly scented with the delicacy of narcissi under the robust tang of the salt. She went down to the low gate at the end of the garden and leaned on it, looking at the sea spread below like a sheet of crumpled tin foil. The moonlight wasn't strong tonight, not strong enough to show up the headlands and cliffs in any detail. There was a faint amber glow like phosphorescence shining along the horizon, and somewhere amongst the thinning spume of cloud an aeroplane was drumming softly toward silence. Was there really going to be war? Was some evil and loathsomely all-powerful monster going to wind the strings of their lives round his bloated fingers and set them moving into the grotesque and slavish puppet dance of his own invention?

"Sherida? You're keeping your promise, I see, about not exploring on your own after dark, along the cliffs."

Mallory's solid bulk had come up beside her so silently that she hadn't seen him, and her heart missed a beat.

"Yes, I'm keeping it, but as much from cowardice as anything else. I think it looks rather frightening out there and yet fascinating."

"Does it?" He was leaning over the little gate beside her, and she felt that he hadn't listened to what she said. "Tell me about yourself, Sherida. Why do you do this kind of job? It must be deadly dull."

"Perhaps it is sometimes, but it certainly hasn't been dull here at Bastions."

"No? Well, perhaps there is a certain amount of interest in being plunged into the middle of a group of strange people and being able to watch their lives as an impersonal spectator. It must be a bit like watching a play."

"You know I didn't mean it like that," she said quietly, and he looked at her and shook his head.

"Yes, of course I know that. I'm sorry, Sherida. You're so much one of us now that we don't think of you as a spectator, we expect you to share everything with us. What do you think of Catherine?"

He was in a curious mood tonight, Sherida thought, jerking from one subject to the other, with a flavour of bitterness tinging everything he said.

"I like her tremendously, as much as I've ever liked anyone. You do too, don't you?"

"Yes." He was staring at the sea again, and his expression was curiously heavy and troubled. "I'm almost as fond of her as I am of Jane and Christine. Sherida, has Leah ever talked to you about Catherine being a foundling from an orphanage?"

"No, never. But I've heard Mrs. Brastock discussing it," Sherida said, and Mallory made an impatient movement.

"That old gossiping wind machine! I've got a great respect for Leah's judgment in most things, but her bosom friendship with Mabel is one of the few things I don't understand, kind as she was when Leah had her accident. Did you feel at dinner tonight Mabel was talking at Catherine when she started on the Bassett murder case?"

Sherida didn't remind him that it was Leah who had started the subject originally, and in fact she didn't believe that Mallory had forgotten it.

"Perhaps," she said carefully. "Or perhaps she was simply so full of her titbit of news that she never thought of hurting anyone's feelings. I don't think Catherine took it like that anyway. Won't they be wanting you back at the bridge table, Major St. Aubyn?"

"I suppose so." He sighed and shook out his pipe against the gate. Red sparks scattered away on the wind and fell like minute stars over the edge of the cliff. "Do you remember how I asked your advice about Jane?" he went on abruptly.

"Yes, but I'm afraid I haven't been able to help much. Jane doesn't talk about herself very easily, and I don't want to pry."

"No, of course not. But she seems happier lately, though I don't quite know why. Simon Crowdy doesn't appear to take much more notice of her than he did before. I expect you've guessed that Jane's in love with him."

"Yes, I had guessed." She hesitated and then asked slowly: "Would you mind if she did marry him?"

"Because he's divorced? No, I don't think so, but Leah has qualms about it. She's so desperately anxious for all the children to be happy and successful that she can't bear any of them to take the slightest risk about anything. It's natural, I suppose, but it's rather a contrast to the way Rosanna would have treated them. She had a sublime belief in everyone's ability and right to manage his or her own life. Unconsciously she was a pioneer of all the modern child-psychology principles of free self-expression and liberty. Well, I must get back to my bridge. Don't catch cold out here."

It was an odd conversation, Sherida thought as she stood for a moment longer by the gate, a vague, seemingly pointless and rather disconnected conversation, but she could dimly see the train of thought that had, in Mallory's mind, linked up his random comments and questions. That link was Leah.

Mallory went back to the drawing room and slid into his seat at the bridge table where Mrs. Brastock, Jane, and Mr. McReady were just finishing his dummy hand. Mrs. Brastock looked up at him with an expression of welcome as though he had been away for weeks, and with a gleam of curiosity illuminating that welcome.

"Oh, there you are, Mallory! We were beginning to wonder where you'd got to, and whether our bridge is so terrible that you had to get away from it for a bit. Is it raining yet?"

So she knew he'd been outside, Mallory thought as he lit his pipe again and looked casually over the results of the hand just played.

"No, the wind is dropping," he said. "Sorry if I was away rather a long time, but I thought it safe to leave things in your expert hands, Mabel. You seem to have been more expert than usual. Congratulations."

"Thank you, Mallory. By the way, doesn't Sherida play bridge? I should have thought she would, she's got a good bridge-player type of face. She looks as though she could concentrate on a subject and think out her moves ahead."

The gooseberry-coloured eyes were wide and bland, and Mallory smiled back into them.

"Yes, she's intelligent—and that's why I don't think she cares much for bridge. Can I get a drink for anybody?"

He moved over toward the table where the drinks were set, and as he passed the back of Leah's chair she reached up a hand and caught his.

"All right, darling?"

There was a question in her look, and Mallory raised his eyebrows.

"Yes, of course. Why?"

"Well, you were away so long I wondered—I thought perhaps you had a headache and didn't want to play any more."

"No, I'm not suffering from a headache." Mallory drew his hand away from under hers quietly and smoothly. "I went outside for a breath of fresh air, and Sherida and I were looking at the headland in the moonlight. Shall I get you something to drink?"

"No, thanks, darling, I'll have it later. I'm sorry, Simon, what did you say?"

He looked at her quickly across the bridge table, his eyes sharp and alert and he saw her hand shake as she picked up her cards. She gave him a faint, tired smile that nobody else noticed before she bent her head over them again.

18

THE REVOLVING SUMMERHOUSE at the end of the lower lawn made an excellent outdoor office for Sherida to work in when the spring weather's mildness hardened into the first glaze of summer heat. She could swing it round to face the sun, the clump of cedars at the back made a sturdy shield against any wind, and in front of her was spread the long flower borders and centre beds, just flaring into gaudy brilliance.

Perhaps that was why it wasn't too easy to concentrate this morning on shorthand notes and piles of letters; the hot vividness of a mass of Iceland poppies or the scent from a newly opened border of velvet dark petunias and prim verbena had a way of thrusting themselves between her mind and her work. There were very young thrushes experimenting with their wings across the open spaces of grass and two ladybirds dawdling gravely in single file across her writing table.

But there wasn't any need to drive herself too hard this morning; in half an hour she could clear up everything. In the last few weeks she had noticed how oddly the secretarial work Leah gave her was dropping off and becoming more casual. The ardent letters from admirers were left unanswered; two offers for further series of "Faith Hope" lyrics were turned flatly down; the personal replies she wrote to troubled and lovelorn damsels who asked her for advice grew fewer and rarer.

Leah was losing interest in her work, and Sherida wondered why—and how she might be affected if all Leah's literary ambition guttered out suddenly and her "writing" were let slide. It might mean that she would decide, in that case, that a private secretary was an unnecessary luxury in these lean, war-threatened days, that she could be dispensed with. And that would inevitably mean leaving Bastions—how would she feel about that?

Sherida pushed the bunch of notes aside and lit a cigarette. From here she looked at the house at an angle, set cornerwise against the Canterbury-bell blue of the sky. That was one of the great charms of the place, that it had been designed and built to no set plan, with no conventional formality ruling straight lines and dictating a neat pattern. One could picture the Señor Don Ramón Sebastiano marching saturninely through the grounds, a gaunt black figure of alien determination, and with a wave of a bony, olive-tinted hand commanding a lawn to be created there, a pool to be placed here, a new wing to be built on at that haphazard angle simply because he knew he would like the view it would provide him with. An inconsequent, easy-going house that had accepted her as one of the family.

And what about the people living in it? Up on the paved terrace outside the drawing-room windows Leah was sitting in her chair, with Mrs. Brastock and Cicely Burnham in attendance, and all three of them were finishing off fancy work for one of the stalls at the forthcoming church bazaar. Neither Leah nor Mrs. Brastock was talking much, but Cicely's voice was blown thinly down the garden upon the breeze, and it had the fretful sound of an angry and frustrated sea gull's cry.

"Of course I know the obvious way to attract men. If I were to peroxide my hair and make more of my figure than I do and wear my nails like talons I'd have them round me in shoals, but because I'm offering something real and sincere and idealistic, they're bored with me. And every one of them is exactly the same without a single exception—yes, even your model Keith, Mabel darling. Personally I think his is a particularly dangerous age for a man, single or married, to be always running off on A.R.P. business for the day to this and that town. You can call me cynical if you like, but I'd be—interested in these little jaunts of his if I were you."

There was no answer from Mrs. Brastock. Sherida could imagine her with her gooseberry eyes congested and her voice muted with rage; but Leah spoke in a cool, amused tone of voice.

"You know Mallory often goes on these trips too, Cicely. Do you, out of your infinite experience of men, consider that he's at a 'dangerous age' too?"

"Yes, I certainly do." Cicely's dulcet tones shrilled a little with resentment. "Because he's not only that, but he's in a dangerous position as well, and every attractive girl realizes it. He seems to them to be fairer game than even the average susceptible husband out on the spree."

And there abruptly, as she probably realized the outrageousness of what she had just said, she was silent. Sherida heard the faint rumble of Leah's chair as she moved it over the uneven flagstones.

"I think I've had enough of doing patchwork for one morning," she said quietly. "Shall we go inside and have some coffee? Oh, here's Christine. Push me over the bumpy bit, darling, I always get stuck in that rut. By the way, have you seen Sherida down in the garden? She might like some coffee if she's finished those letters."

"I think she's gone out along the cliff," Christine said quickly. "I believe I saw her going out of the gate, so I suppose she has finished. You look tired, Leah, you shouldn't slave so at those stupid things for the bazaar."

The voices and the creak of the chair faded away along the terrace and into the house, and Sherida put her cigarette out thoughtfully. Not two minutes before Christine had passed up through the garden, and though she hadn't made any sign at all as she went by she must have seen Sherida in the summerhouse, must have known she was still there when she answered Leah's question. Why had she told that deliberate lie?

There was no doubt at all that Christine heartily disliked her, but what Sherida couldn't quite understand was the sense of uneasiness, almost of nervous suspense, that the consciousness of Christine's hostility set up in her own mind. It was absurd to let herself be worried by an overemotional schoolgirl's hysterical animosity that was probably rooted in the drastic treatment meted out to her once or twice, but sometimes in spite of her common sense Sherida felt herself shaken by a half-superstitious fear of Christine. There was something implacable in her narrow face, something of the hardness of the granite landscape in the look that came into her eyes sometimes. One felt that her emotions hadn't the shallowness of the schoolgirl age but were rooted as deeply and dangerously as an adult's. That must be some quality she inherited from her mother, for Mallory certainly wasn't capable of any great hatred, and Christine was.

In Leah's sitting room coffee was consumed in an atmosphere of rather uneasy trivial conversation, and after five minutes Cicely murmured something about doing a job of work in the garden at home that had been neglected for a long time, and departed with Christine. Leah and Mrs. Brastock were left alone together, Leah idly smoking a cigarette and doing nothing, Mrs.

Brastock feverishly concentrating on the business of turning out yet another rag bag in search of scraps. There was still a faint salmon-pink flush on her face, and since Leah said nothing in a particularly cool and deliberate way, she had to make the opening move in a voice aggressively loud and defensive.

"I hope you aren't annoyed with Cicely for what she said, Leah. I suppose she did it in a clumsy way, but she only meant to be kind and to give you a friendly word of warning."

"A friendly word of warning?" Leah spoke softly.

"Yes. I was going to tell you myself if she hadn't started the subject. These national-service business jaunts of Mallory's—haven't you noticed yourself that they very often coincide with Sherida's free afternoons when she generally goes off by herself on a bus or for a long walk? You must have, Leah."

Across the brilliance of the day a curious tarnishing was spreading, faint as the first film of mould upon a polished surface, and the sea's colour was turning slowly opaque and dead. Leah lit a fresh cigarette from the stub of the old one and answered in the same gentle, toneless voice.

"Yes, you aren't the only person with eyes in your head, Mabel, and other people besides Cicely have an elemental knowledge of human nature. I didn't need to have the news broken to me gently by either of you."

"You mean to say that you—you realize what's going on?" Mrs. Brastock's fat, pale hands stopped their aimless ferreting amongst the pile of scraps. "But why—why don't you do something?"

"Didn't Cicely put the whole thing very neatly into a nutshell just now out on the terrace, when she talked about Mallory's 'dangerous position'? If Cicely can look facts straight in the face so can I. I know what she meant."

"But Leah, it's unthinkable! Do you mean to sit there and tell me that you know all about it and that you aren't going to do anything to stop it?"

As the day outside was changing swiftly, with a kind of furtive secrecy, so change came over Leah's face. Its plump, smooth sweetness tightened and stiffened until cheekbones and jaw were sharply outlined, the haggardness of age pinched it, and her eyes were blank and depthless as glass marbles. She sat with the cigarette limp and forgotten between her fingers, staring out at the sea, stretching now in meek expectation of the coming storm to the sharply etched horizon that showed like a steel wire drawn tightly across the base of the sky.

"Just remember one thing, Mabel," she said. "I love Mallory —that's the mainspring of everything for me. I love him enough to see reality for him as well as for myself—and that means loving a man a good deal. I want to go on living here as his wife, I want to cling to what's left to me, and I'm wise enough to know that I can only do that on—terms."

"Terms!"

"His terms." She ground out the cold cigarette savagely in the ash tray. "Never put into words of course by either of us, but understood all the same as though they were written down in black and white. The terms are that I must be sensible and tolerant, that I should look at things from his point of view, and that I should see myself very clearly for what I am—three quarters of a wife, perhaps less than that."

There was no change at all in her own rosy colour, but Mrs. Brastock had turned an odd light orange in the face; the blood rushing into it seemed to absorb the sallowness of her skin.

"But it's horrible, Leah! You're his wife, and he can't expect you to put up with—with——"

"He's left it entirely to me to decide whether I can put up with it or not, and I have decided. I don't see that it concerns anyone else."

"It concerns your friends that you should be insulted and humiliated in your own home. I would never have believed anything like this of Mallory unless I'd heard it with my own ears. If it had been the other way round he'd have expected you to stand by him."

"He has stood by me in every possible way—except the one," Leah said slowly. "And I've no patience with people who rant and rave at the idea of one law for men and another for women. You might as well object to having different laws for English-

men and Zulus; there's got to be a difference, because they belong
to different species."

The flush had faded out of Mrs. Brastock's face, and her
hands were weaving vaguely amongst the scraps again, but there
was a hungry gleam in her eyes.

"I don't understand how anyone can be so magnanimous.
But leaving Mallory out of it, Leah, what about Sherida? What
sort of a creature is she to come into a house and behave like
this?"

"What sort of a creature she is doesn't really matter to me;
I'm not interested in her personally. Mallory's been happier and
more settled these last few weeks than he has been for months,
and I'm grateful for that. Yes, I'm genuinely and deeply grateful, Mabel, and it's no use blethering to me about pride and self-
respect. I'm afraid the basic emotions of my life are much less
refined and high-flown. I want Mallory to be contented and,
crudely, I'm ready to swallow the reason why he is contented."
She brushed a blowing strand of hair back from her forehead
and smiled. "And remember, Mabel, I'm putting you on your
honour not only not to breathe a word of this to a soul, but not
to hint at it either. I won't have you looking at Mallory or at
Sherida with an air of shocked and outraged virtue. If I can
accept the situation philosophically and tolerantly, it surely isn't
too much to ask my friends to do the same. If it's green-flowered
linen remnants you're looking for, there's one under your nose."

"I don't know what to say," Mrs. Brastock mumbled helplessly. "It's been such a terrible shock to hear that Mallory——"

"It can't be such a shock, my dear, when you were going to
break the news to me gently about what's going on yourself.
Give me those bits and I'll cut them up to the right size, and
let's talk about something else. How long is Cicely staying this
time?"

Neither of them heard Christine get soundlessly up from the
cushion on the lawn beyond the curve of the bay window. She
moved away from it on tiptoe in a queerly stiff, sleepwalking
fashion, her face chalk white, the pupils of her eyes so enlarged
that they were swallowed up in blackness.

"So that's why I've always hated her," she thought. "I did from the first, I hated her so much that I felt sick. I wish I could be sick, but it wouldn't stop me hating her, that's what hurts all the time . . . I hate her so . . ."

She dropped down on the grassy slope of the bank slanting to the lawn and, lying on her face, drove her teeth into the back of her hand until the pain made her stop. Then she sat up, staring dully at the scarlet marks ridged against the faint brown of her skin.

"I wish she were dead," she said aloud. "I wish they were all dead. I'm the only one who cares, who understands. If Leah and I were alone together she'd be happy, nothing would ever hurt her. . . . I wish Sherida were dead."

Presently she got up and went down the garden, but when she came in sight of the summerhouse she swerved sharply away from it down a side path and took the longer way round by the river to the cliffs. Below their edge the sea lay now like a lead shield, giving back no lustre to the brooding sky, and down in the cove Sherida was standing on the edge of the beach idly throwing pebbles into the pale shallows for one of the dogs. Christine stared down at her, fascinated, her mouth a little open, her thin body trembling, the hand with the crimson marks smeared across it beating unconsciously against her thigh.

"I wish she were dead," she said aloud in a sharp, high voice, as though she wanted Sherida to hear, but the faint stir of air lifted it over the cliff top out of earshot above the cove.

19

THERE FOLLOWED three extraordinary days of sullen heat and silence. Cornwall lay like a landscape enclosed within the heavy glass globe of a Victorian paper weight; by day the air was thick as cobweb, at evening the clouds, mahogany and bronze red, piled themselves laboriously into bastions across the sky, at night the quietness was stretched so tight that one expected to hear it rip open at any second. The headlands stood thunderously black out of a sea that dragged itself in weariness up and down the beaches, its frayed edges leaving scum instead of freshness, and in the garden the twisting of a leaf, as a bird brushed against it, set up a brittle, metallic whispering.

"Cornwall in a quiet mood," Logan said, "is rather like a Blackpool fun fair after closing time; there's something eerie and unnatural about it. You look tired, Catherine. Is it the heat?"

They had climbed up on to the headland facing the Plume, whose silver streak had a tarnished, dejected look, and now they were sitting on the cliff edge leaning against rough tussocks of grass while a few sheep cropped and munched indifferently round their feet. It might have been the hard, bilious light from the sky that gave the effect, but Catherine's face looked pinched and pale and smudged with shadow round the eyes.

"No, I don't really mind the heat," she said. "But all the same I think I'll go back to London at the end of this week, Logan."

"In this sort of weather you'll find it fearfully tiring, even for a few days. What is it—another exhibition in the air, or a portrait commission? It's hardly the sort of weather for getting down to work, and surely either could wait."

"No, it isn't either," she said slowly. "And I didn't mean that I was going up for only a few days. I meant for some time."

"I see," Logan said thoughtfully, and they neither of them looked toward each other. A sort of embarrassed, self-conscious wariness had come down between them like a bank of fog, and they both seemed to be intensely absorbed in the scenery for a moment.

Far below them, across the pewter sea; a tiny ship no bigger than an insect swimming feebly in an effort to save its life was wending an aimless and laborious way along the coast, and suddenly there must have been a stir of wind in the air, for the surface of the water was crumpled.

"But why do you want to go away just now?" Logan asked carefully. "What are you trying to say, Catherine?"

"I don't know," she answered listlessly. "I wish I did."

This tiredness that was engulfing her was mental as well as physical; she couldn't make herself concentrate, she couldn't make herself or life feel real. All she could fix her mind on now was the maddening munch-munch of a sheep's jaws as it chewed and the minute progress of that water beetle of a ship.

"Catherine," Logan said slowly and clearly, as though he were speaking to a child or a foreigner who didn't understand his language very well, "things are pretty slack at the office just now and I could get part of my holiday, a fortnight of it, straight away. We could go up to London together at the end of the week and get married quietly and have a short honeymoon somewhere, and it needn't be anyone's business but our own. Wouldn't that settle everything?"

She knew of course what he meant by "everything"—Leah. It was difficult to concentrate her mind on Leah, but she made a desperate effort.

"I don't think it would, Logan," she said at last after a long pause. "It would only make people believe that I was afraid of something but hadn't the courage to face it, and they'd be right, wouldn't they? Besides it would hurt Leah terribly if we slipped away and did things like that, and you can't do that. After all, she loves you, and she crippled herself saving your life."

She didn't know what odd impulse made her say that in such a flat, gentle voice, as though she were trying to be cruel. Logan looked at her sharply and shifted his back against the rough hump of earth and grass.

"You don't have to remind me of that, I can remember it," he said briefly. "Well, if you won't marry me straight away, either in a registrar's office in London or in full panoply down here in the village church, what do you want to do? Have you any plans, Catherine?"

She tried not to hear the sarcastic and bitter note in his voice that suggested nerves stretched to danger point. She couldn't be angry with him for the way he spoke, because she could see so clearly how idiotic and obstinately senseless her behaviour must be, and yet there was something inside her that had taken command of the situation now and wouldn't be ousted until it had had its way.

"Yes," she answered quietly. "There's something I want you to do for me, Logan, and as soon as possible. I want you to go to the—the institute where the Maitlands found me, and I want you to ask them to give you all the details about me. They must know something."

"If they did," Logan said with an odd, unusual patience, "wouldn't the Maitlands have been told, so that they could tell you if you particularly wanted to know?"

"Yes, and that's what worries me, Logan. If they were to tell me that my father was a soldier on leave from France in the last war and my mother a barmaid, or that he was an unfaithful married businessman and she was his typist who couldn't cope with the situation, I shouldn't mind so much. It would give me a sort of background, even if it's only a sordid, common one. But they insist that they don't know anything at all, and I can't believe that. If you go there and explain all the circumstances, Logan, and that you have a right to know, they must tell you."

"But if it isn't a right that I choose to exercise?" he said, and she moved impatiently.

"Well, then, it's my right, and I do choose to exercise it. If you won't go, I will."

He sat forward with his thin, sunburnt hands linked round his knees and a tough blade of grass between his teeth, and for the first time since they had begun talking like this, Catherine looked at him and thought, "God knows how I've ever found the courage to do this, but I suppose it's the courage of despair. We can't go on like this, and Leah knows it, and in a way I'm grateful to her for forcing this on me. I'd never have faced it if I hadn't been made to, and yet I wouldn't have dared marry Logan, not knowing. One of my cowardices is bigger than the other, I suppose."

She waited for him to answer, and the tiny ship, with a last effort, rounded the next headland and went out of sight, leaving the sea desolately empty, sinister in its renewed dead calmness that had a faint, rusty light on it slanting through mildew-coloured clouds.

"All right," Logan said. "If you really want me to, Catherine, I'll do it. But it doesn't matter to me if your father was a hangman, and I'm the only person whose opinion matters at all. Shall we head for home now? It looks as though it might rain at last."

He held out his hand to her, and she came to her feet lightly, leaning her weight against him for a moment, and the thought flashed into her mind, "Wouldn't it be much easier for us and everybody else if we were to cut out this marriage business altogether that means so much fuss and turmoil? I've got my London flat and a career that's going to give me complete freedom if I persevere, and I believe he'd give in about it after a time and we'd save endless complications."

For a moment it seemed simple and obvious, and then she drew away abruptly from him. That would be the biggest confession of cowardice of all, and it would mean something horribly frightening. It might mean that the unknown wild beast of the jungle, heredity, was stalking her quietly and had crept so near that his breath was hot against her cold face.

"It's thundering," she said. "Let's hurry, Logan."

20

IT WAS A HOT afternoon for golf, uncomfortably hot, but in a mood of obstinate unreasonableness Jane took her clubs out onto the scrubby nine-hole course that twisted its way through thickets of impenetrable bramble and gorse, and started a solitary round. Her mind was so far away from what she was doing that she hardly ever saw her ball after she had hit it, and found it only because it had never gone far enough to be lost. But there was a kind of savage satisfaction in hacking at the tough prickles and smiting the iron-hard earth, and she needed the outlet.

She was in the grip of a mood that wasn't quite unhappiness or fear but was poised uncertainly between the two, so that she had been driven out of the house upon this forlorn and physically uncomfortable effort at distraction. Queer how the atmosphere of a house could change suddenly, become tainted with something faintly sour, as milk is tainted by thunder. That was what had happened at Bastions; but what was the thunder that brooded in the air inside the old house?

It was, she thought, chiefly the change in her father during these last few weeks that disturbed and frightened Jane, because he had always been the one sure and solid prop in life, the one utterly dependable factor. To see him restless and nervously on edge was to feel the very foundations of Bastions shake beneath one's feet. And Leah had been odd too lately. The bloom of her good temper and courage was as flawless as ever on the surface, but one had the impression that it didn't go so deep as it once did, and sometimes it seemed to Jane that there was something almost furtive in her serenity. She smiled as readily as ever, but not so much with her eyes, and they were always watching—but for what?

"She's horribly unhappy about something too," Jane thought as she battered her ball out of a tussock of wiry grass. "And I believe Christine knows why. Why on earth don't I ask Leah straight out what's wrong and if I can't do something? I love her just as much as Christine does, and I'm older. Old enough, I suppose, to guess what's wrong without being told. But Leah's right about me, I'm undeveloped and babyish and younger in heaps of ways than Christine. And yet I'm old enough to know— or at least to imagine—that I'm in love."

She took a blind whack at the ball, mis-hit it, jarred her arms as the club head skidded along the unyielding ground, and felt childish tears of rage sting her eyes. Leah had been like that all this week, obviously finding it very difficult to control her temper when trivial things went wrong, when her lighter refused to light or a knitting needle snapped between her fingers. If only it would rain so that this suffocating pressure of cloud and threat could be relaxed; but the sky seemed to have solidified and generated such a heat that raindrops falling from it would surely be sizzled into dryness before they reached the parched ground.

Simon, standing in the bay window of the small clubroom waiting for his partner to make a belated appearance, saw Jane's solitary figure toiling up the shallow hill of the third hole before it dipped into a small valley and then rose again on the steeper slope of the fourth. He watched her idly for a moment, wondering why she should bother to put so much exertion into something that was so obviously giving her very little pleasure, for the set of her shoulders looked tired and depressed and rather cross.

"Excuse me, sir," the club steward said behind him. "Mr. Lawrence has just rung up to say that he has been delayed in getting over by a puncture and won't be here for half an hour or so, and that if you find a game with someone else he will quite understand."

"Oh!" Simon said. "Well, I'll probably go out and join Miss St. Aubyn, so if he likes he can come out and catch us up."

He hadn't really any particular desire to hurry out and attach himself to Jane, but there was something forlorn about her figure that touched him a little and compelled him to make an effort to cheer her up. He swung his clubs across his shoulder and walked slowly over the scraggy turf, expecting at every moment to see her ahead of him on the further slope, where he could hail her; but there was no sign of her, and when he reached the lip of the shallow saucer-shaped hollow, there was no sign of her there either.

That was odd, because she hadn't come back in her tracks and the only rough here was down the narrow gully leading to the sea, and it would have to be a very wild and right-angled slice that landed one's ball into it. She seemed to have vanished mysteriously into thin air.

"Jane!" he shouted. "Jane, where are you?"

There was silence for a moment, and then a faint voice answered him from the gully, undoubtedly Jane's voice.

"I'm down here. I've lost my ball."

He picked his way through the prickly tangle and the massed bramble bushes that shrouded the steep slope, and came upon Jane sitting disconsolately on an outcrop of rock, her face rather white, her fingers pulling gingerly at one shoelace.

"What on earth are you doing down here?" he asked, and then sharply: "You've hurt yourself."

"It's nothing," she answered. "I sliced a perfectly new ball down here and thought I'd better look for it, and put my foot in a rabbit hole. It's only a bit of a twist."

"I should think," Simon said mildly, "that you were so hot and tired that you didn't know what you were doing. I'll get your shoe off."

Her ankle and foot had swelled up so violently that it was bulging over the top of her brogue, and she set her teeth a little as he got it carefully off.

"It's more than a sprain," he said briefly. "You may have broken something. I'll carry you up to the clubhouse and drive you home."

"Oh—no!" Jane said under her breath with a movement that was like a recoil. "I mean—I can perfectly well walk if you'll give me a hoist up the steep part."

She stood up and tried to put her weight on the foot, but sat down again abruptly, looking whiter.

"There you are," Simon said. "You don't imagine I'm going to let you walk on an ankle that may be fractured? I've got a professional reputation to protect, even if you've got a moral one. Is that what's bothering you?" He smiled down at her suddenly, his eyes amused, and she reddened.

"Of course not! Only—well, Cicely's playing golf today with Mr. Brastock, and if she sees you carrying me back to the clubhouse you know the sort of things she'll say. That it must be nice to have such obliging ankles, not like hers which only get twisted when there's nobody within reach but the butcher's boy or the dustman." She tugged viciously at a tough blade of grass and avoided his eyes. "I suppose I ought to be used to Cicely's remarks by this time and not mind them, but sometimes I do feel like strangling her."

"I know." Simon's eyes were suddenly serious. "Look here, it's quite simple, and we needn't go near the clubhouse. I'll carry you up to the seventh to the edge of the road and then fetch the car down and pick you up. Will that do?"

"Yes. I'm sorry to be such a nuisance. I ought to have been on the lookout for rabbit holes, knowing there are hundreds of them down here, but I was thinking about something else. Am I horribly heavy?"

He had picked her up easily, and as he did so he could feel her whole slight body going stiff and rigid, as though she were determined, even when he carried her, to preserve her self-sufficiency and independence.

"I may manage to stagger to the seventh without collapsing," he said, falling in with her childish and embarrassed method of carrying off the situation. She was so young that she firmly believed that flippancy was a dependable shield against every moment of awkwardness. But why in heaven's name should she feel awkward and self-conscious about being carried a hundred yards or so in his arms? "There you are," he said and put her down on a slanting grass bank on the edge of the narrow, stony road. "I'll fetch the car."

She watched him out of sight round the bend of the lane and then felt a queer shiver run all over her in spite of the stifling heat of the afternoon. The clouds had dropped lower in thick, curdled layers faintly tinged with sultry pink, and when she looked up at them two fat, warm splashes of water spattered on her face, but within a few seconds the faint hissing in the brittle grass had stopped.

It seemed to Simon, driving back to her, that her figure looked particularly small and forlorn under the enormous and threatening arch of the storm-clotted sky. She must, he thought, have come out alone like that to work out some problem of her own or to escape from something. The atmosphere of Bastions? He had noticed lately that there had been something strained and taut about it.

"Here we are," he said and put her into the back seat with her foot up. "And there was no sign of Cicely to inquire into my mysterious movements with the car. Comfortable?"

"Yes, thanks. You must think I'm very childish," Jane's tone was resentful and apologetic at the same time. "I always seem to be making a fuss about nothing, don't I? I suppose it doesn't matter in the least what Cicely says. Leah's often pointing out to me that I dramatize things far too much, that it's a sign of an inferiority complex and no confidence in oneself, and she's right. When people tell me I'm a fool or underdeveloped mentally, I firmly believe it."

"And that's exactly what Leah's telling you," Simon said unexpectedly. "Why believe her?"

"But—if Leah doesn't understand people and how to manage life, who does?" Jane said slowly. "She's brought us up, and she's so frightfully wise and understanding."

"There's nobody in the world who can say flatly that she understands anybody else from top to bottom. It just isn't possible. Why not try understanding yourself, Jane, instead of accepting a sort of predigested version from Leah? You might make quite a surprising discovery. Now don't try to stand on that ankle, I'll take you in."

The ankle was slightly fractured in one place, and Jane was relegated to a long chair on the terrace, since the storm still didn't break. The laburnum was opening, its yellow brilliance almost shrill and garish against the world's dour greyness, and the scent of the roses lay thick as honey outside the sitting-room windows. But Jane submitted herself to the dullness of inactivity with a surprising mildness, and Sherida had the feeling that she was glad of the definiteness of being bound to one spot, of having her own restlessness forcibly held at bay.

Why was everyone so restless? Logan had gone off to London suddenly on Monday, and Catherine had packed a suitcase and gone to visit friends at St. Ives the day after, and Mallory was hardly ever in the house, except for meals. He said he was worried about the ever lowering political and world situation, but again Sherida, with a new intuition that had come to her lately, sensed that his restlessness and depression had a more personal source. And Leah had given up any attempt at work. Sherida found herself responsible for answering all her correspondence, almost for the writing of the "prose-lyrics," though Leah did scrawl a rough idea down occasionally and pass it over to Sherida to be polished into shape.

"You know exactly what's wanted," she said, "and I believe you do it far better than I ever did. 'Crocus Tea Party' was a gem, and I believe you've missed your vocation, Sherida."

Leah spent the day sitting out alongside Jane, and Simon coming in during the afternoon found them with their heads together over a complicated knitting pattern for a baby's shawl for the church bazaar.

"How's the battered golf player?" he asked lightly. "She hasn't experimented on that ankle, has she, Leah? And by the way, I've brought over a prescription for a tonic for you, Jane, which you're going to swallow to the last dregs. I've been longing to give it to you long ago, but you never asked me, and I'm too proud to tout my own tonics amongst my patients."

"I'm sure I don't need it," Jane murmured, but she smiled, and there was colour suddenly in her face. "I know your tonics, Simon. They taste like ink and bad eggs."

"If Jane took tonics every time she looked peaky and thin," Leah said quietly, "she'd be a walking dispensary. I've done my best to fatten her and get some colour into her face, just for the sake of my own reputation and pride, because no stepmother likes to have her stepchild looking semistarved, but it hasn't been much use. By the way, Simon, I don't think those sleeping pills you gave me are very much use; I've had some bad nights lately, and I want you to do something about it. I can stand about a week of them on end, but after that it becomes rather an effort to keep going. I meant to tell you yesterday about it, but you didn't ask, and I forgot. I think I'll go in and have a rest now if you don't mind."

She turned her head and gave him a tired, heavy eyed smile of apology, her golden head resting against the blue cushion as though the weight of it exhausted her, and there were dark shadows under her eyes.

"Leah, why didn't you tell me?" Jane said. "Everyone's been fussing ridiculously over me without noticing you were looking tired."

"But, darling, I don't mind," Leah patted her arm. "I quite realize that when you've got a permanent invalid on your hands you get bored with constant enquiries and fusses and you don't notice things so much as you did in the early days. If Simon can produce something that will give me one really good night I shall be perfectly all right. Shall you be over tomorrow, Simon, or do you think Jane's ankle is going along all right? I can't help worrying when you come so often, it makes me feel there must be something wrong."

"Of course there isn't," Simon said almost sharply. "She'll be able to walk on it in a couple of days. I don't think I'll be over tomorrow, but I'll drop in a fresh bottle of pills this evening. I'll push you in."

"Thank you, Simon, but I can manage. It's good exercise for me, and if I get really tired I may sleep better. Stay and have some tea, won't you? I may not come in."

There was a moment of silence as she slid her chair away over the levelled lintel of the door into the back lobby, and presently her door shut and Jane said slowly:

"I've been worried about Leah, Simon. She doesn't look well, and it must be awful not to be able to sleep. I'm glad Christine moved down to the ground floor; that's company for her if she feels rotten. Can you give her something really strong?"

"Nothing stronger than she's having now, but if she thinks it is she'll probably sleep the clock round. There's a lot of autosuggestion mixed up with sleeping drugs." He lit a cigarette and added thoughtfully: "There's no need to worry so much about Leah, you know, Jane. She's extremely strong really, and she'll probably live to be a hundred without any effort at all."

"Simon!" Jane gave him a startled look. "But what about her bad attacks? It's queer you should say that, though, because only yesterday Leah was talking about that—about how long she'd live, I mean. Oh, not morbidly or affectedly, but quite sensibly. She says her one horror is of living to be a toothless old bundle of decrepit bones and useless flesh that has to be pushed about endlessly by people who are bored to tears with the job. It seems horrible even to think of Leah being like that, as well as impossible. She couldn't get old in that way."

"But she will," Simon said thoughtfully, his eyes on the swinging, theatrical tassels of the laburnum at the top of the terrace steps. "She will, Jane, and she's honest and clear-sighted enough to realize it. Do you know what the most dangerous and fatal emotion in the world is?"

"Love?" Jane suggested under her breath, but he shook his head impatiently.

"No. Pity. Pity can spoil and twist thousands more lives than love ever does. Don't let pity do that to you, Jane. It's a blood-sucker; it makes you pour out everything and gives nothing at all back, until you become an empty husk, a walking blown eggshell. I'm not afraid of loving someone, but frankly I'm terrified when I find myself pitying them. I don't think I've time to stay to tea. Good-bye."

His departure was so abrupt that it left Jane with her mouth half open and words unspoken. What a strange way for him to talk, she thought as she watched him swing down the terrace steps, almost as though he were afraid of something. There seemed to be fear in the air for everybody, and she shivered a little in spite of the hot, sunless pressure of the sky.

"Has Dr. Crowdy gone?" She jumped a little as Christine came silently out of the door behind and stood beside her. Christine had developed the habit lately of sliding about the house as noiselessly as a ghost, so that one never knew when she was standing just behind one, listening and watching with those burn-ing, black-pupilled eyes of hers that were sizes too big for her narrow face. "Did he overhaul Leah properly?"

"He—no, not exactly," Jane said. "She told him about not being able to sleep in spite of the pills, and he's going to give her some other ones—stronger."

"He seems to have been very casual about it." Christine was staring at Jane accusingly. "He must have noticed how ill she's been looking, but all he does is fuss about your ankle."

"Christine, Simon is a first-class doctor, and if he thought Leah looked ill he wouldn't waste a second in finding out what was wrong and looking after her. I don't think you're quite qualified to teach him his business."

"He doesn't sleep near to her and hear her tossing about all night and sometimes crying," Christine said slowly, her hands clenched. "None of you hear that except me, and I ought not to tell you. Not that you can do anything."

"But what's the matter?" Jane said desperately. "Why should she cry? Why is she unhappy? I don't understand."

"No?" Christine's smile was faint and patronizing and contemptuous, and it gave Jane that feeling of being an immature child measured against Christine's instinctive, age-old wisdom. Never in her life had Christine committed the foolish, childish blunders and *faux-pas* that had been Jane's lot until a comparatively recent date. Christine had never announced at the top of her voice in the middle of a tea party, as Jane had when she was ten, that she longed to be grown up and do adultery. It had taken her a long time and much lecturing from Leah to understand that "adult" and "adultery" had very different meanings, but somehow she felt that Christine would never have needed to have the difference explained to her. "Where's Sherida?" Christine went on abruptly. "I haven't seen her all the afternoon."

"She's gone over with Daddy to that big A.R.P. meeting. She's going to train as a warden."

"She seems to be finding plenty of time for outside things, apart from the work she does for Leah," Christine said sulkily, and Jane shifted impatiently.

"Leah's hardly doing any writing just now, I don't know why, and she's lost all interest in her correspondence corners. I think she's going to give them up when the contract has run out."

"Well, I suppose Sherida's training as a warden will come in useful wherever she may be," Christine said casually with a sidelong look at Jane, but she refused to rise to the obvious bait.

"We'll all have to turn our hands to something like that," she said. "I think I'll go in now, it's dismal out here. I can hop if you'll give me an arm."

The congested weight of the storm broke through the thick crust of clouds early that evening, and by the time Sherida went up to bed at half past ten the noise outside was so tremendous that she could scarcely hear herself think.

The solid beams and sturdy brickwork of the house were shaking and vibrating under the onslaught of wind and rain and thunder, but there was nothing frightened or abject about it; rather one could feel its defiance and tough resistance bracing themselves with a kind of excitement. One Atlantic storm more meant very little to Bastions, which knew exactly how to plant itself against it, how to come through unscathed while other less experienced houses greeted the morning with dishevelled slates and wobbling chimneys.

It was too wild to open the window, but Sherida turned out the light for a moment and stood by the drawn back curtain. The glass was thickly patterned with torrents of rain, and the blackness of the sky didn't yield even the dim outline of trees, but every moment or two lightning forked in white-and-blue zigzags earthwards, and the fresh smell of wet-soaked ground and thirst-quenched trees came strongly into the room.

This might be a relief, she thought, not only to the heat-baked earth but to overstrained nerves. The St. Aubyn family were Cornish born and bred, and they reacted to the weather as sensitively as the Cornish birds and flowers. Mallory's restlessness and curious aloofness from everyone for the past week or two might be linked up more with that than with any personal unhappiness. All the same Sherida had to admit to herself that it was disturbing, almost frightening to see Mallory's solid tranquillity shaken. In the months she had been at Bastions she had grown to think of him, as the whole family did, as an impregnable rock of dependability and calmness.

There was a horizon-splitting flash of white hot lightning that made her flinch back from the window, and in the split second before the answering crash of thunder she heard an odd sound outside her bedroom door, a muffled, furtive sound like scuffling. As the thunder hit the house with a mailed fist of noise, she opened the door quietly and came face to face with Christine wearing a dressing gown and holding a small torch whose wavering circle of light was fixed apparently on the keyhole. Her pale red-gold hair swung loosely over her face that became a pale blur in the darkness of the passage as she hastily switched the torch out.

"Christine, what on earth are you doing here?" Sherida asked. "I thought you went to bed early with the beginnings of a bad cold. Is anything wrong?"

"Of course not. I couldn't sleep," Christine's voice was defiant. "And then I thought I heard Jane calling for something, so I came up to see what she wanted."

"You must have remarkably good ears to hear Jane calling from her room right upstairs through a closed door in the middle of all this row. I didn't hear anything, and I'm much nearer than you are. And Jane's room is at the other end of the corridor."

"I know that!" Christine's fingers were clutched round the torch, but Sherida could see that they were trembling. "But surely I can walk about our own house without having to—to explain everything to you, Sherida."

"Of course," Sherida said casually. "Only when I find someone snooping round my bedroom door with a torch I rather like to know what it's all about."

She used the contemptuous word deliberately, knowing that it would sting Christine's pride. "Snooping" wasn't the word she wanted applied to her dramatic nocturnal activities, and she answered with angry, childish shrillness.

"I wasn't snooping! I wondered if you were awake and if you'd heard Jane calling, and I was coming in to ask you."

Suddenly Sherida found her pitiful in her thin, taut clumsiness, and she put a hand on her arm and drew her inside the door.

"Look, Christine," she said gently. "I know you don't like me, and I'm sorry about it. I get on so well with all the others, and I can't quite understand why I don't with you. Couldn't you tell me what's wrong?"

But it was no good; the bewildered childishness of Christine's face hardened into blankness and stubbornness, and she tugged the cord of the green dressing gown tighter round her narrow waist.

"Nothing's wrong," she said briefly. "I suppose I don't make friends as quickly and easily as the others do. I can't really help it, I'm afraid. I suppose Daddy has gone to bed?"

"I haven't the least idea," Sherida said quietly and without any hesitation, although she had heard Mallory go along to his room down the opposite corridor half an hour before. Christine had laid a little trap for her, and she had no intention of walking into it.

But it wasn't until Christine had muttered an ungracious good night and departed that it occurred to Sherida to wonder exactly why such a trap should have been set for her by a girl of Christine's age; what her meanderings about the darkened house with a torch had really signified.

Leah's bedroom door was slightly ajar when Christine passed it, and though she went on tiptoe, Leah's voice called to her softly.

"Is that you, darling? Is anything wrong? Come in and talk to me, I can't sleep for the noise."

The bedside lamp with its rose-red shade was on, and she was sitting up against her pillows with a swansdown cape over her shoulders and a cigarette in her mouth, but her eyes looked sunken and dark-circled.

"Haven't those sleeping things done you any good?" Christine asked as she perched herself on the edge of the high white bed. "Can't you try to get off?"

"I'm not bothering about it; I don't really want to sleep, because when I do I dream such strange, nightmarish things," Leah said slowly and patted Christine's hand. "You look as though you needed sleeping stuff yourself, Chris. But how do you manage always to be awake and around just when I'm feeling lonely and need you most?"

"Do you really need me, Leah?" Christine said eagerly. "Sometimes I wonder if I'm a nuisance hanging round so much, because I'm not grown up and I—I'm not like Jane."

"No, you aren't like Jane because you're Christine, and I don't want you to be anybody else, darling. You may not be quite grown up, but I can talk to you as I can't to the others. I—I feel much more as though I really were your mother than I do with the others, and I believe you feel like that too, don't you?"

"Yes." Christine's eyes were enormous in the nervous pallor of her face. "There's something special between us, isn't there? I wish I could do something for you, Leah—I mean something important and tremendous. Oh, I wish I could!"

She lay down along the edge of the bed, her slight body fitting into the narrow space, her cheek against Leah's shoulder that felt smooth and round even through the thick cape. Leah's blue eyes were thoughtful.

"Darling, perhaps one of these days I'll ask you to do something like that for me. At any rate I know there's somebody who really cares, who would help me if I needed help. I'll count on you, Chris. Now run along to bed, and don't lie awake reading or thinking too much. I suppose everybody has gone to bed?"

"Yes. I—I went upstairs just now to see if Jane was all right, and I saw Sherida. She hadn't gone to bed though; she was still dressed and she looked as though—as though she were sort of waiting for something."

She didn't look at Leah as she said it, but she felt Leah's hand tighten on her arm.

"Oh!" she said, very softly. "But I expect it was just the noise of the storm that kept her awake. We're all rather restless to-night."

"But it was different somehow with Sherida." Christine sat up suddenly, pushing the fine hair back from her face with both hands. "Leah—why do you keep her on here? You don't really need a secretary; Jane or I could do everything for you. Somehow, since Sherida came here, everything has been different—funny. If she were to leave, wouldn't—wouldn't you be much happier?"

Leah took another cigarette from the open silver box beside her bed and lit it deliberately, in silence, and Christine's mouth trembled childishly.

"I know I oughtn't to have said that; I suppose it's impertinent because I'm so young. But I—I feel I do understand some things in a grownup way."

"I know you do, Christine. I don't mind you saying that . . . it's a relief to be able to talk honestly to someone. All the others seem rather infatuated by Sherida, but you're sensible and clear-sighted enough not to be." The smoke ring she had blown floated gently above Leah's golden head. "But I can't get rid of her just now, darling; it wouldn't be the right time or the right way. Don't worry, I know the best way of doing things, and I don't want anyone upset. If everyone else likes her and I don't, I'm in the minority."

"But it's what you feel that matters," Christine said with anger in her voice. "They ought to think of you. I—I could kill anyone who hurts you, Leah."

She was trembling again, and Leah laid firm hands on her shoulders and gave her a little shake.

"Christine, don't talk like that, it frightens me. It isn't right for anyone to love a person so much that they'd commit murder for their sake. And yet"—she smiled and pushed Christine's silky hair back from her forehead—"it's rather comforting and nice to know that someone does care like that. Now go to bed and don't tell anyone you came in here so late, darling. If you do, Daddy will begin to think I'm a bad influence on you and you'll be bundled off to a finishing school to be drilled into the shape of a nice, normal, healthy, unimaginative English schoolgirl. Good night— and bless you."

There was a convulsive emotionalism in Christine's final hug and kiss before she departed at last, and Leah, with a tired gesture, stubbed out the half-smoked cigarette and switched out the light. She was tired, in a queer, drained way that left her feeling cold and empty, as though vitality and strength had passed from her to Christine. And she knew that unconsciously that was what she had been trying to do. There was something about Christine that affected her queerly; she wanted to dominate, to possess her as she never could any of the others. Even Andrew, her own child, had a sturdy independence that looked at her with calm grey eyes and pursued its own course untroubled by pity or sentiment. Christine was like a harp on which one could play any tune, and sometimes her own fingers ran away with her and she had to twang the strings and hear the melody she had chosen. But she was a little frightened tonight at the theme she had composed and heard re-echo in Christine's stifled voice.

21

LOGAN CAME BACK from London two days later looking quiet and rather preoccupied. Leah was alone in the garden when he arrived and came down to join her, and she gripped his hand tightly for a moment, smiling at him.

"It's nice to have you back, Logan. Had a good time in London? You needed a change."

"It was all right," he said briefly. "Pretty hot and sticky till the weather broke, and everyone's a bit on edge over this war business. It's a question of being more than on edge now, though; we've got to be on our toes and ready."

"Do you think there's going to be war, Logan?"

"I don't think, I know. I expect to find myself ploughing along a dusty French road any day now."

Logan was in a Territorial battalion, and in recent months they had been putting in more than their usual quota of training and manoeuvres over the sullen moors and along the steep Cornish lanes.

"Oh dear!" Leah said softly and with a little catch in her breath. "It must be dreadful for Catherine, poor child, feeling this looming over you both. Is she going to stay in London? I should have thought, all things considering, that she'd have wanted to see as much of you as she can just now. But she's a curiously austere girl temperamentally. I mean, she doesn't indulge in emotions and sentiments as other girls do, does she?"

"Not in public," Logan said briefly. "Yes, she's staying in London for the time being. How is Jane's ankle?"

"Getting on very well. She walks about without even a stick, but Simon is still making rather a fuss about it. I don't think he can be overworked, he seems able to spare so much time to come over here to see her."

Logan, glancing at her, saw a furrow cut itself down the centre of her smooth, sun-browned forehead, and there was something sulky and troubled about the droop of her mouth.

"A little fussing won't hurt Jane; it may do her inferiority complex good. I'll go and clean up before tea. Where is everybody?"

"They'll all be in for tea, except Mallory and Sherida. He's organizing all the local A.R.P. now, and Sherida is training as a warden and helps him with secretarial work and files and things. It's a good thing my efforts as an author don't take up too much of her time."

Again that acid note in her voice, and her hands jerked suddenly, sharply at the knitting she was doing, so that the ball bounced off her lap and rolled away under the table. Logan retrieved it for her, and as he put it into her hand she looked up at him and said slowly:

"I'm sorry. I'm afraid everyone is finding me rather bad-tempered these days, and I know they've got enough to worry about without that. But it's this war—you're all getting ready for it, learning new jobs, undertaking new responsibilities, but all I can do is sit and knit ridiculous balaclava helmets that no self-respecting soldier would ever wear. And now I've done my little grouse, there's an end of it. Go and get washed for tea, we'll have it in five minutes."

For a moment he felt pity for her catch at his heart and mixed up with his pity a dangerous emotionalism. He could understand so well what torment her physical imprisonment meant to her just at this time when every able-bodied and intelligent woman was training and planning for war. She should have been at the head of the local Civil Defence units, she should have been swinging about the country on long, swift-moving legs, organizing, directing, suggesting. But those wide-palmed, strong-muscled, sun-tanned hands of hers could do nothing more than manipulate knitting needles. The courage she needed to face war with was of a brand and quality that none of them would be called upon to show, and she had to be helped. Catherine had been right in refusing to accept his idea of sneaking away to London and getting married there half secretly. It wouldn't have been fair to hurt

Leah in another way when already she was striving against her own private agony.

"Nobody can accuse you of grousing," he said quickly and dropped an unexpected kiss against her warm cheek before he ran up the terrace steps to the house.

He went up the stairs to his room wearily, feeling depression weigh against his spirits, and a kind of hopelessness. Remembering that moment when the Pullman windows began to slide away from the platform and Catherine's pale, grave face, he found himself thinking, "Well, what comes next for us?"—and there didn't seem to be any answer at the moment. He had felt that it would be like this from the first; he had known the message he would have to bring back for Catherine from that rather gaunt red-brick institute where a rosy-faced, brown-eyed matron had interviewed him over their record ledgers. The entries relating to Catherine Maitland were extremely brief.

On September 15, 1916, a policeman patrolling late at night in the neighbourhood of the local church had heard the cries of a baby, had investigated with his torch, and had found a four-months-old child, wrapped in a shabby but spotlessly clean white shawl, yelling its head off under the seat in the porch. The baby's clothes had all been much darned and worn but carefully washed and ironed, and there wasn't the smallest sign of identification amongst them. Those were war days, and life was chaotic and hard pressed for the police, and nothing had ever been found out about the abandoned baby.

"Naturally," the matron said, "we explained all the facts to Mr. and Mrs. Maitland when they saw the child and wished to adopt her, but they understood them fully and accepted all the risks and possibilities. I believe it all turned out very successfully and happily, Mr. St. Aubyn."

"Yes, it did," he said abruptly. "I expect you know that Catherine Maitland is well on the way to becoming a very well known artist, and I told you that she and I are going to be married very soon. This was just an idea of hers—born of natural curiosity, I suppose."

"I can understand that." The matron's eyes were sympathetic.

"I wish we could have told you something, Mr. St. Aubyn, but since we can't, I should tell Catherine to put the whole thing out of her mind for good and all. We are what we make of ourselves, after all, and Catherine doesn't need to worry about who or what her real parents were. Give her my love and that message."

That was what he had done, his eyes watchful as he looked at her, but her face had been unbetrayingly expressionless.

"I see," she said quietly. "Thank you, Logan, I suppose that's all we can do. I'll write to you in a day or two, but I don't think I'll come home with you just yet."

That was how things stood now; he didn't know what was going on at the back of her mind, what she was really feeling, what she was going to write to him. . . .

"Logan? I thought I heard you arriving." Jane put her head round his bedroom door and limped in on her plastered ankle. "It's lovely to have you back," she said, and then stopped short at the sight of his face. He had been so deep in his thoughts about Catherine that he hadn't had time to rearrange it, to cast the worried look out of his eyes. "Is anything wrong?"

He waited a moment before he answered, looking at her hard, and it seemed to him suddenly that she had changed a good deal in the few days he had been away; that she had suddenly outgrown her rather pathetic immaturity and childishness. She met his eyes steadily, and he held out a hand to her.

"Jane, I want to ask you something. I feel I can talk to you because I think you'll understand. It's about Catherine. Why is she frightened of Leah? She's never been anything but sweet and kind to her, making her almost one of the family. And yet—Catherine is frightened of her."

Jane moved away from him a little and stood by the window, swinging the blind cord to and fro softly.

"Aren't we all rather frightened of Leah?" she said at last and went on quickly as Logan made a startled movement. "I mean we love her and pity her, but mixed up with all that there is a sort of fear—fear of not seeming grateful enough for what she did for us when she saved our lives, fear of not meeting our obligations properly. Don't you think that if Leah were perfectly normal we'd be much more—well—honest with her about things?"

"I suppose we should." He was puzzled. "But that's natural, Jane. One always treats an invalid more gently and considerately than one does a normal person."

"But it's fear that makes us like that, more than pity. How much do you really pity Leah? And how much does she trade on it?"

"Jane!" He stared at her, his face blank with surprise. "I've never heard you talk like this about Leah before. I always thought you were the one of us who was most inclined to dedicate your life to looking after her."

"I love her—of course I do—and I'm terribly sorry for her." A queer stubbornness came into Jane's face. "But I'm beginning to understand something about Leah that I didn't before. Naturally she's a terribly active, alive, strong-willed person, and she's got nothing to vent her energy on—except us. Instead of winning tennis and golf tournaments and organizing the countryside, she can only organize us. That's why Catherine is afraid of her, and I think you knew it before you asked me."

"Yes," Logan said slowly, fumbling for his pipe. "Yes, I did, Jane. But what is one to do about it?"

"I suppose each one of us has to decide that for ourselves. I mean—whether loving Leah and being sorry for her is going to be the most important thing in our lives or not. I think Simon will be over any moment, so I'll go down."

She closed the door softly behind her, and Logan pulled at his pipe and lighted it mechanically. Yes, there was no doubt that, most extraordinarily during a very few days, Jane had completely grown up.

22

THE STORM HAD BEEN like a gigantic vacuum cleaner run to and fro across the sky, sucking up every vestige of dingy air and sombre colour. There were clouds, but they floated high in the blue air in great snow-white masses, like loose-petalled and over-blown camellias, and the sea had come to life again in a fury of peacock green and ultramarine and rainbow arcs curving over the rocks.

But for some reason that she couldn't define, Leah hated the change in the weather, almost longed for the colourless, leaden dull days before the storm. This shining, vibrating dragonfly day that seemed to be shaking its wings in perpetual ecstasy of living tightened something in her breast and made her throat ache.

"I'm running up to town," Mallory said at breakfast. "I may have to stay overnight, but if I do I'll ring you."

"More A.R.P.?" Leah asked with the faintest upward movement of her firm eyebrows, and he nodded briefly.

"Partly. They've built some specimen home shelters, and I want to have a look at them. I'll combine it with several other jobs. Do you want anything done?"

"No, thank you, darling. I know you really won't have any time to spare, and anyway Sherida's going up today to do some shopping for me and interview some editors. Didn't you remember?"

Sherida hadn't come down to breakfast yet, but all the others had, and they were absorbed in newspapers or their own letters, and nobody paid much attention to Leah's question, but Christine's hand, holding a marmalade spoon, gave a little jerk, and she dripped some of the juice over the edge of the plate.

"Sherida going up to London?" Mallory said blankly. "But I didn't even know she was going. Is she catching the 10.18? But what about coming back? She's not going to have much time for all those jobs, surely."

"She's staying the night, darling," Leah said smoothly. "That will give her all tomorrow as well. Here she is."

Sherida had got her hat on, a round-brimmed amber-gold straw with a green feather slanting sharply backwards, and she was wearing amber ear studs. It was the first time she had been up to London since she came to Cornwall, and it was rather fun to get out of suitable-for-the-country clothes into something smarter, something that gave her a feeling of sleek good grooming. Her dark hair was drawn away from her ears into smooth whorls, and she had used a coral lipstick. Everybody looked at her, and as she felt the surprise in their eyes a faint deepening of colour came into her face. But was there any need to feel embarrassed and faintly guilty because she owned one smart hat and knew how to wear it?

"Sorry I'm late," she murmured as she slid into her seat between Logan and Jane. "It's such ages since I've dressed up to go to London that it took me longer than I expected. Not that I am particularly dressed up," she added quickly. "This hat is two years old."

"Well, it doesn't look it," Jane said. "It's a duck of a hat."

Mallory looked at her across the table with his slow smile that started in his eyes before it reached his mouth.

"That hat ought to add guineas to Leah's new contract," he said. "I'm going up to town too, Sherida, so we can travel together. There's no need to hurry over your breakfast, I'll go and finish some letters."

"I've finished too," Leah said quickly. "So have you, haven't you, Christine? Come and help me turn out that wool drawer."

She and Christine went, and Logan pushed his chair back and stretched out his legs with a sigh.

"If you've got time, Sherida, between doing Leah's jobs, will you ring up Catherine? She'd love to see you, I know, and you've got her number."

"Yes, of course I will, Logan. I'll ring her up as soon as I get there."

She didn't ask him if there was any message he wanted her to give Catherine, and he didn't say any more, but she knew why he had asked her to see her. He wanted, in a roundabout way, to know how Catherine was because something had happened between them while he was in London, something discordant and disturbing.

Leah didn't see them go off in the car to the station. She was absorbed in sorting out the wool drawer with Christine, and when she heard the sound of the car starting up at the front of the house she didn't even raise her head, but Christine, unravelling a tangle of red wool, gave it a tug that broke the strand.

"Leah? Good morning, my dear, I hope we aren't making too

early a morning call." Mrs. Brastock and Cicely had arrived un-announced through the garden door, and in spite of the fresh coolness of the morning Mabel Brastock looked flushed and tousled, but Cicely was neat and sedate and faintly amused as Mabel scurried on. "Did I see Mallory going off just this moment in the car with a suitcase? Is he going away?"

"To London for a night. Christine darling, will you see to the dining-room flowers for me? They looked horribly wilted at break-fast."

There was a moment's pause until Christine had closed the door fretfully behind her, and then Mrs. Brastock burst out again.

"Leah, has Jane gone up to town with Mallory? I only saw the car as it passed, and there was someone with him in a yellow hat."

"And you couldn't remember whether Jane has a yellow hat?" Leah said pleasantly. "No, you're quite right, Mabel, she hasn't. That was Sherida. I told you she was going up to London for a couple of days to attend to business for me."

"But Leah—you mean she and Mallory have gone up—to-gether?" Mrs. Brastock's gooseberry-coloured eyes went rounder and wider, and Cicely smiled faintly. "Well, upon my word, if I'd been you, Leah, I'd have told Sherida that she needn't come back to Bastions."

"And I can see in Cicely's eyes," Leah said quietly, "that if she were me she'd tell Mallory not to come back, wouldn't you, Cicely?"

Cicely shrugged her shoulders delicately and screwed up her smooth forehead.

"Well, knowing something about men, it seems to me that if you allow them enough rope to hang themselves with they gen-erally hang your self-respect first. I don't——"

"You don't know what you're talking about, Cicely," Mrs. Brastock said bluntly. "Self-respect! If you hadn't had so much self-respect that you felt you were taking the bloom off your idealism and innocence even by letting Osbert Grimes kiss you good night, you'd have been married to him by this time."

"Perhaps Cicely had too much self-respect to marry a man called Osbert Grimes," Leah said lightly. "Incidentally I'm not

trying to lure Mallory into hanging himself. He had no idea
Sherida was going up to London today; we only decided about
it late last night. Now do you want any further information about
the movements of my family?"

"Well, really, Leah!" Mrs. Brastock stared at her, and hard
patches of salmon pink spread themselves angrily across her plump
neck. "I'm your closest friend, and if I can't ask a simple question . . . Well, never mind about it. We came over to ask if
Jane is well enough to come to lunch tomorrow."

"Jane's out in the garden," Leah said. "You'd better ask her,
Mabel. I don't know what she's doing tomorrow, but I have an
idea she's going out to tea with Simon and his sister—she's staying
with him. She doesn't have to ask my permission to accept invitations, you know."

Mrs. Brastock got up from her chair and hauled down the
raffia-straw beehive-shaped hat that was gradually sliding to the
back of her head.

"I think we did come too early," she said. "You're in an odd
mood this morning, Leah darling. Never mind, we'll find Jane,
but I don't suppose she'll want to do anything so dull as lunch
with us if she's got an exciting engagement like that for the afternoon. Cicely, we must get down to Miss Huggett's early if we
want to order those cakes. Perhaps you'd go on and do it for me."
Cicely with a cool nod went back into the garden, and Mrs.
Brastock paused for a moment beside Leah's chair and squeezed a
warm, soft hand heavily over her shoulder. "It's all right, my
dear," she said in a stage whisper. "Of course I understand
everything, and I think you're being very brave and sensible. It's
the best way of dealing with it. Oh, here's Dr. Crowdy's car! Isn't
Jane's ankle getting on properly? Good morning, Dr. Crowdy.
I'm just going to speak to Jane for a moment, but I won't hold
her up if you're visiting her professionally."

"I'm not," Simon said easily. "I came to see the Major about
those gas lectures he wants to arrange. Is he anywhere about?"

"He's gone to London for a night. Good-bye, Mabel, come
and have coffee with me tomorrow morning. Sit down for a
moment, Simon, and have a cigarette. Has Marian arrived?"

"Yes." He sat down and stretched out his legs. "With the news that she's joined the A.T.S. and is hoping for a commission. Whether we like it or not we've got to look this war business in the face, I'm afraid. It's going to mean big upheavals."

Leah lifted her head and looked at him sharply, her mouth suddenly tight.

"For us down here? I suppose it will in some ways."

"For some of us. I'll be called up pretty quickly for the R.A.M.C. And the funny thing about a war is that it practically does away with any future for most of us, and yet we all start thinking seriously about the future straight away. I've been doing that myself." He put his hand down and scratched one of the dogs' sleek, affectionate heads. "There's something I want to tell you, Leah, but I expect you've guessed it already. I'm going to ask Jane to marry me before I'm called up."

Leah was sitting with her back to the brilliant morning light and the flying legions of soap-bubble cloud, and her face wasn't very easy to see, but her stillness was petrified even though her hands went on working at the wool winding. It was the rest of her body that became suddenly frozen.

"Marry Jane!" she said in a low, clear voice that was tinged with amusement. "Good heavens, Simon, you are an impulsive person! It's scarcely less than a few weeks since you thought of Jane as nothing but a child."

"People grow up in less than a few weeks sometimes," he answered quietly. "But Jane isn't twenty-one yet, and I thought I ought to tell you about it, Leah, and find out if you approved."

"But you know that I don't—and neither does Mallory. You're nearly twenty years older than Jane and you've been married before. I'm being frank with you, Simon, because I feel you want me to be. Even for nineteen Jane is an absolute child—don't you think she'd bore you after a little while?"

"No, I don't think she'd bore me. Do you mind if I smoke my pipe?" She shook her head, and he began filling it slowly. "I'm sorry about this," he went on quietly. "I hoped that you and the Major would have made your own judgment of me, quite apart from the business with Sibylla—whom you didn't know. Well, there it is, and I'm going to ask Jane to marry me."

The ball of scarlet wool dropped out of Leah's hands as though her strong fingers had gone suddenly numb, but neither of them noticed it as it rolled away across the floor.

"You can't," she said. "You can't do that, Simon. I—I want to explain something to you. Do you remember the very first time you came to see me professionally after the accident? Do you remember?"

"Yes, of course," he said gently, and she went on, her voice rough and hoarse.

"I knew then exactly what had happened to me. . . . I didn't need anyone to tell me. I was going to be kept alive as a sort of medical specimen for doctors to poke and prod about and gloat over. What—what was inside me, what I felt about it, didn't matter. I could live on for fifty years in agony, in prison, in torment, but nobody would care so long as I could be kept alive so that you doctors could boast about me and show me off to each other. I didn't want to live—I didn't mean to live, and when I make up my mind about a thing it generally happens. Do you remember telling the nurse to keep me from moving even the top part of my body?"

"Yes, I remember." He was looking at her now, his deep-set eyes staring straight into hers, the pipe forgotten in his hand.

"But I wasn't altogether paralyzed. I could drag myself a few inches this way and that in the bed, and when the nurse went out of the room, I meant to drag myself to the edge and over it. That would have finished things once and for all for me, wouldn't it?"

"Yes." He dragged his eyes from hers abruptly and struck a match for the unlit pipe, and his hands were perfectly steady.

"I didn't have a chance that day. I wasn't left alone long enough. And then, in the evening, you came in again to see me —do you remember? It was raining, and the wind was rattling the windows, and I could hear the sea smashing against the rocks. It sounded angry because it hadn't quite finished me off, and I was angry with it. And then—you came in, Simon, and after you'd finished examining me and had gone away I suddenly found that I didn't mind living after all, that I didn't want to die, that I wanted to survive almost on any terms—even though I knew perfectly well what they were. You saved my life, but it wasn't entirely because of your medical skill, and I thought you knew and understood. Didn't you?"

The appeal in her eyes was terrible; it turned their blueness almost black, and her face looked haggard and queerly thin, as though the firm bone structure underneath had softened and given way. He couldn't look at her eyes.

"I understood that you were a very brave person," he said slowly. "I know that you did as much to save yourself as I did— perhaps more."

"But why—why? You know why, Simon. I didn't throw myself out of that bed because of you. I felt that you didn't think of me as just a patient, a hunk of medically interesting flesh and bone. I thought later on"—her voice faltered and thickened, and she put up a hand to her throat—"I thought you felt a little like that too. . . . You can't marry Jane."

"No," he said very slowly. "I don't think I can." He got up and stuffed the pipe into his pocket. "Good-bye, Leah. If I'm called up I'll hand you over to my successor, and he'll have all my notes."

He went out through the empty hall. There were jars of early mimosa and red tulips standing on the tables, and he could hear Jane's voice down in the garden talking to someone. Jane's voice . . . it seemed to come to him from another world, the world that had been in existence before he knocked on Leah's sitting-room door and heard her say, "Come in, Simon." Wherever he looked he could see against the sunshine the tortured blackness of her eyes, the way her wide-palmed, strong-fingered hands gripped the arms of her chair. She was probably sitting there like that still, holding her breath, wondering whether she had forced her will on him, whether she had driven in the rivets of his fetters truly.

Did he remember the day he had come to see her after the accident! Yes, he remembered every detail of it, the helpless, limp pathos of her athletic body lying brokenly against the pillows,

the wet streaks of golden hair plastered across her brown forehead, the lost bewilderment in her eyes. He had remembered
them for years in a sentimental, blind, adolescent way, as though
he were an immature schoolboy, and he wanted to forget them
and knew that he never could. Her will was so strong and sure
of its purpose that it wrapped itself silently, secretly, like a
spider's thread around his life and Jane's. He would go away
from Cornwall, but he couldn't take Jane with him; there were
some things that couldn't be explained even to her, and Leah
knew it. There was a great deal that Leah knew.

He went down to join Jane, and she looked up at him with a
quick smile that lit up her eyes in the way that was so exactly
like Mallory's.

"Hullo, Simon! I've walked miles on the ankle this morning,
and it doesn't even ache."

"That's good. The plaster can come off at the end of the
week, but you must go easy on it. I—I'm sorry, but I've got to
postpone our tea party tomorrow afternoon, Jane, if you don't
mind. I've got to go up to London suddenly."

It was quite an ordinary thing to say, but there was something in his face that took the smile out of Jane's eyes.

"It doesn't matter," she said. "I expect you're very busy—
too busy for tea parties."

"In a way—yes. I'm going up to town to get myself into the
R.A.M.C. as soon as possible. I hope they'll get a move on so
that I can get away soon. Don't try and do too much yet, Jane.
Good-bye."

She had been cutting tulips when he came down to talk to
her, and a great sheaf of them, their jewel-bright cups sheened
with wetness, lay in the crook of her arm. She stood staring at
them, wondering how red and flame and orange gold could so
swiftly turn to drab greyness—or was that only her eyesight?
She knew what he meant as though he had shouted it into her
ear, but she didn't understand. There were things in Bastions
that she never would understand, and they all seemed to centre
around Leah's own sitting room, where he had gone before he

joined her in the garden. There was no use either in trying to understand or to struggle.

23

SHERIDA HAD DINNER with Catherine in a little Soho restaurant that evening. They had a quiet table in a corner near an open window, and a pale golden evening sky hung like gauze above the grey streets below them.

Catherine was wearing a dark red frock and a white straw hat with a schoolgirl brim over her forehead, and Sherida couldn't in honesty have said that she looked well. But on the other hand there was a tranquillity in her eyes and smile that reminded Sherida of a person who has come through a severe illness and is still tired, but sure of her own recovery.

"How are they all?" she asked. "Did you come up alone?"

"No, the Major is in town too on A.R.P. business, and we travelled up together, but he'll be going back late tomorrow and I'm going at midday. Everybody is all right, but rather restless, I think. It's all this war atmosphere; it penetrates even into Bastions."

"Yes, I can imagine that." Catherine twisted her long-stemmed wineglass round and round thoughtfully. "It's hard on Leah, especially if all the family want to scatter about the place in war jobs. Of course Logan will be the first to go." Sherida deliberately said nothing, and after a moment Catherine went on softly. "I think I'll travel down with you tomorrow, Sherida, and go home. I've rather changed my plans these last few days. The St. Aubyns won't mind, will they, if the first wedding in the family is a fairly quiet one?"

"The first wedding? Catherine, I'm so glad, and they all will be too. The Major said he hoped you and Logan wouldn't get it into your heads that times were too risky and uncertain for getting married."

"It wasn't only the times I had to think about," Catherine said dryly. "There were—other things."

"The other things don't exist at all, Catherine; you're just imagining them. I expect Logan's told you that often enough, and I'm glad you've believed him at last."

"I suppose I ought to be grateful in a way for all this threat of war," Catherine said thoughtfully. "It's made up my mind for me by cutting life in half in a sort of way. The back half doesn't seem to matter so much now. It will be fun to come home with you. Logan doesn't know yet; I'll send him a wire after dinner."

Logan met them at the station, and it reminded Sherida of that first evening of her arrival. There was the same wind, and the fierce, tawny-gold light shining under a straight bank of violet-red cloud was the same, though the air was warmer. Queer how one could come to feel perfectly at home and happy in the most desolate place once it had become familiar and friendly. London had been stuffy, and the sharp, salty air was rich as wine, bringing colour at last into Catherine's pale cheeks. She had been white all the way down with a strange nervousness, but it left her as soon as Logan's hands closed over hers.

"So you didn't find such a lot to do in London after all," he said, and she shook her head.

"I didn't find anything at all to do in London, Logan. I thought there was a good deal more to do down here. That's to say if you've got time for it."

"I'll make time. . . . Hullo, Sherida, I'm glad you looked Catherine up. Hop in. We'll look in at home, Catherine, and then I'll take you on. Leah would love to see you."

So he had told Leah exactly what she had said in her telegram, Catherine thought, as she got into the front seat. Well, it had been wise of him; it left her no more loopholes now, it made the thing settled and definite.

Leah was sitting beside a small log fire, since the evening had turned crisply chilly, and she had changed for dinner into a blue dress with a short-sleeved sapphire-blue coatee, and there were sapphire studs in her ears. She looked faintly regal and as though she were doing honour to a special occasion, and her smile was warm as she held out a hand to Catherine.

"Hullo, my dear! Come and get warm and have a glass of sherry, you must be frozen. It's lovely to see you home again so soon; we were afraid you'd gone off for longer than any of us liked, weren't we, Logan? It must have been Sherida's persuasiveness." She took the sherry glass and lifted it, and the diamonds winked from the rings on her hand. It always seemed to Sherida oddly incongruous to see jewels glittering on Leah's strong hands. "This is almost more of a celebration than the day you announced your engagement," she said. "Here's to the wedding day, Catherine. So it's going to be very soon?"

"I think so. It seems rather a waste of time to wait any longer, doesn't it? And one doesn't want to waste time these days. Thank you, darling."

She sipped the sherry, her eyes meeting Leah's steadily—more steadily, she knew, than they ever had before. In the hall the telephone rang, and Leah said over her shoulder: "You answer it, will you, Christine?" Christine went into the hall and came back in a moment with her small mouth primmed up and her face expressionless.

"It was Daddy. He's not coming down till tomorrow, the morning train, and he has to go straight on to a meeting. He wants Sherida to meet him at the station with his notes so that he needn't come home, to save time. If she's free to go . . ."

"But I don't——" Sherida began to say, but Leah cut her short with a faint smile.

"Of course you'll be free, Sherida; I shan't want you for anything, and you'd better go along to the meeting with Mallory, he's sure to want you to take more notes for him. Come in after dinner, Catherine, and we'll talk about wedding plans. Not that the bridegroom's parents have much say in them, I know, but still we'd like to hear all about them."

"We haven't really made any yet, have we, Logan?" Catherine said. "And we don't want anything very big or fussy, just a quiet country wedding with our real friends coming to it. How's the ankle, Jane? You haven't told me yet."

"Oh, it's getting on splendidly!" Jane said, and she finished her sherry quickly. "Dr. Fortescue's taking the beastly plaster off tomorrow and shall I be glad!"

"Dr. Fortescue?" Catherine looked at her quickly. "Has Simon Crowdy handed you over to him?"

"In a sort of way. Simon's gone up to London to try and get a commission in the R.A.M.C., and he expects to be called up very soon. We'll all miss him."

She said it with a quiet deliberateness, and Leah put her sherry glass down on the polished table with a little click.

"Simon's an extremely restless person," she said lightly. "He gets enthusiasms and gets over them with equal rapidity, and he's easily bored. I'm surprised that he's stuck this place as long as he has, knowing him as well as I do. Privately, just between ourselves, I've always thought that Sibylla, or whatever her name was, must have led an exhausting life with him and that she must have been a nervous wreck by the time they got themselves divorced. See you later, Catherine dear."

In the car as they drove through the gathering dusk that was warm amethyst shot with rose and topaz, Logan asked softly:

"What made you change your mind so suddenly, Catherine? Was it anything Sherida said?"

"No, I suppose it was something Hitler said. Funny that a man shrieking his head off leagues away in Munich should settle people's lives for them, isn't it? You haven't changed yours, have you?"

"No. And now you see, don't you, that there was nothing on earth to be afraid of, that your imagination was simply bullying you like a Gestapo agent. Now that you've turned round and given him a sock on the jaw, he won't bother you any more. Leah's terribly pleased that the wedding is going to be at once."

"Yes, I'm sure she is—and there's nothing on earth to be afraid of, as you say. I'll drive over about half past eight."

When Logan came back into the empty lounge hall of Bastions, Jane was going slowly upstairs to change for dinner, and he went up with her, his hand through her arm.

"What's all this about Simon Crowdy going off to join the

R.A.M.C.?" he asked. "It was the first I'd heard of it when you told Catherine."

"Was it?" Jane paused on the half landing to rest her ankle, which was aching tonight, perhaps because in her restlessness she hadn't been able to sit still all day but had been perpetually wandering about the garden or the cliff top, though she hadn't ventured down any of the steep paths yet. "I thought Leah would have told you. He only mentioned it yesterday when he looked in to put me off going to tea today because he was going up to London to try and fix it. Leah's right about him, I expect —he must find life and the people here very dull and boring, especially after being married to Sibylla Massey. She was an actress, you know, and I saw a photograph of her only the other day, and she's a beautiful, exciting-looking sort of person. I'm terribly glad about you and Catherine, Logan."

They were moving slowly on up the wide, shallow stairs, but Jane paused again to look down into the hall. It was a deep well of soft, mellow light that picked up high notes of colour here and there, a deep azure-blue jar of fresh laburnum that was like a globe of golden light in itself, the vivid scarlet of a guard officer's tunic in one of the portraits, Leah's jade-green Spanish silk shawl flung casually over the arm of a chair.

"It looks like a stage setting, doesn't it?" Jane said. "As though the footlights and arc lights had just been switched on and the curtain run up, as though this were the moment of emptiness just before the players come on. Why is everything holding its breath, Logan? Not only here in the house but everywhere."

"Because everything is holding its breath, I suppose. The curtain is just going up, Jane, on something pretty big and dramatic. Catherine was right about not wasting time."

It was odd that Jane should sense that air of tension and expectancy that gripped Bastions. It was easy enough to put it down to the political and world situation beyond the four sturdy walls, but he knew—and he thought she knew too—that Bastions was waiting for a more personal and isolated drama to open. And the house, in its calm, wise fashion, would look on at it and remember other dramas played out in these same rooms in other ages, and this new one wouldn't seem very important or original. Human nature couldn't be original if it tried; that was the tragedy. He opened her bedroom door and switched on the light for her, and she gave his arm a little squeeze.

"Catherine is a darling. But Logan, before you get married, don't let her talk to Leah alone too often or too much. And have the wedding very soon. . . . I'm going to be hours late for dinner if I don't hurry."

He went on along the corridor to his own room, wondering what she meant by that cryptic remark, wondering what had changed Jane so oddly, not in the space of days but almost within a few hours. Since yesterday she had been different, with that queer, withdrawn look in her eyes, that older tightness about her mouth, that note of faint irony and mockery in her voice. What had happened since yesterday? . . . Simon Crowdy had announced that he was going to throw up his practice and join the R.A.M.C.

He changed quickly and went downstairs again, and as he lighted a cigarette at the bottom of the stairs Leah called to him from her sitting room.

"Is that you, Logan? Come in and talk to me till the others come down. I changed early."

She was sitting in her chair beside the small wood fire, and it struck Logan suddenly that he had never seen her look as well and as attractive as she did tonight. There was a kind of brilliance about her, a glow that was triumphant. Her colouring, the gold of her soft hair, the blueness of her eyes, the flush in her cheeks were like victory signals hung out at her masthead, and he thought admiringly: "She's wonderful to be able to look like this, considering what her life is and what she's got to put up with. Nothing else matters when you compare them with her courage."

"You're looking grand tonight, Leah," he said, smiling down at her affectionately. "And happy. I hope that's got something to do with Catherine and me. Has it?"

"Darling, of course it's got everything to do with you. I'm so thankful it's all come out right, because frankly I was beginning to worry about things between you two. Catherine was behaving in such an odd, unnatural way for a girl in love, but I'm sure you understand her, and she's such a sweet child." She ran her fingers through the waves of hair over her forehead and made a rueful little grimace. "I've got something to confess that I'd clear forgotten. Mabel and Cicely are coming over after dinner tonight to play bridge."

"Oh lord!" Logan said frankly. "Must they? No, I suppose they can't be put off now. But there's one thing I wish you'd do, Leah, and that's suggest that they keep off discussing the Bassett murder."

"The Bassett murder? But why?" Leah's eyes were puzzled, and then light dawned in them. "Logan, you don't mean to say that Catherine imagines for a split second that we're linking her in our minds with any possibility like that, simply because Mary Bassett is a child adopted from an orphanage too? It's fantastic and idiotic. You must try and teach her not to be so supersensitive about some things, my dear, otherwise you'll find life rather trying."

"I have tried," Logan said reluctantly. "Perhaps it wasn't the actual subject as the way Mabel Brastock brought it up. I don't know—anyway, Catherine's got over that bother in her mind now, otherwise she wouldn't be marrying me."

"You mean she's decided that it doesn't really matter who or what her parents were?"

"Yes. And it doesn't, does it?"

He looked Leah very straight in the eyes, and she smiled and patted his arm.

"Of course not, Logan, and don't look so thunderous about it. The whole idea is so preposterous that I can't take it seriously. And it's rather difficult not to discuss the Bassett business, there's such a lot in the papers about it and the coming trial. But I'll head poor Mabel off the subject if she starts on it. And don't look alarmed, I won't do it too blatantly, or else I suppose poor Catherine will imagine that's another sort of innuendo and hit at her. Let's go in, shall we? I wish Mallory had come home so that he could have been here tonight at this little celebration, but he seems to be rather preoccupied with other things these days. It will be good news for him when he gets back."

24

CORNWALL WAS CERTAINLY a country of moods, Sherida thought, as she drove the small car down next day to the station to meet Mallory. Today there was no brilliance, no sharpness of colour in anything, and yet there was no sombreness or gloom either.

Clouds banking themselves in smooth-edged, velvety folds across a gentle dove-grey sky were lilac and silver white; the moors and hills curved away in all shades of petunia and lavender and dark lapis blue, and the only shrill note anywhere was the cry of the gulls circling watchfully above the granite tors. But this wasn't the foreboding and heavy stillness that threatens a thunderstorm; it was the grave, contented quietness that heralds summer rain whose faint, sweet, distant scent makes the flowers lift their faces more eagerly toward the sky and the slim grasses shiver a little in expectation.

Sherida parked the car outside the little station and sat at the wheel with her arms folded over it, waiting for the train to come in. Perowen, moving darkly past with a load of sacks on a trolley, vouchsafed her a dour and unsmiling greeting, and she felt that here was acceptance and condescension indeed for which she should show adequate gratitude. She smiled and said: "Good morning, Perowen. It looks like rain, doesn't it?" but this was a long, long way beyond the boundary Perowen had set as the limit of his recognition, and he made no answer but trundled up the rough slope onto the brief stretch of platform.

Sherida, watching the curve of the railway line round the foot of the next rocky hill, remembered her first coming to Cornwall and how utterly empty the world had seemed as she waited in the wind and the harsh golden evening light for someone to meet her. Now the world, her world, was almost too full of people. It was queer and uncanny to think that at any moment she might be ejected from it, that it and its inhabitants might suddenly disintegrate and disappear forever from her life. It all depended on those few words that Leah might so easily say at any moment, quite casually as though they were quite unimportant—as of course they were to her. She might say them this evening or tomorrow morning. "Sherida," she might say, "I've been thinking it over, and really it doesn't seem right of me, these days, to have a resident private secretary, considering how little writing I'm doing. Of course I'll give you a first-class reference and you can stay with us until you find another post."

And nobody could accuse her of being unjust or even unfair if she did say that; she had everything to support her. And after she had said that brief, reasonable sentence—what then? Sherida couldn't think about that without coldness sliding down her spine and her throat contracting. Yet it had to be faced. Her footing in Bastions was as insecure and tenuous as the grip of a single strand spun by a spider upon a twig. The least puff of air, the brushing of a hand might destroy it. Then there would be another job, probably in London in some big noisily clacking office. The St. Aubyn family would fade, as the images fade from the surface of a photograph that hasn't been set properly.

She would lose Mallory, she would lose his nearness and presence, the work they did together, the queer, torturing pain and joy that everything to do with him gave her. Inevitably she had to lose him one day, but not yet . . . not yet, she thought desperately and knew she was being an unutterable fool.

The train whistled round the bend and slowed in, disgorging from two opening carriage doors Mallory and his suitcase and a bent old woman with a black bonnet on her meagre white hair and a battered brown-paper parcel clutched under one arm. What was an old woman like that doing alighting at a place like this, miles from anywhere? Perowen vouchsafed her not even a look as he went to take Mallory's case, and she trudged off up the stony lane, the brown-paper parcel gaping to reveal the straggling leg of a pair of red-flannel bloomers.

"Hullo, Sherida! Thanks, Perowen. Here you are." Mallory gave him a shilling, and Sherida made a movement away from the driver's seat, but he shook his head. "No, you drive. This must have been a nuisance for you, and I'm sorry. You can get the bus at the crossroads to take you back; I'm afraid I haven't time to go all the way home."

"It's all right." She started up the car, hesitated, and went on quickly. "Mrs. St. Aubyn said she didn't need me any more today, so if I can be any use—I mean if you want any notes taken or anything like that at this gas demonstration, I can come with you. But only if you really want me."

Mallory took off the soft hat that he wore at a rather rakish angle and settled himself deeper into the seat with a faint sigh of contentment.

"That's fine. I would like you to be there, you're so good at remembering things, and I've got to get all this gas-protection stuff right. We can have lunch afterward and take it easy coming home. How is everyone?"

"Very well. You missed the great excitement yesterday. Catherine came down with me from London, and she and Logan have decided to have the wedding very soon."

"Catherine's decided, has she?" Mallory said thoughtfully and groped in his pocket for his pipe. "Well, that's a good thing. Is Leah pleased?"

"Delighted," Sherida said briefly. "Everybody is. Doesn't the air smell lovely?"

High in the silver grey light a kestrel was hovering on sharp-pointed pinions, and the familiar grove of ancient beeches, grouped in their stately and Grecian isolation on the crest of the slope, had a black solemnity.

"Cornwall is a queer country," Sherida said suddenly. "At first it's so unfriendly, almost resentful, as though it didn't want you to like it, and then it simply can't help making you fall in love with it. But it still gives you the impression that it doesn't care in the least what you feel about it. It's exasperating. Logan warned me when I first arrived."

"And you have fallen in love with it?"

"Yes—terribly. I can't imagine living anywhere now where the country's flat and green and the weather is good-tempered and the sea behaves politely and runs round promenades and under piers as though it were a trained animal in a circus. I don't wonder Cornish people are a bit 'fey.' "

"Do you think my family are fey?" he asked as he struck a match for his pipe, and Sherida slowed down a little.

"In some ways, yes. Jane is. Do you remember some time ago you asked me if I could help you to find out if Jane is really happy? I haven't been able to do much, I'm afraid. She doesn't talk easily."

"And if she did I don't think you'd tell me," Mallory said with a faint smile. "It wasn't a wise thing to ask you, Sherida. I ought to be able to understand my own family, and I think I do."

She knew that by that he meant that he understood what Jane's secret unhappiness and problem was, but it wasn't a thing they could discuss, because Leah came into it.

The gas lecture and demonstration took place with an air of calm, cold, horrible efficiency in a small hall whose windows were wide open upon the silver shimmer and rustle of light rain and the scent of wet lilac and the voices of thrushes digging for worms in the juicy brown earth. The audience sat in rows on hard school benches, numbering amongst them a large sprinkling of elderly maiden ladies in round raffia-straw hats and long drab mackin-toshes, and they were told about different forms of gas that would burn holes in their flesh or turn their skin bright blue or tear out their lungs. They took down notes in neat little books in neat little handwriting, and when they emerged from the hall they got briskly on their bicycles and pedalled off to the butcher and the baker and the grocer with exactly the same expression of placid unconcern on their rain-spattered faces. Mallory stopped to speak to one of them while she rearranged quantities of parcels in her bicycle basket.

"It's very noble of you, Miss Allcock, to turn up to the lecture. Are you arranging a gasproof room at Hollyhock Cottage?"

"Oh yes! It's all rather tiresome, isn't it, but I do feel every-body ought to be prepared." Miss Allcock wedged a wrapped-up haddock into the space between a parcel of khaki and a bottle of salad oil. "I'm afraid I haven't got very used to my gas mask yet," she confessed with a look of guilt in her faded blue eyes. "But I'm trying to break myself into it. I haven't much time during the day to wear it, so I—I put it on every night when I'm having my bath, and really it doesn't feel at all uncomfortable now. Good-bye and remember me to dear Mrs. St. Aubyn."

"It's a strange world, isn't it," Mallory said dryly as he and Sherida walked across to the small local hotel for lunch, "when middle-aged spinster ladies have to sit in their baths in gas masks so as to get used to them? Let's have some sherry."

The hotel lounge was tiny, with low timbered beams and faded prints of horrific-looking shipwrecks hanging round the faded red walls, but the sherry was mellow and dry, and out of the window they could see blue sky shining through a great tear in the gossamer fabric of the rain cloud. Suddenly the taste and smell of gas that still seemed to be clinging to the sweet air vanished from it, and Sherida felt her spine warming up, and Mallory smiled across at her.

"That's better. You looked quite white and pinched when you came out of that lecture, as though it had frightened you. Did it?"

"In a way—yes. Perhaps one isn't so much afraid of the dangers of war as the—the changes it means. I didn't think about that until Logan came down from London and seemed so sure that it had to happen." She put the empty sherry glass down on the table and went on quietly: "For one thing it would probably mean my leaving Bastions, wouldn't it? Mrs. St. Aubyn wouldn't need me, and I ought to be doing something less pleasant and—well, more necessary, I suppose."

They were alone now in the little lounge; everyone else had drifted off to lunch. Sunlight slanting through the torn clouds stretched dusty shafts of primrose yellow across the worn red-plush armchairs and the grim pictures. A green jar of wall-flowers standing in the middle of the table beside them scented the smoky air with honey. It was odd that wallflowers should blossom in the spring, Mallory thought; they were essentially an autumnal flower, so rich in colour and presence and scent that in their vicinity all other spring flowers looked faintly anemic and bloodless. He remembered that he had thought, when Sherida first came into the hall of Bastions, that she looked like a wallflower, with her dark hair and tawny brown eyes and glowing colour. And like the wallflower she made everyone else look colourless.

"Don't go until you have to," he said in a low voice. "We'll all miss you so much. . . . Somehow it's difficult to imagine Bastions without you now. . . . You must be hungry, let's go in and sample the cold beef, it's good here."

25

THE WEDDING DAY had been settled, the little white-and-silver invitation cards sent out, and in the shabby, comfortable dining room of the Maitlands' house Catherine spent hours unpacking presents and ranging them along the enormous carved Victorian sideboard. Christine had come over to help her, and she was unwrapping a parcel now with something of the excitement of a child undoing a Christmas stocking.

"Another hors-d'oeuvres dish," she said triumphantly, holding up the glass and silver tray, and Catherine sighed faintly.

"The fifth. People seem to imagine newly married couples are going to live entirely on hors d'oeuvres and fish. Tie the card onto it, will you? Did you see what Cicely sent us from London? It came this morning. Cicely believes in being just about as downright as the beginning of the marriage service."

Cicely's gift was an elaborately enamelled, pink-basketed baby's weighing machine, and the card attached said baldly: "If you don't think you'll have any use for this do please change it for something else. With best wishes, Cicely Burnham."

"With malice and envy, she means," Christine said bluntly. "I hate her. I wish she weren't coming to the wedding."

"I don't; I'm rather sorry for her," Catherine said as she cleared up string and brown paper, and she added gently: "You tire yourself out hating so many people, Christine. I believe you hated me once for some reason or other. Didn't you?"

A thin stain of pink came into Christine's face, but she answered bravely.

"I didn't exactly hate you—nobody could. But I was kind of muddled about you and Logan—I mean about you getting married. I didn't know whether Leah was pleased. But now I'm sure she is, so everything is all right."

She was so childishly frank in her explanation that Catherine smiled as she set about another parcel.

"This looks like another fish slice. You love Leah, don't you?"

"I adore her. She's the most wonderful person in the world."

"But Christine, you're nearly seventeen, and soon you'll be grown up and you'll have to think about your own life and what you want to do with it. You can't always be wrapped up in Leah."

"I don't see why not." Christine abandoned her unpacking and sat on the window seat with her thin legs curled under her and her cheek resting on her hand. "I wish Jane would get married to somebody quickly so that I'd be left at home to look after Leah. I suppose Jane is fond of her, but she doesn't really understand her, not the way I do. She doesn't feel that Leah's unhappy, even when she seems to be most cheerful and brave. She doesn't know when she needs helping through a bad time, the way I know it. I'd do anything in the world for Leah."

Catherine, glancing at her, was suddenly uneasy at the sombre, enlarged blackness of Christine's eyes and the way her immature mouth shut into that thin, tight line that was almost invisible. Did Leah realize the extraordinary and unhealthy power she had over Christine's imaginative, childish mind? Yes, Leah did realize it; Catherine was sure of that. Sometimes she had noticed Leah looking at her in a speculative, satisfied way, as though she were surveying a piece of her own handicraft that pleased her. There was something deliberate in the way she was quietly moulding Christine's personality into a shape that was still obscure and undeveloped but already faintly sinister. But what on earth could there be that was sinister about a girl of sixteen with long legs and a thin face and silky red-gold hair drifting against her cheeks?

"Another fish slice," Catherine said resignedly. "From Simon Crowdy. I'm disappointed; I should have thought he'd be more original. Are you going to stay to lunch, Christine?"

"No, I must get back." Christine unfolded her legs and pulled down the skirt of her short pink linen frock. "I'll come back at half past two and help with the rest of all this."

"Then why not stay to lunch? It will save you that long pull up the hill on your bike in this wind."

"No, I promised Leah I'd be back," Christine said quietly. "She'll be all alone for lunch if I don't go. Jane is over at the Evanses', and Sherida is working down at the billeting place, and Daddy—Daddy's out somewhere." Again that withdrawn, secret look came into her eyes. "I don't mind the hill or the wind. Oh, by the way, I've got a message for you from Leah. She wants you to come over and have tea with her this afternoon if you've got time. Can you?"

"This afternoon? Yes, I'd love to. Is it a tea party? I want to know if I've got to dress up."

"Oh no! It's only you alone. I've got Girl Guides at four, and none of the others will be in. Good-bye."

The wind was rollicking and boisterous today, bumbling about the sky like a giant puppy whose paws are too big to be manageable. The laburnum shook its golden tassels in delicate and shocked protest at such rough handling, and the gulls, swaying on straining, outstretched wings, squawked angrily. Christine, bent double over the handle of her bicycle, fought her way up the hill breathlessly, stubbornly. Along the cliff road she could feel the breaking spume blown upward stinging sharply against her face, and all along the coast there were rainbows curving from rock to rock like paper decorations hung up for a party.

No, Leah shouldn't be left to eat her lunch alone in that big dining room whose emptiness must be like a hand squeezing her heart. None of the others cared—they were selfish and heartless —but at least she'd know that one person loved her enough to ride a bicycle a mile uphill in a gale so that she shouldn't be lonely.

"Darling, you shouldn't have come back," she said to Christine when she came in, still gasping a little for breath, her hair flattened in fine streaks across her forehead like a kitten's fur. "Didn't Catherine ask you to have lunch there?"

"Yes, but I didn't want to stay. I wanted to come home to be with you." Christine pressed her cold cheek for a second against Leah's warm one. "And Daddy's always lecturing me about not taking enough exercise, so I feel rather virtuous. Besides I love a nice, cozy lunch alone with you."

"Do you? But you shouldn't, Christine. You ought to be out enjoying yourself with other young people."

"Bother other young people! I hate them all, and you know I do. I'll just get tidy for lunch."

"All right. Did you give Catherine my message about coming to tea this afternoon?"

"Yes, and she said she'd love to." Christine's voice floated back to her from halfway upstairs, and Leah folded up her knitting slowly, smiling a little.

Catherine walked over to Bastions, feeling the need for fresh air after the hot afternoon of struggling with more parcels and name cards and thank-you lists and acceptances. In spite of the suddenness and the supposed quietness of the wedding, the whole proceedings seemed to be piling up monstrously. So many people couldn't possibly be left out, and the reception was to be in the garden of Bastions, since the Maitlands garden wasn't large enough to accommodate a marquee in case of rain, and her original idea of an afternoon dress and hat for the ceremony had been quietly submerged in a smother of white satin and old lace and tulle. Well, the first wedding in the St. Aubyn family couldn't be expected to be too quiet and unobtrusive.

What a glorious colour the sea was today; arrogant, truculent peacock blue rising at the horizon into a crescendo of emerald and cobalt. All the rocky crags and pinnacles and headlands were like taut harp strings against which the fingers of the wind swept rhythmically, creating a violent, urgent melody of sound. She turned in at the gates of Bastions, almost reluctant to go indoors from such aliveness.

"Catherine, this is nice of you, to spare time to come over and keep me company when you're so busy." Leah had had tea brought into her own sitting room, and she gestured to Catherine to pull up one of the comfortable armchairs. "I don't seem to have seen anything of you this last week, and I thought this afternoon, when everybody else is out, would be a good opportunity for a talk. Besides I want to give you this, with my love."

There was a flat red leather case on the table beside her, and she put it into Catherine's hand with a smile, and yet Catherine felt a queer chill as she pressed the spring catch and opened the lid. On pale blue satin a string of pearls shimmered pinkly, and Catherine stared at them and felt queerly tongue-tied.

"I don't know what to say," she managed at last. "They're so lovely. But—they're your pearls, Leah, and I don't feel I ought to have them."

"My dear, I have no sentimental attachment to them, I assure you," Leah said lightly. "They weren't given to me by Mallory or anyone like that. As a matter of fact a very grumpy and crabbed old great-aunt left them to me, and they're much too young for me. Middle-aged people shouldn't wear pearls, though they all do. If they only knew what a thin, scraggy, yellow neck looks like with a string of perfect pearls draped round it! But they'll look lovely on you, and I want you to have them."

"It's sweet of you," Catherine said slowly as she closed the case again. "I'll wear them at the wedding."

What a strange person Leah was. Had all the hostility and quiet resistance of the past months been entirely her imagination? She couldn't believe that somehow; she couldn't believe in this mellow little domestic scene, with herself sipping tea alone with Leah and thanking her for a gift of highly valuable pearls.

They finished tea in an amiable spate of discussion about the wedding and the bridesmaid's dress for Christine and the decorations on the wedding cake, and the tea tray was cleared away. Catherine picked up the yellow beret she had flung aside when she came in and stubbed out her cigarette.

"I'm afraid I'll have to be going now, Leah. It's been lovely, and I still don't know how to say thank you for your wedding present."

"I don't want you to try. But before you go, have another cigarette, Catherine, and sit down a minute. There's just one thing I want to tell you, and frankly I've been putting it off to the last moment because—well, because I wish I didn't have to. Not that it's anything that matters now in the very least," she added quickly. "I want you to understand that and promise me, before I say anything more, that you won't let it matter to you. It's only that it's something I know you've been wanting to know for some time, and, as it happens, quite by chance I can tell you. But you do promise, don't you, that you won't be silly and melodramatic about it?"

"It rather depends what it is, doesn't it?" Catherine said quietly as she took the cigarette. "But I'll try not to be either silly or melodramatic."

"I didn't mean that quite." Leah smiled ruefully. "Only I know what a sensitive child you are. It's about you, Catherine, about your people, your own mother and father."

"Yes?" Catherine bent her dark head over the silver cigarette lighter. "Do you know something about them?"

"Yes. I only found this out within the last few days, as I told you, quite by chance, and even now I'm not positive about it. I've got a legal friend up in London, Scott Tracey, who has been concerned with some rather famous Old Bailey cases, and he tells me about them sometimes because I'm so interested in the human-nature angle of crime. You know he was staying with us last week end."

"Yes, I met him." Catherine remembered Scott Tracey, a tall, boney, eagle-nosed man with piercing grey eyes and a craggy brow jutting out from a thatch of rusty grey hair. She hadn't liked Scott Tracey or the cold, summing-up expression upon his face when he had talked to her when she sat next him at dinner on Saturday night.

"Yes, of course you did. And he was terribly interested in you,

Catherine, so interested that he talked to me about you next day. And he showed me this."

She laid a newspaper cutting on the table in front of Catherine. Above the letter press there were two slightly smudged photographs, of a youngish man with a heavy-jawed, low-browed, brutal face, and a girl in an old-fashioned cloche hat pulled down over her ears. Her eyes went to the print.

"Norvill Butler," she read, "who was arrested last night for the brutal murder of Julia Brent and her child. The body of Ann Butler, Norvill Butler's wife, was recovered early this morning from the Thames at Maidenhead, and she is believed to have committed suicide. Up to date no trace has been found of the Butlers' baby daughter, and it is believed that Mrs. Butler jumped with her into the river."

"Well?" Catherine said gently. "What did Mr. Tracey say about this cutting?"

"He said—Catherine, he may be utterly wrong, but he's a man with a very keen, accurate mind, and he doesn't put ideas into words unless he's pretty sure that they are more than ideas. He knew the Butlers well by sight, because he defended him in another case a year before this business, when he was accused of the manslaughter of another girl. Ann Butler was in court every day during the case, and he studied her carefully. And when he met you, he told me it was like meeting a ghost face to face. Don't you see the likeness?"

Catherine stared at the right-hand photograph. Under the shadow of the ugly hat the face was very young, square at the cheekbones, pointed-chinned. The eyes looked as though they might be brown, and the hair curved in stiff points against the cheeks was dark.

"Do you mean the likeness to me?" she asked softly.

"Yes. Here's another photograph without a hat; it shows more there. It startled Scott, and he's not a man who is easily startled."

Again that pathetic, tragic-eyed face, this time with the dark hair cut in a heavy fringe across the forehead. Startling—yes, it was.

"But—the institute wasn't at Maidenhead."

"It wouldn't be, my dear. I can understand that girl's thoughts and feelings so well. She knew Norvill Butler couldn't escape this time. Julia Brent had been his mistress for four years, and her child was his. Perhaps she wanted more money from him or tried to blackmail him, but that wasn't wise with a man of his type. He went back late at night after leaving her, got into her flat, and battered her and the child to death."

Catherine didn't move or speak, and Leah shook the ash off her cigarette and went on thoughtfully:

"Ann Butler must have known what had happened when he went home, before he was arrested, and she couldn't face it. I feel sure the first person she thought of was her own child. There must be a way of escape for it from all this horror and sordidness, and she found that way. I think she travelled all night with—the baby, getting as far away from home as she could. She left it where she knew it would be found and taken care of, and she left no clues of any sort, so that the break might be complete. Then she travelled all the way back to London and down to Maidenhead, and she was very clever still. All through the journey and when she walked along the riverbank, where she was seen by some people, she carried a wrapped-up bundle in a shawl, a bundle that looked exactly like a sleeping baby. It was taken for granted, when her body was recovered from the river, that she had jumped with the baby still in her arms; she meant them to think that, and nobody ever bothered to think anything else, least of all to connect an abandoned baby found miles away in a small country town with her. You see, she was absolutely determined on one thing, and that was that her child should never know that her father was hanged for a particularly ugly and callous murder."

It might, Catherine thought, have been Scott Tracey himself telling the story in calm, well-ordered, and carefully telling phrases to a judge and jury. It was all so level and undramatic and yet vividly, cunningly pictured. One could follow that anguished, haunted-eyed girl, with the thick fringe curving over her wide forehead, all through those bitter, elaborately planned hours. One could see her so clearly strolling casually along the towpath beside the green river with the bundled-up shawl cradled in her arms and a queer sense of triumph and satisfaction softening her misery.

"But there was one thing she forgot," Catherine said softly. "And that was that her daughter might grow up to look exactly like her."

"Catherine, you've got to be sensible about this." Leah's tone was brisk and unemotional. "For one thing it may be entirely an extraordinary coincidence, and Scott may be completely wrong."

"Do you think he is? Wasn't there anything else?"

"Well—only a small thing but rather strange, perhaps. He's a very observant person, and he noticed that one of Ann Butler's thumbs was different from the other. It was about a quarter of an inch longer." Her eyes went to Catherine's square-fingered hands, and Catherine quietly measured her two thumbs against each other; the left-hand one was noticeably shorter than the right-hand one. "Even that isn't conclusive," Leah went on obstinately. "And if it is, what does it matter? Supposing you had been told about your parents, Catherine, what difference would it have made to your life? You'd still be entirely yourself, Logan would still want to marry you, and we'd still love to have you as one of the family. I hope I've made that perfectly clear, because I wouldn't for the world have told you this if I hadn't thought you understood it."

"I do understand," Catherine said, and she pulled the yellow beret onto her dark head and stood up. "You've been very kind about it, Leah, and I'm glad you told me. I must go now."

"And don't spend any more time thinking about it." Leah gave her cold hand an affectionate squeeze. "I only told you because I thought you'd be—well, interested, but in an almost impersonal way. These two people who have both been dead for years don't mean anything in your life. You're forgetting your present, my dear."

"Oh yes!" Catherine looked down at the pearls lying rosily in their bed of satin, and she closed the lid. "You have a safe here in the house, haven't you? If you don't mind, would you let me leave them here with you until the wedding? I've got nowhere to lock them up properly at home, and I'd worry about them."

"Well, if you like," Leah looked at her sharply. "Perhaps they would be safer. Aren't you going to stay till Logan gets home?"

"No, I can't, there's such a lot to do at home. Good night, Leah."

"Good night, Catherine dear, and come over tomorrow if you have time. I want to be quite sure you aren't going to be silly about all this. But I'm sure you won't be, for Logan's sake."

"No, I won't be silly. I'll come over some time."

She went through the hall and down the curving path between the big trees that were closely woven shadows now against the pale amethyst sky. A few early stars hung here and there, and the wind, tired with its frollickings, had sunk to a drowsy murmur and stir of air amongst the young leaves. There was a new moon too, an enormous, delicate pointed double horn of bright ivory, so fragile-looking that an extra puff of wind might blow it away altogether.

Norvill Butler, double murderer, seducer, brute, who was hanged by the neck in Wandsworth jail, and Ann Butler, timid, bewildered, half crazy with fear, whose body had been fished out of the Thames on a dank autumn morning. As a matter of interest, she knew now who and what her parents had been; she knew now what blood and heritage and family history were hers. Norvill Butler had been a flashy young commercial traveller with a too large and colourful signet ring on the third finger of his left hand and too much glistening pomade on his slicked-down hair, and Ann Butler had been a scared little shopgirl who got herself into a mess with him and wasn't brave enough to face the consequences alone, who preferred marrying him and accepting all the misery and sordidness of the marriage to keeping her freedom and cutting her losses, who wasn't brave enough to accept the inevitable, who abandoned her baby to strangers in a strange town and then made her own easy escape by way of the river. Catherine remembered the whole story now, more of it than Leah had told her. The Butler trial figured in a collection of famous murder cases that stood in one of Mr. Maitland's bookshelves. Had they had any inkling of this when they chose that particular baby out of the neat row of cots in the Institute nursery? No, it was obvious that they hadn't. Scott Tracey was the only person in the world who had drawn the frayed threads together into a horrible pattern.

It was very cool on the cliff top. The grass had the movement of bottle-green water flowing quietly; the white breakers below were ghosts dancing restlessly to the piping of the wind; the gulls had gone to bed.

She took off her hat again and lay down with her face, which was strangely burning hot, pressed against the cold, dewy roughness of the turf, but when she closed her aching eyelids the only thing she could see against their dark weight was a shapeless black bundle dangling wildly at the end of a rope. The grass seemed to flow over her in smooth, inky waves, and there was a salt taste in her mouth.

She understood so many things now that had puzzled her before, things about herself. Her queer, intense capacity for anger and hatred. She had known moments of anger when everything had turned red in front of her eyes and a clenched fist had hammered against her temples from the inside, and yet she knew she had never betrayed it. And hatred—the way she hated Leah. That had frightened her often, that black abyss of hate that could at moments gape in front of her, into which she felt her whole being and self-control hurtling helplessly. Norvill Butler must have known anger like that when his plans went wrong, must have known hatred like that when he felt Julia Brent's soft flesh pulping under the blows of the poker he had used to batter the life out of her.

And her cowardice, her eternal doubts and uncertainties and nervous qualms that Logan called "imagination"—she knew who had bequeathed those to her now. Ann Butler had always been cowed and frightened and helpless, down to the last moment.

Presently Catherine got up and tidied her ruffled hair and powdered her nose in the darkness. The hot blood had faded out of her face now, and she wasn't even trembling. She didn't want to leave this solitary place on the cliffs whose emptiness and silence was like morphia, numbing and tranquillizing. She didn't even think of Leah, sitting in her chair in that warmly lighted room at Bastions, with her firm hands always busy with writing or sewing and her golden hair shining and her rounded cheeks dimpling sweetly, almost childishly, when she smiled. There was a point when thinking and feeling were petrified into one solid, icy substance that was determination.

Mrs. Maitland was still cutting the strings of parcels when Catherine came into the dining room, swinging the yellow beret in one hand.

"Darling, you shouldn't be bothering," Catherine said. "I meant to get back earlier, but Leah and I were talking such a lot and I didn't realize it was so late. And then I lost my beret along the cliff path and went back to look for it. Leave all that alone now."

"But I like doing it." Mrs. Maitland put down the scissors and looked at Catherine and smiled. "Darling, I'm so glad you went to tea alone with Leah today, without a crowd of other people, without even Logan there. I know you've always had an idea in your head that she didn't want you to marry Logan, but you don't feel like that now, do you?"

"No," Catherine said softly as she unknotted a length of string. "No, I'm sure that Leah is perfectly happy about everything now."

"And she's such a charming person," Mrs. Maitland said sentimentally. "She's never let her own tragedy make her self-centred and petty-minded. She deserves to be a happy woman."

"And what about the others?" Catherine thought. "Mallory and Jane and Logan and Christine—don't they deserve any happiness? Or is it only to be the happiness that Leah doles out to them and thinks fit for them?"

"I must go and get tidy," she said aloud. "If Logan rings while I'm upstairs, Mummy, tell him I don't think I'll come over this evening and that if he comes here he'll find me terribly busy."

She went on upstairs, still swinging the yellow beret and wondering in a flat, impersonal way, "If you'd known all those years ago, when you saw me in that institution cot, that my father had been hanged for murder and my mother was a neurotic, spineless coward, would you have adopted me? I don't think so. If you'd known, it wouldn't be me walking up these stairs now. I wonder what I would have been doing. Banging a typewriter in some stuffy city office, I suppose, for two pounds a week. Perhaps the baby you might have chosen instead of me is doing that now. It doesn't seem fair to her."

The telephone rang as she reached the top of the stairs, and Mrs. Maitland answered it and called up to her.

"It's Logan. Are you coming down to talk to him?"

"Darling, I'm so tired I can't get all the way down the stairs again. Give him my message."

Mrs. Maitland murmured into the telephone and then hung up.

"He'll come over later, and he's worried about you tiring yourself out so."

"But I haven't done anything all day. I've spent the whole afternoon having tea peacefully with Leah, and that isn't particularly exhausting."

She closed her bedroom door and leaned back against it without turning the light on. The darkness was soft and comfortable, the darkness that covers a room that is lived in and familiar and dear. Darkness can have such a quality of friendliness and strangeness, and the darkness of Catherine's room had always been her friend, so that she had never feared it, even as a small child. Lying curled up in bed, she had thought about fairies and the good angels whose wide, shadowy wings folded themselves like a canopy round her at night. Rosanna had told her stories both about the fairies and the angels. Why had Rosanna died? She, the most insubstantial and shadowy of women, had been most desperately needed at Bastions. If there was a ghost there, it wouldn't be that of some tough old Elizabethan buccaneer; it would be the ghost of Rosanna looking helplessly down at the terrible mistake she had made of dying.

Catherine turned the light on and began brushing the bits of grass out of her hair.

26

JANE RAN INTO Simon Crowdy at the village post office next day. The plaster was off her ankle, and she could get about easily with a stick to help her. She came out of the post-office door with the dogs crowding against her legs and almost collided with him as he hurried in.

"Oh—hullo!" he said. "How are things? Not walking about too much yet, are you?"

He looked not at her face but at her ankle, and she felt her whole body trembling with uncontrollable anger. So that was it —back to the old, casual, patronizing friendliness that made him talk to her and look at her as though she were still ten years old.

"It's perfectly all right, thanks," she answered coolly. "What's your news? Are you going to desert us for the R.A.M.C.?"

"I hope so." There was a snap in his voice, as though she were a precocious child asking impertinent questions. "You're not walking all the way home, I suppose?"

"No, Daddy's picking me up at the crossroads. Are you going to find time to come in and see us? Leah isn't very well this morning. She's got a bad head, and she looks very under the weather. I know she won't send for you, knowing how busy you are just now, but if you do drop in it would be a relief to Daddy."

What was making her say all this in such a cold, controlled voice? Why did she want to make things worse for herself by forcing him to come to Bastions when there was no need? Leah's headache was a very mild affair, and Mallory wasn't in the slightest degree worried about her.

"I'm sorry to hear that," Simon said briefly. "But unless I'm really needed, and Leah's the best judge of that, I don't honestly think I've time to come round. Keep an eye on her, though."

He nodded abruptly and pushed by into the post office, and Jane limped down the road to meet the car. This was all very strange too. A few weeks ago one would only have had to breathe it in Simon's hearing that Leah wasn't looking up to the mark and he would have been round to see her within half an hour, on any feeble, trumped-up excuse. But today, when he was definitely told that she wasn't well and that Mallory was worried, he didn't seem to care.

It was like one of those nightmares, Jane thought wearily, in which perfectly familiar people behave in the most fantastic and unnatural way. Once, years ago, she had had an awful nightmare, dreaming that Leah had attacked her with one of Mallory's heavy, loaded riding crops and was beating the life out of her. She had wakened, wet with the perspiration of sick terror, and the hideous vividness of the dream, of Leah's contorted face and twisted mouth, had haunted her for days afterward, and she had felt a sense of personal shame and guilt because she was capable of dreaming such a thing about Leah, of all people. Now everybody was behaving in a queer, twisted way, as though normal life had merged quietly into the illogical, grotesque world of nightmares.

Simon bought his stamps and stood on the post-office steps for a moment, watching Jane progress slowly down the twisty village street to the old crossroads where the sturdy, rough-hewn granite war-memorial cross stood defiant against the pale sky. Why had she tried to force him to go up to Bastions? He didn't for a moment believe that Leah wasn't well; that was unimportant. It was Jane's motive that puzzled him, and his own feeling of shrinking revulsion from going into Leah's bedroom and laying his fingers on the pulse in her firm wrist. He couldn't ever do that again, though he didn't know how he could avoid it. Supposing she did send for him? He didn't believe that any woman, after the scene in her sitting room, could show such crudity of purpose, but with Leah he was out of his depths now. She reminded him oddly of a certain ancient stone poised high up on the moors in solitary authority on a purple tor. To the casual eye it was just a moss-grown, time-weathered, picturesque old rock, but suddenly, if the light shifted, it became different. Under the smooth green moss strange old signs and symbols carved upon its face eons ago sprang to life with a kind of evil urgency, as though they refused to be obliterated. They were undecipherable, incoherent marks, and yet their significance was clear enough. And then abruptly the sunlight would shift and they would fade away and there would be nothing again but mellow tinted lichen and an air of venerable, serene dignity. Simon often thought, with amusement, of picnic parties happily eating their sandwiches there, quite unaware of those secret symbols leering down upon them from behind the monolith's respectability.

Not that he wasn't to blame for what had happened. From the first he had used things outside the scope of his medical knowledge and skill to save Leah's life, and he had used them deliberately. He was a quick character reader, and he understood Leah instinctively. She liked adventure and experiment and fresh fields of conquest, and she didn't want to live if those highways were closed to her forever. Almost without thinking, he had realized that there was just one incentive that would stir up her desire to live, and he had frankly thrust it in front of her. She would hold herself back from death if she believed that he wanted her to live, not so much because he was a doctor as because he was a man, and he hadn't stopped to think of consequences when perhaps his play-acting might become too real to both of them. He hadn't allowed for the fact that if her will were strong enough to keep her literally back from the depths of a grave cut out of the bleak Cornish soil, it was strong enough to achieve other things upon which she had set her heart.

If it hadn't been for Jane's broken ankle and that moment when he carried her across the golf course and felt the lightness and thinness of her in his arms, he might never have realized where Leah's will and his acquiescence were leading him. As it was, he had come up against a solid brick wall.

"Good morning, Dr. Crowdy." He jumped a little at the sound of Sherida's voice as he realized that she was standing in front of him and that he was blocking the post-office doorway.

"Oh—good morning, Miss Binyon. I'm sorry, I seem to have

taken possession of the doorway. You should have given me a good hack on the shins to wake me up."

"Were you so far away?" She glanced casually down the length of the ramshackle village street to Jane's figure in the distance, waiting patiently beside the memorial cross. "I think we're all a bit absent-minded these days," she added almost gently. "I hear you may be leaving Cornwall."

"I hope it's a certainty," he said savagely. "This is a queer part of the world, Miss Binyon. Sometimes I believe the locals' stories about hobgoblins and ancient presences hovering about the moors." He hesitated and then asked abruptly: "Will you be staying on here once things really start happening, Miss Binyon?"

"I wish you'd call me Sherida," she answered inconsequently. "I'm afraid you'll think me desperately stupid, but I haven't got my mind tuned in yet to the certainty of war. I haven't thought about what I'll do."

"It will make big changes at Bastions, of course. I'm afraid the family will get scattered all over the place, what with Logan going and the Major."

"Major St. Aubyn!" Sherida stared at him. "But he can't be called up, he's over age."

"You can't imagine the Major, can you, being satisfied with sitting in a remote village in Cornwall, waiting to herd a few old women and children into an air-raid shelter? Of course he'll move heaven and earth to get back into the army in some capacity, and he'll be needed. That will leave only Jane and Christine at home, and it's going to be a big responsibility for Jane. If you stayed on at Bastions it would be an immense help to her."

He was speaking almost pleadingly, and he avoided Sherida's eyes. But she felt anger against him rising inside her. If he cared twopence about Jane he couldn't shift the responsibility of looking after her onto someone else.

"I'm afraid the point is that it doesn't really depend on me whether I stay on at Bastions," she said smoothly. "Mrs. St. Aubyn is the person who has to decide that. She hasn't said anything about plans yet, but I've no doubt she's got them all ready in her mind."

"Yes, of course." Simon looked suddenly tired and grim. "I only meant that I hope you'll stay if it's left to you to decide. By the way, is Mrs. St. Aubyn really feeling ill today? Jane seemed worried about her."

Mrs. St. Aubyn? That was new and strange; Sherida had never heard him call her anything but Leah.

"Feeling ill? No, I don't think she is. She said she had a slight headache at breakfast, but it seemed to have gone by the time we'd finished. I don't know why Jane should be worried."

Simon didn't answer for a moment. Somehow he had known from Jane's first words about Leah that she wasn't telling the truth; that she was merely trying to get him to go and see Leah. Why? Had she believed that he wouldn't go, not even if he were told that she wasn't well? If that had been a trap he had fallen into it, but he couldn't imagine where the result got Jane.

"Perhaps she's in the mood to worry about things," he said and made a move toward his car at last. "Good-bye for the present—and keep Jane as quiet as you can for a bit."

Sherida bought her stamps and came out into the empty little street again. It was really warm today, with long honey-coloured pools of sunlight lapping against the grey walls of the stone cottages, and wallflowers and nasturtiums making a gay show in the rugged little gardens. Turning off through a tiny side lane, she walked up to the cliff where the church stood very near the edge, so near that a great chunk of the old churchyard had toppled one stormy night into the cove below, so returning to the sea the bones and dust of many seamen whose drowned bodies had been buried there.

Along the Cornish coast the churches had a habit of crowding to the cliff edge, as though they felt that they were nearer there to their real congregation and the men they served than standing safely inland. The ancient slabs of granite that marked the graves showed the strength of the prevailing winds as clearly as the trees by their uniform leaning over, and salt had crusted over with white many of the rough epitaphs. The square church tower sat solidly down on the small building, and inside there was a smell of the sea.

It hadn't occurred to Sherida that Mallory might be sucked into the war. She sat down in a carved pew and stared at the window over the altar. The stained glass spilled ruby-red and emerald-green and cobalt-blue stains over the stone floor, and a brass eagle lectern glared back at her with a fierce, penetrating eye.

Perhaps that was the best and only solution. Queer that she and Simon, both talking so casually about the coming of war, had both been groping in their own minds toward a settling of their own personal problems. She didn't know what Simon's problem was; it must be a big one if he was so easily defeated by it, as defeated he was.

A sound behind her made her turn her head quickly, and she saw Catherine standing in the doorway. Coming in from bright sunlight, Catherine didn't notice that there was anyone else there, and for a moment her face had the empty, alone look of a person who thinks she is by herself, who shows no emotion and so does not have to struggle to hide it. Her face was very pale, but the colour of her mouth was a hard, defiant crimson. Then she saw Sherida as she came out of the end pew, and she spoke casually.

"Hullo! Am I interrupting a private session with Providence? I'm sorry."

It didn't sound like Catherine saying that, but her eyes challenged Sherida to be shocked or to remonstrate, and she did neither.

"Not particularly. Perhaps it was more of a private session with myself."

They went outside together, and Catherine said, still in the same impersonal, half-mocking tone:

"I suppose a lot of people are suddenly rushing into churches to try and make a last-minute bargain with God, but I'm afraid I don't think that's very honest—or effective. In fact I don't believe we've much say in anything that happens to us, and so I'm worrying less than anybody. Prayers aren't going to stop Hitler or fate. Is Leah having a day off from literary effort?"

"Leah's 'writing' is more or less of a family myth now," Sherida said quietly. "In fact I don't really know why she keeps me on at Bastions. I'm eating my head off and doing nothing except get the Major's A.R.P. notes into shape for him."

"Don't you know why she doesn't tell you she doesn't want a private secretary any longer?" Catherine asked with a slow, queer smile that frightened Sherida a little. "I should have thought it was pretty plain. But if you haven't guessed it, perhaps I'd better not tell you. There aren't many things Leah's afraid of, but I've found out one of them. She's afraid of Mallory going away. I must get home to lunch. Come and see us soon."

"Simon's right about Cornwall," Sherida thought as she watched Catherine climb lightly over the crumbling stone wall and walk springily away across the short turf. "It does things to people—it's doing something to Catherine. What in heaven's name did she mean?"

And all the time at the back of her mind a little voice was whispering urgently: "Perhaps I can guess what she means, but I'm not going to let myself, because it isn't true."

She began to walk slowly homeward along the cliff path, and today, in spite of the sunshine and the tranquil blueness of the sea, there was something unfriendly about the familiar scenery. To look down over the sheer drop to the jagged black rocks where the surf boiled and steamed whitely made her giddy as it never had before. There was cruelty here under the beauty; suddenly she felt homesick for the comfortable flatness and safety of a London street, for the unemotional quality of grey office buildings and tube stations and Lyons' Corner House. One lived too dramatically in Cornwall; it was like being perpetually in the middle of a setting for one of the wilder and more turbulent operas.

The car picked her up at the corner of the hill. Jane was in front with Mallory, and Christine was behind with the dogs sprawling over her lap and overflowing shopping baskets wedged round her feet.

"Give me something to hold," Sherida said and reached out a hand for a pile of new books that Christine was clinging to. "Those look nice. Is that a new Agatha Christie?"

"Yes, they're for Leah. They're perfectly all right, thanks."

For a moment Christine raised her hand as though she would actually push Sherida's away by force, and there was a shrill pink flush in her cheeks.

"She hates books that have been fingered and messed about by other people before she starts to read them," she said swiftly. "I'm the same; it spoils a new book if it isn't all crisp and stiff and shiny when you first open it."

"I wasn't exactly going to finger them," Sherida said dryly. "Give me the stuff for the black-out curtains then—or does Mrs. St. Aubyn object to them being messed about before she starts sewing them?"

"I didn't—no, of course not." Christine pushed the bundle of dark blue material onto Sherida's lap, and her eyes were suddenly full of frank hatred. "Jane, did you ask Dr. Crowdy to come up and see Leah?" She leaned forward to speak to Jane, ignoring Sherida. "I saw you talking to him."

"Only for a couple of minutes." Jane didn't turn her head. "I told him Leah had a headache, but he didn't seem to think it was anything to worry about, especially as Leah didn't ask for him to come up. He's too busy to have time for trivial things now."

"Trivial things!" Christine's tone was blankly astonished. "But he can't possibly consider one of Leah's headaches a trivial thing! It might mean she's going to be really ill. I don't think much of a doctor who——"

"Christine, Leah's health isn't entirely in your hands," Mallory said sharply. "If a doctor is needed he'll be sent for, and at the moment he isn't. Don't for heaven's sake start a great fuss and agitation over Leah's headache; she detests that sort of thing, and it's bad for her, it only makes her worse."

Christine sank back in the seat, her hair falling loosely over her cheek, her thin hands clutching the precious books so tightly that her knuckles were bleached.

"He can't be bothered any more," she thought, with a sort of clogged passion making her head throb. "He doesn't care any more about Leah and whether she's well or ill—because of Sherida. Perhaps he hopes she will be ill . . . that she'll die. He can't think of anyone but Sherida, and Leah can't send her away because she's afraid he'll think she's mean and petty and jealous. It's horrible . . . it gets more horrible every day, and I can't bear it."

Jane spoke over her shoulder, feeling someone had better say something to ease the uncomfortable, edgy tension in the car.

"Did you get Leah's sleeping pills from old Brabham, Chris? He didn't make any fuss about a second bottle of them, did he?"

"No. It was written on the prescription that she could have them again. But they don't seem to be much use, Leah's hardly sleeping at all. Can't she take a double dose?"

"Christine, for heaven's sake, do you want to kill her?" Jane turned round furiously. "That stuff's dangerous, and Simon's given the strictest orders that she's never to have more than one in twenty-four hours. You talk about as sensibly as Andrew sometimes."

"Well, if you heard her tossing about hour after hour, not able to sleep, you'd feel pretty desperate," Christine flashed back, with an emotional shake in her voice. "None of you do hear her except me, and she never tells you how awful it is. There must be something we can do."

"Dr. Crowdy is doing the best he can, Christine." Mallory spoke with an unusual gentleness in his voice. "I know Leah has some bad times; we all know, and we all wish we could do something more to help, but we can't. Perhaps none of us are sleeping very well just now, anyway; there's a lot to think and worry about."

He pulled the car up at the steps, and in silence they went into the house with their parcels and baskets, Christine still gripping the new books as though she defied anyone to wrest them away from her, and she went straight in to Leah with them. Leah was writing letters at her desk, and she looked up with a smile.

"Hullo, darling! Got my books? That's lovely. I'll have a snug afternoon in the garden with a hectic thriller, and I hope it will send me to sleep. Chris, what's the matter? You look so white."

"It's nothing." Christine dropped the books on the table and began pulling viciously at the string that tied them together. "I hate everyone, that's all. Jane saw Dr. Crowdy, but she didn't ask him to come up and see you. At least she says she did, but he said he was too busy or something. That's a queer thing for a doctor to say."

Leah was carefully removing a blob of ink from the end of her fountain pen, and she answered with her head bent.

"That was stupid of Jane, and she had no business to try and bother Simon Crowdy about me, and I'm glad he had the sense not to pay any attention to her fussings. My headache's completely gone, and I feel perfectly well."

Why had Jane said that to Simon? To see how he would react to the possibility of her being ill? Well, it was pretty clear how he had reacted; he had practically refused to come up to Bastions to see her.

Christine had gone off rather sullenly to get tidy for lunch, and suddenly Leah's fingers slipped and the fountain pen spluttered ink over the letter and her fingers. Her hands closed over it again, and she dug it into the inkwell until the nib bent and buckled, and when she took it out at last, it was ruined forever and she was trembling. That was all that was left for her to do now; she could only take her revenge on inanimate things like badly working fountain pens and pencil points. She could only exhaust herself in these useless, pointless fits of rage that had no result but a few blots of ink on her fingers, but there was nothing she could touch that really mattered now.

"Leah? How's the head? Are you coming in to lunch?"

She drew a piece of paper quickly over the scrawled letter and the damaged pen as Mallory came in, and her eyes were tranquil when she looked at him.

"Yes, of course. It wasn't anything but a touch of neuralgia. Had a busy morning?"

"Yes, fairly. I've got to go up to London day after tomorrow for a couple of nights. Will you be all right?"

"I? Darling, of course, why shouldn't I be? I've got to break myself in to seeing less and less of you, I suppose, now that you've got so much responsibility on your shoulders. I'm glad you've got Sherida to help you with all the hack work."

"Yes." He turned his back on her and stood by the window, staring out at the sea. "Leah, do you really feel you need a private secretary-companion living here, now that you're dropping so much of your writing and correspondence?"

Leah was mechanically trying to straighten the twisted points of the pen nib, and suddenly the warm colour ebbed from her face.

"Do you mean that you think I oughtn't to keep her on here? That it's useless extravagance?"

"No, I didn't mean that exactly. I know a secretary is a great help to you, but perhaps we could find someone older and less valuable to the war effort than Sherida to do a job like this. She's young and strong and capable, and I feel she may be hankering to leave and join one of the services, but feels that it might seem ungrateful to us."

"She's never said so, has she? How would you manage all your A.R.P. work without her?"

"I ought to be able to keep a few notes and instructions in order without the help of a secretary to do it. Besides"—he straightened his shoulders a little—"I feel a good many older men could do my job perfectly well while I might be useful at something else that's a bit more military. That's what I'm going up to see Kenmuir about, he may be able to pull strings and find me something."

"Oh!" Leah said very softly and smiled. "I see. But darling, if you're going off to join the army again, leaving a houseful of women to look after themselves, Sherida would be more useful than ever. I can't do much, and Jane's young for responsibility. If Sherida stayed on I'd feel much happier about everything. Why not leave her to decide? If she wants to go she'll tell me surely."

"Yes, I suppose she will. But if she does, I don't think it would be fair to try and persuade her to stay. Are you coming along to lunch now?"

"In a moment. I must ring up Mabel first."

Mallory went out of the room, but Leah didn't touch the telephone. She was fingering the pen very gently now, and she felt so tired that her hands would scarcely move. The effort of holding back the desperate appeal she had wanted to make had been physically exhausting, but she was glad she had conquered the humiliating impulse. Better to go on imagining that if she had made it there might have been some response than to know for certain that there was nothing there now but pity. Pride would carry her on through this thing, pride and wit, but pathos and sentimentality would be no help. If Sherida stayed on at Bastions, Mallory, even if he got this prospective war job, would come back sometimes. There was no one to come back now but Mallory; she knew that Simon would never set foot in the house again if he could possibly help it. She put the broken pen away in a drawer and with a deft movement swung her wheel chair toward the door.

Logan brought Catherine over to dinner, and Sherida, watching her, could see no sign of the queer mood of the morning. She looked young and vividly alive and gay in a coral-red frock with a lipstick that matched. Tomorrow afternoon she and Logan were going over to take possession of the old converted coast-guard cottage on the cliff looking toward the Plume, which was to be their home. Logan was renting it for a year, with an option of buying it at the end of that time, and there was no doubt that they were lucky. Noel Prentice, the author who had converted the cottage into a week-end hideout, had done the job expertly and thoroughly. The rough grey granite and weathered slate exterior had hardly been touched, but inside the fittings were almost luxuriously up to date, and the oddly shaped, cream-washed rooms were going to give Catherine's artistic sense of decoration and furnishing a perfect background to work on.

"What about help?" Leah asked her. "Is Mrs. Perowen going to 'oblige'? She isn't a bad cook."

"She'll come for a couple of hours three mornings a week, but that's all I'll need in the way of help. Logan's hardly ever home to lunch, and that will give me time to get my nose well inside Mrs. Beaton's and produce something really succulent for his dinner."

"I don't care what it is, darling," Logan said, "so long as you don't give me calf's head. Do you remember the evening in

London at your flat when I went to forage for something and opened the larder door and came face to face with a pallid, grinning head on a plate with its tongue sticking out at me?"

"I know. I wasn't very partial to that calf's head myself, and nothing would induce Betty to go set foot in the larder as long as it was there. She said it rolled its eyes at her and flapped its ears, and somehow I never managed to make myself dissect it; it reminded me too much of John the Baptist, and I felt like a cannibal. I think we had it there four days, and then Mrs. Winkle had it given to her as a birthday present and took it away wrapped up in brown paper. I won't give you calf's head. By the way, what's the latest news about the Bassett trial? Wasn't it the first day yesterday? I wondered if there'd been any exciting developments."

They were in the drawing room having coffee now, with the windows wide open upon the soft amethyst-blue dusk that was faintly varnished with the honey-yellow light of a young moon. Logan, just striking a match for Catherine's cigarette, hesitated imperceptibly before he answered her, but Sherida, looking at him, saw the relief and pleasure in his eyes, and it seemed to her that everyone in the room drew a little breath of thankfulness. This was the first time Catherine had brought up the subject of the Bassett case herself, and she did it so easily and naturally that there wasn't a shadow of doubt that she didn't any longer connect it in her mind with anything personal. Leah glanced up from her knitting to give her a warm, approving smile that was like a message flashed at her privately, and Logan, after that tiny pause, said cheerfully:

"There's been nothing very sensational. I'm afraid public opinion is rather against Mary Bassett, she's always been such a surly, bad-tempered girl in spite of the Bassetts' amazing kindness to her. Isn't it marvellously warm this evening!"

"Yes, it feels as though summer had come." Catherine had moved over with Logan to the window. There was a scent of syringa on the air, and the terrace flagstones shone dimly with dew. "So warm that I really must bathe tomorrow. Sherida, don't you go swimming some time in the morning? Can I come over and plunge in with you?"

"Yes, do. I'll be going in about eleven o'clock if there's plenty of sun."

"And come up afterward and have coffee with me," Leah said. "You won't have much time once you start settling into your own home to bother about visiting mother-in-law." She folded up her knitting and ran her fingers through her bright hair. "And now, people, I think I'll slip away to bed. I'm feeling lovely and drowsy, and if I seize the opportunity I may get a really good night. No, nobody's to move," she added quickly as Mallory put down his pipe. "I don't want to break up the party. Kate will look after me. But I'd like you to come in and say good night, Catherine dear, in about half an hour. Will you?"

"Of course," Catherine said, smiling back at her with very bright, unwavering eyes. "I hope you have a lovely night."

There was a shifting about of the party after Leah's chair had gone. Sherida went off with Mallory to his study to type notices, Jane departed to wash her hair, Christine curled up with a book on one of the lounge settees, and Catherine and Logan went out into the garden.

"I can't help it," Logan said softly. "I know the world is in a bloody mess and it's not much use planning things, but all the same I'm happy tonight. I suppose it's because I'm perfectly sure that at last you've stopped being an overimaginative, oversensitive goose. Funny how it's one's own little personal problems and worries that matter most, even when the world's on the verge of a pretty hideous sort of war. You'll never worry about that ridiculous idea of yours about yourself and Leah again, will you, Catherine?"

"No." She shook her head and blew a smoke ring neatly up into the blue-and-silver air. "Never again, and that's a promise, Logan. But there's one thing I can't help being a tiny bit curious about. I wonder how you would have felt if, when you went to ask questions at that institute, they'd answered you quite firmly and definitely with the information that my real parents were—well, worse than just morally weak and spineless. That my father, for instance, had been hanged for murder or that my mother was the proprietor of a brothel. What would you have done?"

"I told you ten thousand times before I went that nothing on earth would make any difference. Can't you believe that yet, Catherine?"

"Yes, I can believe it for myself," she said slowly. "I don't think anything would make any difference to the way you feel about me, personally. But what about—children, Logan? You might not have cared much what your wife's people were, but wouldn't you mind a good deal what your children's grandparents were?"

Logan didn't answer for a moment. He was sucking at his pipe and sniffing the night air, and his face refused to look anything but young and happy.

"Perhaps. But if it had come to that I'd have been perfectly willing to cut out a family altogether. The sort of world you bring children into is more important anyway than who or what their grandparents were, and this isn't the sort of world I'd choose for my children. Not," he added hastily, "that I'm suggesting we should do that. Somehow I feel you and I between us may manage to make life passably pleasant for our offspring. But it would have been an excuse if we'd decided not to produce infants who might develop homicidal mania. Do you think you ought to go in and say good night to Leah now?"

"Yes, I'll pop in. Wait for me here, Logan. I ought to go home then."

Leah was in bed, sitting up with a rose-pink woollen and swansdown jacket over her shoulders, and she was carefully applying clear rose-pink varnish to her square-tipped, well-kept nails. She looked up with a smile as Catherine closed the door.

"I'm sorry to drag you away from Logan on such a romantic night of moonlight and flowers, my dear, but it's only for a second. I just wanted to tell you how terribly happy I am that you haven't let what I told you—and I still can't forgive myself for telling you—spoil anything. Afterward I worried myself sick thinking that you mightn't be as sensible and level-headed as I believed you were. You've not breathed a word to Logan about it, have you?"

"No," Catherine said lightly. "I'm not quite brave enough for that. But in a roundabout sort of way we've been discussing whether we'll have any children. Logan rather thinks that this isn't quite the kind of world he wants to bring babies into, and I agree with him. So that's probably how it will be."

"Oh!" Leah said softly and carefully finished one smooth thumbnail. "Well, I think you're right, Catherine, though it's a pity. But after all Logan's children would inherit this place and count for a good deal down here, and it would break Mallory's heart if there were any more tragedies in the family. It's brave of you to face it like that, my dear." She put the brush back into the bottle and waved her hands up and down to dry the varnish. "Good night, Catherine, and I'm going to sleep well because I'm so happy about everything."

"Good night," Catherine said quietly and closed the door. It was queer to stand there in the corridor for a moment with the solidity of the door behind her, knowing that she would never see Leah again. Already in a strange way her image had faded and grown blurred, so that Catherine couldn't quite remember what she looked like. The room behind her with its high hospital bed and bright eiderdown and rose-shaded bedside lamp had melted into limbo. Time and space were fluctuating oddly about her, so that she could have sworn that she caught a glimpse of Rosanna's childish figure in its brief, round-necked flowered frock and open sandals passing across the brightly lit lounge, that she heard a scamper of feet on the stairs and knew that they were the feet of Logan's unborn children.

She picked up her coat from the hall stand and spoke to Christine, still hunched over her book at the end of the deep settee. "Good night, Chris. Say it for me to the others, they all seem busy."

"Yes, don't they?" Christine looked up at her, and Catherine thought with a shock: "The child really looks ill and haunted, as though she'd been seeing ghosts." Christine pushed the drooping hair behind her small ears impatiently. "I'll tell Daddy. He seems too busy in the study with Sherida to be disturbed. Is Leah all right?"

"Yes, perfectly. I expect she'll sleep the clock round."

"No. Round about midnight I'll go in and give her some sleeping stuff. I have to do that every night now. Jane and Daddy say she ought to try and do without, but that's so cruel. They don't know the sort of nights she has now since——" She stopped abruptly and opened her book again. "Good night."

The faint wind and the breaking surf made music all along the cliffs as they walked across them, arms linked. Cornwall was tired of being sullen and bad tempered and violent tonight. Like a repentant woman who wants to make up for her sullenness, she had put on her best array of sapphire blue and silver, her brightest stars, her most enchanting cloak of shadows. Her voice said: "Look at me, I can be beautiful, can't I? And I can be gentle and sweet-tempered, and I mean you to love me and forgive me."

Logan put his arms round Catherine in the porch of the Rectory and lifted her a little off her feet. Her cheek was cold against his, but he thought it was only the fresh night air that made it like that.

"Good night, my sweet. Don't do too much tomorrow and have a nice, long laze in the sun on the beach with Sherida, it will do you more good than unravelling teaspoons and grapefruit glasses from tissue paper. Happy?"

"About everything—like you. Good night, Logan."

Sherida and Mallory put the last of their papers away at half past ten and lit cigarettes and went out onto the terrace for a stroll before turning in, though Mallory nowadays never went to bed until one or two o'clock, and it seemed to Sherida that he needed sleeping tablets more than Leah did. He noticed that when the moonlight struck lightly on the top of her head it turned her hair an odd, copper-beech colour.

"Are you still happy here, Sherida?" he asked her abruptly. "Now that you've got to know us really well as a family, do you still feel we're pleasant people to live with?"

"You sound as though you expect me to say that I didn't," Sherida answered softly and he shrugged his shoulders.

"You must get bored sometimes at being so tangled up in our personal and domestic affairs. Christine's tantrums and Jane's miseries and Leah's headaches and my fits of the grumps—you must get very sick of being eternally involved in them. Don't you? Don't you ever long for independence and a life of your own?" "I've pretty well summed up what a life of my own would be like," Sherida said slowly. "A bed-sitting room in a dingy house in Marylebone or Bayswater and a nightly routine of stocking washing and hair washing and the nearest cinema once a week. That isn't so glamorous, is it?"

"Not glamorous, but more personal somehow. Besides you're the type of girl who could get a really interesting and responsible job anywhere. I always feel that Leah got you here rather under false pretences. Any faded spinster who can type with one finger could do all her work for her. But of course it wouldn't be so pleasant for us. I expect you've discovered by this time that we're a selfish family. And yet our selfishness doesn't seem to make us particularly happy." He knocked his pipe out against the stone balustrade, sending a flight of tiny red sparks winging away across the lawn. "We're all too idle, that's what's the matter with us," he went on abruptly. "We'll all be the better for a good hard job of work to do that doesn't leave us any time to think about our Cornish feyness and mystical temperaments. Leah's always been right about that, and I'm looking forward to my job of work."

"It's definitely settled, is it?" Sherida asked steadily.

"I hope so. I had a letter today, and I'm going up next Tuesday for an interview at the War Office. I hope that will mean a rush order for kit and the feel of a camp bed under me again. If by any chance I don't pull that off, well, I'll have to look about for something else. I've got to get away, Sherida."

She felt her heart thumping suddenly, suffocatingly, and her throat tightening. He couldn't be trying to tell her that—she wouldn't let him even if he were.

"I can understand every man feeling like that now," she said. "And every woman too. If—if Mrs. St. Aubyn doesn't really need me here I feel I ought to join one of the women's services. Only I don't want to let her down."

She wanted him to understand that if it were a question of one of them leaving Bastions, she would be the one to go.

"I know," he said. "But I'm hoping that if I get this job you won't rush off just yet, Sherida. I'd feel happier about everything knowing you were still at Bastions. I'm the one who feels useless and at a loose end. I think you ought to go in now, the dew's heavy. Good night."

"Good night." She walked round the terrace and into the house by the side door beyond Leah's rooms, and Leah, still awake, heard the click of her heels and the soft sound of the door closing. She could piece everything together from that: the enchanted, moonshot darkness, the scent of the flowers opening their throats to the dew, the red glow of Mallory's pipe, the slow footfalls of two people pacing up and down the terrace, the casual "good nights," Mallory's continued strolling alone.

Christine, still brooding over her book in the hall, raised her head as Sherida came through and stared at her with such a fixed intensity and such a cold hatred that for a moment she was startled and shocked before Christine looked down at her book again.

"I must have imagined it," Sherida thought. "She's in a nervy, melodramatic mood, and she's always acting a part. Probably she's imagining herself as Lady Macbeth or someone equally doomed and violent." Aloud she said cheerfully: "Good night, Christine."

There was no answer from Christine; her chin was sunk, and the loose hair flapped over her eyes, and Sherida went on upstairs, feeling suddenly that Mallory was right about the difficulties of becoming involved in the lives and temperaments of a whole family who were complete strangers to begin with. She was too tired tonight to struggle with Christine's moods, too tired to think much about anything. None of them mattered except Mallory, and she was all in a confusion about him. Did he want her to leave Bastions, or to stay when he had got his army job? Did he want to go on seeing her, or did he want to finish everything, the everything that was so pitifully little. Her head was throbbing, and there were queer cold shivers slipping down her spine when she got into bed.

27

WHERE THE SEA curved into the little cove at the foot of Bastions' cliffs, it was a deep, cold jade green laced with white, but farther out it melted into grey-blue, shot with violet. The sun was hot, beating down into the hollow tucked under the granite heights, but the wind was strong, and beyond the shelter of the two horns of the bay it was definitely rough, heaping the waves up into splinters of broken spray against the jagged rocks.

Sherida enjoyed her bathe. The water was freshly, sparklingly cold and bracing, but she was still too tired to stay in long, and after ten minutes of floating idly up and down on the swell of the waves beyond the surf, she came in, leaving Catherine still swimming energetically.

"I'm not coming in yet," she shouted. "It's glorious and I'm feeling strenuous. I'm going to swim out to the flat rock and sun-bathe there for a bit."

"All right, don't hurry."

Sherida stretched herself out on her towel on the sand, with a cigarette, and her face turned up to the comforting glow of the sun. She had slept badly, and her mind and body were still in the grip of this curious listlessness and lethargy. She wasn't very interested today in what anyone else was doing, and in the sunlight she fell asleep, feeling almost glad that Catherine was leaving her alone for a bit so that she didn't have to talk.

"Hullo! You're going to collect a pretty rich coat of tan, not to speak of crimson, before the morning's over. You ought to turn over and baste the other side a bit."

She came out of her doze to find Logan folding himself up cross-legged beside her with a towel slung round his neck.

"Good gracious, what on earth are you doing here?" she asked sleepily. "I thought you were going to struggle this morning with some rich old miser's will."

"So I was, but she rang up cancelling the appointment till this afternoon, when I've got to go over and sit by her bedside and do the job, so I trundled home for an early lunch on the way. Catherine gone home?"

"Catherine? No, not yet." Sherida yawned and filtered hot sand through her fingers. "I only stayed in ten minutes, but she was feeling energetic and she stayed in a bit longer. I wonder she isn't cold though, she's been in nearly half an hour already."

"But where is she?" Logan said quietly, and he slid his pipe into his coat pocket.

"In the cove somewhere or still sun-bathing on the flat rock. She said she was going to swim out there and—Logan, what's wrong?"

His face had turned a queer colour as the blood ran out from under the sunburn, and he was on his feet.

"Catherine is a rotten swimmer," he said very softly. "And she's never swum out as far as the flat rock in her life. And the tide's going out."

She hadn't time to haul herself up before he had wrenched off his tweed coat and heavy brogues and in trousers and shirt was in the water, taking a running dive through a giant fan of white surf that was just breaking with a great swoosh.

"Logan! . . . I'll come too. I didn't know . . ."

Sherida's breath went as the next breaker hit her, and underneath it she could feel the imperious tug and drag of the outracing tide. A rotten swimmer . . . but she hadn't known, how could she? Catherine had been so matter-of-fact and natural, as though swimming out to the flat rock at the mouth of the cove were an every-day exploit. Why . . . why?

She had to fight to keep her breath and her head against the suck of the tide, and she was a strong swimmer. Coming up from under another smother of foam and shaking the salt wetness out of her mouth and eyes, she felt her fingers touch pinnacles of rock and clung to them. She had reached the flat rock whose smooth surface jutted out of the sea and could easily be climbed onto. A voice shouted to her from ahead.

"Stay there, don't come out any further! I'll yell if I want help."

"Can you see her?" she cried back, her voice breaking, but there was no answer from Logan.

She hauled herself up the shallow rocks onto the top and stood up, trembling. It was much rougher out beyond the mouth of the cove, and the blueness had gone out of the sea, leaving it drably olive green and sullen. It was impossible to see anything . . . but there was a dark speck in the trough of a wave, Logan's head. He seemed to be swimming straight out into the Atlantic, and suddenly Sherida plunged back into the sea and began to fight her way shoreward. It was an eternity before she felt ground under her feet and, half sprawling under the angry smack and wallop of the surf, struggled up the beach to her towel. She was at the foot of the path up the cliff when she saw the leisurely figure of Mallory strolling down it, and she hardly had breath to shout.

"Get a boat!" she gasped and waved a hand toward the sea. "Catherine's out there and Logan . . . looking for her. . . ."

There was always a rowboat kept pulled up on the beach above the tide line, in case of accidents. Mallory had it down the beach and afloat before she had recovered her breath, and she sprang after him.

"I'll help. They're right out beyond the flat rock. At least Logan is . . . I don't know if . . ."

She couldn't say "if he's found her." Mallory's face was grey and grim, and he didn't answer as he lifted the boat over a breaker and tugged at the oars. Sherida was gripping a pair too, unconscious of the suddenly cold wind cutting through her wet bathing dress. They scraped past the flat rock and rounded the rocks; there was nothing to be seen anywhere.

"O God!" Sherida thought. "It's my fault. I should have known. I should have stayed awake and with her. If both of them . . ."

"What's that?" Mallory said sharply. "Over there? Yes, it's someone. Pull to the right."

They were pitching and heaving wildly. Up on the cliff someone else was shouting, and there were people running, but neither of them took any notice. All their concentration was bent on that tiny black dot amongst the waves . . . but only one dot. The muscles of Mallory's arms stood out like whipcord, and Sherida's spine was cracking. Was it Logan?

"Hold her steady, I'm going in. It's Logan, and I think he's got her, but he's about all in."

The boat rocked as Mallory shot away from it, and Sherida fought to keep it head on to the in-sweeping waves. She hadn't time to look and see what was happening; she mustn't get swept away from them.

"I'm all right," a voice said chokingly. "Hang onto her. Keep her steady if you can, Sherida. I can make it, I think."

She hauled on one oar and with the other hand clutched at Logan as he heaved himself exhaustedly over the side of the boat until it tilted dangerously.

"Steady! It's all right." He dragged it round in time to face the next wave and then hung over the side. "We must get her in somehow."

Catherine was small and light, but she was a dead weight as they dragged her out of the clutching water. Mallory didn't follow but waved toward the shore.

"I'm all right. Get her back as quick as you can. They'll pick me up."

They had launched a second boat from the beach, and it was plunging out toward them. Logan shouted something and went on rowing, though his face was dirty white and his breath was coming in long, broken shudders. A burst of surf shot them up onto the beach, and before it could suck them back he was out with Catherine in his arms.

"Help me, Sherida. You know artificial respiration. We must take turns."

Catherine lay face downward on the sand, her dark hair clinging wetly to her blanched face, her hands trailing limply, her body inert as seaweed under their toiling hands. There was sweat running down Logan's face along with the drops of sea water.

"Let me take a turn. Rest for a moment."

He let her work for a minute and then pushed her hands away.

The other boat was rushing up the sand on the crest of foam; there were other people now running down the beach.

"I'm here, Logan. Leave it to me."

Simon was there somehow, pushing them both away. Someone wrapped something round Sherida's frozen shoulders, and she saw that it was Mallory and that it was his coat he had put over her.

"It was my fault," she whispered. "I didn't know when she said she was going out to the flat rock. I didn't know. It was my fault."

"It wasn't anyone's fault. Here, have some of this." He pushed a flask into her hand, and she swallowed a few drops of brandy and choked. "Go up to the house and get some clothes on, you'll die of pneumonia."

"I can't go . . . not till I know. Logan—I'm sorry."

His face was so utterly blank and bewildered and old that it was scarcely his, and Mallory put a hand on his shoulder.

"Sit down and drink some of this, you're all in. Crowdy's doing everything he can."

Logan sat down obediently like a child and drank some brandy and didn't seem to notice what he was doing.

"I don't understand," he said dully. "She knew she wasn't a good swimmer, she knew she couldn't get back from the flat rock, even if she reached it. I don't understand . . . Sherida, what did she say?"

"Don't talk now," Mallory said quickly. "Yes, Simon? All right."

They had brought a stretcher down from the house and blankets. Catherine's weight hardly bent the canvas. Her dark hair was brushed back now from her square forehead, and the blue veins shone like threads of azure across her temples, and her lips were faintly blue too. Sherida stood up and felt her legs buckle under her, and Mallory put a hand through her arm.

"Hang on to me, you're all right. Can you manage, Logan?"

There was no sunshine now; all the sky was curdled with pale silver grey, and the horizon was olive green with banking clouds. The little procession wound its way up the steep cliff path, and at

the top Leah's wheel chair rested dangerously near the edge of
the cliff and Christine was clinging to it, her eyes terrified in her
white face.

"What's happened?" Leah said in a very low voice. "Who is
it?"

The stretcher and Simon passed her without a word; he didn't
even look at her, but Logan stood dead still in front of her.

"It's Catherine," he said quietly. "I think she's dead. She swam
out too far and got caught by the tide. It was a queer thing to do,
wasn't it, when she knew she was a bad swimmer?"

Nobody else spoke at all. Logan and Leah were staring at each
other, and she had turned as grey as he was, and suddenly it
seemed to Sherida as though her sturdy body shrank in the chair
and grew small and shrivelled and frightened.

"It was—silly of her," she said, and her lips moved as though
her brain wasn't controlling them, as though they were the lips of
a ventriloquist's doll.

Logan made a stiff movement and went on toward the house,
and Sherida felt the pressure of Mallory's hand on her bare arm.

"Come along, Sherida, you must get warmed up somehow.
Christine, look after Leah."

They went up through the garden, and Leah's chair came last
with Christine still clinging to its back, and the rain swept in
abruptly from the sea in a curtain of steel grey.

28

SHERIDA WOULDN'T GO to bed. She had a hot bath and a
violent rubdown, swallowed a cup of scalding hot coffee with
more brandy in it, and came downstairs into the hall. Mallory
and Jane were there, standing by the fire that had been lit, and
Mrs. Maitland was sitting huddled on the sofa.

"Sherida, tell us what happened. We don't know."

She tried to tell them as clearly as she could, remembering as much as she could, but there was so little.

"I didn't know she wasn't a good swimmer when she said she'd go out and sun-bathe on the rock. I thought . . . she was enjoying it so much. And then I fell asleep till Logan came down. I shouldn't have . . ."

"My dear, it wasn't your fault, you aren't responsible in any way," Mrs. Maitland said gently. "I think I know how Catherine felt, so alive and strong and happy that she felt she could swim to the end of the world and back again without any trouble. She's like that. Come and get warm, you must be terribly cold and shaken still."

Sherida thought she would never be warm again as she held her hands out to the fire. Where was Leah?

"Logan's up there still," Mrs. Maitland went on gently. "He won't come down. They're doing everything."

But it was two hours since they had brought Catherine into the house, and if in two hours . . . A door opened and shut upstairs, and Mrs. Maitland clutched suddenly at Sherida's hand and clung to it. Simon Crowdy came downstairs lightly, wiping his face that was damp still with exertion.

"There's a chance," he said. "She's breathing. I've rung up for a nurse, and she ought to be here in half an hour. I'm going home to get some things I need. Logan and Jane will stay with her; she's still unconscious. I'll only be ten minutes or so."

Nobody moved for a moment, and then Mrs. Maitland got up shakily.

"I think I'll go and tell Leah," she said. "She's worrying herself ill in bed."

Two days later Catherine was moved over in an ambulance to the Rectory and her own room. Simon said he didn't think it would hurt her, and she was fretting to go.

"From her room here," he said to Logan, "she can see the sea and hear it all the time, and I think it upsets her. The Rectory is much farther back, and she won't be reminded of it all the time."

He didn't add that for his own sake he wanted Catherine

moved away from Bastions where every visit he made meant strain. There was always Jane somewhere about the house, behaving perfectly naturally, quiet as she usually was, but with something in her eyes and an older look about her mouth that pierced his heart. And there was Leah, genuinely ill from shock, with her face drawn with pain and the blueness gone out of her eyes; they looked grey as the sea did under the shadow of cloud. Simon went in to see her very briefly, if he possibly could with Jane or Christine, and his eyes never met hers directly, though once when they were alone together she said in a low voice:

"Simon, I realize I shouldn't have told you what I did. It wasn't because I meant anything to be different. Can't you——"

But he cut her short quietly and finally before she could finish the sentence.

"I'm very busy, I'm afraid, and unless you really feel any worse and ring me up, I won't come in till the end of the week. Goodbye."

Christine, coming in after he had gone, found Leah lying back on her heaped pillows with such a drained, white look on her face that she was frightened and clutched at her hand.

"Leah, what is it? Are you feeling worse?"

"No, I'm better." Leah's voice was hoarse. "I'm better, but I wish—oh God!"

There were tears rolling down her face, and her whole body was stiff and taut. Christine caught her breath.

"Leah . . . Leah, darling, don't look like that. Can't I do anything? I don't care what it is."

She sat on the edge of the bed with her arms round Leah, and slowly the tenseness relaxed and Leah shivered.

"Chris, I don't know what I'd do without you. To know that someone loves me, thinks about me . . . I believe it's the only thing that keeps me going. I'm all right, darling, don't worry."

She pushed her hair back from her forehead and wiped her eyes.

"All this is just silly nerves and the strain of Catherine's accident. There's so little I can do to help, in fact I make a nuisance of myself by falling ill too. But tomorrow I'm going to get up, and

I've told Dr. Crowdy I don't need any more fussing over by any-one, and I mean it. Go and fetch me the *Times*, will you? I haven't had it today."

"Haven't you? But I asked Sherida to bring it to you. I'll fetch it."

They couldn't even be bothered to take Leah the morning papers, Christine thought dizzily as she went off to find them. They left her lying there hour after hour, alone, feeling she was a nuisance. Everyone thought of Catherine, who was perfectly all right and anyway deserved all she got for being such a fool as to go swimming too far out on an ebbing tide, but nobody remem-bered that Leah was ill because she had deliberately risked her life to save someone else. Christine felt physically sick and ex-hausted with the violence of her fury, but there was nothing she could do to ease it.

Catherine's bedroom window at the Rectory looked out on the peaceful green filigree of beech trees spread against the sky, and one couldn't hear the sound of the sea here; the only noises were the murmuring of bees and the cooing of the pigeons and doves in the old stable loft.

It was a week since the day she had been dragged out of the sea, and tomorrow she could get up and sit in the garden, and this evening Logan was coming to sit with her. She picked up a hand mirror and retied the green ribbon round her hair and rubbed a hand against her face to rouse a little colour in it. But there was still a queer, brittle unreality about everything, and sometimes she couldn't be sure that she had been hauled out in time, that she was still alive. Being alive meant things that she didn't want to face, things that were too big and tiring for her.

"Can I come in, darling?" Logan's head appeared round the door. "I managed to get away a bit earlier. And here are some of our finest roses."

They were delicate blush rose pink and palest lemon yellow half-opened buds on long, fragile stems, and one couldn't believe that the rocky, stern-tempered soil of Cornwall had produced anything so frail and timid.

"They're lovely. Pull up a chair. Tomorrow I'll be out of this old bed and getting back to normal."

"Will you?" Logan sat down across the chair, leaning his arms on the back, and his eyes seemed to pierce through her. "I mean will things be normal, Catherine?"

"Of course, why shouldn't they be? I'm not going to let people go on fussing over me after tomorrow, not even you."

She was putting the rosebuds into a long glass vase on the table beside her bed, and her back was half turned to him.

"Catherine," he said quietly. "Why did you try to do it?"

"Do what, Logan?"

"You know. Drown yourself. You're a bad swimmer, and you've never ventured out as far as the flat rock in your life even on a perfectly calm day, let alone a rough one. You went out there deliberately, not meaning to come back. Why?"

She put the last rose into the vase and looked at him and knew that he meant to sit there watching her until she told him, and she was too tired to struggle.

"Because I don't want to marry you," she said softly. "I can't marry you, and that seemed the simplest way for everybody. I didn't want to argue about it any more, and you would have argued."

"Why can't you marry me?"

The inexorable flow of his questions were like whips beating her; she could feel her flesh shrinking and wincing, and she couldn't stand it.

"Because you couldn't stand having a hanged murderer and a spineless suicide for your children's grandparents, that's why," she cried. "My father was Norvill Butler, who was hanged for a brutal and horrible murder of his mistress and his own child, and my mother was his wife, who abandoned her baby in a railway station and then went and drowned herself in the Thames. That's why it was so easy for me to swim out to the flat rock. You ought to be thankful my hereditary instincts only went as far as that."

"Who told you this, Catherine? Who told you your father was Norvill Butler?" She was silent, her face suddenly tight, and he leaned closer to her. "It was Leah, wasn't it? She told you because she thought you ought to know. How did she find out?"

"A friend of hers told her," Catherine whispered. "That friend of hers from London who came to stay with you. He knew them— the Butlers; he defended Norvill Butler when he was tried for manslaughter before, and he remembered Ann Butler very clearly. He said it was like seeing a ghost when he saw me, and he was right, he had some newspaper photographs to prove it. And then there was something else, something final. My thumbs . . . Ann Butler's left thumb was shorter than her right one too."

"I see," Logan said quietly. "Scott Tracey told Leah all this, and he had the photographs with him when he came to stay with us. And Leah told you."

"She had to, Logan. Then she left me to decide what I was going to do. I didn't let her guess."

"She didn't have to guess, she knew what you would do." Logan got up and put the chair carefully back in its place. "I'm going up to London tomorrow, Catherine, to talk to Tracey."

"It's not much use, is it? There are the photographs and my thumbs, and Leah put the whole story together, and any fool could see that it's true, that it's exactly what happened. And she said your father would feel it so terribly if anything else went wrong in the family, with his grandchildren, for instance. It's no use, Logan."

"All the same I'm going up to London tomorrow." He bent down and kissed her lightly. "And you'll give me till tomorrow evening, won't you? I promise I won't argue about anything after that."

He was so matter-of-fact and practical about the whole thing that Catherine looked at him, her eyes puzzled, before she nodded.

"All right. Good night, Logan."

He went down the steps and started up his small car deliberately, moving more slowly and carefully than usual. He had to do that to get control of himself before he arrived back at Bastions. He must control himself until tomorrow evening. And when he walked into the hall and saw Leah in the lounge, sipping a sherry, he was able to answer her perfectly normally when she asked how Catherine was.

"She's much better, and she'll be up tomorrow. In a few days the Maitlands are going to take her off into the country some-where for a change."

"Miles away from the sea, I hope," Leah said. "Poor child, she must want never to set eyes on it again. Has she told you how she came to do anything so silly as to swim out beyond the cove on a rough day?"

"I don't think it's good for her to talk about it," Logan said as he moved towards the stairs. "By the way, I'm going up to town for the day tomorrow on some business, and I'll be seeing Scott Tracey. Any messages for him?"

He turned on the bottom step of the stairs and looked back at Leah with a faint smile, and the sherry glass in her hand shook suddenly.

"Are you? I didn't know you had professional dealings with Scott. Your firm must be coming along, Logan. Give him my love."

He nodded and went on upstairs, still smiling a little, and Leah put the sherry glass down abruptly and wiped away a few drops that had spilled over her hand. No, she hadn't known that Logan's small and rather insignificant firm had any connections with Scott Tracey. But it didn't mean anything; Logan couldn't have come back from seeing Catherine looking so calm and normal if he had any idea of the truth. Logan was too young and immature yet to have such iron control over his emotions. And Scott wouldn't say anything; he had probably forgotten all about it by this time, though he must have seen the brief paragraph in the papers that said that Catherine Maitland, the well-known young artist, had had a narrow escape from drowning in a bathing acci-dent in Cornwall. But Scott had a cautious, highly trained legal mind, and he wouldn't say anything, even if he did remember. Leah poured out another half-glass of sherry and sipped it slowly, and Jane came downstairs, looking faintly worried.

"I've just put Sherida to bed, Leah. She isn't a bit well, and I think she's got a bad chill or something. She's shivering one moment and hot the next, and her throat's sore. If she isn't better by tomorrow, perhaps Simon ought to see her."

"I thought she looked rotten at teatime," Leah said. "But I

expect it's a sort of reaction from that awful day. Make her stay in bed and stuff her well with hot drinks and fruit juices and she'll probably be all right. Mallory, Sherida isn't well."

"Oh?" Mallory said, and he filled his sherry glass. "I don't wonder, she's been working hard, and she didn't have a good rest after Catherine's accident. She must have needed it badly. Tell her not to move till she's really feeling all right again, Jane."

It was no use, Leah thought wearily. He was too expert now to be caught like that into any sort of betrayal. He seemed to sense traps even before she laid them. Logan was coming downstairs again for dinner, and he was still smiling in that queer, secretive way, as though some private and rather macabre joke amused him. She found it difficult to eat any dinner.

29

IT WAS so hot next day that Catherine sat in the garden after dinner, feeling the warmth still rising from the sun-baked ground, with a smell of grass and honeysuckle flavouring it. The big trees ringed the garden with quietness, and the sky was a deep, ardent lilac, holding the light lovingly still in its transparent depth.

She heard Logan's car drive up and his footsteps round the tiled path to the garden, but again that far-awayness swept over her like a sea fog, blurring everything. In a moment she was going to know, but it didn't seem to matter.

"Hullo, darling!" he said and kissed her in his swift, light way. "I'm glad you've had such a grand day for your first outing. It was boiling in town."

He unfolded a canvas chair and set it beside her, but she didn't look at him, and her mouth was dry. This gentleness with invalids was more cruel than kind. Why could she think only of little, trivial things? That he couldn't have had time for any dinner if he had come straight from the station; that if tomorrow evening had the same colours she might try to paint the old house, dusky against the amethyst-and-topaz sky; that her hair was still looking very limp and flat about her head.

"But I had a busy day," he said in the same even, calm voice. "I had lunch with Scott Tracey at Simpson's. He's written you a letter, but it's too dark to read it out here. Shall I tell you what's in it?"

"A letter—to me? Why should he write to me?"

"I asked him to because I knew you wouldn't believe what he said if I simply repeated it to you. I'll tell you what he says, and you can read it for yourself afterwards. He says that he believes that somehow or other you got the impression that he connected you with the Norvill Butlers and their child, but he can't understand why, because he's never had such an idea in his head."

"But he said to Leah . . . he told her himself . . ."

"Wait a moment, Catherine, and listen. He says that for a moment he was struck by a certain resemblance between you and Ann Butler; you have the same shaped face and eyes and colouring. He admits that and that it's quite striking and that he mentioned it to Leah some time during the week end. But he had no photographs of the Butlers with him when he came down here, and he didn't know them well."

"But Leah had the newspaper cuttings; she showed them to me. She said . . ."

"I'm telling you what Scott Tracey said, and that's more important than what Leah said. Then I told him about the question of your thumbs being slightly different lengths. He said he hadn't the faintest idea that Ann Butler had the same oddity in her hands, and in fact he found out definitely that she hadn't. He knows the doctor who made the post-mortem on her, and he rang him up then and there. He said that there was no question of Ann Butler's thumbs being different lengths; that's a peculiarity that's entirely original to you."

"I don't understand," Catherine said helplessly. "Even without that—it might be true."

"It's absolutely impossible for it to be true, because the body of the Butler baby was recovered from the river near Maidenhead three months after Mrs. Butler drowned herself. It was identified positively by the shawl wrapped round it and a silver locket it wore round its neck with its name and date of birth engraved on it. Ann Butler jumped into the river with her baby in her arms, and they were both drowned. Leah never noticed the report of that in the papers, and she didn't know. But it's all written here, Catherine, under Scott Tracey's signature. And now there's nothing to argue about any more, is there?"

For a few moments she felt exactly as she had felt when she surrendered herself to the urgent pull and command of the sea; everything floated away from her under an immense blue-green wave of peace and comfort, but just as before, Logan dragged her back almost roughly to reality. She felt him picking her up out of the chair.

"I'll take you in now, and you must go to bed. I'll go home for half an hour, and then I'll come back. Your people won't mind me dossing down in the spare room for a few nights, will they?"

"Logan, are you going to stay here? But Bastions——"

"I'm going to set foot in Bastions just once more, and then never again," he said in a voice that wasn't his own. "The cottage is waiting, Catherine. We can get married any time and move in next week. No arguing!"

She clung to him weakly, trembling suddenly as she realized what she had so nearly lost and deliberately thrown away because of her own weakness. She, who had always prided herself on her independence of will and strength of mind, had let herself be driven to this thing simply by the persecution and force of a stronger will.

"No arguing, Logan. Never again."

"I'll be back in half an hour," he said quietly as he put her down outside her bedroom door.

Bastions was very quiet when he let himself into it. All the doors were open through the house to cool it, and the heavy brocade curtains swayed faintly, and from the sea it must have looked like a beacon of light and comfort and happiness with its brightness streaming out into the closing twilight.

"Hullo, Logan! We thought you'd missed your train, but there's some dinner waiting for you if you want it."

Christine had come suddenly out of the drawing room, but he brushed past her toward Leah's rooms.

"I don't want any, thanks. I suppose Leah's in bed."

"Yes, and you'd better not go in, Logan. She's had a bad day, and she's very tired and ought to get to sleep early. Please leave her alone; it can't be important."

She was trying clumsily to bar his way, her eyes suddenly frightened, but Logan pushed her to one side mechanically without answering and went straight into Leah's bedroom, closing the door softly behind him. She had just finished her dinner on a tray and was lying back on the pillows doing nothing, her hands spread limply on the thin cover, her eyes fixed on the open window. The sound of Logan's coming in made her move sharply, and she stared at him for one split second in panic, until she recovered herself and smiled at him. The dimples in her firm cheeks were less noticeable now.

"Hullo, my dear! Your train must have been very late; I was getting quite worried. Have you had anything to eat?"

"No." He came up to the high bed, moving very lightly in an almost catlike way. His eyes were very bright, and his light hair was untidy, streaked across his brown forehead. "I've been over to see Catherine."

"Oh!" Leah moved her hands at last and picked up a piece of sewing. "She's been up today. How does she feel?"

"All right. Leah, where did you get those photographs of Ann Butler that you showed her?"

"Photographs? You mean some newspaper cuttings?" She snipped a thread neatly. "Logan, I've been feeling dreadful about all that, and I hoped you'd never know. She's told you, I suppose, poor child! Scott Tracey gave them to me when—when we were discussing Catherine."

"No, he didn't," Logan said softly. "You forget that I had lunch with Scott Tracey today, Leah. He's never kept any press cuttings about the Norvill Butler case. You had them or you found them somewhere. You've got an agile, imaginative mind, and you were able to work up quite an exciting little drama out of the photographs and the cuttings. You passed the story on to Catherine, and you knew she'd try to commit suicide, didn't you? Didn't you?"

Leah put the sewing down again and looked at him, and her whole face was crumpled and trembling and colourless.

"Logan, try to understand how I felt. I—I believed it was true about Catherine being the Butlers' child. There was the extraordinary likeness between Catherine and Mrs. Butler, and the baby's body was never found."

"But it was," Logan said. "You can't have read the papers very carefully on the morning of December 10, 1916, Leah. They reported the recovery of the baby's body and that it had been identified as the Butler child."

"No, I didn't know that." Leah lifted herself a little on the pillows. "But can't you understand? I was thinking of you and Mallory and what might happen if you married Catherine and had children, Logan; it was because I love you—you might be my own son."

"And so you tried to murder Catherine," he said, still in the same queer, gentle voice. "You might just as well have swum out there with her and held her head under the water. And it wasn't because you cared twopence about me, Leah. It was because it amused you and gave you a sense of power. You're a helpless invalid in a wheel chair, but you've still got the power to commit murder and control my life for me. You thought——"

"What's all this, Logan?" Mallory had come into the room before either of them noticed him. "Leah, what's the matter?"

She held out her hands to him, and the tears were streaming down her face.

"Mallory, for God's sake stop him saying these horrible things. . . . Make him understand about Catherine. I never dreamed she'd try to kill herself. I thought she'd find some way of breaking off the engagement and going away from here."

"You knew there was only one way for Catherine of doing that, and you depended on her taking it." Logan opened the door. "Good-bye, Father, I'll be over at the Rectory for the next few days until Catherine and I move into the cottage. I'll ask Jane to send my things over."

He closed the door with a smooth, noiseless movement, and they heard the front door slam behind him so violently that the house shook a trifle and then was very quiet again.

"Mallory, you can't believe him! After what I did for Logan, saving his life, bringing him up all these years——"

"It's getting chilly," Mallory said. "I'd better shut the windows."

He closed them carefully and pulled the curtains across deliberately, his back to her. She made a wild gesture that sent the sewing and the small workbasket onto the floor in a heap.

"Mallory, for God's sake, say something! You're not even listening to my side of it. I suppose it was cruel of me in a way, but after all Catherine had the right to know and decide for herself. I didn't try to persuade her to do anything. I didn't——"

She stopped short, breathing jerkily. Mallory opened the door into the sitting room and spoke over his shoulder.

"Good night, Leah, I expect Christine will look in to see if you want anything."

Leah put up her hand and switched off the bedside lamp. The room was swamped in pitch darkness, thick and heavy as black plush; she couldn't hear anything for a moment except her own breathing. She was still lying there, like a clockwork doll whose mechanism has broken, when the door opened a slit and someone crept into the room and across to her bed.

"Don't put the light on," Christine whispered. "Not if you don't want to. I'll stay with you, Leah darling." She slid herself along the narrow edge of the bed, pressing against Leah so that some of her young warmth crept into Leah's cold blood. "I know what's the matter. It's Daddy, isn't it—and Sherida? I've known for ages. It's beastly, but I'll—I'll help you somehow, Leah."

"I don't think anyone can," Leah said dully. "Stay here a little while, Christine. It's a great comfort to me."

"I'll stay all night if you want me to. Go to sleep and don't worry, everything is going to be all right."

She raised herself on one elbow and stroked Leah's hair back from her forehead, and she was like a mother comforting a sick child. Leah's eyelids closed slowly.

30

MALLORY AND JANE both wanted to send for Simon to see Sherida, but she was unexpectedly obstinate in her refusal to have him bothered about a mild chill. Her temperature was only in the region of 100 degrees, and her bones ached, but a few days in bed would set her right. She didn't feel capable of dragging Simon back to Bastions and whatever it was that was so hard for him to face there.

Kate brought her a light breakfast, and presently Jane came in, her face white and rather strained. She had a bunch of deep blue larkspur in her arms, and she began arranging them in a tall cream pottery jar, but Sherida could see that her mind was far away.

"Did Logan get home last night?" she asked for the sake of something to break the silence and Jane's fierce concentration on her own worry. "I never heard him come up to his room."

"Logan?" She pushed the last spire of vivid blue into the jar and put it on the low table by the open window. "Yes, he came back just after dinner, but he only stayed about half an hour. Then he went away again."

"Went away again? Back to London?"

"No, he went over to the Rectory to stay with the Maitlands." Jane sat down suddenly, and there were tears in her eyes. "Sherida, something awful's happened, but I don't understand it all. Logan rang me up this morning and asked me to pack his things and take them over in the car to the Rectory. He's going to stay there till next week, when he and Catherine can get married very quietly, but the reception and everything is to be cancelled. He won't come back here at all."

"But Jane darling—why? He must have given you some reason."

"Yes, he did, in a sort of way. It's Leah—he won't come back into the house as long as she's here. He said that Leah told Catherine something that wasn't true, that she'd made up, and it was something so dreadful that she knew it would make Catherine—try to drown herself. It was something that she'd invented about Catherine's own parents." She got up abruptly and went back to the window. "I couldn't have believed it if I hadn't heard Logan's voice change when he told me. It was frightening—he sounded as though he could kill Leah—Leah, of all people!"

"Has your father said anything?" Sherida asked softly, and Jane shook her head.

"No. But when I told him what Logan had said, he simply nodded and said he knew and that he'd see about cancelling all the wedding invitations. And he hasn't been in to see Leah this morning. Sherida, what's been happening to us these last few months? I've felt as though—as though something cruel and horrible was stalking about the house."

"And you've been right," Sherida thought. "Something cruel and horrible has been following you everywhere for years, but you're only just realizing it, you and Logan and perhaps Mallory. It's worse for him though—you'll never know how terrible it is for him." Aloud she said quietly: "Jane, some people have a frightful craving for power, dominion over other people, and it's a kind of game with them to see how far they can exert it. I'm afraid Leah is like that, since her accident."

"You mean that because she lost her physical power and attractiveness, she had to find something to put in its place?" Sherida was surprised at Jane's quick understanding. "Yes, I suppose that's what it was. But to do a thing like that to Catherine, who's almost been one of the family, whom she's known since she was a little girl! How can I go in and see her, Sherida, knowing what she's tried to do to Logan and Catherine?" Her eyes darkened suddenly in her pointed face, and Sherida guessed the thought that had flashed across her mind in the wake of those words, like a thunderbolt hurtling out of the sky. "And what she's done to me and Simon. Something that she's succeeded in this time." But what could she say to Jane to guide her though this black tangle?

"Talk it over with your father, Jane. I know it's a frightful problem. Perhaps one ought to pity Leah."

"Pity her! We've always pitied her. When she saved my life and Logan's she—she laid the cornerstone of a kind of temple, Sherida, a temple of worship of herself. I believe that day, when she swam out to us, she was almost glad, because, whatever happened, she'd laid the foundations of that temple. Saving us didn't really matter." She looked at Sherida. "Do you know, I've been wanting to say that to somebody for quite a long time. You're not to move out of bed today. I'll bring you up something nice and hot at eleven."

Strange happenings in the old house—had it ever watched stranger? But months ago Logan had warned her that Cornwall was a queer land where old passions and impulses and emotions still had their powers over people. If Leah had lived in a red-brick suburban house in the sedate mildness of Kent, none of this might have happened. Something had come in to her from the thundering Atlantic and the slashing gales and the devil-possessed storms, and she had surrendered herself to it.

The day slid away drowsily, though Sherida didn't sleep much and her temperature rose a little toward the evening, though she didn't tell Jane when she brought up her evening soup and hot toast. They didn't talk much; she left the tray and smiled at Sherida and went downstairs again, and it seemed to Sherida that her bewilderment and fear had gone. Had she decided how to tackle the problem of her future relations with Leah? But how could anyone find a solution to such a problem?

She was drowsing again with her light out and a bad headache throbbing across her temples when there was a light tap on her door and Christine came in with a little tray.

"Oh, hullo!" Sherida murmured, surprised at this apparently amiable visit. She switched the light on and saw that Christine was carrying a glass of hot milk and a small bottle.

"How are you feeling?" Christine put the tray down carefully, and there was something childishly awkward and embarrassed about her movements. "It's miserable for you being seedy like this, just when the weather's so lovely. You've still got a temperature, haven't you?"

"A scrap of one, but it isn't anything. It's nice of you to come in and see me."

One couldn't snub a child who was trying, clumsily, to make up for her sulks and bad temper. Christine could be very appealing when she chose to be, when that delicate pink flush came into her cheeks and her eyes looked huge and brilliant, as though she were excited.

"I meant to come up earlier," she said, "but I seem to have been dashing round doing all sorts of things for Leah. She's sent you up something too. This." She held out the small bottle, and Sherida saw that there were two pink tablets in it. "It's some of her sleeping stuff, and if you take one now you ought to sleep eight solid hours and wake up perfectly all right. If you're not asleep in an hour you can take the other one. It's perfectly safe, because it's Dr. Crowdy's prescription. Leah's so anxious for you to have a good night."

"It's very kind of her," Sherida said, a shade doubtfully. She hadn't a great fancy for sleeping tablets, but perhaps it would be pleasant to sink into oblivion for eight blissful hours. "All right." She smiled at Christine. "Do I take it now?"

"Yes, straight away. And drink down all the hot milk; that helps it to act quicker. That's right."

Sherida obediently swallowed the pink tablet and drank the hot milk that had a faintly malty flavour and was comforting to her swollen throat.

"That's lovely," she said as Christine took the glass from her. "Thank you, Chris, I think you're a good doctor."

"I—I wanted to do something for you," Christine said, and suddenly, to Sherida's surprise, her face seemed to quiver and crumple like a child's on the verge of tears, but she was out of the door before Sherida could even say good night. She switched the light out and dropped back into the depths of the pillows, feeling sleep flood into and over her senses like an anesthetic. It was a heavenly feeling of rest and forgetfulness, and she let herself float away on it acquiescently.

Mallory sat up late that night in his study with a pipe and a book, though in the course of hours he only turned over a couple of pages. In the last few weeks a touch of grey had come into his thick hair at the temples, and he looked older and rather tired. He only had the reading light on at his elbow, and beyond its small pool of radiance the room was in shadow, a rich amber shadow generated by the morocco bindings of the books on the shelves and the mellowed colourings of the old pictures. Everyone else had gone to bed. Was Leah asleep? He hadn't been in to see her all day, and he might not be able to bring himself to see her even tomorrow. He felt like a man who has been badly shell-shocked and is still dizzy and confused. He had been over to see Logan. The wedding would take place very quietly and privately, with no guests or reception, in five days' time.

"I shan't come home at all," Logan had said, and Mallory had nodded. Logan was right; all the virtue and comfort had gone out of the house, and it had become nothing but an empty shell, a roof and four walls under which unhappy people had to go on living.

This room seemed full of ghosts tonight: the ghost of Rosanna with her pointed, elfin face and fine, flying hair and odd, noiseless movements; the ghost of Leah as she had been, swinging in here rosy and wind-blown after a round of golf, bringing a scent of the open air with her; the ghost of Sherida as he had seen her that first night with her hat in her hand and her dark hair ruffled and her eyes quietly alert and interested. A curtain seemed to have risen on a stage setting when Sherida came in, but none of them had realized it. Yet if she hadn't come, all this would still have happened, Catherine would still have tried to drown herself, Simon Crowdy would still have decided to leave Cornwall, Jane would still have gone about with tired, defensively expressionless eyes. It was merely that the tempo of the play seemed to have quickened with Sherida's coming, as though Leah had become afraid of something suddenly.

It was past midnight; he ought to go to bed and try to get some sleep. He knocked out his pipe at the open window and stood for a moment looking at the red-bronze moonlight that paved a broad highroad across the sea. Why did Cornwall hate the women he brought to Bastions, and always wish them ill? He shrugged his shoulders and started to close the windows, and heard someone coming downstairs with a rush, clumsily but in desperate haste.

"Daddy! Daddy, ring up Simon quickly and tell him to come over at once. Hurry!"

Jane's face was greyish white, and she was clutching a dressing gown round her anyhow over her pyjamas.

"Is it Leah?"

"No . . . it's Sherida. She's terribly ill, sort of unconscious and breathing queerly. He'll be up still."

He dialled Simon's number and heard an answer within a few seconds and spoke briefly.

"He'll be over in five minutes. I'll come up with you. What happened?"

"I went to bed, and then somehow I felt uneasy about her, as though I ought to see that she was all right before I went to sleep." Jane was limping up the stairs unevenly, clinging to his arm. "I went along to her, and the moment I opened her door I knew something was dreadfully wrong. She was breathing in gasps, and though I shook her and shook her she never moved. I'm frightened."

"It's all right, Jane. Simon will be here any moment now."

In Sherida's room the light was on and she was lying deep in the bed, one arm curled above her head, and her breath came roughly, heavily, as though she had to struggle to keep it going.

"We can't do anything till Simon gets here. What's this?"

He picked up the little bottle with the one pink tablet in it.

"I don't know. Oh, it's one of Leah's sleeping tablets, but Sherida hasn't got any, and she doesn't like sleeping stuff. I don't know. . . . There's Simon. Simon, hurry!"

He came up the stairs three at a time and went straight to Sherida, and Jane put her hand into Mallory's.

"Overdose of veronal," Simon said briefly. "Pretty big overdose too. I'll just telephone home for some things. Can you fetch them in the car, Major? She'll have them ready for you. Get me some hot water, Jane."

Christine's bedroom door was open when Jane came down again to the kitchen where the boiler was kept up all night.

"Jane, what's wrong? I thought I heard a car outside."

"It was Simon's car. Sherida's terribly ill. Bring that other jug of hot water up, I can't manage two."

"Sherida—ill?" Christine said very softly. "But she was perfectly all right when I took in that hot milk. What is it?"

"An overdose of veronal." Jane put the heavy jug down on the table for a moment and stared at Christine. "There was a bottle on her table with one of Leah's sleeping tablets in it. I didn't give her that."

"Did you say—one tablet?" Christine brushed a hand across her forehead, and Jane didn't notice that it was wet, but not with water. "Oh, Jane!—Leah wanted her to have a good night, so she asked me to give her one of her sleeping tablets, and I put five into a bottle and took them up to her. She had one straight away and she said she'd take another in an hour if she didn't get to sleep. There were four tablets when I left her. . . ."

"Come on," Jane said and picked up the jug again. "There's no time to worry about how it happened now. If I hadn't felt nervous about her and gone in last thing to see her . . . I may have been too late even then. Hurry!"

At five o'clock Jane went into the kitchen and made tea and carried it out on a tray into the hall. Mallory was there, still dressed, his face haggard and stiff, and Simon was coming downstairs.

"The nurse will be with her," he said. "It's been touch and go, but I think it's all right now. Sit down, Jane, and don't carry any more heavy trays or I'll beat you. I'll pour the tea out, and I hope it's strong."

Mallory's hand shook a little as he took the cup.

"You think she's really all right, Crowdy?"

"Yes, we got to her just in time. If Jane hadn't gone in when she did—another half-hour would have made a difference." He took his own cup and sat down on the sofa close to Jane. "How in heaven's name did she come to have veronal tablets? She doesn't look the sort of girl who'd take anything like that."

"She doesn't," Jane said quickly. "That was Leah's idea, so that she should have a good night. She sent Christine up with some, and Sherida took one, and Christine left the bottle by her bed in case she needed another. There were four left in the bottle, she says."

"But I don't understand," Mallory said, and he got up suddenly and called softly down the passage. "Christine! Come here, will you?"

"Yes, Daddy."

Christine had dressed completely, had even brushed her hair neatly and tied a pale green ribbon round it to keep it from flopping into her eyes. There were two hard, bright spots of colour on her cheeks that looked as though they had been painted there, and the pupils of her eyes were dilated enormously.

"Christine," Mallory spoke gently, "we want to know about this sleeping-tablet business. You took them up to Sherida?"

"Yes. Leah and I both thought she ought to have a good night, so I put five tablets into another little bottle and——"

"Why five?" Simon put in quietly, and she stiffened.

"I—I don't know. I just shook some out into it from Leah's bottle. Sherida knew all about how to take them. She had one with a glass of hot milk, and I left the bottle on her table so that she could take another if one didn't work. Leah does that, so I knew it was all right."

"What do you think can have happened then?" Mallory asked.

"Happened? I don't know. I suppose in the dark she meant to take one more and—and made a mistake."

"You took five tablets upstairs," Simon put in almost casually. "Sherida took one straight away, and there was one left in the bottle when Jane went in. That means she took four tablets, a double dose." He lit a cigarette thoughtfully. "That would have made her ill, certainly, but not as dangerously ill as she is. She's had at least a treble dose of the stuff, and that would mean six tablets. Where did she get the other two from?"

"I—I don't know. Why should I? I only——"

Christine's frightened whisper was interrupted abruptly and sharply by a voice calling down the passage.

"Christine, where are you?" Leah's wheel chair appeared suddenly from her rooms. She was dressed, but her hair looked wild, and there were heavy black circles under her eyes.

"What on earth are you all doing?" she said in the same high-pitched, uncertain voice. "I heard you asking Christine all sorts of questions, as though you were policemen putting a prisoner through a sort of third degree. It's not fair on the child."

"We aren't third-degreeing anyone, Leah," Mallory said quietly. "We've got to find out what happened to Sherida, and Christine was the last person to see her."

"But she's a child, she's not responsible for anything that happened. Christine, come here." She held out her hand, and Christine went to her mechanically. "Darling, you're stone cold and you're shivering like a leaf. Go and put your cardigan on and lie down for a bit, you aren't needed here and you've been up for hours. Go along. I'll come in and see you presently."

"I don't think I want——" Christine began to say and then stopped short, stared from face to face, and then with a confused, stifled sound fled down the passage. . . . Leah gripped the arms of her wheel chair till the nails looked whitish mauve.

"I don't know how you can be so cruel, Mallory," she said. "To Christine of all people. She's such a sensitive, easily frightened child, and this is all horrible for her. For heaven's sake leave her out of all this sordid business. If you want to know what happened to Sherida, I can tell you. She may have taken those extra sleeping tablets by mistake, or she may have taken them deliberately. Girls in the middle of unhappy and hopeless love affairs do things like that, no matter how level-headed they may seem. You know what I mean."

Her eyes were fastened on Mallory's face with a sort of starved passion that made it look old.

"You mean she tried to commit suicide—like Catherine,"

Simon said unexpectedly, and Leah unclasped her hand slowly and stretched out the stiffened fingers.

"Perhaps. Or it may have been an accident. Christine told you she left four tablets in the bottle."

"But Sherida has had more than four tablets, Mrs. St. Aubyn. Are you sure there were only five put into the bottle?"

"Five?" Leah looked past Simon out of the window. The summer daylight was brightening and quickening across the garden, and the early risers amongst the birds were warbling with a certain smugness. "I can't be sure. Christine shook some out of my bottle into the smaller one. If she says there were five —but she may have made a mistake."

"A number of people seem to have made mistakes last night," Mallory said thoughtfully. "But somehow I don't think Sherida made any. You'd better go back to bed, as there isn't anything more we can do. Sherida is being looked after all right. You'll look in again, Crowdy?"

"Yes, about lunchtime. If the nurse wants anything she can ring me. You'd better go and rest, Jane, you look done in."

He went out of the front door, leaving an odd silence behind him. Everybody seemed to be trying to avoid Leah's eyes, but she didn't move her chair. She was staring at Mallory, and there were burning patches of colour blotched on her cheeks.

"You must promise me, Mallory, to leave Christine alone," she said. "She's not a child who can stand being nagged at and frightened. She——"

"Why should she be frightened about anything? Nobody's suggesting that she's responsible for what happened. But wasn't it rather careless to ladle out veronal tablets in that casual way, even to Sherida? Christine said you sent her up with them."

Mallory did look at her at last, and the red faded out of her face.

"Yes, I suppose it was careless of me, and I accept full responsibility for that. I only wanted to make sure Sherida had a good night's rest. I think I'll go back to bed now. Christine will help me."

Mallory pushed her chair as far as her own door and left her there. She ran the chair silently into the room, and Christine, who was lying on the sofa, sat up with a terrified jerk.

"Oh—it's you. I didn't hear you. You must get back to bed, Leah, you look awful. Let me help you."

It might have been a doll that she was undressing, Leah sat so still and submissive, her body a dead weight when Christine and Kate helped her into bed. The sunlight poured into the room now, and the sea gulls were screaming and wheeling over the lawn as the dogs chased them away from the remains of their bones. Christine tucked the sheet carefully in round Leah and patted her hand.

"Now try and go to sleep, and nobody shall disturb you till lunchtime. If you want anything I'll be just outside on the terrace; I'm going to sun-bathe on a rug there after breakfast. Would you like some tea and toast before you settle down?"

"No, I don't want anything. I only want to go to sleep."

Leah turned her face to the wall and closed her eyes, and Christine tiptoed out of the room. Her legs were trembling under her, and her throat ached as though something tight were tied round it. The house was very quiet again; Simon had gone, the others were back in their rooms, the nurse was upstairs with Sherida, only from the kitchen came a faint, cheerful clatter of plates and a sound of voices. But out of her bedroom window she saw Mallory walking slowly up and down the terrace with his pipe in his mouth, and as he turned at the end to come back, she shrank away from the window out of sight and began to undress with trembling haste, her face white as milk.

Simon came back just before lunch and again in the evening, when a thick scarlet-and-bronze sunset flaring across the west sucked all the light away from the earth, so that it lay black and sombre along the edge of the sea. He came downstairs to Mallory, waiting in the hall, and nodded briefly.

"She's doing very well now, and there's no more need to worry, but it was a close call. I've let Jane go in to see her for a moment."

"Has she said anything about last night?"

"Not very much. I don't suppose she can remember anything

in detail yet. But one thing she's perfectly sure about, and that is that she didn't take another sleeping tablet after Christine gave her one and left her. She says she thinks she went straight off to sleep then and there."

"I see," Mallory said slowly, and Simon changed the subject abruptly.

"Jane said something about Christine not being well and staying in bed all day. Would you like me to have a quick look at her?"

"No. No, I don't think you need bother," Mallory said. "She's nervy, and all this excitement has probably upset her a bit. It's better not to make too much fuss about it with her."

"I agree. Well, if you want me you've only got to ring up, but Sherida will be all right."

His alert eyes met Mallory's straightly for a moment before he went out to his car. Mallory drew a hand wearily across his forehead, knocked out his pipe, put it still warm into his pocket and went to Christine's room. It was almost in darkness with the curtains closely drawn, and there was no sound from the bed as he opened the door.

"Christine, you're awake, aren't you? Good heavens, what a stuffy room! You'll always have a headache if you lie cooped up in an atmosphere like this."

He crossed the room vigorously and wrenched the curtains back, letting in a flood of stormy evening light that made Christine wince and protest feebly.

"Oh, Daddy, don't! The light makes my head worse. I don't want anything."

"But I do. I want to talk to you, Christine." Something in his voice made the faint colour ebb out of her face as she sat up in bed, pressing her thin body tightly against the pillows, her eyes terrified. "And I'm not going to leave you till you tell me the truth," he went on. "What exactly happened last night about those cursed sleeping tablets?"

"What happened? I—I don't know. I told you all about it. Daddy, I don't want to talk about it, it's horrible. Is Sherida ——?"

"She's better," he said quietly. "But not out of the wood yet."

"Do you mean that she might still—die?"

"I imagine that's what Dr. Crowdy means when he says that."

Her thin fingers were clutching the sheet up round her chin, pleating it feverishly into folds, and under her eyes there were blue-black shadows smeared like patches of ink.

"Christine," he said gently, "I want you not to be frightened to talk to me. There are a lot of things that I understand better than you think. How much you love Leah, for instance."

"Oh, I do!" She caught her breath childishly in a sort of hiccough. "It's—it's dreadful to love somebody like that and want to help her and yet feel that you can't. It's nearly driven me crazy, watching her being so miserable and nobody caring much or understanding. I had to find a way to help her—I was the only one and so I——"

She stopped dead, and he could see that she was shaking all over. He sat on the edge of the bed and put a hand on her shoulder.

"So you did—what, Christine? Tell me. Something about Sherida and the sleeping tablets? Was that really Leah's idea?"

"To give her one to help her sleep, but not—not anything else. Daddy, I swear Leah didn't know about anything else, she hadn't the faintest idea! You can't think that she had."

"Yes, I believe that. But what happened?"

Suddenly Christine went limp and blank-eyed, and her voice came in a whisper.

"I suppose you—everybody guessed. I put five sleeping tablets in the glass of hot milk I took up to Sherida, and she drank it all when she took the sixth one."

"You wanted to murder her," Mallory said slowly, and a vein stood out on the side of his forehead. "Why? What harm has Sherida ever done you, Christine?"

"She hasn't done anything to me. But Leah—she's made her desperately unhappy, she's hurt her terribly. Since Sherida came, you and Leah . . . Leah knows that you don't . . . she couldn't stand it and I couldn't either. Oh God, I wish I were dead . . ."

She collapsed in a heap with the sheet dragged over her head, and the low bed trembled with the violence of her tears. Mallory didn't move for a moment, until he had got control of himself. But his anger wasn't for Christine, sobbing under the bedclothes. It was for Leah, who for weeks had worked quietly and methodically on the child's nervously intense emotions. She had been another harp for Leah's restless fingers to play a tune upon. He put out a hand and stroked Christine's tangle of fine, silky hair that was just visible above the sheet.

"Christine, listen to me. I guessed all this, but I wanted you to tell me yourself. I think you realize what you nearly did, but it's all right, Sherida's out of danger now. Simon told me before I came in. She's going to get well."

The heaving and shaking lessened a little under his hand.

"Is that true? I haven't——"

"Yes, it's absolutely true. You haven't killed her."

"Daddy!" Christine emerged from under the sheet, her face streaked with tears and still twisted queerly. "Daddy, I didn't think . . . I didn't mean . . ."

She clung to him, sobbing again, but in a more childish way, and he held her tightly and patted her awkwardly, trying to find the right words.

"Christine, try and get hold of yourself, darling. I told you not to be afraid to tell me, and I meant it. I told you I understood a lot of things. If Sherida had died—but she isn't going to, and I don't think I need talk about that. I think I know that Leah drove you to doing this horrible thing. Didn't she?"

"Leah?" Christine lay still against his chest, and he could almost feel her thinking, realizing. "Yes, she did," she went on under her breath. "She never said anything, but she—she made me feel I had to do something, anything, it didn't matter how awful, to Sherida. But all day I've been thinking about Sherida, how sweet she's always been to me. If I'd stopped to think I'd have known she couldn't do what—what Leah said she was doing. Could she?"

"No. There are things I can't explain to you quite, Christine, about people, but Sherida couldn't do what Leah made you think she was doing. And Leah knew that."

For a moment Christine's quietness and stillness alarmed him. Had she fainted or collapsed? But she spoke again, softly.

"Yes, I know that now too. Leah just wanted to—to see if she could make me do that for her. Daddy, I don't want to see Leah again."

And in Christine's face, in the older-than-her-age clearness with which she saw things now, he realized that she was receiving a punishment more stern than anything he could devise. The golden image of Leah had tottered and fallen into a heap of dusty plaster, and Christine was like a person coming painfully out of a trance.

"We'll see what we can do," he said haltingly. "Would you like to go and stay with Aunt Meg at Exeter for a bit? I could wire her that you haven't been well and need a change and you could go tomorrow."

"But I can't stay there altogether."

"No." Inspiration came to him suddenly. "But while you're there I could arrange for you to go to this finishing school in Somerset. You know several of the girls there, and you could learn typing and shorthand and cooking, or whatever you're interested in."

"Could I? Would they have me?"

"I imagine so. If there's going to be war, you'd be of some use to somebody by the time it happens. You can't say that you're that now, can you?"

"No," she said simply. "I know I'm not. Daddy, does Sherida know? But even if you don't tell her, I think she will."

"Yes, I'm quite certain she will. That's one of the things you've got to face for yourself, Christine. All I can say is that Sherida is a very generous person—though it's asking a lot of her generosity to forgive what happened. You can only hope that she'll understand." He got up from the bed. "I'll send that wire to Aunt Meg now, and you can catch the early train tomorrow morning. Good night."

"Daddy." She put out her hand halfway toward his and then drew it back sharply. "You—you talk about Sherida forgiving me, but what about—you? I can't bear——"

"It's going to take time, Christine," he said quietly. "You're not a child, and you realize what you nearly did. I can't treat you as though you were six years old and had confessed to some babyish sin that can be forgiven and forgotten in five minutes. All I can say is that I do understand how it happened. Good night."

He wondered whether she would start weeping again after he had left her, and for a moment he listened at the door, but there was no sound on the other side of it. Perhaps within a few minutes she had outgrown her childish habit of hysteria and self-dramatization. He moved quietly along the corridor to Leah's bedroom door, tapped on it and went in. She was reading a book, and she put it down quickly as he came in. She had, he thought, during the day, pulled herself together a good deal. Her cheeks looked pink and smooth again, and her hair was brushed softly back from her forehead, and she smiled at him.

"Darling, I was hoping you'd come in with the news. Is it good? Simon's been again, hasn't he? What does he say?"

"She's better, in fact she's out of danger now," he said and saw her relax her breath in a little sigh of relief.

"That's wonderful. What a ghastly twenty-four hours it's been, especially for you, my dear. I hope this is going to be the last of these upsets for us."

She had incredible courage and nerve, he had to admit that, he thought, as he watched her picking up her role of affectionate understanding wife whose eyes sent him intimate messages of sympathy across the room.

"I hope so. By the way, I've got a message for you from Christine. She didn't actually ask me to tell you, but I know she wants you to hear it. She never wants to see you again."

It was grotesque, the way Leah's mouth hung open and all the life in her face and eyes was frozen into utter vacancy. She couldn't even speak.

"She realizes," Mallory went on quietly, "just what she tried to do—murder someone by deliberately poisoning her with an overdose of veronal tablets. There were five dissolved in that glass of hot milk she gave Sherida to drink, and she swallowed the sixth with it. You guessed that, didn't you? And Christine knows now that you made her do it; that for weeks you've been working on her blind adoration for you and her oversensitive imagination, until she tried to murder Sherida almost without knowing it. Christine realizes all that now, and she's going away to stay with my sister, Meg, tomorrow, and from there she'll go to some sort of finishing school. Please don't try to see her before she goes."

Leah's jaws moved at last, stiffly as though they were half paralyzed.

"Christine's gone mad. . . . Mallory, you can't believe . . ."

"Oh, I know you didn't in plain words suggest that she should put those tablets in the glass of hot milk. But you made it all so obvious and easy for her that she couldn't refuse to see what you meant. You gave her to understand, didn't you, that Sherida and I were carrying on a love affair, here in Bastions under your nose?"

"I—I thought—it seemed to me——" Leah's throat worked convulsively.

"You were partly right," Mallory said softly. "I love Sherida, and I believe she cares for me. But that was the beginning and end of it for us. I'm going to get a war job, and she was either going to stay on here or join one of the women's services." He took his pipe out of his pocket and began filling it slowly. "You'll have Bastions pretty well to yourself, won't you? I'm going, and Logan's gone, and Christine is going. There's only Jane left, and I don't see why she should stay, she's got as much reason as any of us to go away. I'd better see if I can find a competent house-keeper-companion for you who can run things. You needn't worry about that, I'll arrange everything so that you're perfectly comfortable and free of worry, even when war comes. Good night."

Sherida, opening her eyes after a long, dreamless sleep, focused them a trifle dizzily for a moment on a figure standing beside her, and as the mist of heavy drowsiness and confusion cleared she saw that it was Mallory.

"The nurse let me in for half a second," he said. "How are you feeling?"

"I'm all right." She yawned and stretched herself, and suddenly she did actually feel energy and vitality bubbling again through her body, in spite of the faint swimminess about her. "I'm perfectly all right," she said again, smiling at him. "I'll be up tomorrow. I'm sorry to have been such a nuisance, but I——"

She stopped short, not smiling now, and he met her eyes steadily.

"Yes," he said. "That was it, Sherida. It wasn't anything to do with you. Christine's told me. In a way I suppose she was out of her mind, or rather under the complete control of a stronger one. She's broken free now, and I think she realizes what she nearly did. You must decide how you feel about her."

"About Christine?" Sherida closed her eyes for a moment. "But there's nothing to decide, Mallory. I can understand too. Poor Christine! She needed something like this to pull her together. Tell her not to worry."

"All right. She's going away to stay with my sister tomorrow. I ought to have taken things in hand for her months ago; it's all been my fault as much as anyone's. Take it easy, Sherida."

The nurse hadn't drawn the curtains yet, and when he had gone Sherida propped herself on her elbow and looked out at the dark sweep of the sea under petunia banks of cloud still faintly smouldering in streaks of sulky crimson along the horizon. It had been a hot day, but in spite of that the air in the house felt cool and fresh, as though a sea wind had swept through it, clearing out staleness and the faint flavour of rot that had hung on the atmosphere. She never even thought of Leah as she curled up deep down in the bed and went to sleep again.

31

THE FOG CAME UP in the night, moving smoothly and soundlessly like a black panther stalking its prey through jungle grass. In the morning the world had become a thick white canvas upon which, here and there, the vague impression of trees and roofs was sketched smudgily in blurred charcoal. It was like the world at the beginning of time before anything had taken definite shape out of the primeval mists and chaos of limbo. The voices of the gulls, invisible in the upper air, had a lost, bewildered quality, the silence was like marble upon which tiny sounds were chiselled sharply into a pattern of sadness.

And yet here and there, when the fog wore thin for an instant, there were flashes of colour, an opal glitter of clouded sunlight, the blue mass of Canterbury bells with the tongue of every blossom hung with a diamond clapper, the dapper glossiness of a blackbird methodically working over the grass in search of worms.

Everybody seemed astir early in the house. Sherida lay and listened to the various sounds and knew what was happening. There was the car coming up to the front door and then driving away; that would be Christine going off to catch the train to Exeter. She hadn't had the courage to come up to see Sherida before she went, but perhaps that was asking too much of her moral pluck. There was another and smaller car going off; that was Mallory bound for his A.R.P. work.

Ten minutes later another car arrived, and Simon came upstairs briskly into Sherida's room.

"You're convalescent," he said briefly. "You can get up for a bit tomorrow, but don't try to do too much yet." She realized that he was staring at her hard. "Have you any idea how all this happened?"

"Yes," she answered quietly. "But it isn't anyone's business, is it, since I'm alive and kicking still?"

"No, of course not, it's your affair entirely." She saw that he understood and that in a grudging, dour sort of way, he approved. "I hear Christine has gone away to stay with an aunt."

"Yes. She was getting so nervy and overimaginative that she needed a long change. The Major hopes to send her from there to a training college, so that she can take up something properly."

"He ought to have done that months ago." Simon dug his hands deep into his pockets and rocked backward and forward on his heels. "And I gather that the Major is pretty sure of this war job and that you won't be staying on at Bastions."

"No," Sherida said thoughtfully. "I think I shall be leaving pretty soon."

"That means that Jane will be left here all by herself with Mrs. St. Aubyn," he said abruptly. "That's going to be rather lonely for her, isn't it?"

"I've been worrying about that, and so has the Major. But it's difficult to know what to do, isn't it? Someone has to look after Mrs. St. Aubyn."

"But it shouldn't be Jane!" Simon said violently. "She's the last person who ought to be expected to sacrifice herself to Leah. If it hadn't been for her and——"

He stopped short, staring down at the carpet, with a dark ferocity stiffening his face, and Sherida didn't say anything.

"I suppose things will be worked out somehow," he said quietly. "Curse this fog, it's going to hang me up all day. I won't come in again till day after tomorrow, if you go on all right."

She heard his car rattle away down the drive, and then the silence of the fog closed down again smoothly. There was no sound of Jane all the morning, but at lunchtime Mallory's car came back and Sherida could hear him coming upstairs. He put his head round her door, and there were drops of wet clinging to his face and hair.

"How's it going, Sherida? Has Simon been?"

"Yes. I can get up tomorrow, and that's the end of all the fussing over me. I believe I've been all the better for a couple of days and nights of solid sleep. Was it awful driving?"

"Pretty bad. But in a way I enjoy getting the better of a Cornish fog. I didn't—what on earth is that?"

There was a queer noise coming up from downstairs, a hurrying of feet and the cry of a voice that sounded choked and frightened.

"Daddy! Daddy, are you upstairs? Come down quickly."

"It's Jane. Yes, I'm here. What's wrong?"

Sherida scrambled out of bed and into a dressing gown, though her legs nearly buckled under her and she had to cling to the bedpost to keep on her feet. She could hear what Jane said from the bottom of the stairs.

"It's Leah . . . I don't know where she is. Kate says she got up and dressed half an hour ago and said she'd stay in her sitting room for lunch. But she isn't there now, nor anywhere in the house, and the door onto the terrace is open."

"The terrace door?" Mallory came downstairs with long steps, and Sherida followed him, clinging to the banisters. "But she must be somewhere! She can't have gone out into the garden on a day like this; you can't see more than a couple of feet."

"She has gone out," Jane said in a low voice and put her arm through Sherida's. "Sherida, you ought not to be down here. Look, put this coat on, and don't come outside."

She put one of Mallory's heavy tweed coats over Sherida's shoulders and pushed her toward the sofa.

"Stay there, you can't do anything. I'll go out with Daddy."

There were scared servants moving about outside in the fog that billowed into the house in thick, smoky gusts. Mallory was moving quickly, staring at the wet-smeared flagstones of the terrace.

"Yes, she's out here somewhere; here are the wheel marks of her chair. Leah! . . . Leah, where are you?"

The voices died away down the garden. Jane followed them slowly, her eyes fixed on those marks that were smudged across the sticky wetness of the paths. They led straight down the garden and out onto the cliff. Mallory was standing there, and he put a hand on her arm as she moved mechanically to his side.

"For God's sake be careful, Jane. Keep behind me, I know where I am. Here are the wheel marks. Leah! . . ."

A gull screamed back at him angrily, but the sea was oddly silent, as though it were hiding, pretending it wasn't there at all. They went forward cautiously, step by step, peering into the fog ahead of them. Every grass blade was familiar to Jane out here, but she felt as though she were in a lost and unknown world.

"Wait a moment!" Mallory said sharply. "The edge is only a few feet away now. Leah, for heaven's sake say where you are! It's dangerous to be out here like this."

For the first time they heard, far below them, a wave breaking gently, tiredly, along the rocks, and Mallory gripped Jane's arm tightly.

"Stand still," he said in a low voice. "You can see now."

They were within three feet of the sheer cliff edge where the solid earth and its coarse covering of grass stopped abruptly and space fell away in a confusion of swirling mist that was faintly thinner and lighter-textured. The wheel marks of the invalid chair went straight to that edge and then ceased. Behind them Kate gave a muffled gasp, and Mallory spoke in the same low voice.

"You two men come on down the path with me. Go back to the house, Jane, and ring up Simon and then wait there. We shan't be long."

He didn't tell her to get anything ready, he simply gave her a push, and she went slowly back to the house where Sherida was waiting, huddled on the sofa, with the tweed coat wrapped round her.

"They've gone down to the cove to bring her up," Jane said flatly. "She's gone over the cliff in her chair. I must ring up Simon—but he won't be able to do anything."

Sherida put out a hand and touched her cold one as she passed, and then she heard her voice, calm and controlled on the telephone.

"Simon, Leah's had an accident, can you come straight over? She went over the cliff in her chair. . . . She must have gone out alone for some fresh air and got lost and confused in the mist. Yes, I'm all right, but you'll hurry, won't you?"

She came slowly back to Sherida, and it was impossible to tell what she was feeling; her small face had a shuttered look.

"He's coming at once. You'd better go back to bed, Sherida; you can't do anything and I'm all right."

"Perhaps I will; I expect I'll be in the way down here. But if there is anything I can do, come and tell me."

She went upstairs to her own room and stood at the window, looking out into the mist. There was a faint, luminous quality in it now, and the sound of the sea came more clearly, as though a thick curtain had been lifted between the house and it. There was another sound too, the slow trample of feet on the path below. The men came into sight, three of them carrying a stretcher with Mallory walking behind. There were coats spread over whatever lay upon the stretcher, and it was heavy.

Sherida stared down at it with a queer dryness in her mouth. It was hard to believe that that was all that was left of Leah. And yet there was a kind of dignity about the little procession, a certain proudness. Defeat had never been a thing that Leah could face, and she had her own way of striking her flag. Simon had driven up to the house, and Sherida saw him hold out his hand to Jane as the stretcher passed them and grip it hard for a moment before he went into the house. Mallory hadn't looked up at the window, hadn't turned his head, but she felt that he knew she was there, looking down on the fall of the curtain. Or was it only just being slowly rung up?

A breath of fresh air touched her face lightly, showing that the wind had shifted into the west, breaking up the mist. High overhead there was a sudden gleam of blue, swift and bright as the flash of a bird's wing, and sunshine slanted down jubilantly across the front of the house.